Praise for Debb

'Emotional, beautiful, wonderful. Debbie Johnson at her finest'
Milly Johnson

'Romantic, heartbreaking and packed with Debbie's trademark warmth and wisdom'
Catherine Isaac

'A rollercoaster of emotions. Absolutely brilliant and beautiful'
Alex Brown

'A very special, hugely affecting novel that you'll return to time after time. A future classic'
Miranda Dickinson

'A beautiful story with emotional twists that pulled at my heartstrings'
Jessica Ryn

'Utterly spell-binding, it sent shock waves through my heart'
Cathy Bramley

'This book is a triumph'
Woman's Own

Debbie Johnson is an award-winning author who lives and works in Liverpool, where she divides her time between writing, caring for a small tribe of children and animals, and not doing the housework. She writes feel-good emotional women's fiction, and has sold more than 1 million books worldwide. She is published in the USA, Canada, Australia, India, Germany, France, Italy, Turkey and the Ukraine. Her best-sellers include the *Comfort Food Cafe* series, *Cold Feet at Christmas*, *The A-Z of Everything*, *Maybe One Day* and *The Moment I Met You*.

Also by Debbie Johnson

Forever Yours
The Moment I Met You
Maybe One Day

Falling For You

Debbie Johnson

First published in Great Britain in 2023 by Orion Fiction,
an imprint of The Orion Publishing Group Ltd,
Carmelite House, 50 Victoria Embankment,
London EC4Y 0DZ

An Hachette UK company

1 3 5 7 9 10 8 6 4 2

A CIP catalogue record for this book is
available from the British Library.

ISBN (Mass Market Paperback) 978 1 4091 8809 4
ISBN (eBook) 978 1 4091 8810 0

Typeset by Deltatype Ltd, Birkenhead, Merseyside

Printed and bound in Great Britain by Clays Ltd, Elcograf S.p.A

www.orionbooks.co.uk

For Margaret Johnson, much missed x

Chapter 1

There are some things that would be so useful in modern life, I often wonder why nobody has bothered inventing them yet. With so many clever people in the universe, surely someone should have come up with more quick fixes? More ways to smooth out the niggles of everyday existence?

For me, this list includes, but is not limited to, the following:

- Shoes that come with retractable high heels – one minute you're all tall and swanky and looking professional, the next, you pop the pointy bit into a cunningly designed compartment concealed in the sole, and you're walking on air in comfy flats. No more shoving ballet pumps in your handbag.
- A breathalyser attached to my phone that automatically shuts it down if I'm over the limit – no more drunk texts or 3 a.m. phone calls that you eventually remember the next morning; you know, the ones that come back to you in fragments like a dream sequence and are so embarrassing

they make you want to put your head in a blender.

- A very specific GPS app that could help you locate things that are missing in the house – for example, 'your car keys are in the fridge', or 'the TV remote is down the side of the big sofa', or 'your sanity is in the recycling bin'. You'd be able to choose the voice it used, so it was Chris Hemsworth saying it in his Thor voice, rather than someone who makes you feel like your mum's nagging you.
- Some kind of video game – possibly social media-based, like maybe on TikTok with some cool music? – that gives teenagers points every time they actually manage to put a pair of dirty pants in the laundry basket instead of leaving them on the floor. It could be huge – like Grand Theft Auto with gussets instead of guns.
- A delivery system – possibly by drone – that can bring an iced coffee and a box of cheesy chips to your car when you're stuck in long traffic jams. And while we're on that subject, a car seat that doubles up as a commode for lady drivers – I know, that's a bit gross, but there's nothing worse is there? You're stuck in a snare, wondering when you're going to get home, wondering if you'll ever get off the motorway, and even worse you're absolutely busting for a wee?

I think I've peaked with that last one, now I come

to think of it. Anyway – your list might be different, depending on your circumstances, and some of these might even have already been invented without me being clued up enough to notice, but I'm sure you see what I mean. There are just so many ways that life could be improved.

I'm the sort of person who struggles to assemble flat-pack furniture, so I'm never going to become an inventor. If I was, though – if I had a sudden change of fortune – I'd give it a go. I have so many ideas.

Even more tempting than the ones on my list, the thing I'd really love to have is some kind of early warning system for what your day is going to throw at you. Like a weather forecast but for living. Not so much 'Cloudy With a Chance of Meatballs', but stuff like 'mainly boring, but with a sudden spike in adrenaline at 8 p.m. during the National Lottery draw', or 'predominantly stable but with some tears edging in after dinner'.

We wake up every morning, and we go about our business. We eat, we wash, we dress, we get grunted at by our children, we go to work. We do these things over and over again, without ever knowing what that day has in store for us. How the hours between opening our eyes and closing them again might unfold.

We don't wake up assuming that something amazing is going to happen, or something terrible, or something so mind-bendingly weird that our lives will never be the same again. If we had some idea, some inkling, some intuition, someone telling us in that Thor voice that we needed to be careful, then maybe everything could be calmer. We could take a different turn in the road, and avoid the banana skins lying in wait for our unsteady feet.

I say this, but part of me also wonders: what would we miss out on if we never took the occasional tumble? I think that sometimes, just maybe, you need to lose your balance before you can find it again. That we need to take a few steps back before we can move forward.

The day that everything changed for me started like any other day – and it ended with me losing everything I owned, everything I planned for, everything I thought I held dear. Everything I assumed I needed.

Ironically, it turned out to be the best day of my life. I can say that now, with hindsight, and the distance of time and experience. Back then, though, I thought I'd never get up again, never find that balance. Back then, I felt like giving up. Like lying down on the ground in a foetal ball and crying for help that I couldn't ever see coming, waiting for a cavalry that was never going to gallop across the horizon. I felt alone, and scared, and helpless.

Now I feel none of those things, at least most of the time. If I'm stuck in a small place with a wasp, maybe all three, but only on a temporary basis. Now, I am stronger and more confident than I have ever been – and it all started on the day I lost everything. I wish I could go back to then-me and reassure myself, tell myself it would all be OK in the end. Just give myself a great big cuddle. But then-me probably wouldn't have listened – I was too lost, too closed off. Clinging too hard to the things I thought kept me stable.

Maybe that's another thing I'd like to invent, now I come to think of it. A Hindsight Machine – one that sounds like someone comforting, maybe Oprah Winfrey or Dwayne 'the Rock' Johnson or Mrs Weasley or whoever makes you feel safe – telling you to take a deep breath. Telling you that it's not as bad as it seems. Telling you that everything will be all right in the end – that when you fall, there will always be someone to lift you back up. That, in a year's time, this will seem amusing, or irrelevant, or actually exactly what you needed, even if you don't feel like that right now.

So, this is my story. A story of falling, and getting back up again. Of stepping back, and moving forward. Read it in whatever voice you like – for me, that will be my own voice.

The voice that I've finally found, and the voice that I finally listen to.

Chapter 2

My name is Jenny James, and I'm having a very bad day. In fact, it's such a Very Bad Day that it probably deserves capital letters.

It started with my son, Charlie, screaming at me because the internet was down. Charlie is eighteen and, more often than not, the light of my life. He is a thoughtful and gentle soul, empathetic and emotionally intelligent beyond his years – unless something gets between him and the information superhighway. When that happens, he becomes a complete bastard.

Even though it's not my fault, I somehow end up being the one who gets yelled at. I suggested sluggishly that he tried calling the company that actually provides our broadband, but that had about as much effect as when I ask him to pick his own dirty socks up off the bathroom floor – i.e., zero. Isn't it weird how this current generation is connected to the matrix twenty-four hours a day, but they're scared of talking to an actual human being on the phone?

From that point on, nothing improved. I laddered two pairs of tights trying to dress myself while exhausted, and had to patch the second pair up with nail varnish.

Which wouldn't have been so bad, but the tights were black and the nail varnish was neon pink.

After that, the fun really kicked in – the milk was sour, I broke a nail trying to hook breakfast out of our ancient toaster, and I discovered when it was too late to retreat that we'd run out of loo roll. There was definitely some there the night before, which meant it had disappeared into Charlie's room – and that's something that no sane mother likes to contemplate.

Welcome to my life – 8.30 a.m. and already a complete disaster zone.

I open the front door and am greeted with torrential rain. This doesn't come as a surprise, as I have been greeted by torrential rain every single morning for almost a month. It is early July, and the great British summer is probably leading to a rush on ark-building supplies. It's the kind of weather that is so bad, it gets its own segment on the local news every evening – Freak Summer Storm Update, with nifty graphics and the weatherman finally getting his shot at the big time.

Up until now, it's just been rain – but I have a vague memory of there being warnings about today reaching peak crappiness, with strong winds and scary weather symbols pinging up all over his little map.

As soon as I am outside, I feel it. My hair blows up around my face, and I have to hold my skirt down with my hands. The shrubs are shaking, the wind is whistling over the clifftops, and the sea is wild and angry. In fact, it's furious – maybe because the internet is down again, who knows?

Our little cottage is on the coast in Norfolk, and on less disgusting days, emerging from it always lifts my spirits. It's perched near the edge of a cliff, far enough away not to be scary, close enough to feel exhilarating.

In front of the house, we have a long strip of garden that meanders down to join the coastal path, a cute little gate at the end. When the sun is shining, it's breathtaking – endless views out over the sea, dazzling light and shade playing on the waves, the only sounds those of nature. And sometimes Charlie on his Xbox.

We've lived here for the last eleven years, and it is a haven. I grow my own strawberries and raspberries, and have giant sunflowers on the patio in terracotta pots, borders bursting with lupins and cosmos and nasturtiums. Beautiful purple-blue aubretia is rooted in the rocks around us, cascading in a riot of glorious colour. We have a vegetable patch, and harvest carrots and potatoes and onions and herbs. I can lose days to gardening, and to sitting out on the patio at the little table, a cup of coffee and a good book on the go.

We're tucked away at the end of a half-hearted lane, miles away from real traffic, our only neighbours a nearby farmer who keeps donkeys in his field, and occasionally lets space to families on camping trips.

It's a little slice of heaven, on a less disgusting day. Today is not one of those days, and everything looks grey and damp, my flowers flattened by the weight of the rain, the path outside mired in mud. The waves are crashing in to the shoreline so powerfully that spray is bouncing up over the clifftops, pirouetting into the air before they are lost in the downpour.

I glance over at the field next to us, glad to see that the donkeys have all been taken into their stables. I notice the solitary motorhome that's been there for the last week, and hope the man who lives in it has wellies.

Actually, I kind of hope he's knee-deep in mud – the first day I saw him, I waved and shouted good morning, because that's what you do when you live in the middle of nowhere. He just returned my wave with a half-hearted nod and closed his van door, as though horrified at the thought of seeing me. I have this effect on men.

I struggle over to my car, an ancient Nissan Micra. It starts on the third try, which I take as a good sign. It really should be chugging off to its final resting place in the heavenly scrapyard, but, as ever, I can't afford a new one. I can never afford much, to be honest – which is fine. I've never been especially bothered about stuff, about things – but it would be nice to shed some of the stress.

It takes me about half an hour to get to the small town where I work. I'm an office manager for a company that makes carpets. Have to be honest, it's about as interesting as it sounds, but the people are nice and it's steady work.

I was only eighteen when I had Charlie, and soon discovered that my clutch of GCSEs and one year of A levels wasn't going to get me very far in the workplace. In the Olden Days – the days before I became the me that I am today – I had dreams of being a writer. Maybe a journalist, or a novelist – something creative and important and fulfilling. Now, I dream of other things. Things like loo roll and still having some money in the bank at the end of the month.

When Charlie was two, his dad left us to go and 'find himself'. Apparently he thought he'd find himself somewhere in Europe, and took off with a backpack and the last of our money, leaving me a note saying he'd be back when he was a 'better version of himself'. That was sixteen years ago, and he still seems to be a work in progress.

I am past the stage where I harbour any resentment or anger about it – in fact, it was probably for the best. Sometimes, being on your own is easier than being with the wrong person. If you live with someone and expect them to help you, it stings when they don't. When they're gone, you know you have to do everything yourself, so you just get on with it.

One of the things I got on with was doing a course on office basics – how to use computers and spreadsheets and software, that kind of thing. It was a bit different than going to some fancy uni and lounging around discussing philosophy and Shakespeare, but it was definitely more useful at that stage of my life. It meant I could work, and earn money, and eventually find a job that paid enough for me and Charlie to move here. To this soaking wet corner of paradise.

There is never much spare cash, after I've paid the rent and the bills, but it is enough. Charlie has had a stable life, if not a wealthy one. He's been rich in love, I like to tell myself. School trips have been tough, and I've become an expert at hunting down acceptable clothes in charity shops, and OK, I do cut my own hair – but it's a nice enough life. We have each other, and the cottage, and Netflix. I mean, what more could a girl want?

Well, I think, as I arrive at work – maybe an umbrella.

There is a strange silence in the office as I enter, and at first I think the Big Boss is in, which always makes everyone go quiet. There are eight of us working here, which is just about enough to make the tea round challenging, but it's generally a pleasant atmosphere. The business had been run by the same family for donkeys' years, but they recently sold it to a big national company. Mr and Mrs Hedges, the previous owners, are now living in a villa with a pool in Lanzarote, and getting more and more orange every day. They eat out every night, start drinking at lunchtime, and send us all pictures of them singing in karaoke bars on a regular basis. As retirements go, they are living the dream.

It's been an adjustment for us, being owned by The Man. We have things like Performance Reviews and Targets and HR Assessments now. We also have a regional manager, a thirty-something man called Tim who likes to have us all sit in the meeting room and give us inspirational pep talks about the carpet business. Two things you would never expect to hear in the same sentence. We're all supposed to tweet about carpets as well, but so far none of us have bothered – one reason to be grateful for the dodgy Wi-Fi at least.

I am hanging my wet coat up on the rack, wondering why it's so quiet, when my colleague Barb walks over to me. She looks pale, and her mascara is smudged. For me, this would not be a big deal – I try to make my make-up last a few days, if humanly possible. For Barb, though, it is a sure sign of impending disaster. She's one of those perfectly tidy women who always have healthy food in clean Tupperware boxes for lunch.

'Are you OK?' I ask, wringing out my hair. 'Is Tim here?' I whisper the last bit, looking around as though I might find him hiding behind a potted plant.

'Haven't you seen the memo?' she asks, her eyes swimming with tears. Now that I look at her more closely, I see that the pink combs in her hair are also slightly askew. The end of the world is nigh.

'Erm ... no. I've only just walked in.'

'Oh. I thought you might have checked your emails at home.'

No, I think – I did not have the kind of morning that lent itself to a calm checking of emails. I was too busy ignoring Charlie's meltdown and managing my own chaos and using the last strip of kitchen roll in the loo, even though I know I shouldn't because it might block it, and then I'll have to get the landlord out. Again.

'The internet was down,' I say, because Barb doesn't need to know any of that. 'What is it?'

'They're thinking of closing us down,' she says, each word laden with disbelief. 'Too many overheads and not enough productivity apparently. It's between us and a branch in Kidderminster!'

'Kidderminster?' I echo, frowning. 'Where the f— flip is Kidderminster?'

Barb doesn't like swearing, and I am a respectful human being, so I try to keep my foul-mouthed tendencies in check around her.

'I don't know . . . I think the Midlands? Does it really matter? It means we could all be out of a job, Jenny!'

She's right, of course. It doesn't matter. Kidderminster could be in Nepal, or on a hellmouth, or at the bottom of the Grand Canyon – it makes no difference. I am still pondering it, though, because questioning the geography of small towns in the United Kingdom is easier for me to handle than the panic that I know will soon engulf me if I let it.

I have made some poor choices in my life, and I have taken some wrong turns. All of them led me to Charlie, who I can never regret, but it has not been easy. Leaving my own family wasn't easy. Raising a child on my own wasn't easy. Finding stability in the wreckage wasn't easy, nor was being both mum and dad to a growing boy. Bringing up another human being when you barely feel capable of looking after yourself is tough, you have to make so many decisions all alone, accept consequences all alone, budget and plan and cry all alone.

The only way I've got through all of that is by employing a coping mechanism that I call Just Don't Think About It. I should probably write a self-help book: 'Life getting you down? Just don't think about it! Facing a divorce, bankruptcy or an existential crisis? Just don't think about it!'

Of course, I have to think about something else instead – this time, the precise location of Kidderminster. Our rivals in the cut-throat world of carpets.

'I need to get a coffee,' I say, patting Barb on the arm. I haven't had any, due to time constraints and the lack of viable milk in my own home. I bet that never happens to Barb. 'Then I'll read the memo. Don't worry, Barb, it'll be all right.'

'Do you think so?'

She asks me this with such sincerity, such hope, that I am momentarily taken aback. I know that my life is a whirling dervish of insanity, but she doesn't – she believes the calm and positive front that I put on when I am around other people. I am Jenny James, Office Manager – the woman who always knows where the spare staples are and makes sure the printer doesn't run out of ink and checks everybody else's paperwork for them.

'Yes, I do,' I reply, putting as much oomph into the claim as I can. If Barb disintegrates right now, I'll join in, and we'll both end up crying. It will be a decision that will work out badly for both of us.

I nod at the rest of the staff but stay silent as I make my coffee, drinking it out of a World's Best Granddad mug simply because it is the biggest one in the cupboard. If there'd been a bucket handy, I'd have used that instead.

I settle down in the small office that is my domain and log on to my computer. First things first, because I have a clear sense of my priorities right now, I google Kidderminster. It turns out to be a market town in Worcestershire. Clearly a hotbed of evil.

Next, I check my emails, and open the dreaded memo. I scan through it, but learn little more than what Barb has told me. It is couched in corporate terminology to soften the blow and make it all seem more reasonable – benchmarking, economies of scale, blah blah blah - but the cold fact remains: the axe is hovering over our heads, and Tim is wielding it. A decision will be made next week, it explains, and all staff contacted in person.

I am scared, and I am worried, and I am starting to feel a little tremble in my hands. I have worked so hard for the small life that we have, and I sense it starting to crumble around me. It's not like this is my dream existence, but the thought of starting again makes me feel weak.

I tell myself to stay calm. That I am not the same person I was all those years ago. That I have skills, experience, a decent CV, references. That I will be able to find another job.

Except . . . well, times are tough, aren't they? It always feels like times are tough, but right now it's true. You can't watch the news without there being some story about redundancies or factory closures or the soaring cost of living. There was a piece in the local newspaper – the free one that comes through the door – recently about there being 120 applications for one job at a McDonald's on the retail park.

What if I end up being one of those people, fighting for a minimum-wage job? What if I can't afford the rent, or petrol, or, heaven forbid, Charlie's Spotify account? I already shop at the cheapest places I can tolerate, and there just isn't much slack – there are very few ways I can cut back without making life a complete misery. I budget for one bottle of wine a week as my own luxurious treat, and right now I feel like I could do with increasing that, not cutting it out.

When Charlie was little and his dad left, we lived in a series of one-room bedsit flats that have left me haunted. Most of the people who lived in the same buildings were nice, just down on their luck – but some of them were not so nice. Some of them were scary, and aggressive, and intimidating. Looking back, I understand that many of them had problems with addiction or their mental health, but it didn't make it any less terrifying.

It was a horrible period of my life, and I can't contemplate going back to it. It took me years of graft and many missteps to get to where I am today, to our cosy cottage and a sense of security that now feels threatened. Even if Charlie is now eighteen and thinks he's all grown up, he's still my baby, and it's my job to give him the very best that I can.

I bloody hate Kidderminster. And Tim. And carpets. And the whole damn world.

The rain is crashing against the windows, and a crisp bag flies up in the wind and splatters across the glass. I stare at it – cheese and onion. My least favourite crisps. A bad omen.

I see Barb looking in at me, a questioning expression on her face. I force a smile onto mine, and give her a little wave. I hope it is a wave that says 'look how calm I am, it's all fine!' not a wave that says 'the end of the world is nigh!'

My phone pings, and I pick it up, fighting the urge to throw it through the window. It is rarely good news.

I find a smile when I see it is a message from Charlie. 'Sorry I was a dick this morning,' it reads. 'PS – the internet is back. And the milk is off. And we need bog roll.'

I reply with a series of random emojis that have no meaning whatsoever. My mood is complicated, in the way that only a stream of small cartoon faces can ever express.

As soon as I've finished my reply, the phone pings again. This time, it's not so pleasant. It's from the bank, informing me that I am 72p past my overdraft limit, and that if I don't pay in this grievous amount by midnight, I'll be charged £25. I consider replying, but there are no emojis that fully convey the way I feel about this. Now I'll have to go to the bank later and put a pound in, one of the last twenty of them in my purse – but it's payday soon, I remind myself. Though how many more paydays I'll have is a matter of some conjecture right now.

The day moves slowly, all of us quiet and gently downtrodden, flattened like my lupins in the rain. We are kind to each other, there are more teas and coffees than normal, and we all get on with our work. Heaven forbid our productivity rates should slump at a time like this.

It is hard to concentrate, and I have to redo several pieces of work because my mind has suddenly taken on the characteristics of one of those baboons who try to pull your windscreen wipers off at safari parks. Leaping all over the place, loud, smelly, nimble, bare-arsed.

I keep finding myself dragged back to those bedsits, and each time I do, it gets worse and worse. I imagine Charlie falling in with drug dealers or gangs, and myself becoming an alcoholic, and before long we are both just toothless drudges, like the poor people in those Hogarth paintings of gin mills.

My resilience is low, and I am glad to be working in an office full of other people. While I am around other people, I will be able to hold it together. While I am around other people, I will be able to smile and joke and fully inhabit my Brave Face. I will be able to stay strong for their sake, if not my own. I am aware, of course, that eventually I will be alone – that I will be back in my little cottage, on the edge of the world, with a glass of wine and a luxurious new multipack of bargain-basement toilet tissue.

Then, I will have to face up to this. I will have to think about the future, and finances, and all those sorts of grown-up things that make me want to run screaming into the hills. My life might not be a party, but it is solid – Charlie is solid, and that's what matters. Keeping his life on an even keel, where all he has to worry about is the occasional internet break, is the most important thing in my universe. He might think that his life is boring, but he has no idea how lucky he is – boring is a luxury, a privilege. Boring takes effort.

After what feels like at least ten days, my shift is over. We all troop out of the building, Barb staying behind to lock up, with promises to take care and stay cheerful and not think the worst. I have a weird vision of a group of strangers, somewhere in Kidderminster, doing exactly the same.

Charlie has messaged me to say he is in town, and he will meet me for a lift home. We make our arrangements, and I go about my very pressing business – the bank, the shops and a luxury spa with full body massage, detoxifying facial and a glass of cucumber water. That last one was a lie – the closest I'm getting to a spa any time soon is standing in the rain and looking upwards.

Our small town is nice enough, a strange mix of the usual soulless modern high street shops and a few rows of old Tudor buildings that have survived from days of yore. Of course, these are the buildings that feature on all the postcards, and on the websites of the people here who boost their income by hosting tourists.

There are a few tourists around today, and my heart aches for them. Families with young children mostly, toddlers jumping in puddles, soaking-wet parents looking exhausted and bedraggled as they wander around the shops and the one amusement arcade. This is probably not the holiday they'd hoped for. This is not what England in July should be like.

By the time I get back to the car, Charlie is already there. He is leaning against the bonnet looking at his phone, shielding it from the worst of the downpour with his hands. As ever, I feel a little jolt of surprise when I see him.

I know this isn't an uncommon feeling among

parents, but it only feels like yesterday that he was a baby. Then, the day after that, he was starting primary school. Maybe a week after when he started losing his first teeth, and calling me Mum instead of Mummy, and making new friends at high school. Now he is huge, hairy and hungry – all three, all the time.

I am a person of averages – average height, average build, average attractiveness. I have long brown hair and blue eyes and the only thing about me that ever gets commented upon is my smile. I'm told it's a cracker, and was once offered a job as a croupier in a casino purely on the basis of it. I should probably consider a new career as a smile model, as it seems like I might be needing one soon.

Charlie, though, is very much his father's son – at least when it comes to appearances. He is already over six foot tall, still slender from the terrifying growth spurt he had last year, with wild dark curls that make him look like a young Heathcliff. His eyes are deep brown, like his dad's, and he has that half-man, half-boy vibe that kids of his age always seem to display. Keeping up with his need for new clothes and new shoes has been a fun time recently, and I will be financially relieved when he stops doing this growing-up thing.

I still can't believe that this gorgeous young dude came out of my body, and I am flooded with love as I approach him.

'Did you get the bog roll?' he asks, barely tearing his eyes away from the screen. Ah, the magic of parenthood.

'I'm fine thanks, son, thanks for asking. My day was good, nice of you to inquire.'

He pulls a face and rolls his eyes in patented teenaged fashion but doesn't fight me off when I give him a hug. My coat is a shabby affair, frayed at the cuffs and repaired at the hem. I am wet and hot and probably look terrible. He is wearing a really nice Regatta jacket that I picked up in the sales that seems to be keeping him toasty. Mama's Little Soldier.

We climb into the car, and I ask him how his day was – because it was definitely better than mine.

'All right,' he answers, twisting his long legs to get comfortable. 'Met some of the gang. Did some hard drugs, drank ten pints, hooked up with some exotic dancers . . .'

'Ah. The usual stuff then?'

'Yeah. Plus, I was looking for a job.'

I pause as he says this, biting my lip. He is eighteen, and it would be good for him to have a job. He wanted one earlier, but I was keen for him to do well in his A levels. To be able to go to uni – to build the kind of life he deserves; the kind I turned my back on. It has been a touchy subject between us – we don't disagree about much, but this is one of those things. We had a spectacular row about it, where I pointed out he needed to concentrate on his studies, and he pointed out that I was 'an emotional vampire trying to live my life through his'. It blew over, as these things do, but the fact that he is looking for work pretty much straight away after his A levels tells me it has not been forgotten.

Now, though, I have to accept that it would be good for him – both as a human and as a person who lives with me, the possibly soon-to-be-unemployed mum. Things are different now – and he might not be able to rely on me forever. It hurts to even think that, but it's true.

I hide all of this from him, and simply ask: 'Find anything?'

'Not yet. There was a kitchen porter job in the hotel, but I wasn't keen on that. Dangerous.'

'Really? How? I mean, I know there are sharp knives and stuff . . .'

'Nah, Mum, it's not that. You know when you watch a film or a TV show, and there's a bad guy being chased? They always run out through the kitchens, don't they? And the cops chase them, and all the poor staff get knocked over or hit with frying pans or flying bullets . . . dangerous.'

He winks at me to show he is joking, and I reply: 'Yeah. You're right. Lots of brutal gun chases in small towns in Norfolk. What's the real reason?'

'Pay was rubbish and the nights were late. Like, after the bus late.'

'I'd always come and get you, you know that!'

'Mum, you're usually in bed by ten!'

'I know . . . but I'd wait up for you, Charlie. You know I would.'

He pats my hand and nods. 'I do know, Mum. Thanks. And once I get a job, I can pay for driving lessons, and that will be cool. Can we go home now? I'm really soggy.'

I turn the key in the ignition, realising that it is that weird temperature where it's too warm to put the heating on, but too wet to feel warm enough. It'll be a jiggle with the buttons all the way home, balancing tropical heat against a steamed-up windscreen. Life, eh? Full of challenges.

Except, I soon find out, getting the air con right won't be one challenge that I need to face today – because the car doesn't start. I try again, and again, and again. I swear a bit, and remind myself that I filled it up only a week or so ago, and wonder if I've somehow got a flat battery. This is, unfortunately, the extent of my mechanical knowledge.

'The car isn't starting,' says Charlie, frowning.

'Really? You think?'

'Umm ... is there enough petrol in it?'

'Of course!' I say, a bit too sharply.

He raises his eyebrows and wisely remains silent. He is, I know, thinking about a time a few years ago when I was trying to budget a bit too carefully and driving on fumes for a day. We ended up stuck at the side of a country lane in weather very similar to this while I walked to the nearest garage – which was four miles away. Happy times.

I try the key again, but nothing happens. No sound, no gas, nothing at all. I sit still, and feel my fake sense of 'everything's OK' float away from me. My hands are gripping the steering wheel so tightly that my knuckles are white, and I have bitten my lip so hard that I taste blood.

'Do we have ... I don't know ... like, the AA or something?' asks Charlie quietly.

I shake my head, feeling tears start to sting. No, of course we don't. That would be an unnecessary expense. I'm sure that's what everyone thinks until they're stuck in a car park in torrential rain with a broken-down car.

'It's OK,' I say, shaking my head to clear away the impending panic. 'I'll sort it tomorrow. Or the day after when I get paid. For now, my darling child, we will have to get the bus!'

He makes a gagging noise, but laughs as he gets out of the car again. I grab the shopping, button up my wet coat and join him.

He stares at the car – Nina – and pulls a face.

'It's a bit of a crap car, isn't it, Mum?'

'Don't say that, you'll hurt her feelings!'

I stare at Nina, with her dents and scratches and muddy undercarriage. With her complete lack of co-operation. I feel annoyed now – I mean, what use is Nina if she can't fulfil her primary function?

'You're right,' I say, giving one of her tyres a kick, 'it is a crap car. Come on, let's go.'

I start to think my luck has changed when we manage to get the bus with a minute to spare. The route that goes the nearest to our house only leaves once an hour, so it feels like a better omen than cheese and onion crisps. I don't usually believe in things like omens, but it's been that kind of day. I wouldn't be surprised if a giant crow flies through my window tonight and drops dead at my feet.

I embarrass Charlie by getting him a child's ticket, and we snag a couple of seats, settling in for what I know will be a bumpy ride. It takes ages to get out of town, then we go up and down winding country roads that often present many exciting entertainments – small floods, maverick sheep, overgrown hedgerows that block the path, passengers who get on and try to pay their entire fare with 2p pieces and bubble gum.

It's not especially comfortable, especially as every human being on the bus is wet and steaming. It's like being in a grimy sauna. I use my hand to wipe a patch of window clear, but all I can see is rain.

'So, did anything else happen today?' I ask, keen to distract myself from my own thoughts.

'Kind of. You know Eric?'

'Yes. You've been friends with him since year five, of course I know him.'

'That was rhetorical. Anyway, he came out on Snapchat.'

'Oh. But hasn't Eric always been gay? I mean, didn't most people already know that? What difference does saying it on social media make?'

Charlie gives me a disgusted look, and replies frostily: 'Yes, we knew, Mum – but now it's official. It's not just something his friends and family know about, it's something he's proud of. And I think it's a pretty brave thing to do.'

'OK, love,' I say quickly. 'I suppose I still think of Eric as the kid who ate all the doughnuts at your tenth birthday party and threw up on the bouncy castle, so

I struggle to engage with his sexuality. Or coming out on Snapchat.' I am only thirty-six myself, but I often feel the generational gap between me and Charlie's pals. The way they live a lot of their lives on social media, their obsessions and passions and the fact they have a whole new language. It's not that I'm right and they're wrong – I just don't quite understand it.

'Well, it's a big deal, Mum. It's not easy to be different, is it?'

'I don't know, love. I'm very boring myself. But, look, that's great – I'm all for whatever makes him happy. Should we send him a card or something?'

I'm not quite sure if I'm joking or not – I don't really know the protocol for Charlie's era - but he assumes I am.

'People have been oppressed for hundreds of years, Mum, just for being who they are, and it's important that we all try to change that – you don't have to make a joke out of everything, you know? Some of us actually give a shit about other people.' With this, he inserts his earbuds with an element of fury that surprises me.

Wow. I've somehow managed to alienate my beloved son in about three sentences, without even trying. I know from experience that once the earbuds are in, and the arms are crossed, and he is looking in the opposite direction, that there is no point trying to converse with him.

Anyway, I think, closing my eyes and leaning back, maybe he's right. Maybe I do make a joke out of everything, even when it's the wrong thing to do – even when there is absolutely nothing funny going on at all. In fact, that's what I've been doing all day. It's another coping mechanism, and sometimes it even annoys me, never mind the people around me. But Charlie isn't quite old enough or experienced enough to understand that sometimes, if you don't laugh, you cry – and if I start crying now, I might never stop.

Charlie blanks me for the whole journey, and I take it. No point arguing with a sulky teen – they have a way of dragging you down to their level anyway. Before long I'd be snapping 'whatever!' and sticking my tongue out at him. My phone is out of charge, so I amuse myself by making up fictional life stories about my fellow passengers. Absolutely scandalous what some of them get up to, I tell you.

We get off the bus, Charlie still quiet, walking the regulation five paces behind me to show me he's still at battle stations.

The bus stop is almost a mile from our house even with shortcuts, and the weather is still as delightful as it has been for the whole of the day. For weeks and weeks on end. I can't even remember what sunshine feels like – it's a vague memory, like a flashback in a film, the way your skin glows and the light lifts your mood. Plus the exotic way your hair actually stays dry all day.

My work shoes aren't ideal for this kind of trek, some of it down a muddy footpath tumbling with tree roots, but I've done it enough times to know it passes quicker than you expect as long as you don't think about it too hard.

I put my head down, into the rain and the howling wind, and tell myself that it will all be OK soon. Before long, we will arrive at our little cottage. It will be cosy and welcoming and safe and dry. We will hang our coats up over the bath, and I will make us beans on toast for dinner, and I will have my glass of wine. I will talk to Charlie about Eric's announcement in an open and curious way that shows that I am, deep down, an empathetic and emotionally evolved human being – not just an old lady in a tatty coat who makes inappropriate jokes all the time.

He is a good lad, and he will accept that, and it will also be true. We will be friends again, and all will be right with the world. I'll start looking at other jobs, just in case, and we will find a way out of this mess.

It will all be OK once I am home, I know. Once we're inside the walls of the cottage, our refuge from the weather and the worry and reality.

Except, of course, for one small fact. As we emerge from the end of the footpath and into the field, my sense of relief almost palpable as I visualise kicking off my shoes and unhooking my bra strap and pouring that wine, I see one very strange thing.

My little cottage, or at least the version of it I left this morning, simply isn't there any more.

Chapter 3

I freeze, and Charlie walks straight into the back of me. He tugs out his earbuds and looks as though he's about to make a snarky comment until he sees my face.

He follows my gaze, and his mouth drops open.

We are about a minute's walk away from our house – or at least the place where our house used to be.

Now, there are crumbling walls, a roof tilted sideways and sliding away down the side of the cliff, which has encroached all the way inland. It's a skewed, slanted fun-house version of our house, as though time has fast-forwarded a hundred years to when it is falling apart.

I can't quite believe what I am seeing. It is like something from a disaster movie, and I blink rapidly in case I am having some kind of stress-induced hallucination. It doesn't help. My home is still a wreckage of bricks, pipes and shattered tiles. The cliff face has still moved.

The wind is screaming and the rain seems even more dense than before, my feet getting sucked into the mud of the field because I've been still for so long.

A wild gust lifts the roof momentarily, and it seems to float in the air like a kite, before crashing down again. The tiles shatter and break, slipping away and down, into what would once have been my garden but is now just the new edge of the cliff.

The whole cottage has sunk low, parts of the walls completely gone, the rest reduced to crazy paving leaning and shaking to one side.

'Mum ...' murmurs Charlie, grabbing my hand. 'What the fuck has happened?'

I grip his fingers and shake my head.

'I don't know. The cliffs ... they've eaten our house!'

'But the cliffs weren't that close! There was the garden, and the vegetable patch, and the coastal pathway that everyone waves to us from when they're walking past ...'

I nod. There were all of those things, once. But now, they are gone. No more garden, or vegetable patch, or pathway. Just the sludgy brown edge of the cliff, and our home slipping away – down, down, down, onto the beach, into the sea, out of existence.

I drop my shopping bags, and run towards the house. I have no idea why – I don't think I'll be able to stop it, but some instinct just makes me run anyway. I cover the field in about thirty seconds, water splashing around my legs with every step, hair plastered to my head, wind whooshing like thunder in my ears.

As I get closer, I see the entire front of the cottage is gone. The rest has collapsed and is inching down in the same direction. The chimney has sunk in the middle of it all, and only one doorway is left standing. It's the door into the back kitchen, the one we use when we come home this way, and it is so odd, freakishly upright in the middle of the carnage, bright red and wavering in the wind. A door we'd have been walking through minutes from now, sighing with relief at being out of the rain. Now it is a door that leads nowhere, nothing behind it but smashed glass and twisted metal and ruined plasterwork.

I see flashes of colour against the deep poison-grey of the sky, bright pops of vibrancy that catch my eye. The cushions of our burgundy sofa, now covered in rubble. The remnants of our pale blue curtains, the ones I made myself. Smashed plates and mugs, yellow and cream. Flapping gingham material that used to be a tablecloth. It's a rainbow of destruction.

There is a trail of the weirdest items scattered around: paperbacks from my bookshelf, open, pages fluttering in the wind; the toaster I was battling with this morning lying on its side; clothes flying and flapping; a torn box of cornflakes, its contents dancing in the air. CDs and DVDs I'd picked up cheap at charity shops are lodged in the mud. My bed, along with its pretty floral duvet cover, is hanging half on land, half over the cliff, and the toilet has somehow landed on top of it.

I see Charlie's Xbox rolling away towards the edge, his old school textbooks and his desk, legs snapped, the only things remaining from his room.

I am paralysed by all of it until I notice the photographs. Loose, flying, wisping through the air – precious pictures that I can never replace. Pages torn from albums, the stray ones I'd tucked inside the covers, spiralling in a chaotic dance, caught in swirling wind currents.

I can buy a new sofa. I can make new curtains. I can sleep anywhere – but I can't ever get those pictures back. I run towards them, trying to snatch them from the air, grabbing at random and trying to collect them. I am jumping and stretching and crying, desperate to save as many as I can.

I hear Charlie's voice somewhere nearby but a million miles away, shouting: 'Mum! Stop! Leave them ... you're getting too close to the edge!'

He doesn't understand. These pictures are pre-digital. These pictures are priceless. These pictures are all I have to remind me of Charlie's childhood – there is no dad around, no family, nobody to reminisce with. Nobody else with a camera. It has always just been me and him, and if I lose those photos, I lose those memories. I lose that part of us. I have to get them.

I'm aware of one of my shoes coming off, getting stuck in the squelching mud, a strange sucking sensation as I leave it behind. I see a picture of Charlie on his fourth birthday, wearing a badge that is almost as big as his chest, and I try to snatch it. I miss, it flutters away, flying out of my reach.

I feel my balance deserting me, and have that dizzying moment where you know you're going to fall, the adrenaline surging up into my brain. I stagger, throw my hands out in front of me to break my descent, barely aware now of Charlie's voice and the relentless drive of the rain.

I am grabbed from behind, held, lifted, pulled back to collide with someone's body.

'It's OK! I've got you …'

I glance over my shoulder. It isn't Charlie. Charlie is metres back, a look of horror on his face, dark curls squashed flat to his head.

I look up into the face of a stranger … or maybe not. He looks familiar, but I can't place him.

'My photos!' I protest, struggling to try to get free.

His arms are firm around me, and he physically lifts me up into the air and starts to walk backwards. I am half-carried, half-stumbling, watching forlornly as I see Charlie's birthday badge picture blown away into the bleak distance.

'We'll get them,' the man says, having to shout to make himself heard over the wind, 'I promise. But for now you need to be safe. You need to stay away from the edge, and you need to talk to your son.'

Part of me wants to fight him off, to push his arms away, to scream at him. But the rest of me knows that he is right. I look up, and nod.

'Come on,' he says, taking my hand and leading me away from the chaos. From the carnage. From my entire life.

I reach out to grab Charlie's hand in my other, and together the three of us make our way across the field. It is a battle every step of the way, impossible to predict which way the gusts will come from, our bodies assault-ed from every angle.

The man leads us on, and I see that he is taking us up towards the big barn where the donkeys live. Next to it is the long white motorhome that has been here for a good few days now, and the pieces fall together – this is his motorhome. He is the man who has the little dog, and sits on his steps with a mug of tea every morning, even in the rain. The one I have categorised as 'rude and to be avoided' in my mind. And now here I am, clutching hold of his hand, breathless, soaked, confused.

After what feels like an hour, we finally make it. He lets go of me, and opens the door to the van. He holds it firmly, stopping it from flying wide, and gestures for us to get inside. I push Charlie through first, then stagger up the steps myself and follow him.

As soon as the door is closed behind us, the silence almost hurts my ears. I can still hear the storm, but it is removed, it is distant, it is shut out. The windows are rattling, and the place is rocking gently – nothing that feels like it might result in us flying away like Dorothy's house in the *Wizard of Oz*, but a gentle sway that reminds me of the force of the weather out there.

All three of us stand, still and silent, caught for a moment in our communal shell-shock.

That moment is broken by a blur of movement from one of the other rooms, a flash of black as a tiny creature hurtles towards us. My eyes snap wide, and I step in front of Charlie, going purely on instinct, dropping into some kind of weird boxer's stance.

'It's OK, Mum,' says Charlie, laying a hand on my shoulder, 'I think I'm safe.'

I look down, and see a black-and-tan daschund jumping up at me. It has its front paws on my shins, and is most definitely longer than it is tall.

I reach down and pat its head. It snuffles its muzzle into my hand, and my fingers find the silkiest, softest, floppiest ears I've ever encountered. Weirdly, it immediately makes me feel better.

'This is Betty,' the man says, leaning down and scooping her up into his arms. She nestles into him and licks his face, and I see that her tiny body is trembling.

'Bless her,' I say, giving her another stroke. 'She's terrified.'

'So am I,' Charlie replies, moving in to scratch those amazing ear. 'What the fuck happened out there?'

I don't have it in me to reprimand him for his language. He is an adult, and he is also correct – in some situations, only the word 'fuck' will suffice.

As if to back that up, an especially loud shriek of wind gives us all another gentle nudge.

'Don't worry, we're fine,' says the man, seeing my expression. 'I moved it around to the side of the barn as soon as the wind got bad. I'm Luke, by the way.'

As he talks, he opens an overhead cupboard and pulls out a stack of towels. We all take one, and the act of rubbing my own hair makes me realise exactly how wet I am. In fact we're creating puddles on his floor.

We are in what seems to be the living area, and it is surprisingly spacious. There is a table that looks as though it folds back up, a banquette-style sofa that probably doubles as a bed, and a compact cooking area with a hob and microwave. Beyond the contents, though, it feels really nice and lived-in – there are gorgeous framed photos on display, showing beautiful sunsets in beautiful places, and a small shelf lined with fossils and seashells and pressed flowers in glass. A battered acoustic guitar is propped up by the window.

I see a scattering of well-worn paperbacks, a newspaper folded open to the crossword, a pair of binoculars and a clearly much-used *Guide to British Birds*. This feels like a proper home, not like a holiday home. Despite the fact that there are three wet people and a dog in here, it doesn't feel too cramped, and it even smells nice – probably due to the small tribe of scented candles in glass jars and tins that are grouped together on the table. My eyes run over the labels: bergamot, lavender, mint, rosemary and sea salt.

I can imagine, under better circumstances, how nice this would be – a cosy night in, reading a book by candlelight, everything close by and tucked away. Safe and cocooned. Everything I once associated with my own home, which is now halfway down a cliff that didn't even exist this morning.

I thud down onto the banquette, suddenly running on empty. Suddenly and totally exhausted, numb, incapable of staying upright for a moment longer. There was so much damage out there – even the stuff that hadn't fallen was wrecked, coated in debris, buried beneath the bricks that once protected us, the roof that should be over our heads.

Everything has gone. Our clothes, our furniture, our books and games and precious photos. Our passports and paperwork and phone chargers and the laptop and the Xbox. Our bedding and towels and curtains and food and pots and pans and the slow cooker I never even use. Our flowers and our vegetable patch and our little patio set and my own scented candles. Our shoes and coats and Charlie's collection of random baseball caps and my few items of jewellery. The cookie jar shaped like an owl; the trophy he won for the Good Citizen Award in year six that I've embarrassed him with ever since; his GCSE certificates; all our fridge magnets.

So many things, all gone. A new one seems to crowd into my mind every second, and I feel the panic starting to rise. The panic, and the grief – because these aren't just things, are they? They are memories. They are moments. They are the physical manifestation of a life lived together. And now they are lost.

It's the thought of the baby scan picture that finally pushes me over the edge. I always meant to put it in a frame, along with the pictures of Charlie as a newborn, but somehow I never did. I just kept it, in an envelope, tucked inside one of the albums. I know it was just a fuzzy black-and-white outline, I know I have the real thing in front of me right now, and I know it is silly to react like this – but that is the loss that makes me cry. I feel big, fat tears rolling down the side of my face and don't even have the energy to wipe them away.

Charlie kneels down in front of me and pats my hands. He looks distraught, and about twelve years old, and I see that he is trying to comfort me even though he is still an overgrown version of the baby in that scan photo. I squeeze his hands in return.

'I'm all right, love,' I say, as calmly as I can. 'I'm

just in shock. And sad. It'll all be OK, I promise. I just needed to have a little cry, it seems …'

'You never cry, Mum,' he replies, still looking uncertain.

Hah, I think – as if. I cry all the time. I just do it when I'm alone, because nobody wants their child seeing that, do they? Us mums are supposed to be invincible, unbeatable, unsinkable. We stay strong for the sake of our kids, even if that means we have our meltdowns in private.

Luke has remained silent so far, watching this mini-drama unfold before him. It has taken perhaps five minutes.

'Tea?' he asks now, raising his eyebrows in question.

I nod, and wonder if he has any brandy. I don't think my much-anticipated bottle of wine will have survived today's events somehow. Another loss to mourn – alas, poor Chardonnay, I knew him well.

Charlie sinks down next to me and we sit together, wet and shaking, holding hands. Betty jumps up to join us, and she is such a sweet little thing, I even consider a smile.

I glance at Luke as he goes about his business, filling a kettle, getting mugs. The kitchen is tiny but perfectly formed, everything in its place, little storage cupboards built in all over. He is a big man, I realise, and he takes up a lot of the space.

I have seen him before, of course, and part of my brain had registered that he was a good-looking human – but his standoffishness completely obliterated that aspect.

Now, things are different, and I find myself seeing him in a much more appreciative light.

He is as wet as we are, a black T-shirt with the logo of a rock band on the front plastered to his body, a pair of faded Levis dark with rain and mud. He has dark hair, so closely cropped it is almost shaved. He has the tanned skin of the outdoors type, the kind of nose you see on statues in museums, and a wide mouth. I stare at him as he concentrates on what he is doing, and wonder how old he is – there are creases on that face, laughter lines around the green eyes, a certain lived-in quality that speaks of challenge and experience.

He meets my gaze, and I am suddenly embarrassed. I know nothing about him, and he is not a stranger on a bus. I am silly to be trying to make up a backstory for him. He is clearly a seasoned travelling man, without a care in the world – I am simply filling in the blanks, pondering his life to stop myself thinking about my own.

As though I have manifested it, he produces a bottle of brandy, and holds it up. I nod, and he glugs a generous splash into my mug. He glances at Charlie, and I fight off the urge to say no. He is eighteen, and he has had a Very Bad Day as well.

Luke sits opposite on a small footstool, and we are silent for a few moments. The mug is warm against my palms, the brandy is warm against my throat, and it is helping.

'I called 999,' he says, once we have all savoured our first mouthfuls. 'They told me they'd get people out here as soon as they could – there's been a pile-up on the Norwich road, and all kinds of accidents because of the storm. They're sending people out to cordon it all off, and to close the beach, in case ...'

'In case my house falls on a dog walker's head?'

'Yeah. That. It started getting bad about an hour ago, stuff flying around from your garden – but this ... this happened pretty fast. It was like the sea just swallowed the cliff, it all collapsed, and then the cottage started to shake, and bit by bit ... it fell. I'm so sorry. But at least you weren't there – I saw your car was gone, but there was still a moment where I wondered, and that's why I came down to check.'

'Thank you,' I murmur, really meaning it. 'That was both kind and brave, running towards the disaster instead of away from it. I'm not sure I'd have done the same. And I know it's lucky, really, that we weren't in – we might have been, but my car broke down in town and we had to get the bus. I was pretty annoyed about that at the time, but ... well, maybe it saved our lives, now I come to think of it ...'

For a moment my mind drifts to a dark place; a place where me and Charlie were at home, getting ready for a quiet night in. Where Charlie was gone, along with his Xbox. It's been an absolute shit of a day, but it could definitely have been worse.

'Do you have a phone charger?' I ask, suddenly aware of the fact that I need to start thinking about some practicalities.

Luke nods and retrieves one from a drawer.

I root my phone out of my bag and find, naturally enough, that it doesn't fit. Charlie's, however, does. Success.

'What will you do?' Luke asks, frowning. 'I mean, in the short term?'

'I was thinking maybe a brief period of anxiety followed by a full-blown panic attack ... but after that, well, I don't know. I have to speak to the landlord – he lives in London. I have to speak to my work colleagues and tell them I won't be in tomorrow. I have to ... find somewhere for us to live?' The last few words trail out limply, as though they ran out of energy halfway to being spoken. It's all too much. It's too big, and too weird, and too insane.

'That's long term,' says Luke, looking at me with concern. 'For now, let's take it one step at a time. Get warm. Drink your tea. Make your phone calls. You can always stay here for the night if you need to. Betty won't mind.'

A small smile makes its way to my lips, and I see Charlie has scooted Betty onto his lap. She's like a canine comfort blanket.

'Again, thank you. I'm Jenny, by the way, and this is Charlie. Nice to meet you, and sorry it took my house falling off a cliff for me to introduce myself. I should have done it ages ago. Brought you some home-baked cookies or something ...'

Charlie snorts in disbelief next to me, and I have to grin. He is right. The best I would have managed would have been a plate full of artfully unpacked Oreos.

'That's OK,' replies Luke seriously. 'I'm not exactly Mr Sociable, to be honest. Plus, I don't eat cookies. I only eat what I can forage in the wild. I live off nature's bounty.'

'Really?' I ask, finding it hard to imagine. My idea of foraging is the bargain fridge at the supermarket.

'No,' he says, grinning. 'Though I am honing my mushroom-gathering skills.'

He has a great grin, warm and infectious, which comes as something of a surprise. Both me and Charlie laugh much more than the joke called for.

For just a moment, I forget my new reality. I forget the wreckage, my lost belongings, my impending redundancy, my financial strife. We are both safe and well, here in a cosy place, sipping brandy and fondling a small dog. It could definitely be worse, and I need to focus on that instead of letting my mind race ahead too far.

Betty suddenly jumps off Charlie's lap and starts barking at the door. It is a much bigger bark than you'd expect from a dog of her proportions. Her whole body is shaking as she wags her little tail.

'She's a killer,' I say, as Luke gets up and opens the door.

Outside, there is a man in a hi-vis vest, his fist raised as though he was about to knock on the door. His hard hat is blown to one side, and his eyes are screwed up against the wind. Luke gestures for him to come inside, and quickly tugs the door shut behind him.

It now does feel a bit cramped in here, and Luke clears

the items from the table, and folds it back up against the wall, hooking it securely to create more space.

'Hi!' says our visitor. 'Shocking out there, isn't it?'

'Um ... yes?' I reply. I'd say that having your house fall down definitely qualifies as shocking.

'I'm Bob. From the council.'

He is wearing a hard hat. And his name is Bob. So, automatically, I start humming the *Bob the Builder* theme tune, and hope that he can fix it. He doesn't react – maybe he's heard it before.

'Are you the property owner?' he asks, looking around. I'm guessing that Luke fits more into the mental image of a man who lives in a van than I do. And once upon a time, just a few hours ago, I was wearing office clothes and looking more respectable. Now I only have one shoe and I'm covered in mud.

'We rent it,' I reply. 'Or we did. Not much left now. Do you think there's anything that can be done to salvage it?'

'Oh no, I wouldn't have thought so,' he says blithely. 'Certainly not today. There are people on the way to make the scene safe, cut off the gas and electric, that kind of thing. We don't won't an explosion on top of everything else, do we?'

'No. We really don't,' I say, my eyes widening. Bob is clearly not someone who is good at reading the room.

'The main thing now,' he continues, 'is to make sure nobody gets hurt. I've done a quick survey and it looks as though the worst is over, and there won't be any more land loss. The storm is peaking, and tomorrow the forecast is much better. Then we can do a proper assessment and take things from there.'

'Will we be able to go back?' asks Charlie. 'And, you know, see if we can find any of our things?'

'I can't say at this stage. We have dealt with this kind of thing before on this coastline, but it's usually a lot more gradual. It usually happens over days or even weeks, which means we can do a planned evacuation, give people time to pack. This ... well, this wasn't that, was it? I've not seen this happen before.' He sounds genuinely intrigued, like this has all presented him with an amazing puzzle to solve.

'Wow. We just got lucky, I suppose,' I say, feeling a stirring of annoyance. I control it, because none of this is Bob's fault.

'It's the weather,' he says thoughtfully. 'Climate change is real. What happens in a big storm like this, the cliffs get eroded. We saw it with the Beast from the East in 2018. This time, though, it's on top of weeks and weeks of rain, which has softened everything up. That process has probably been going on for a while. We get quite a few landslides when the precipitation is heavy and constant. So, you've got the rain, the erodibility of the cliffs here, and the erosivity of the waves being whipped up. Between those things, plus the geology, the local currents, the groundwater levels ... well, I suppose it was the perfect storm.'

I meet Luke's eyes, and he shakes his head. It's not just me imagining it – Bob has said those last words with a total lack of irony.

'Totally,' I reply. 'Pretty much the best storm I've ever seen.'

He nods eagerly, glad that I agree. 'For now, I need you to stay away from the building. I've classed it officially as being structurally unsafe.'

I blink, assaulted with images of cracked walls and the crumbling plasterwork and the roof flapping in the wind like one hand clapping. The toilet, perched on my bed. 'I have to say, I think you're right,' I answer. It is better than what I wanted to say, which was a heavily sarcastic 'No shit, Sherlock.'

It is only just sinking in, now, how close I'd come to being structurally unsafe myself – running around out there near the new cliff edge, trying to save photos. I wasn't listening to Charlie, and in that moment, I hadn't been at all concerned with what might have happened if I'd slipped in the wrong spot and followed my lupins into the sea below. I shudder at the thought.

'Right,' continues Bob, all business. 'Well. My team is on its way, as are the emergency services, so for now we need to get you somewhere safe for the night. Do you have family you can go to?'

It is a simple question, of course, but it has a complicated answer. Yes, I have family – but they live hundreds of miles away and I haven't seen them for almost two decades. We're not what you'd call close.

Bob doesn't need to know any of that, so I just shake my head. I see a moment of sadness flitter across Charlie's face, and bite my lip. He has always wanted a bigger family, has always envied the chaos of his friends' lives, the tangle of siblings and grandparents and cousins and aunts and uncles. Whereas I've been content with our solitude – I chose it, after all – he has often said he always wished he had more relatives around him. He doesn't understand that the upsides come with steep downsides, or how the people you love most in the world can also be the ones who hurt you the worst.

I feel a wash of melancholy, probably a combination of everything that has happened today and the brandy – yet another perfect storm.

'We can get you to a hotel,' Bob continues, oblivious to the swirl of emotions he has unleashed. 'Find you some clothes, the basics. Maybe you could make me a list of what you urgently need, and I'll see what I can do?'

'Um ... how much will it cost? The hotel?'

I hate the fact that I have to ask. I hate the fact that I am worried about my card getting declined, about embarrassing Charlie, about the money that I don't have.

'Nothing. We have a fund for things like this, don't worry. It won't be the Ritz, and you shouldn't hit the minibar, but your accommodation and food will be covered.'

'No minibar?' I repeat. 'Not even those stubby tubes of Pringles or a Toblerone that costs a tenner?'

'Umm ... well, under the circumstances, maybe the Pringles? Anyway. I'll leave you to it, and come back in a bit for that list. Are you OK here for the time being?'

He glances between me and Luke, obviously uncertain of the dynamic here, of how we relate to each other's lives.

'They'll be fine here,' says Luke, my Good Samaritan in a Motorhead top.

Bob nods and leaves with a jaunty wave. The wind almost blows him off his feet as he steps outside, and Betty barks at it, just to be safe.

'Am I imagining it,' I ask, 'or did we just make Bob's day?'

'I think you did,' Luke replies, smiling. Weird how he's been distant and grumpy until now, and in the midst of disaster there's a whole new side to him. 'He'll probably be talking to people in the pub about this for years.'

'Yeah. I wonder if he's married? Maybe he'll go home and start saying "heightened levels of erosivity" to his wife . . .'

'The dirty bastard.'

We all laugh, but it is strained. Luke has done his best for us – he has physically removed me from a stupidly dangerous situation, rescued me from my own recklessness, and he has kept us safe and warm and given us strong liquor. But these are not pleasant circumstances, and this is not a pleasant social occasion. It is a disaster zone.

I feel brittle, taut, like a string that could snap at any moment.

'It'll be OK,' says Luke firmly. 'It might not feel like it now, but it will. You'll feel better after a shower, and some sleep, and maybe some more brandy. I'll be here for the next week, and I'll help in any way I can. Plus you have Betty on your side now, and in my experience there are very few situations that she can't improve.'

Right on cue, Betty licks my hand. I hope he's right.

Chapter 4

Bob the Not Builder is a man of his word, and he arranges a taxi to take me and Charlie to the glamorous location of a service station with its own version of a Travelodge. It has a dodgy neon sign outside it that is on the blink, announcing to the world that it has free Wi.

'At least it has free Wi,' I said to Charlie, as we walked to the lobby.

'Yeah. But the kicker is it's £100 an hour for the Fi,' he replied.

Before we left, Luke insisted on handing me some cash, 'just in case you need the Toblerone'. I was hesitant to accept it – Luke lives in a motorhome, he doesn't exactly seem dripping in wealth. I felt that he had done enough, that the kindness of strangers can be taken too far – but one look at Charlie's face told me he was right.

He was pale, exhausted, a faint tremor on his lips. The boy was going to need a Toblerone for sure, or maybe a bag of fish and chips. Luke's money also meant that I had enough to call off at a supermarket and pick up a phone charger, which is most definitely one of life's essentials these days.

The hotel was expecting us, and greeted us like refugees – which I suppose we were. The staff on reception had already got together a package for us: basic toiletries, toothbrushes, a box of spare clothes that had been left behind in rooms and never reclaimed and, in an especially kind touch, a bottle of red wine. I felt like kissing both the bottle and the receptionist.

We were escorted to a decent-sized twin room on the first floor, and told to make ourselves at home. Goodness, I thought, please don't let that be true – it was a pleasant enough hotel, but it was far from being home. We both showered, and I hand-washed our undies in the sink using shower gel and, before we both collapsed, went in search of food.

The restaurant was still open, and we were told it was all being paid for by the council. Now we are sitting here, among people with normal lives, people who presumably still have homes and possessions. It all feels so strange. The storm has indeed calmed, but the sky is still grey, already dark and gloomy by 9 p.m., perfectly suiting our mood as we sit at a small table by the window with plates full of pizza and garlic bread.

Charlie, always hungry at the best of times, is wolfing his down like a man who has been starved for a week. I see the immediate effect – he seems stronger the moment the first bite of pepperoni hits his tongue. I, on the other hand, am finding it impossible to stomach more than a mouthful. I am just too tired, too stressed, too on edge. A million thoughts are swirling around in my mind, none of them good. You don't realise how much stuff you have – how much stuff you need – until you lose it.

I am chatting to Charlie, trying to keep his spirits up, but at the same time I am mentally cataloguing everything we need to replace and how much it will cost. Multitasking at its finest. I am trying to avoid cataloguing the things that we can't ever replace – the pictures, the knick-knacks, the items that have no financial value but are the ones I will miss the most. I wish I was sitting at my own kitchen table, with its gingham cloth and the little jam jar I'd filled with wild flowers. I wish I was eating beans on toast rather than this feast, looking forward to nothing more exciting than finding something to watch on TV.

As we'd travelled home on the bus earlier today – could it possibly still be the same day? I wonder – my problems had seemed overwhelming. The threat of losing my job. The few days left until payday. A minor spat with Charlie. Now, looking back, I'd give anything to go back in time and only have those problems to deal with. I suppose that's always the way in life, isn't it? A lesson to live in the present, even if it seems less than ideal. In fact, I'd better enjoy this pizza, before Godzilla and King Kong decide to fight their last and greatest battle in rural Norfolk and we become collateral damage. You never know – it could happen.

'Mum?' says Charlie, interrupting my thoughts. I can tell from his tone that it's not the first time he's said the word. 'Are you OK? You look a bit . . . wrecked?'

'Ah, thank you, son,' I reply, forcing a smile onto my

face. 'Always nice to know I'm creating a good impression. I'm all right, yeah, just, you know, thinking about stuff.'

'You always tell me it's a bad idea to think too much.'

'And it probably is – but there is a lot of stuff to think about right now, and I'm trying to do it before I fall asleep for a thousand years.'

He nods and puts down his fork. He stares at the table, at the remnants of our meal, and says: 'It's nice here, isn't it? Great food.'

I glance around and see a few business travellers, some tourists probably on their way to somewhere else, men who look like they're on a stopover on their truck-driving routes. It is nice, in a generic refillable-coffee-machine kind of way.

'Yep,' I reply. 'I'd give it two Michelin Tyres.'

He frowns, not getting the reference, but not wanting to show it.

'Michelin is a restaurant guide,' I explain. 'And a company that makes tyres. That's what makes it a hilarious joke. You can look it up on your phone, and then it will become real to you.'

'Oh. I see. Is this going to be one of those "the younger generation never get off their phones" conversations? The one where you tell me that in your day, you used to play on rope swings for twelve hours and drink water straight from the sewers and play rounders in the park even though you had a broken ankle and it never did you any harm?'

My mouth twitches in amusement; we have had

versions of this conversation many times. It is a game we regularly play. 'Yeah. You young people and your phones, it's a disgrace. I bet you don't know how to do anything without your phone.'

'No, we don't. I have to google "wiping your own arse" every time I go to the loo.'

'Wouldn't surprise me. I bet, before long, everything will be replaced with phones.'

'Like what?'

I screw up my eyes and try to think of a silly example – we both need the distraction; we both need a few moments of levity.

'Like bins. I bet you don't have bins in the future.'

'No, we'll just use our phones.'

'And chairs.'

'You're right, we'll just sit on our phones. They're really comfy.'

'And Pot Noodles.'

'Mum! Don't be ridiculous – some things are sacred, and we will always have Pot Noodles …' He reaches out and squeezes my hand, grinning. 'We'll be all right, Mum. We can still make each other laugh, so all is well in the world.'

He is being so brave, so grown-up, so mature – he is comforting me, consoling me, trying to get me to see the bright side. This is a whole new dynamic to our relationship and I'm not totally sure how I feel about it. He is my baby, my child, my responsibility – I am the one who should be looking after him, not the other way around. I know none of this is my fault – I didn't create the storm or the cliffs or the sea – but I still feel terrible, as though I have let him down.

'But your stuff, Charlie. I'm so sorry ...'

''S'OK. Eventually, I'll get new stuff. And it is only stuff.'

'Even your Xbox?'

'Well, that's part of my soul, like Voldemort and his horcruxes, but less creepy. I carry my Xbox within me, wherever I go ... but one day, maybe I'll upgrade. You can help me pick a new username, it'll be like a whole new world.'

'I vote for DickBagBallFace.'

'I'm not sure that'll fit. Could abbreviate it to Dick? What do you think?'

'I think,' I say, leaning across the table to give him a big and undoubtedly embarrassing kiss on the forehead, 'that you are the best human in the whole world. I love you, and I'm proud of you, and right now I even like you.'

'Wow. The L word. Thanks. So ... what happens next?'

'In life?'

'More like tonight.'

What I would like to happen next is for me to curl up in a ball in my nice clean bed and sleep. Lord knows I need it. But I also know that with my mind in its current hyper-aware state, there is no way that I will manage it. I will just lie awake, tossing and turning and thinking and crying, and that will not be good for me or for Charlie.

'I think you should go back up to the room and chill for a bit,' I say, watching with astonishment as he demolishes a whole slice of garlic bread that was left on the plate.

He holds up a hand to gesture for me to wait while he finishes chewing. Charming.

'And what will you do?' he asks. 'Hit the bar, go clubbing?'

'Probably, yeah. I'll be twerking on the tables within the hour. But, before that, I have some boring stuff to do – phone calls to make, things to sort, that kind of thing. I'll follow you up in a bit, OK?'

He yawns, hiding his mouth with his hand, and replies: 'I was going to argue, but you're right. I'm knackered. See you in a bit.'

He stands up, and once again I marvel at his ridiculous height. He is wearing a pair of tracksuit trousers from the hotel box of abandoned garments, and they are about three inches too short. He gives me a hug, and I pass him the keys.

'He was nice, wasn't he? That guy from the motorhome? Luke? You'd made a few snarky comments about him being rude before ...'

'Yeah. Well, he kind of was, to be honest – but maybe that was just the surface, and underneath he's really nice. We'll have to pop in and thank him. Maybe take him a little "ta for dragging us out of the storm" present.'

'Didn't look like he needed much, did he? One of those people who seems totally sorted. Maybe something for Betty instead.'

He's right, now I come to think about it. Luke might live in a motorhome, but it is a spacious and pleasant motorhome, perfectly equipped for a presumably adventurous life on the open road. Luke might not forage for his food, but he does give off a self-sufficient vibe – possibly a 'don't bother me' vibe, which is how I'd first thought of him. Betty will definitely be an easier buy – bag of dog treats, squeaky toy, boom.

'That's a great idea love. Now scoot!'

Charlie nods firmly, and leaves, giving me a little wave over his shoulder. I notice a teenaged girl who is eating with her parents follow him with her gaze as he heads to the stairs, and it makes me smile. My son – the accidental heartbreaker.

Once he has gone, I relocate to the small bar area with a glass of wine, taking my now wonderfully charged-up phone with me. I spend an hour or so making calls: first to Barb, who is aghast at this strange turn of events and promises to help in any way she can. I can't help thinking that this kind of thing simply wouldn't happen to a woman like Barb. Her house wouldn't dare fall off a cliff.

I leave a message for the landlord, and am not especially looking forward to that conversation. I register my claim with our insurers, not at all convinced that they will pay out, but refusing to imagine what will happen if they don't. I check my emails, and stalk a few people on Facebook, and I read the online news report about 'a severe cliff-fall on the local coast'. It's weird, reading the words and seeing the picture that seems to have been taken with a drone, and knowing that it is my home they are talking about. That their breaking news is my breaking life.

The photo isn't too clear – probably not ideal weather for drone photography – but I can vividly see the wreckage of my once-lovely home – the roof has finally given up and come off completely, the red kitchen door is still somehow standing, the cliffside is strewn with my furniture. I can make out yellow tape cordoning it all off, and vans parked up nearby.

I scroll away quickly – it is too upsetting. I fear it will overwhelm me, so I move on. I browse the internet for a while, doing that mindless tumble from one link to the next that we've all become familiar with. The online shuffle. I read a few articles, check out a few websites and then finish my wine.

I still don't feel like I'm going to be able to sleep, but I can't stay here forever. I gather my belongings, say goodnight to the staff and head up to the room.

I try to creep in quietly, but Charlie sits up as I close the door behind me. His curls are all over the place, and it's so adorable, he'd be mortified if he could see it.

'You all right?' he asks groggily. 'Not going dancing?'

'Nah. Hadn't got my dancing shoes.'

I point to my feet, and the bright pink Crocs that I found in the box. Beggars, choosers, et cetera.

I head into the bathroom and use a strange toothbrush, and a strange towel, and look into the mirror to see a strange woman. I am dressed in clothes I don't recognise, and my eyes are dark and tired. I look dreadful.

That is, I decide, understandable. This has not been the kind of day that lends itself to an immaculate beauty routine.

I take off the clothes I don't recognise and climb under sheets that are not mine, in a bed that is unfamiliar. I can hear the sound of cars outside as people top up on petrol and buy late-night snacks and go on with their journeys. For everyone else, this is a stopping off-point – for me, it is the beginning of a whole new and frankly terrifying stage of my life.

'Hey, Charlie?' I say, as I pull the duvet up to my chin and try to create a snuggly feeling to comfort myself.

'Yeah?'

'I'm really pleased for Eric. You're right, it is brave.'

There is a pause before he replies, and perhaps he is thinking the same as me – that that conversation now feels like it took place in another lifetime.

He grunts, but I can see the glimmer of a smile from the light creeping through the curtains.

'Go to sleep, Mum!' he answers, amusement in his voice.

And, amazingly, I do exactly that.

Chapter 5

It is three days before we are allowed back to the place that we used to call home. We woke up the morning after it all happened to be confronted with dazzling sunshine and dry skies; the first day without rain for a month. I kind of felt like the world was mocking me, watching the local TV news raving on about the impending heatwave, doing wrap-up pieces that featured the storm damage but focusing on all the good times ahead. Fire up the barbie, get your shorts on, don't forget the factor 50. If I ever meet that weatherman, I might punch him in the face.

We continued our stay at the hotel, and are now so familiar with the staff that they feel like part of an extended family. I have had meetings with Bob, and I have talked to the man in London who owns – owned – our cottage. He was amazingly laid-back about it all, but I'm assuming that our cottage was just one of a larger portfolio of properties, that maybe he was insured, that maybe he's a multi-squillionaire, that for some reason this is not the same kind of disaster for him as it is for us. I have no idea which. He has offered us another place to stay, but it is in Essex. Charlie was all for it, as he believes the entire county will be awash with 'super-hot reality TV stars', but it's not really a feasible commute.

I have been looking for somewhere more local to rent, but it is difficult – at the moment I don't have money set aside to pay for security deposits and advance payments, all of which you need to get a lease. I might get my deposit back from the multi-squillionaire landlord, but I'm not sure when. To add to the mass of 'not sures' that make up my life, I also don't even know if I'll have a job for much longer.

I have, however, got my wages, which takes some of the short-term strain away. I've cancelled the direct debit for my rent, because, well, you know – the house fell off the edge of the world. I've no idea if the landlord will object, or in fact even notice, so I am not going to raise the issue. There is a time to be single-minded, and this is probably it.

It's been a very weird few days. Everyone has been so nice, so supportive, done everything they can to help. Barb turned up at the hotel the day after with a suitcase full of clothes for both of us – she has a son a few years older than Charlie and raided his cast-offs. They're in better nick than Charlie's original wardrobe, so he's pretty pleased. Me, not so much – Barb wears a lot more florals and lace than I am accustomed to, and while I really appreciated it, I am still walking around feeling like I've been snatched and put in someone else's body. I feel a trip to the charity shop coming on, this time for me and not the Incredible Expanding Boy.

But at least today, we are heading home. Kind of.

As the taxi pulls up at the edge of the lane, I feel a sense of constriction in my chest, a tightness in my throat. I know it is only a physical reaction to my emotional dread, but it is still unpleasant. I hide it from Charlie, and we make the familiar walk up to the cottage. Or the cottage-sized space. We are armed with gloves and heavy-duty bin bags to either collect anything we want to keep, or clear up things we don't – maybe a bit of both.

There are still signs of the work that was done here – the yellow tape, now cut down but still trailing on the ground; large heaps of rubble where brickwork was cleared; a giant skip filled with random items from our home. I see the corner of the sofa sticking up, and it makes me deeply sad: abandoned and unloved, dumped in a skip after years of loyal service. Years of providing a comfy spot for us to rest our weary limbs, a cushioned home for our bottoms. Years of watching TV and reading books and eating our dinners – and now a sad end, cast aside and presumably destined for the tip.

It is only a sofa, I tell myself. The shops are full of them.

I take a deep breath and force myself to walk on. Charlie is silent at my side, and I think it is affecting him much more deeply than he expected as well. He's seemed okay at the hotel, but seeing this in person is completely different.

It is eye-searingly sunny, warm in that way that makes you long for a swimming pool and a cocktail. Insects are buzzing around us, and I can hear the donkeys braying in the distance, the waves gently lapping against the shore. It is the kind of idyllic summer afternoon that I have enjoyed so much over our years here, and it seems unreal that just a few days ago, this same spot looked like something from an apocalypse movie.

My hair is sticky around my face, and I wish I had a bobble to tie it up with. I wish I had so many things, but as we near the was-cottage, I realise that I don't have many things at all. Bobbles are the least of my worries, I think, as I survey the scene.

The walls that were halfway down last time I saw them, stubs sticking up from the earth, have been demolished completely. The red door is now lying flat on the ground. The roof has been removed and stacked to one side, half-covered in a tarpaulin. Part of the area has been cleared, the bit nearest to the edge of the cliff side, but the rest still looks like it's been hit by a bomb, like the old black-and-white news images of the Blitz.

We walk closer, our feet crunching over broken glass, smashed pottery, snapped shards of plastic. The ground is scattered with debris – fabric so muddy and torn it is beyond identifying, trampled floorboards, plaster, patches of carpet. A lot of the furniture must have gone over the edge, but my bedside cabinet is still there, lying on its side, the door thrown open and hanging on by one hinge.

'Wow,' says Charlie, walking closer to the foundations of the cottage.

You can still see the outline of the floor, the way the rooms that no longer exist were laid out. The bath is still here, filled with roof tiles and bricks, the shower curtain trapped between them. It's a nice shower curtain – white with pale blue stripes. The whole bathroom was done in those colours, white tiles and blue towels, a mirror edged with seashells we'd collected on the beach, a little cabinet I'd painted blue and white to match. It was jaunty and vaguely nautical, once. Now it's a shipwreck.

Charlie leans down, rooting in a pile of rubble, and comes up looking triumphant. He holds aloft a small metal cup, and yells: 'Hey, look! My Good Citizen of the Year trophy! All is not lost!'

I know this calls for a certain response, so I force myself to laugh. Maybe this will be the first of a series of small victories – maybe we will rescue more, salvage some precious items from the destruction. Maybe not absolutely everything is gone.

I join him in the space that was the cottage, keeping a careful eye on the jagged glass that once formed windows, and look around. Up close, the details are almost comical – a frying pan with no handle sitting next to a fancy hat I once wore to a wedding; one of Charlie's old football boots on top of the shattered screen of the TV, as though the Invisible Man stamped on it. A spatula wedged in the ground like a plant, sticking upright. The bag full of Christmas decorations I kept in the cupboard under the stairs has burst open, random strands of tinsel and tangled fairy lights strewn over the ground. I pick up the fairy that we put on top of the tree – she is battered, and the poor thing only has one wing, but I reckon she will live to fly another day.

I put it into one of the bags, and Charlie adds his trophy. We continue to pick through the remains of our home, and it is a surreal experience – the skylarks are singing, the sun is shining, the sea is a gentle shimmer below us, and I have just discovered my Nigella cookbook in pristine condition, hiding beneath a far less lucky one by the Hairy Bikers. Nigella goes in the bag – she's a keeper.

We do actually manage to salvage quite a few clothes – some are beyond resuscitation, but others just need a good wash. Sadly, the washing machine is in the skip, but I know how to use a launderette. Charlie finds a few of his video games, though he has nothing to play them on, as well as a can of Lynx Africa – because no party is complete without that. It's a hot day, and we are working hard, and I laugh as he pulls off the lid and gives himself a quick spritz. Livin' the vida loca.

Other random survivors include a packet of wholemeal pasta that I bought when I was trying to be healthy and never ate because I don't actually like it; several DVDs of the classic romcoms of Hugh Grant; a half-full tub of multivitamins; and, bizarrely, a pile of travel brochures. I used to keep them in the bathroom to read while I was having a soak, taking comfort from pictures of exotic places and planning luxurious fantasy holidays that I couldn't afford but enjoyed imagining. I throw those away – there seems even less point to them now.

There is one big win as we excavate our home, though, which gives me even more comfort than fantasy holidays. For years, I've kept a wooden crate in the bottom of my wardrobe, which I creatively called my Special Things Box. Despite its name, it doesn't look very special – at least not on the outside. I always meant to paint it, but was too busy doing other things and it remained plain. The inside, though, is a different matter. I spot it on its side near the new cliff edge, which is now fenced off and draped in neon-coloured warning tape. The lid is still on, and my heart skips a beat as I make my way carefully towards it. I lean down, pick it up, feel a surge of joy as I judge its weight – this is not some cruel trick, it seems like the contents are still in there.

I carry it over to the side of the field, and sit down on the grass, where I feel more safe. The cliff edge has obviously stabilised or they wouldn't have let us come out here, but it still gives me a touch of vertigo, emotional and physical, to get too close. The image of me chasing those photos in the storm is still a bit too real for comfort.

Charlie ambles over and collapses by my side. He wipes his forehead and takes a glug from his water bottle.

'What have you got there?' he asks, nodding at the box in front of us.

'An Aladdin's Cave of delights,' I reply, opening it up. There is some mud on the lid, but the interior is clear. I root around inside, and pull out a tiny baby's sleepsuit decorated in dinosaur print. I hold it up and Charlie laughs.

'I don't think it'll fit me now . . .' he says, smiling.

I lay it down on the grass, stroking the soft fabric, remembering so vividly the first time I put him in it

– his dad was still around, but neither of us knew what we were doing. We were still children ourselves, and I was terrified every time I put one of his little arms into a sleeve that I would somehow snap it like a twig.

Tucked away in one corner is the plastic wristband he wore in the hospital as a newborn, worthless to anyone but me. I take out Charlie's record book from when he was a baby, its red plastic cover containing all the scrawled numbers that immortalised his weight, his length, his development. There is a school report from Reception, where the teacher praises his bright smile and kindness and eagerness to learn. A poem he wrote for me on Mother's Day when he was ten, when he rhymed 'heart' with 'fart' in a typical little boy move. A cutting from the local paper when his Primary was School of the Week and he was one of the kids on the photo. His first shoes, and his first tooth, and a lock from his first haircut.

'This is getting kind of creepy,' he says, inspecting the collection. 'It's like a museum of me.'

'It's not creepy!' I say, feigning outrage. 'All mums do this ... I think.'

'Do they? Do you think your mum has a collection like this, then?'

I grab the water bottle from him, trying to buy myself a few extra seconds before I speak. The honest answer is that I don't know. I haven't seen my mum for such a long time, and we did not part under the most ideal of circumstances, and it hurts to even think about. There are times in your life when you desperately want a hug from your mum – like, when you give birth as a teenager, or when your partner leaves you with a toddler, or when your house falls down. Times when only the solace of maternal arms will do – that childlike sensation of knowing that everything will be all right. Mother Magic.

I try to be a good mum to Charlie, to make him feel safe, to sprinkle his life with my own version of Mother Magic – but I haven't had it myself for years. I still remember it, though, that simple feeling of love and comfort. The certainty that whatever is wrong, Mum will be able to fix it, or at least make you feel better about it if she can't. Things got complicated between us, things were said and done, and I did what I thought was right. I still miss that feeling, that solace – but I now recognise it as a fairy tale. Mums can't fix everything – they just fool you into believing it. It's not magic, it's a placebo.

Charlie doesn't understand why I'm estranged from my family, for a pretty good reason – I've never explained it to him. It felt justified when he was younger, when there was no way his forming brain could understand the complexities of the situation, the wounds dealt and the wounds received, the tangled web of pain that is cobwebbed all over my family dynamic. Now, of course, he is an adult – and clearly looking for answers. One day, I will try to give them to him – but not today.

'I don't know, love. Maybe,' I say simply. 'It's not just a museum of you, though – there is some stuff in here of mine if you want to see it?'

'As long as it's nothing that'll make me sick in my mouth.'

'I can't promise that ...'

I pull out a small wad of pictures, ones that pre-date Charlie, and pass them over. He flicks through them, and I watch as he looks by turns amused and thoughtful.

'It's weird, Mum, thinking about you as a teenager – how old were you in these?'

'About fifteen, I suppose, sixteen maybe. That's me and my then best friend Lucy, and her cousin, who I think was called Sian.'

'Why are you posing like that? Why are you all pouting?'

'We were trying to be the Sugababes ...'

He frowns, obviously unsure of the reference, and I am momentarily saddened to think that his generation has missed out on the glories of 'Round Round' and 'Push the Button'.

'Were you still living at home back then?' he asks quietly. He knows I left my family when I was very young, but little more than that. When he was younger, I know he accepted that reality, as kids do – but I also know that he is no longer a kid and has more questions than I am ready to answer. Especially now.

I just nod my head, stay silent, and he gets the message. I see a flicker of annoyance cross his face, see him manage it. I know I'm probably only delaying having to talk about it all, but I'll settle for that today.

'So what's this?' he says, pointing at a small pile of exercise pads, covered in my loopy teenaged handwriting, doodles and the ubiquitous love hearts enclosing the initials of our young heart-throbs.

'Ah, well – those are my early attempts at novels.'

'Novels? You? I mean, I know you love reading, but you've never mentioned writing before ...'

He's right, I haven't. When I was younger, it was all I ever wanted to do. I wasn't sure if I saw myself as a journalist or an author or a poet, but definitely something that involved words. I was always to be found scribbling away in those notepads, coming up with ideas, creating what I now see was very pretentiously written teenaged drivel. I used to write love stories for my friends based on their favourite pop stars or actors or real-life crushes, filled with excruciating scenes about lingering glances and heated kisses.

'It was just a phase,' I say nonchalantly, 'although I still wouldn't mind being in the Sugababes.'

In truth, of course, all of those youthful hopes and dreams had to be abandoned when I became a mother. When I fell pregnant, it was all so romantic, so hopeful, so wrapped up with the way I felt about Rob, Charlie's dad. I was swept away in some kind of juvenile fantasy that was utterly destroyed by the reality of having a newborn. Later, when I was alone, there was even less chance of finding the time or the space to write – it was a full-time job keeping us both alive, and finding a way to support us. I had more important things to do than create some kind of fantasy world, and more important things to spend my money and time on than buying notepads and wasting hours on end achieving nothing at all. I probably would have missed it, but I didn't have time.

I don't say any of this to Charlie, though – I don't ever want him to feel that he was in any way a mistake, or a burden to me.

'I like this bit,' he says, grinning as he flicks through the pages. 'It's about someone called Nathan, looking up from his hoodie with menacing eyes …'

I laugh and grab the exercise pad from his hands.

'Enough! There's some X-rated stuff in there that will definitely make you sick in your mouth. How are you feeling now, anyway, love? I know this is all a lot to deal with.'

He shrugs and tucks a long strand of curls behind his ear. The boy needs a haircut. 'Yeah. It is. It's all really weird. A few days ago my biggest worry was waiting for my A-level results and whether I'll get the grades I need to go to uni. Now … well, actually, now I come to think of it, that's still my biggest worry!'

'Really? Well, don't worry. You're going to smash it. And you'll go off to London, and become a world-leading expert on microbiology, and the world will rejoice!'

'Yeah. Maybe. I know that's the plan anyway …'

'What do you mean, the plan? Is it not what you want?'

He does a good me impersonation at that point, and just looks at me, staying silent. He shrugs, and that's the end of it. I'm probably overreacting.

'But what about you?' he says, gesturing to the disaster

zone in front of us. 'What will you do next, if I'm off at uni?'

I have, of course, contemplated what my life will look like without Charlie. I'd assumed I would have to learn how to deal with long and lonely nights in the cottage – but at least I don't have that to worry about any more. I have no idea what life has in store for me, and don't want to add to any of his stress.

'I haven't decided yet,' I reply, frowning. 'It's a bit of a coin toss between international espionage and resuming my old career as an ice-dancing champion.'

'Or working at a carpet company?'

'No, that sounds too exciting.'

He laughs, and takes the water back. He doesn't know about my job situation, and I don't plan on enlightening him any time soon. There are enough uncertainties in his life at the moment without adding anything else to the mix, and anyway, even I don't know what will happen yet. Maybe it will all be OK – because everything has been going so swimmingly recently.

'Shall we pack it in for the day?' I ask. 'I'm pretty wiped out and I wouldn't mind seeing if the launderette is open, or if the hotel can stick some of these clothes in the wash for me.'

'But why? Barb's stuff really suits you. I especially liked that blouse with the lace collar and the built-in pink bow-tie.'

'I rest my case ... Come on, we'll call in and see if Luke is in. He might well have fled the county by now.'

We grab our bags and heave ourselves up and start

the trek across the field. I see the donkeys are out, no worse for wear, and grazing in their enclosure. One of them spots us approaching and lets out the world's biggest bray, alerting the herd.

As we arrive at the motorhome, I see that Luke is most definitely in. To be precise, he is outside, manning a small barbecue, a table and chair set up in the shade of a green-and-white striped extended awning. There is music playing, something soulful from the Motown era, and the whole scene is one of perfectly content domesticity.

Betty jumps up and gallops over to us, dashing around Charlie's ankles and making yipping noises, apparently pleased to see us. Luke waves and shouts a greeting.

He's wearing khaki combat shorts, the kind with big pockets, and a T-shirt that advertises a surf shack. He smiles, and his whole face changes. He's not exactly handsome, he's a little too weather-worn for that, but the smile is world-class. I am surprised by how much it affects me, that smile – the way it transforms him from the grumpy stranger he used to be to the Good Samaritan he has become. And, if I'm being totally honest, a pretty hot Good Samaritan.

'I was just burning some food,' he says, gesturing at the barbecue with his tongs. 'Can I tempt you to join me?'

'Yes!' says Charlie, before I can even consider replying. Charlie is hungry – what a surprise. He pulls a face at me and takes off with Betty, the two of them chasing each other around the grass. It's wonderful to watch, and I love the way one small dog has turned him back into a child.

'Only if it's no bother,' I add. 'I'm assuming you weren't expecting guests, and it's no problem if you only have enough food to burn for one.'

'Nah, it's fine – I was out hunting this morning.'

'Right. The wild savannah or Tesco?'

'That farm shop on the main road. I am fully stocked on burgers, steak and salmon fillets. Watch this, and I'll get you a chair.'

He passes me the tongs and disappears off inside the van. I make an exploratory poke at the cooking meat, and see that he was lying. He isn't burning it – in fact, it's a nice-looking piece of steak that has obviously been marinated in something extremely tasty. Bit of a sneaky gourmet barbecue vibe going on. I find my mouth watering and realise that I am doing a Charlie.

Luke emerges with a fold-out chair and sets it up for me next to his.

'I only have one spare,' he says apologetically. 'Don't often have visitors. Beer?'

'The answer to that is always yes.'

He grins and pulls a can from a mini-fridge he has tucked away by the steps. He adds a couple of burgers and some salmon to the barbecue and sits down next to me.

'How does this thing work?' I ask, frowning.

'Ah. Good question. Well, there's this little gadget on the top called a ring pull, and if you tug it, an opening appears. Then you put the can to your lips and drink it. Does that help?'

'Ha-ha, very funny. I meant the motor-home, van, whatever you call it – do you have electricity? And, like, a toilet?'

'I do have a toilet, and you are more than welcome to avail yourself of the facilities. And, this is most definitely a motorhome, not a camper van.'

'Is there a big difference?'

'Oh yes. You could actually get shot in the motorhome community for making that mistake.'

'There's a motorhome community?'

'Yeah. It's like the Illuminati. On wheels. So, a camper van is a van that's been modified and had a bed put in, like that. A motorhome is specifically designed and built to be what it is. You can hook it up to a power supply, either on a site or anywhere with electricity if you have the right adaptor, and then you can run on what's called the leisure battery for a while. I mix and match between official sites, and places like this, where I have access to some facilities but get my own space.'

I nod, pretending I understand. In truth, I'm not the world's most practical person, and he pretty much lost me at adaptor. 'Right. Well, I'll probably still call it a van, because it's shorter.'

'True. It saves you a whole two syllables.'

'So, how do you wash and stuff, in a van— motorhome?'

He sniffs his own armpits and replies: 'What are you trying to tell me? There is actually a shower room in there. There's a water tank, which I fill up when needed, and a water heater and a pump, and that means I have a shower and a sink and all the usual stuff.'

'Wow. Just like magic.'

'Well, it is a bit magical, to be honest – the freedom of it. The independence. Having to think about what you really need in your life rather than just being surrounded by … stuff. Though I realise that might be a sore spot for you right now.'

I sip my beer, and listen to the music, and feel the warmth of a sunny day on my skin. I look at Charlie, gambolling around with a cute dog as though he is five again, and smile.

'Well, it probably should be – but I am choosing to live in the moment. Right now, this is nice. So I will accept the magic, even if it's only for half an hour. We've lost a lot, but we still have what matters. At least that's how I feel right now, sitting here drinking beer. That might only last for five minutes, though, I warn you. It's unpredictable, to be honest – I'm fine, and then I'm spiralling into a flat panic, remembering a new thing we need every second, and freaking out about what happens next.'

'And what does happen next?'

'I don't know,' I reply, shaking my head. 'I suppose I need to find somewhere else to rent, but that's all a lot more complicated than it sounds.'

'Anyone you can stay with? Family?'

'Also a lot more complicated than it sounds.'

'Ah. I get it. What has Bob said?'

'Bob has passed me on to the welfare team. They're

really nice, and they're trying to find me some emergency accommodation because, you know, we can't stay at a service-station hotel forever ... but I'm a bit worried about that. I know what emergency accommodation can look like, and I don't think I can cope with that. With a hostel, or a group home. Been there, done that, don't want to buy the T-shirt.'

'Why would you, when the one you're wearing is so very awesome?'

I glance down at my own chest, and am reminded that I am modelling one of Barb's finest – pink background, decorated with two cartoon hedgehogs canoodling and the words 'All you need is love'. Huh. Maybe she's right. Love, and maybe beer. I suppose 'all you need is love, beer, a washing machine, a TV and a roof over your head' would be too long for a T-shirt slogan. 'I found some clothes,' I reply. 'Just need to get to the launderette, maybe tomorrow now. Except I also need to go into work. And look after Charlie. And sort out a million things. I think my head might be about to explode.'

'Don't let it do that,' he says gently. 'You might splatter the steak. Look, I know this is hard – terrible in fact. But it'll all be OK in the end. I'm guessing you've already overcome a few obstacles in life, and this is just the latest. We're resilient, us humans. Take each day as it comes.'

'Yeah. I know. I'm trying. Mindfulness and all that. Except, I always find myself thinking – if you're super mindful, and live in the present, and don't worry too much about the future, then eventually you'll run out of clean pants …' I am rambling, and I'm not sure if it's because of the heat, the beer, the circumstances, or the simple fact that someone is being kind to me. 'So,' I say, trying to rein myself in a little, 'what led you to this way of life, Luke? How did you end up as an old man of the road, travelling life's highways in a van … I mean, motorhome?'

'Less of the old, please; I'm forty-three. And that is a long story, for another time. Let's just say that I reached a crossroads, much like the one you're facing. A moment when everything changed, and I had to make some hard choices. It didn't feel like it at the time, but it was the best thing that ever happened to me. This lifestyle … well, it's not for everyone, and it's maybe not forever, but it's right for me, at this stage. Plus, I'm an adrenaline junkie, and you haven't lived until you've tried to get one of these babies down a narrow country lane, let me tell you …'

He hasn't actually answered my question in any meaningful way, but he has avoided it skilfully. He is a bit of a pro at that, I suspect. I am consumed with genuine curiosity, but understand that some things are just too difficult to talk about.

He gets up, and moves the food around on the grill, a pop and a sizzle sending up delicious aromas. He puts the steak out onto a plate, adds some salad and a roll, and shouts Charlie over.

Charlie responds in exactly the same way as Betty, running at speed, nostrils twitching. His ears aren't as long as a daschund's, though, so he can't pull off the cute flapping thing that she does.

He takes the food and collapses down onto the grass a little way off. His face is red from the sun and the playing, and he swipes sweat from his forehead as he says thank you. I feel a momentary stab of guilt that Luke has given Charlie the posh meat, but that is wiped away when I see how happy it makes my son. He practically cries with joy, muttering about how good it is as he eats. He is easily pleased when it comes to food and has enjoyed being in a hotel, but this is next level stuff.

'So,' says Luke, sitting down again. 'I found some of your things. I went for a walk down on the beach this morning to see what was what.'

'Oh gosh, maybe I should have done that too ... what did you find?'

I am silently hoping it was something useful, and not my fifth-best underwear or a toilet brush.

'It was all pretty grim, to be honest. The council people took away the big items, but there's still some wreckage. Garden furniture, some pillows, what looks like the remains of some kitchen chairs. Nothing that can be salvaged, I'm afraid. But I did manage to gather up some of your photos – after the storm settled, a lot of them seemed to land down there. Pretty muddy, but OK once they dried out. Plus, I found a tied-up carrier bag that seems to be full of documents.'

'Ah,' I reply, feeling a spike of relief, 'you discovered my filing system! That has our passports in it, which is brilliant. And photos ... well, that's even better. Thank you, so much. I am so grateful for everything you've done. You didn't need to bother with any of that, and I really appreciate it. We wanted to get you a present, but we didn't know what you'd like.'

'You're very welcome. Living my old-man-of-the-road lifestyle, it's nice to have a bit of company.'

'Do you get lonely? You don't seem like you're lonely. You seem ... self-sufficient?' I babble.

He grins, and the crinkles around his green eyes deepen. 'Yep, that's me. A self-sufficient old man of the road. You make me sound like one of those survivalists who lives on a mountain and shoots squirrels for dinner ...'

'Well, if the baseball cap fits ...'

He laughs, then stands up and sorts out the burgers. He hands me a plate, and I force myself to pause, fighting the urge to stuff the whole thing into my mouth at once. I can be classy like that.

We eat, and he gets another couple of beers, and I see that Charlie is stretched out in the sun, Betty curled up next to him. He's looking at his phone, and I swear to God it looks like Betty is as well.

'Lonely is a difficult one to define,' Luke continues, leaning back in his chair, 'and I don't think you can tell from looking. Just because I live alone, it doesn't make me lonely. And just because people are married or live in big families, it doesn't mean they're not. You can be surrounded by people who love you and still feel lonely, you know?'

I nod. I do know. I am also now fizzing with

curiosity – what is this man's backstory? Why does he live like this? What happened to make him choose this path? And, really, why is it any of my business? It's not, I know, but I find him deeply interesting – he's gone from being a surly almost-neighbour to this real-life heroic figure who not only pulled me back from a cliff edge, but is being so very kind. 'Yes, I do know,' I reply. 'You're right. I've raised Charlie on my own for most of his life, and I love him to bits. Can't imagine being without him. But there have been times – nights, mainly – where it's been lonely, even when he's lying in the next room. You see other parents at school, and it feels like there's always two of them and one of you. You go on holidays, and the whole place seems full of neat little family units. Even though again you can't tell from looking, other people seem to have these perfect lives, while I'm just scrabbling along doing my best on my own. I wonder sometimes if I should have tried harder to meet someone else, to build a better family for him, if I've let him down in some way ...'

'All parents think that. All parents feel guilty, either for the stuff they have done, or the stuff they think they should have done. In fact, I'd make a claim that guilt is the sign of a good parent – it shows you give a damn. And Charlie doesn't seem to be doing too badly, does he, despite your many failings?'

I pause, and stare at Luke, pointing one finger. 'You are too wise, and too kind, and too good to be true,' I say. 'Are you secretly a serial killer who keeps rope and duct tape on hand at all times?'

'Funnily enough, I do have rope and duct tape on hand at all times – pretty essential kit in a motorhome – but I use it more for minor repairs and hanging out washing than anything criminal. Another beer?'

I really, really want to say yes. I could easily stay here, in this little bubble of calm and music and sunshine, pretending that I'm just another person enjoying a lazy Sunday afternoon with a friend. Pretending that everything is OK. Pretending that I'm not homeless, possibly soon to be jobless, and most definitely clueless.

'Thanks, but no,' I reply. 'This has been lovely, and thanks again for all of your help. I've got the money I owe you, and thanks for that too – it was a bit of a lifesaver. But I think it's time to call for a taxi – you won't know this, but there are only about three in the whole of town and it might take a while – and head back to our temporary des res.'

He nods, and says he's going to fetch the photos and other items he found for me.

I walk over to Charlie and poke him in the ribs with my toe. He's half asleep, his hair splayed over his face.

'Time to go, sleepyhead,' I say. 'These clothes won't wash themselves.'

He groans and rubs his eyes with his fingers. 'Do we have to go? It's nice here ... even nicer now there's a proper view out to the sea, and no cottage blocking the way ...'

I glance out towards the cliffs. He's actually right – you can see for miles, the waves a glittering swell of blue rolling away to the edge of the world. Seabirds are wheeling in the sky, and you can smell the salt, and it is idyllic. Tears sting the back of my eyes as I am washed with unexpected grief. This was my home, and now it is not.

Like Luke said, I am sure I will overcome this. I will rebuild. But it is hard, knowing that I have to leave all of this behind.

'Sadly, love,' I say, tearing my eyes away from the coast I have lived beside for so long, 'we do.'

Chapter 6

The next day, I meet Barb for a coffee while my clothes are in the launderette's giant washing machine. She is horrified that I didn't bring it all around to her, and now she mentions it, so am I – I'm willing to bet good money that everything would have come back not only clean, but pressed, folded and possibly embellished with sequins.

Charlie has gone over to stay with his friend Eric for the night, and I am glad of the break. I love my son and know that he loves me, but there does come a time when being in such enforced close proximity to each other brings significant mutual irritation risk factors.

I am feeling low, in all honesty. The welfare people sent over links to some accommodation they have available, and none of it fills me with joy. Part of me feels ungrateful – they are doing their best, and I can't expect to be offered a mansion with swimming pool and tennis courts – but the thought of taking what feels like a step back from what we had fills me with sorrow.

I have never been in a position to get a foot on the housing ladder – I'd need to stand on a box to even be within touching distance of the first rung. That has never bothered me until now, when I find myself cut adrift, insecure, facing a wobbly future. The only consolation is that hopefully Charlie will be off to uni in London in September, so whatever happens next won't affect him for too long.

I hide all of this from Barb, because she doesn't need to hear it. She is trying to be perky and has also brought me a gift – a £100 card for Marks & Spencer that my colleagues bought for me after a whip-round. It is a sweet gesture, and I am thankful.

'This is lovely, Barb,' I say, as we settle outside the cafe with our drinks. It is another glorious day, and this week's tourists are getting a very different experience than last week's. 'Just imagine how many packets of Percy Pigs I can get with this!'

'Oh I know,' she replies, smiling. 'Enough to put you in a diabetic coma, I'd imagine! How are you bearing up?'

'Not so bad, all things considered. I really appreciate all your support, Barb. I'll be able to get your things back to you soon.'

She waves this off, as though it is of no concern, and I realise that I have actually never seen her in the same outfit twice. Today she is a veritable ice cream of pastel shades, even her shoes.

'So,' she says slowly, sucking her cheeks in afterwards, as though that one word has exhausted her, 'Tim was in this morning.'

'Ah. Did you catch a glimpse of his cloven hooves or was he in disguise?'

She frowns, and I shake my head. I have confused her.

'What did he have to say?'

'It's not good,' she replies, tears appearing in her huge blue eyes. 'They've decided to keep the other office open, and close ours. There was a lot of talk of logistics and supply chains and other things I didn't really understand. We're all in work until the end of the week, but paid for another month, and we'll all either be offered redundancy or asked to reapply for posts in the Kidderminster office.'

'I'd rather die than move to Kidderminster,' I state firmly.

'Really?' she says, looking shocked.

'No, I was just being dramatic. It looks really nice. But ... well, who knows? I suppose at this stage anything is possible. What about you?'

'Oh, well, I won't be going anywhere, will I? Anthony's job is here, and the younger ones are still in school, and I only work part-time anyway. We can cope without it for a while – it's just that I'll miss it, you know? Coming in to work and seeing you all. We have such a laugh, don't we?'

I am momentarily caught unawares by this statement. I don't hate my job, and I like my colleagues, and we definitely make the best of it – but I wouldn't exactly say it's a comedy club. Clearly, it is a whole different experience for Barb.

'I thought maybe you might be tempted, though,' she adds, stirring her iced tea, 'by Kidderminster. Because, you know – Charlie will be leaving soon, and … the other thing …'

She doesn't even know how to say it. It's as though my house has become He Who Shall Not Be Named. I nod to put her out of her misery. I haven't really had much time or head-space to genuinely think about moving, what with everything else going on.

We are both silent for a moment, as though paying our respects to the memory of my former home. We are probably both still shell-shocked by the news about our jobs – I knew it would be landing this week, but perhaps not so early. It is another layer of WTF added to the ones I am already being smothered by, and I am unsure how to react. Literally everything that rooted me here, to this place, to this life, has been taken away from me. I should be in pieces, but I am not – I think I am numbed to it all, and maybe that is a blessing. My own mind has provided me with some much-needed anaesthetic to tide me over.

Or maybe, it sneaks into my thoughts, it is all just pointing me in one direction: change. I've been scared of change for a very long time – all you really want for your kids when they're little is a stable life. Now, my kid isn't so little – and my life isn't so stable. If there are any cosmic coincidences in the universe, maybe this is one of them.

Barb and I chat some more, both of us distracted, probably thinking about different things. I, personally, am adding up exactly how much redundancy pay I might get, how long it will last me and when it might land in my bank account. It will probably be enough to pay for a security deposit on a new rental place, and enough left over to live on until I find a new job – but is that really what I want?

I am excited for Charlie's future, for his time at university, for the next phase of his life – but now I am forced to think about it, I am not so excited about mine. I would have stayed in the cottage, at the office, if everything had retained its status quo – but neither of those is an option anymore. I wouldn't have chosen for my house to fall off a cliff, or to lose my job, but now both have happened, can I really face launching myself right back into different versions of exactly the same thing?

I find myself thinking about Luke, and his van-that-isn't-a-van, and about how he said I am at a crossroads. He was even more right than he knew. I *am* at a crossroads, and I have no idea which way to turn.

By the time Barb has started to make 'I really must be going noises', I have come to a decision. I ask her if she will give me a lift, and she is more than happy to oblige. Now I've been paid, I really need to get Nina fixed – she's slipped down my priority list and is currently still languishing in her parking spot.I will feel better about things once I have my own transport.

We load my washing into Barb's pink Fiat 500 and drop it off at the hotel, and then she is kind enough to drive me to the end of the lane where I used to live.

As I walk along the path and onto the field, I do a bit of googling to confirm statutory redundancy pay, and then make my way to the motorhome. I avert my eyes from the rubble, from the skip, from the debris. I need to start trying to think of the future, and I know I will be easily derailed by a random glimpse of a precious object calling to me from the wreckage.

There is nobody at home at Luke's, and when I knock, all that happens is that I hear a ferocious amount of woofing from Betty. I peer in through one of the windows, and she jumps up at me, bouncing up and down like a yo-yo.

Delightful as Betty is, she's not much of a conversationalist, and I still have no clue if Luke is in and doing something else, or out and about, or maybe just lying on the floor and pretending not to be in so he doesn't have to talk to me.

I do a circuit of the vehicle, and see an empty bike rack on the back. Aha, I think – the mystery is solved. It is like an episode of CSI Norfolk. Maybe I could be a private detective.

It still doesn't help me guess where he is and how long he will be away for, though. I realise that I should have done something sensible like get his phone number before I left last time.

I go over to stroke one of the donkeys – the friendly one who always comes for a scratch on the ears – and tell myself off for being impulsive. Now, I'm stuck out here for no reason and will have to either wait for the bus, which isn't due for another forty minutes, or call a cab. The donkey looks at me with big, sad eyes, and I say: 'Yeah. I know. I don't blame you for judging. I didn't think this one through, did I?'

The donkey remains silent but swishes its tail in what I take to be agreement.

'You're right,' I continue. 'I'm not very organised. I'm like an un-superhero. Like Captain America before the magic potion, or Spider Man before the radioactive venom. I am ... the Amazing Crap Woman!'

'Are you talking to a donkey?' says an amused voice from behind me. 'Does it talk back? Is that one of the Amazing Crap Woman's superpowers?'

I whirl around and see Luke, standing next to his bike. He's so hot, his close-cropped hair is shining, and his arms are coated in a sheen of sweat. He looks fit and healthy and active, like an advert for multivitamins. I hate him a teeny bit just then.

'Hey! You're here! Um ... so far, the donkey hasn't replied. I'm counting that as a good sign, because my life is already weird enough.'

'Is everything OK?' he asks, before he takes a long gulp of water from a bottle he has attached to the frame of his bike.

'Yeah, fine ... sort of. I was just wondering if I could pick your brains about something?'

'Of course, but I need a quick shower. Can you give me five minutes?'

'I have nowhere else to be,' I say honestly. 'Charlie's with a friend for the night. Take as long as you like.'

We stroll back over to the motorhome, and he opens the door to let Betty out. She flies at him in a flurry of licks and yips and he scoops her up for a cuddle. It is quite the contrast, this big, brawny dude and his tiny dog.

'You make a cute couple,' I say, reaching out to stroke her lovely ears.

'I was only out for about an hour and a half, but even if I'm only gone for ten minutes I get this kind of reception ... she's the very best kind of travelling companion. I take her with me when I'm walking, but she has certain leg-based disadvantages when it comes to cycling.'

We make our way inside, and again I am struck by how homely it is, how welcoming. I love the way that everything you need is here, but in miniature. I gaze around, seeing the hidden cupboards and cleverly designed shelving; how every inch of the space has been used. I notice there are fairy lights strung around the top of the sides and imagine how cosy it must be at night-time.

'What's this stuff?' I ask, pointing at the blue matting I see on various shelves and spots in the kitchen.

'Anti-slip mat,' he replies. 'It does what it says on the tin. So, when you're driving, you don't want stuff moving around too much – like the microwave sliding off the counter, or even your phone falling off the dashboard, whatever. You put this stuff on shelves, in cupboards, on surfaces, and it helps keep things stable.'

I reach out and prod it and make a small 'oooh' sound. It's all so sensible, this motorhome stuff. I wonder if my mind could ever adjust to being so practical?

Luke flicks a switch on a small control panel by the door and says: 'I'll be back in a few minutes. Motorhome showers are not luxurious experiences. Help yourself to a cuppa; there are biscuits around somewhere as well . . . Coffee for me, black, no sugar!'

I nod and take the few steps over towards the kitchen area. Further off to the other side is another door, which I assume is for a bedroom, and next to it is the one Luke goes into, bowing his head slightly to fit.

I soon hear the sound of a shower and pause, kettle in hand. This is the closest I've been to a naked man for a very long time – Charlie doesn't count, obviously. I find my mind wandering a little, imagining Luke there, water cascading over his broad shoulders. I blush ferociously and shake myself out of it – inappropriate to the max. I feel like I'm taking advantage of him somehow, even if it's just mentally.

I make a lot of noise looking in cupboards, extricating mugs, opening the little fridge door, humming tunelessly as I do it. I am trying to drown out both the sound of the shower and my own thoughts. As soon as I've made the drinks, I head outside. I need some fresh air, and possibly to sign up to a dating app.

I mean, I've seen other people since Rob left – but nothing that ever amounted to anything. I was too busy, too wrapped up in Charlie, too distrustful, if I'm honest. Every time I met someone, I'd immediately start imagining how it would end before it even began and ultimately never got past a second date. The collateral damage never seemed worth the risk – I didn't want to introduce any potential disruption into our lives. I could hide behind my son here and say it was all for him – but it was also for me. I've never felt quite robust enough to put myself in a position where I could be hurt again.

Now, I have to accept, Charlie is grown up. He will be heading off to start the next phase of his life shortly, and I will no longer be able to use him as a human shield. I am only thirty-six – other women are having their first child at my age, never mind behaving like an old maid. I barely know Luke, and I've already imagined him naked – maybe my body is telling me something.

I decide my body is stupid and that I won't listen to it, at least not right now. I settle down on the steps of the motor home, Betty at my feet, and sip my coffee. It is bright and sunny today, but not quite as skin-meltingly hot, and it is pleasant to sit out, looking across the fields to the sea beyond. I block out the ugly bit in between, the outlines of the skip and the tarpaulin – I need to focus on the future, not get sucked into a black hole of what might have been. My old life is gone, and I need to accept that.

That would be a neat trick if I could pull it off, but, of course, I can't completely manage it. I keep picturing my strawberry plants, mashed and battered, and the pretty terracotta pots full of begonias. They are small things, tiny fractions of what I have lost, but somehow they seem to symoblise it all: the comfort and the calm and the sense of nurture that I felt in my old home has been snatched away from me, and I feel stripped bare. I need to move forward, to make a plan, to embrace change, to have faith in my own abilities – I have done tougher things than this before. But still – I miss my garden. I hate the thought of the living things I'd grown and cared for being destroyed.

I am surprised out of my reverie by a noise to my left. I look along, and a chair emerges from the side of the motorhome. It is surreal, seeing its folded-up legs emerge, like a Salvador Dali painting.

'Here you go!' shouts Luke. 'Grab this!'

I do as he says and take the camping chair in my hands. I stare inside and realise that one of the cupboards in there opens up so you can pass things through the sides of the van. Ingenious. Is there no end to the mind-boggling efficiency of these crazy inventions?

I set up the chair, and Luke joins me. His hair is glistening, and his white T-shirt is clinging to him where he is still damp. He smells fresh and citrusy.

'So,' he says, once we are settled, 'how can I help? You said you wanted to pick my brains about something? I hope it's not something too hard or the pickings will be mighty slim . . .'

'Yes. Right. Well, I'm getting made redundant, or moving to Kidderminster, not sure yet, but I'm leaning towards the first.'

His eyes widen in surprise, but he takes a sip of his drink before he replies.

'You've not had the best of weeks, have you?' he eventually says, shaking his head sadly. 'I'm so sorry.'

'Don't be too nice to me,' I say quickly, 'or I might cry. And no, not the best of weeks – but, in all honesty, probably not the worst, either. Anyway, I am adopting onwards and upwards as my new life motto . . .'

'You have a life motto?'

'Doesn't everyone?'

'No. What was your old one?'

'Um … OK, I was lying. I didn't have one before, and if I did, it'd probably be something like "duck and cover". But onwards and upwards feels better for now. So, as you may have noticed, my home recently fell off a cliff. I am living in a hotel with free Wi. I have no job, and nowhere else to move to. Charlie is off to uni this year, and everything feels very up in the air. Which, now I come to think of it, could also be my life motto, but it doesn't feel as positive …'

He listens, and nods, seeming to understand my need to ramble at this stage.

'So. I don't have much money, but I'll be getting a redundancy payment. It won't be enough to buy a house, and until I get a new job, I wouldn't be able to do anything grown-up like get a mortgage or probably even rent somewhere nice or whatever. Anyway, I was thinking about you, and this place, and the way you live, and wondering if it could work for me as well. I was wondering if I could use the money to buy something like this.'

'OK. Well, what kind of money are we talking here?'

I am oddly relieved that he isn't laughing in my face and telling me I'm stupid, but appears to be taking me seriously. I fill him in on how much money I might have to spend, and he frowns, gazing off into the distance for a few moments.

'Well, that wouldn't be enough to buy one of these.

In the motorhome world, this is the big bad beast – it sleeps six, has all mod cons, pretty much top of the range. It wasn't cheap.'

'Oh ...' I murmur, feeling the disappointment settle over me. It's like all my hope has been smothered by a blanket of reality. It was undoubtedly a stupid idea anyway. I have a never-ending supply of those.

'But,' he continues, seeing my expression, 'you could probably get a smaller one, an older model. People trade up all the time, there are always motorhomes for sale. It just wouldn't be a deluxe version. It all depends on how many compromises you're willing to make, and how much space you could live in. It'd be you and Charlie, right?'

'At least to start with. Then maybe just me. I don't really know. Charlie will be going off to uni, and I always knew things would change – but this has accelerated everything. Maybe I'm just looking for something different. For some kind of sign of how the rest of my life will look.'

'And you think it might look ... mobile?'

'I don't know! I mean, I expected the empty nest thing – it's just that, now, I don't even have the nest. Which sort of leaves me just with "empty", which isn't a nice feeling. You seem so content, and ... well, I haven't thought it through properly, and I am beginning to suspect I was clutching at straws ... I just don't like the idea of renting another place, which won't be as nice as the one we had, and getting another boring job. I've done a boring job for years, and it allowed me to support Charlie, and give us some security, and it was fine. But the prospect of doing it all over again just makes me feel …'

'Trapped? Stuck? Cornered?'

'Yeah. All of those things. Am I being silly? Or selfish?'

'I'm not one to judge,' Luke says calmly, smiling at me. 'I used to have a boring job too … well, no, it wasn't boring, but it was big, and demanding, and it was chewing me up and spitting me out. Things happened in my life that made me see that more clearly, made me realise how unhappy I'd been. I opted out, and I enjoy this lifestyle – but it's not for everyone. You need to not mind solitude, and you need to be willing to accept some practical limitations, and you need to be comfortable with minimalism. Having hardly any stuff around you is fine for most people when they're on holiday for a week or two – it's different when it's permanent.'

'Well, I've got a leg-up on that one, I suppose. I am currently Little Miss Minimalist. But you're right. I don't know if it would suit me. What if I get scared at night? What if something breaks and I can't fix it? What if I get stuck down one of those country lanes you mentioned? What if I start talking to myself and adopt fifteen cats and die alone in a Sainsbury's car park?'

He laughs, and replies: 'Well, that wouldn't be good, would it? I mean, who'd look after the cats then?'

'I know – poor kitties! I'm sorry, by the way. For turning up here and loading all of this on you. I bet you wish you'd gone and stayed on a different field entirely and avoided all of this.'

'And miss out on a monologue from the Amazing Crap Woman? Never! Look, I know this isn't easy. A lot has happened to you in a very short space of time.'

I nod and finish my coffee, placing the mug down at my feet. Betty runs over and sniffs it, decides she's not interested and takes off to investigate a blade of grass instead.

'You're right. It has. It's like I've been cruising along on a nice quiet B road for the last decade, and suddenly I'm in the fast lane on the motorway blasting along ninety miles an hour, with no particular destination in mind. I'm scared I might crash.'

'You won't. And anyway, right now, you're not on that motorway – you've stopped off for a break, haven't you?'

Huh. Maybe he's right. Maybe that's a good way of looking at it – I need a break for sure.

He stands up, and that fresh citrus scent wafts towards me.

'I'm going to get biscuits,' he announces. 'Everything is better with biscuits.'

'That,' I reply, grinning, 'could be your life motto!'

He laughs and picks up my mug. He emerges a few minutes later with a refill and an old-fashioned biscuit tin. It has pictures of little black Scottie dogs all over it, all wearing tartan coats. He opens it up and passes it across. A veritable feast of chocolate digestives and pink wafers and bourbon creams stares up at me.

'That tin was my gran's,' he says, looking vaguely embarrassed. 'Whenever I used to go there as a kid, it was always full of those kinds of treats. When she died, I was about fourteen and we were told we could choose something from her house to remember her by. That's what I emerged with, and it's kind of become a thing – I always keep it full.'

'What a nice idea,' I reply, fishing out a digestive. 'If I believed in such things, I'd say I hope she's looking down at you, proud of your biscuit barrel.'

We sit silently together for a while, and I enjoy the peace of it all. Luke is right: I have pulled into a lay-by and need to relax for moment.

'So,' he says, leaning back in his chair, 'I think I'm going to leave at the end of the week. That's kind of the only rule I have – I don't stay anywhere longer than two weeks.'

'Worried that Interpol might finally track you down?'

'Exactly. I've got away with that art heist in Vienna for so many years, it'd be a shame to blow it now ... but, actually, it's just that now summer's finally decided to arrive, I'm feeling a bit of wanderlust.'

I'm not proud of myself, but my first reaction is utter disappointment. It's selfish, but I don't want him to leave. I barely know him, and maybe that's why this works for me – he has become, in a short amount of time, someone I feel safe talking to. Perhaps meeting someone in the extreme circumstances we met in heightens things, speeds up the process of connection. I have a slight suspicion that he could have saved my life, and he's certainly been a good sounding board. I realise that I will miss him, even though I have no right to, and even though this time last week I'd written him off as a grumpy git.

I gaze over at him, see that he is looking serious and thoughtful, and, despite all of this, also find myself noticing that he has really long fingers, wrapped around his mug. My mind is made of mush.

'Oh, right – well, that's cool. Off on your new adventures?' I say. I think that was the right response – it's definitely better than 'please don't leave, kind stranger who makes me feel less mental'.

'Yes. No idea where as yet, which is all part of the charm. But I was wondering, and this is a completely new thought that has literally just appeared in my mind, so bear with me ... I was wondering if you and Charlie would like to come with me? You could just join me for a week or so, see how you get on with the motorhome, the lifestyle? It could give you a sense of whether it's for you or not. Please don't feel obliged to say yes – it was just a random idea, and I'm sure you have better things to do than take off into the unknown with a complete stranger.'

'One who has freely admitted to having a plentiful supply of duct tape and rope.'

'Indeed. Guilty as charged.'

'But, well ... why? Why would you possibly offer such a thing?'

He frowns a little, and shakes his head. 'Honestly? I'm not completely sure. I've never exactly made myself approachable ...'

'I noticed that. Before, I mean – you didn't wave back or say good morning!'

He grimaces and replies: 'Yeah. I know. But I was planning on staying a few weeks and didn't especially want to end up having to make small talk every time I was out, to be honest – I like staying in places that are empty, I find it simpler to avoid too many people ...'

'Ha! Well, that'll teach you – be careful who you blank or you might end up rescuing them from a world-class storm! I feel bad now, for intruding so much ... and maybe even more confused as to why you're inviting us along?'

'Well, it was all pretty dramatic, wasn't it? The storm? Before I moved the motorhome into shelter, it was rocking our world as well. And seeing what happened to you and Charlie ... I suppose it made me realise that we all need a bit of help sometimes.'

'You don't seem to,' I reply, gesturing around us. 'You seem to have life cracked.'

'Ha! Far from it ... and I did need help, once, a long time ago. Someone I loved, someone I'd hurt, was kind enough to keep me in their life when I didn't deserve it. Kind enough to help me move on. So maybe this is just a messed-up way of paying it back. We all need help sometimes, don't we? It's part of what makes us human.'

'Maybe. I'm not very good at asking for help.'

'You're not asking, I'm offering.'

I'm not entirely sure I want to feel like a charity case and in two minds as to whether he realises what he's letting himself in for. Sharing close quarters with a teenager is not for the weak.

'So, taking me and Charlie on a mobile mini-break would actually be a way of making yourself feel better?' I say.

'Yeah. Exactly. In fact, you'd be doing me a favour!'

I look at him, at this man who has been so kind, at this man who just moments ago I knew I was going to miss. He's right. He is a complete stranger. This is an insane idea.

'It's an insane idea,' I say out loud. 'But, on the other hand, you do have a really good biscuit tin. Let me talk to Charlie about it.'

Chapter 7

I meet Charlie in town at lunchtime the next day. I arrived early to see a mechanic, who has pronounced Nina dead – or at least economically dead. It would cost me more to repair her than she's worth. He offers me £500 for scrap, and I accept. In normal circumstances, I would be sad to see her go, and possibly hold some kind of memorial service with a car-related playlist, but in the inventory of Rubbish Things That Have Happened In The Last Seven Days, it barely registers.

I promise to clear the car out and bring him the paperwork the next day, and then spend a good half an hour rummaging through the boot and the glovebox. Apart from general garbage that I bin immediately – I am a car slattern – I come away with 97p, a Black Eyed Peas CD, a packet of blister plasters and a half-eaten bag of cashew nuts. Party time.

Charlie walks into the pub just after 1 p.m., looking exhausted. His hair is clumped on one side and his eyes are bloodshot and crusted with sleep. He is so pale his skin is almost grey.

'You look good, love – has there been a zombie

apocalypse without me noticing?' I say as he collapses into the booth with me. He lays his head on the table for a moment, then winces up at me.

'Xbox. All night long. I'm out of practice, Mum.'

I ruffle his hair and go and get us both a drink. I order him scampi and chips because I know that's what he'll want, especially after a tough night of virtual warfare.

By the time I get back, he is upright again, gazing at his phone with tired eyes. I pass him his Coke and he gulps at it thirstily – I suspect he forgot to either hydrate or eat while he was away. It prompts a niggling worry about what will happen to him when he is at uni, surrounded by other young people and with a subsidised college bar and no mum to remind him to take care of himself. I am probably not the first parent to feel like this, and I reassure myself that he will survive.

We chat for a few minutes about his night, about Eric, about Eric's family, about other friends' lives. It is so strange, thinking about them all heading off to uni or jobs or apprenticeships – these little men that I have known since they were kiddiwinks.

Eventually, once the food arrives and he inhales his lunch and I make my soup and roll last as long as I can, I broach the subject with him. I have been thinking about Luke's offer all night and am catapulting between 'this is 100 per cent the best idea ever' and 'don't be such an idiot'. I have to make some decisions, and soon – by the end of the week, I need to let Tim know if I am accepting redundancy, let the council know if I am taking up their offer of a flat, leave the hotel and decide whether to go on a road trip with Betty and her pet human. No pressure, then.

'So,' I say carefully, not at all sure about how Charlie will react, 'you know Luke?'

'Um . . . yeah?'

'Well, he's asked if we want to go on a trip with him and Betty in his motorhome. Just for a bit, to see if we like it. I thought we might get one.'

'Like, to keep, not just for a holiday?' he says, looking confused.

'Yes. Because, also, they're closing the office, and I'm being made redundant. I don't want you to worry about it, it's all OK – I'll get a payment for it, and I'm sure I'll get another job quickly anyway. We could even end up better off. So, it'll all be OK.'

Charlie frowns and spears the one chip that was left on his plate, and chews it slowly.

'When did you find that out?' he asks eventually.

'The day we lost the cottage. Well, that's when I was told it might happen anyway. I only found out for definite yesterday.'

'So this is something you've been hiding from me?'

'Not hiding exactly, love. I just didn't see the point in giving you something else to worry about when there was already so much going on, and anyway, it's for me to sort, not you.'

'You realise I'm eighteen, yes? I'm not a baby any more. I don't need protecting, and I don't need you treating me like I'm a kid.'

'I don't treat you like a kid!'

'Yes, you do. You stopped me getting a job when I wanted one. You think I never notice when you're worried about money. And you hide things, like, all the time – like this, and all your family stuff? Every time I ask questions about that you shut me down, even though I don't think I'm being a dick to ask – you just fob me off. Sometimes I think you still see me as a four-year-old, Mum, and it makes me feel like crap! How am I supposed to grow up if you never let me?'

He actually sounds quite angry with me, and I am worried that I might cry. It's been a rollercoaster, and not in a fun way, and I hate rollercoasters anyway. I realise that I am clinging on to my resilience with the very tips of my fingernails. I screw up my eyes and force myself to stay calm.

'OK, you have a point. I accept a lot of that, even though I have my reasons – I'm not perfect, and I'm sorry if I've made you feel crap. But you did walk in here with a teen hangover from playing Xbox all night, so forgive me if I don't always see you as the mature adult you are. Don't give me grief over this, son, because I just don't need it right now. I'm sorry if I've upset you, but it's been a bit chaotic, hasn't it? I've just been concentrating on getting through each day since it happened.'

He is tapping his fingers on the tabletop, and I see he is still annoyed but is also turning my words over in his mind. I see the grown-up battling it out with the pissed-off teenager and wonder who will win.

'All right,' he says quietly. 'I'll let you off for now

– but there are still things we need to talk about, Mum. So tell me about this thing with Luke, as that seems to be something you're actually willing to discuss.'

I bite back my snarky reply and say: 'Well, I went to see him yesterday, while you were at Eric's. Barb had just told me about the redundancies, and it struck me that a motorhome could be the answer for us. It's a weird time, isn't it? You'll be off soon anyway, and we don't have a house, and I'm just not sure what's going to happen next.'

'I don't have to go to uni this year, you know, Mum. I could defer. I could get a job. We could get you settled somewhere else.'

'That sounds like you're planning on putting me in a nursing home, love! And no, Charlie, I don't want that. This is your time, and I want you to enjoy it. Anyway, I've been looking forward to September myself – I'm going to start hanging round in casinos, maybe get some tattoos, possibly buy a hookah pipe and a skateboard.'

'Ha! I'd pay good money to see you skateboarding. So, how would it work, with Luke?'

'I'm not entirely sure it will. But he says there are three beds – he has his own room, and there's one in the living area that pulls out, and one over the driver's cab that you climb up a ladder to get to.'

'I want that one.'

'What?'

'When we go, with Luke, I want the one with the ladder. I might be a grown-up, but who doesn't love a ladder?'

'So, you think it's a good idea?' I ask. I was half hoping he'd hate the concept and I could write it all off. It is a whole new level of change and I'm already dizzy with change.

'Yeah. Why not? If nothing else it'll be a free holiday, and I'll get to play with a dog. Is there Wi-Fi?'

'No idea. Is that a deal-breaker?'

He considers this, and then shakes his head. 'Nah. I think, after last night, I'm ready for something different myself, Mum. And I like Luke, he seems like a cool guy.'

'Why do you like him?' I ask, genuinely interested.

'Well, he stepped up big time, like a low-level superhero. He just has all that good stuff you've always said matters in life – he's kind, seems dependable, like you could trust him. Plus a dog. Maybe this will be good for us.'

'Maybe it will,' I reply. 'So, I suppose it's time to hit the road, Jack.'

'Mum, I keep telling you – my name is Charlie.'

Chapter 8

Once we have made the decision, it is alarmingly easy to uproot our lives. I know this particular phase will only last a week or two, but I realise that I just can't imagine myself coming back here. It's as though something has switched off inside me, and I no longer see the cottage, or this town, as home – I'm not sure I see anywhere as home, which is strangely liberating.

I have accepted the redundancy, declined new accommodation and done everything I need to do. I have been out for a farewell drinks session with Barb and the rest of my colleagues, which ended with a terrible group rendition of 'Don't Stop Believing' on the karaoke, and I have put Bob in touch with my landlord's office so they can work together on clearing the site.

Charlie has made his farewells and we have arranged for any mail to be redirected to Barb's house for the time being. The postman would really struggle delivering stuff to my old address, anyway, what with it not having a door any more, never mind a letterbox.

I have had a very small shopping spree, buying myself a cheap laptop, getting Charlie some new trainers and getting us both head torches – little lights attached to an elasticated headband. Luke assures me they are very useful, but I look so silly in mine that I wonder if it is some kind of prank. We needed a few practical items – extra bedding, as Luke is only equipped for one; toiletries that aren't from a hotel room; new underwear, new pyjamas. It will all be strange, living in a small space with someone we don't know very well, and it will most definitely call for pyjamas rather than my usual approach of sleeping in my birthday suit. I also find us some swimming gear, shorts, and in my case a couple of lightweight sundresses – our friendly neighbourhood weatherman is now predicting a weeks-long heatwave and lots of the clothes we retrieved from the site were winter-wear, now kindly stored at Barb's.

On a less practical level, I splash out on some posh rose hand cream, as everyone deserves a little luxury, and buy a couple of paperbacks from the charity shop. Charlie insists he is happy as long as his earphones are working, so I get him an extra set in case of emergency. He was always losing them at home, they used to live in tangled heaps under the sofa cushions, curled up like nests of snakes. The answer to the ages-old question 'have you seen my earphones?' was always 'have you checked down the side of the sofa?' There will be less places for him to lose them in a motorhome, but I wouldn't be surprised if he manages it.

In a fit of utter indulgence, I also pop into one of the town's bijou gift shops and spend way too much money on a leather-bound notepad that has a little tassled bookmark attached to it. The leather is dark green and engraved with a leaf design. It is a beautiful thing, and even though I have sworn off owning too many things in my brave new world, this one was irresistible. It is a Thing That Brings Me Joy, and as I run my fingers over its cover and sniff it, I feel that tinge of excitement I used to get as a little girl whenever I was starting a new pad or opening a new set of felt-tip pens. Blank pages, waiting to be filled.

When I was a teenager, I often felt lonely – my brother was older and not interested in me, we lived in an isolated place and, in time-honoured tradition, I didn't feel like my parents understood me. I had friends, but my real escape was my own imagination – I'd spend hours disappearing into it, writing my stories, doodling, making up spectacular events that might come along and transform my life. In later years, I've channelled a lot of that into imagining Charlie's future life and into planning luxury fantasy holidays – but maybe now it's time to let myself indulge a little. I think, also, I am acknowledging the fact that my life is made up of blank pages, waiting to be filled. In less than a week, I have lost my job, lost my home, lost most of my possessions. As chances to recreate yourself go, this is top-level stuff.

I feel strangely hopeful as we arrive at the motorhome, ready to embrace the unknown – or, at the very least, give it a friendly handshake and see where we go from there.

Charlie has been low-key excited about it all for the last few days, and I think this trip has given him something to focus on. He has chatted to his father about it, and Rob was full of enthusiasm – he is a man who has never truly settled down, so I'm not surprised. He's been in Paris for two years, which is the longest he has lived in any one place since he left. Charlie hasn't actually seen him for a decade, although they are in regular contact. It's been a hard balance to find – not villainising Rob in a way that would be unfair to Charlie, but also making it clear to Charlie that his father's absence from his life isn't his fault, that he shouldn't feel any sense of rejection. He doesn't seem wracked with daddy issues thus far in life, so I hope that all these years of biting my tongue have been worth it.

We are dropped off in a cab at around 6 p.m. and plan to stay in the van overnight as a practice run. Assuming neither of us runs from it screaming 'I can't take this, I feel like I'm trapped in a cave!' then we will hit the road tomorrow. Yeehah.

We find Luke inside, wearing his trademark Levis and well-washed rock T-shirt, cocooning mugs and plates in bubble wrap.

'Fellow travellers!' he says, holding a mug aloft. 'The shutdown begins ... Come on in.'

We don't have a lot with us – the bedding, and one small bag each – but it feels like we are overwhelming the living area.

Luke lifts up the banquette seat to reveal a large cupboard space beneath.

'I cleared this one out,' he says, 'thought you guys could use it for your things. This also pulls out into what will be your bed, Jenny. And Charlie – you're up top, I believe?'

'Yeah … can I go and see? Not gonna lie – insanely excited about living in a tiny man-cave with a ladder.'

Luke grins and points the way.

We both watch as Charlie clambers up the ladder with long limbs, Betty jumping up and yipping as he goes. I hear him squeal when he reaches the top, his feet disappear and he shouts: 'Awesome!'

'OK, while he's up there exploring – that should keep him busy for at least five minutes – how about I fill you in on some logistics?' Luke says.

I nod, and he gives me a tour of the vehicle, explaining as he goes how to operate the water pump and heater, how to use the weird toilet and the separate wet room shower, how to use the kitchen appliances, and where all the various essential items are kept. There is a lot to take in, and I think I switch off after the first instruction.

'Um … I probably won't remember all of that, you know,' I say, as he walks me outside to show me where the charging plug is and to give me a crash course in how the water tank works. I swear to God he calls something a whale, so in my mind the tank immediately becomes known as Moby Dick.

'I know,' he replies, smiling. 'And you don't need to. It'll all sink in, bit by bit. We might have a few disasters along the way, but such is life …'

'What kind of disasters?' I ask, looking up at him. 'Because you might be joking, but I am a disaster magnet right now. If there is a disaster lurking within a ten-mile radius, it will come flying towards me.'

He glances over at the wreckage of the cottage and nods. Hard to argue the point.

'Well. Like I said, I'm an adrenaline junkie ... but seriously, we'll be fine. There is a thing you can do with the electrics on sites that can be pretty fun – all to do with using faulty appliances or the wrong voltages. It usually just trips out your own place, but I have been on sites where it's knocked us all out. Hence the torches. Then there's the tried-and-tested favourite of forgetting about Fiamma rails – the things that hold up the awnings – and them getting bent out of shape or even blown off in bad weather. It's pretty easy to not notice you've left a skylight open, and once you're driving along at speed, they can get into trouble. Then there's the more mundane stuff – like running out of gas when you're cooking, getting lost, getting stuck ...'

I feel myself pale slightly as he lists these potential pitfalls, convinced that I will tumble spectacularly into every single one of them.

'The main thing to remember,' he says, reaching out and laying a reassuring hand on my shoulder, 'is to try to enjoy yourself. Don't think about the potential problems – think about the freedom, the fun, the wide open spaces. And, hey, if you don't like it, I can just drop you off at the nearest services!'

I am momentarily distracted by the touch of his skin against mine and realise that he hasn't listed at least one of the possible disasters: all three of us, living together in a space that is used to accommodating one man and one small dog. That will be a challenge for each of us in different ways, I suspect – I haven't lived with a man for a very long time and even then not for long; Charlie has only ever shared a home with me; and Luke? Well, I realise, I don't actually know – he lives like this now, but I assume he didn't always. He said he had a big job and a different life and presumably all the trappings – house, car, maybe even wife.

'Are you sure you're OK with this?' I ask seriously. 'You chose this lifestyle because you wanted to be alone, I presume.'

'I did,' he replies, nodding. 'And that is a story for another day – or maybe a night, sitting out under the stars with a campfire and a guitar and a bottle of wine. But I wouldn't have offered if I didn't mean it. I'm not the sort of person who does things they don't want to.'

Our eyes meet, and nothing I see in his expression contradicts what he has said. I have to accept it, and go into this whole adventure with an open mind.

'OK, fine … though I might get you to sign some sort of disclaimer … Can I drive, by the way?'

'Probably not. It's too big, you need a special addition to your licence. But I'm OK with driving, I'm used to it. It'll be nice to have company. The big decision is where we drive to. I came here from the south coast, I spent spring and the early part of summer in Kent and Essex. Where next … well, that's the fun part!'

'What's the fun part?' says Charlie, emerging from the motorhome. His hair is tousled and his cheeks are red; he has been having a good time, and all of the childlike glee makes him look a lot younger. 'Did I miss the fun part? Because, I tell you, that little bed up there is pretty wild … I opened the skylight, is that OK?'

'That's fine,' replies Luke.

'As long as you remember to close it before we set off,' I add wisely. I wink at Luke and add: 'See? I was paying attention!'

'I never doubted it. What's the name of those rails again?'

'Hmmm … it begins with F, and I'm quite tempted to improvise here …'

'Don't swear, Mum,' intercedes Charlie. 'You'll set a bad example.'

'OK. So, I am going to call the rails Frank. And the water tank thingummy is Moby Dick. And the cupboard under my bed is Susan.'

'Susan?' they both say.

'Yes. It felt like a Susan to me. I'm still waiting for the rest of the cupboards to tell me their names …'

'My bed is called Conan the Barbarian,' Charlie chips in, getting into the spirit of things.

Luke frowns, and I wonder if he is having second thoughts. Maybe we're just too mad for him – he'll be chucking us out at the next junction and leaving us in his dust.

'I think you're onto something,' he says slowly. 'In fact, it feels remiss that I've never done this before. I think that from this moment on, the toilet will be known as the Mona Lisa.'

'Oh. How cultured,' I reply. 'What about the shower room?'

'Give the shower room a name? That would just be silly ... So, where to?' he smiles.

Charlie holds up his hand, a bit like he is in school, and says: 'I've got an idea about that!'

'Go for it, love,' I reply, genuinely warmed by the sight of his enthusiasm.

'OK – well ... you know how when it's Christmas, Mum, and we watch a film together every night from Christmas Eve-Eve through to Boxing Day-Boxing Day?'

'The twenty-third to the twenty-seventh,' I clarify for Luke's sake. Funny how families develop their own language after time, isn't it?

Charlie continues: 'Well, why don't we do what we normally do then?'

'Write the names of films down on bits of paper and put them in a Santa hat?' I say, frowning. A little slug of sadness tries to slime its way into my mind; the Santa hat is long gone, of course, along with the DVDs and the TV and most of the Christmas decorations. I salt the slug and urge it to shrivel away.

'Kind of, yeah,' says Charlie. 'What we could do is maybe each of us come up with a list of, like, five places, or books, or films, or food, or animals, whatever, that we enjoy. Then we draw them out, and go there.'

'Well,' I answer, 'I get it with places. Not sure how it'd work with the other stuff?'

'You'd have to be sensible, Mum,' he says, and I try to keep my face straight. Being told to be sensible by your eighteen-year-old son is quite something. 'You couldn't put something stupid like *Gladiator* ...'

'Hush your mouth, child. Don't you dare say *Gladiator* is stupid, you know I have very strong feelings about that film. I will be the mother to a murdered son if you carry on with that nonsense.'

'I know – I don't mean the film is stupid, obviously it's one of the greatest films of all time, I mean if you put *Gladiator*, we couldn't exactly drive to ancient Rome, could we?'

I have always wished that we could. I mean, imagine getting to be one of the spectators in the Coliseum? Watching Russell Crowe tart around in a skirt and having loaves of bread chucked at you? Throw in some tequila shots and it's the perfect night out. It'd be super-popular with hen parties.

'But,' I say, 'we could go somewhere Roman – like Bath, or Chester, or Hadrian's Wall.'

'Exactly! So, if I put *Jurassic World* or whatever, we could go somewhere with fossils. We'd find a connection and go there.'

'What do you think?' I ask Luke, who has been watching our double act in amusement.

'I love it,' he says. 'I might put some bands or songs in. And, actually, you know, just some places as well . . . just bear in mind we might end up doing some crazy zigzags, if one is in Aberdeen and the next is in Cornwall and then it's North Wales.'

'Let's limit it to England then,' I reply, 'and ban Cornwall, because it's too far away and too isolated.'

It is also, I do not say, the place where I grew up.

The place where my family, presumably, still lives. I am more than happy to ban it from our travels.

'Have you got a hat, though? That's a very important piece of the puzzle ...'

He laughs, and assures us that he has a hat, and paper and pens and scissors, and also a whole collection of maps, guidebooks and reference works about the sights, sounds and animals of the UK that we can dip into for inspiration.

We chat for a few more minutes about practicalities – stopping off for food and petrol and gas and water – and plan a last-night chippie run while we are still near civilisation. Luke says it's a tradition of his, and we can't mess with tradition – it would be bad luck. He heads off on his bike to a small village a few miles away, ready to do some hunter-gathering that involves battered cod.

While he is gone, Charlie and I unpack our few belongings, and I practise using the Mona Lisa and operating the shower. None of it is difficult, but it will take some getting used to.

When we are ready, I get the bottle of fizz I have had chilling in the fridge out and grab two glasses. Together, Charlie and I walk down to the place where our beautiful little home used to be.

The view is breathtaking – the sun dappling golden stripes on the waves, seabirds white smudges in a crystal-clear sky, the whole horizon stretching out endlessly before us. A perfect panorama.

I pour myself and Charlie a glass each as we stare out at the edge of the world. I remember all the days, months, years, of living here. Seeing Charlie grow up; his friends coming for sleepovers, the garden swarming with little princess and pirates at birthday parties. Quiet mornings with a good book and a pot of coffee on the patio. Baking wonky cakes, watching movies, pottering around with my plants. The challenges, the contentment, the sense of security it gave us.

'A toast to our former cottage,' I say, raising a glass at the rubble, the skip, the abandoned sofa. 'May she rest in peace.'

'We had some great times here, Mum,' Charlie says sadly. 'I can't believe it's really gone.'

'I know,' I say, giving him a cuddle. 'But it's time to move on – and we will have great times somewhere else, my love. I'm sure of it.'

Chapter 9

I sleep amazingly well that first night. It is all a bit of a tight squeeze, and all a bit foreign and strange, and the three of us are on our very best behaviour. There is one moment, when Charlie goes to use the Mona Lisa while Luke clears up our dishes and I go into the wet room to change into my PJs, where I wonder what kind of madness has gripped me – is this an insane thing to be doing? And if the answer to that is yes, then is it good insane or bad insane? Only time will tell.

When I wake up, though, it is a peaceful and gradual emergence into consciousness – a luxuriously slow process that involves lots of stretching and languid eye-opening, and the comforting sensation of being wrapped up in cotton wool, somewhere safe. It is a feeling I have not had for a very long time, and when I eventually drag myself up, I am awash with an unexpected sense of optimism. It is very early, and the birds are singing, and I have nowhere to be but here.

We all take it gently that morning, Luke showing me how to wrap and pack the remaining breakable items for the journey, Charlie bleary-eyed but happy as he clambers down his ladder, Betty clearly loving all the new human company.

Eventually, we are ready to leave, and Luke is settled in the driver's seat up front. There are three seats there, and they all swivel around so they can face into the main cabin. I have packed away my bed, and on the small table next to me is one of Luke's baseball caps, filled with crumpled-up pieces of paper. It is an exciting moment. We have decided that Charlie will choose, and I am doing a fake drum roll with my palms against the wood.

Charlie dips in to the hat, and pulls out a scrap – a scrap that will determine the next few days of our lives. Yes, I think, it is insane – but so far, so good.

'So,' says Luke from his swivelled chair, 'the deed is done. Where to, Captain?'

Charlie opens up the paper, and frowns. Obviously not one of his, from the look on his face. 'Erm . . . we're going to Wuthering Heights?' he says eventually. 'No idea where that is . . .'

It's not one of mine either, so I look over to our driver for some clarification.

'Ah,' he says, grinning and looking slightly sheepish, 'that's from me. And no, it's not a place. It's a song. And a book. And a film. But for me, it's a song . . . I just got a bit carried away last night.'

'And by carried away, you mean you had two pints of that real ale with the weird name?' I reply.

'It's called Scratchum's Wobbling Frog, which I think is a perfectly reasonable name. But . . . yeah, maybe it did influence some of my choices? We can skip it if you like?'

'No way!' says Charlie, so emphatically that Betty looks shocked and yips her disapproval. 'First rule of Motorhome Club is ... umm ... that doesn't really work ... but let's do it! Isn't it in Yorkshire, the book? Let's go there! And also, while we're making confessions, I had a drink last night too, so some of mine might be a bit random ...'

'You had two glasses of Prosecco!'

'Well, I'm just a lightweight, aren't I, Mum? Not a professional, like you! Yorkshire then?'

I nod, keen to move away from the subject of my drinking skills. *Wuthering Heights* ... I remember reading it when I was much younger. It was wild, and passionate and, truth be told, a little bit creepy. I remember the sense of isolation, the way the Moors were almost a character in their own right. It felt like a landscape that could swallow you whole. I also remember that the Brontë family lived in a small town in Yorkshire, and wonder if we could combine the two, and really get this magical quest off to a rip-roaring start. 'Yes. Let's do that,' I say. 'Luke, head for Yorkshire – and we'll look up the rest! Let the adventures begin!'

He gives me a jaunty salute and turns his chair around. We buckle up our seat belts, the various guidebooks and gazettes spread out on the table in front of us, my new laptop at the ready. Luke presses play on his music system, and I hear what may or may not be Led Zeppelin coming from the speakers. Rock and roll, at just after

7 a.m. The early start, he says, is the key to successful travel.

He drives slowly and carefully away from the field, and I wave at the donkeys as we pass their enclosure. I don't look backwards at our old home – I keep my eyes firmly forwards, because I don't want a random glimpse of the sofa to make me cry again. A quick glance at Charlie shows me he is too engrossed in a book about wild swimming to be having a moment of melancholy. Attaboy.

'OK,' says Luke, lowering the music and navigating the motorhome onto the lane that runs into town, 'I'm going to head for the A17 north, and once I hit that, the route is up to you guys. Choose whichever way you like – doesn't matter if we make detours, get lost, go backwards, drive in circles. The journey, my friends, is what matters!' He grins, and looks delighted with it all. The music goes back on, and I find myself smiling too as I turn to my laptop.

Much to Charlie's relief, Luke has a Wi-Fi set-up that involves an antenna on the roof, a router and a SIM card. I'm told it pretty much works anywhere there is a decent signal. It's all frightfully clever and way beyond my understanding, but I take the blessing and go online. Luke has sent me links to a few specialist sites and blogs about motorhoming, where like-minded souls share tips and details of great spots to stop off. It is, I have been told, very important to find places where you can empty the waste tanks and charge up. I get busy researching the Brontës and the Moors and finding a fun route. I am looking forward to heading inland – I have lived by the sea for the whole of my life, and I love it. But now is a time for fresh experiences.

Sitting across from me, Charlie is now fascinated by a massive tome called *The Modern Antiquarian*. It looks well used.

'This is brilliant,' he says, staring at the pages, 'it's, like, got all of the stone circles and long barrows in it.'

'Cool. What's a long barrow? Is it what giants use in their garden?'

'Ha ha. No. Long barrows are, apparently, Neolithic structures. Some had bodies in them, some were chambers. Nobody really knows for sure exactly what they were used for, but there are some pretty excellent ones still around. I think I could quite get into this. There's loads of Post-it notes in here too, reckon Luke's a bit of a druid on the side ...'

I glance at the pile of books. Some of them are standard – road maps, guides to national parks, that kind of thing. But a few others are stranger – there's one called *Wild Ruins BC*, another about Britain's holiest places. A folded-up *Great British Music Map*; the extremely encouraging *Ye Olde Good Inn Guide*. A veritable delight of weird unknown locations just waiting to be discovered.

After a bit of research, I tell Luke to join another A road, deciding unilaterally that this is not a motorway kind of day. I've been living at a service station hotel for the last week, and the thrill of Costa in takeaway cups has worn off.

Between us, Charlie and I come up with a plan, and

we make our first stop-off after a solid three hours of driving, at a small town in the Peak District called Bakewell. It is extremely pretty, with hilly streets and quaint buildings made of mellow stone and – the star attraction as far as Charlie is concerned – it is the home of the famed Bakewell pudding.

We park the van up, and stroll into the town centre, replenishing ourselves with cake and old-fashioned homemade lemonade. It is another scorcher of a day, so hot on the pavements that Luke carries Betty in his arms so her tiny paws don't get burned.

The town is bustling, and we meander our way up to the churchyard. Charlie becomes our tour guide and informs us that it has Saxon origins, is Grade I listed and has fine medieval misericords. I am unsure as to what misericords are, and I suspect Charlie is as well, so I do not inquire. He stays outside with Betty, inspecting the Saxon crosses and reading the gravestones.

The church itself is blessedly cool and shady, silent apart from the low-level talk of the few visitors inside its walls. I admire the stained-glass windows and the huge font, then stand and stare at the tombs of local dignitaries of centuries gone by. Elaborately carved versions of their living selves are draped across the top, as though protecting them. It is strangely sobering, imagining them as real people, with lives and hopes and dreams and disappointments and triumphs. Now forever trapped in alabaster.

I shake off the momentary melancholy and look around for Luke. I see him standing quietly in front of a lit candle, its flickering flame vivid in the dim lighting. A few others dance around it, and I wonder what their stories are – for every light that shines, there will be a prayer, a promise, a plea.

Luke closes his eyes and bows his head, and I quickly avert my gaze. It feels as though I am intruding on a deeply personal moment, and I move away, giving him space. We may technically live together, but I understand that I barely know this man – he is like one of those alabaster carvings; I can see the outside, but I have no idea what formed him, what lies beneath. Perhaps I will find that out as our lives walk parallel lines, or perhaps I will not – that is another mystery yet to unfold.

When we have all had our fill of culture, we stock up on picnic items and head off to our next stop. This is a place that Charlie suggested after becoming deeply enthused by the concept of wild swimming, and we couldn't have chosen a better day for it. The drive is sometimes slightly terrifying, through narrow winding roads and a pine forest, but Luke assures me he has navigated worse.

We all put our swimming gear on, and Charlie hefts a backpack full of towels and snacks and drinks. It feels a little like we are on holiday, and I wonder if we can possibly maintain this level of excitement for the whole trip. Which of us, I ponder, will be the first to say 'nah, I'm a bit tired, might just crash out in bed today'? From the looks of Charlie as he sprints ahead along the path with Betty at his heels, it won't be him.

'He seems to be having fun,' says Luke, walking by

my side as we follow the trail. We are heading for a pool that is apparently tucked away on the River Derwent, near to the neighbouring reservoir. The air is thick and warm, the trees lining the way casting welcome shade, sheep grazing nearby.

'He does,' I agree. 'Though with Charlie, possibly all teenagers, there does come a point where their batteries run out. At that point, he's likely to just fall asleep, or get really grumpy and blame me for everything, from the fact that he has a blister through to global warming.'

'Ha! Well, to be honest, that probably is your fault ... so, how are you feeling?'

'Apart from hot? I'm OK, thank you. It's all a bit strange, obviously, but I think this is the perfect distraction for us. I can't tell you how grateful I am for you giving us this opportunity. I mean, without you I'd have never tasted that Bakewell pudding ...'

'This is true. I am the Patron Saint of Women Who Need Cake. We'll add that to the mission statement, shall we? Everywhere we stop off, we have to find cake.'

I laugh and tell him I am all for it.

We walk in companionable silence until we reach an old stone bridge, watching as Charlie tears off his outer layers and follows Betty into the water. She clearly loves to swim, and her little brown head is bobbing around like a miniature seal. Charlie jumps in after her and shrieks in a very un-macho way.

'It's COLD!' he yells, splashing around. 'And deep! It's brilliant!'

We clamber down to the rocks at the side of the

riverbank and strip down to our swimmers. I feel a small sliver of embarrassment, and wonder why – I am no supermodel, but there is nothing going on beneath my clothes that is too disgusting. Just a woman thing, I suppose – we're never quite happy with ourselves, are we?

Luke seems to have no such qualms and is almost as fast as Charlie at tugging his T-shirt over his head and ditching his jeans. There is a moment, as he stands by the riverbank, trunks lying low on his hips, where I literally do a double take. He is like a work of art, tan skin, broad shoulders, the lean muscle you get from an active lifestyle rather than a gym. I cover my fluster by turning around and folding all of our cast-aside clothes into neat piles.

By the time I have finished, Luke has jumped in as well, and I go next. The shock of the chill water makes me squeal, but within seconds I adjust and start to absolutely love it. The water is clear and cool and completely refreshing, a gentle current adding a rhythmic flow. We are the only people here in this tiny paradise, surrounded by the majestic hills of the Peak District, banked by lush grass and the hum of insect life.

I lie on my back and float, gazing up at the pastel-blue sky, sun warm against my skin, listening to the sublime song of the skylarks. It is a moment of the purest peace: knowing that Charlie is safe and well and happy, that I am exactly where I need to be, that I have nothing else I should be doing right now.

That lasts for about thirty seconds, before Charlie

dive-bombs next to me and creates a mini-whirlpool of noise and splattered river water. I respond by holding his head underneath the surface, and Betty barks as she darts around us in circles. The peace is over, but the fun has begun.

We end our swim with a lazy picnic lunch at the side of the river, Betty curled up in a ball beneath a tree. It is idyllic, and we spend way too much time there. I remind myself that there is no schedule, that we are not on anybody's clock, that the day is ours to waste as much of as we like. It takes some adjustment, after years of work and school runs and carefully timed comings-and-goings, but I hope I can settle into it. One of the points of this journey is to explore a different way of living, a different way of being – and step one seems to be learning to relax.

The downside of that attitude is that by the time we reach Haworth, the Brontë village, we are too late to go into the museum. We stand outside, though, and look up at the building. It is the parsonage where Emily, Charlotte and Anne lived with their brother when their father was the reverend at the nearby church. Back then, it must have been a strange place – an industrial town, but perched on the edge of wild open moorland, bleak and beautiful at the same time. The building itself is handsome, but somehow also foreboding – to me, there is a darkness to it, the brickwork, the rigid structure of the place. I try to imagine those three women there, to picture Emily, her physical life so small, but her emotional and creative world so vast.

I gaze up at the parsonage from the neat gardens outside, and Charlie says: 'You're going to say "just imagine ..." aren't you?'

It is a joke between us – every time I have dragged him around a National Trust house, or taken him to clamber over ruined castle walls, I will inevitably say 'just imagine this the way it was!' and try to recreate some of the scenes from the past. Charlie plays along up to a point, but usually gets bored pretty soon and plays Candy Crush instead.

'I'm just imagining myself, love. Such amazing talent that lived in this one building. I keep looking up at those windows, and picturing them looking back out at me ...'

He gives me a look that says 'yeah, right, weirdo', and leaves me to it.

The heat of the day has faded, but the sun is still bright, the sky clear. We decide to go on a signposted walk from the parsonage across the moor to Top Withens, the place that is thought to have inspired *Wuthering Heights*.

It is a long trek, but breathtaking. The moors are wild, exposed, somehow alien – it is easy to imagine them in winter, wind-blown and snow-scattered, haunted by Cathy and Heathcliff. We pass the Brontë Waterfall, we climb steep hills, cross stepping-stones and spot kestrels gliding overhead. Iridescent dragonflies skim over water, and the landscape is brightened with luscious foxgloves, wild roses and honeysuckle. Even though we are not far from civilisation, it is eerily quiet out here.

The farmhouse itself is a ruin, but the views are

amazing. Again I find myself 'just imagining' Emily sitting out here, soaking in the primeval terrain, the wildlife, the sounds and scents of nature, feeding them all into her work. Charlie slightly ruins the moment by playing the Kate Bush song on his phone, which makes me laugh but leaves Luke with a slightly startled expression. He is quiet as we make the long trek back to the village.

We decide on a pub dinner, and once we are settled in a corner seat, Betty promptly falls asleep after a bowl of water and some gravy bones. She has been carried for some of the walk but is clearly exhausted, as is Charlie. Mid-conversation, he slumps back against his velvet-topped seat and closes his eyes. Poor baby – he's done more exercise today than he usually does in a month. As have I, and I am feeling it in my knees.

'Are you wiped out?' asks Luke, smiling at me over his pint of shandy.

'Yeah,' I reply, 'but in a good way. Is it always like this?'

'No,' he says, amused. 'Nobody could keep this up for long! When I settle somewhere for a while, like I was when we met, I take it much more slowly. I know I have days or weeks to explore, so there's no need for a list, or a hat . . . I set my own pace. And, before you ask, no, this isn't an inconvenience. I'm enjoying it. I like my lifestyle, but it can be a bit melancholy – seeing amazing things, with nobody there to share them with. So this is a bit of a holiday for me as well. If I'd been on my own, I wouldn't have been able to laugh my arse off watching you dance around the moor to "Wuthering Heights", would I?'

'Fair point. I should have been a ballerina, really, not an office manager in a carpet company.'

Those words feel strange coming out of my mouth. Only a matter of days ago, that's exactly what I was – and yet it already feels like a lifetime ago. A different me, in a different world.

'Can I ask you about money?' I say, needing to broach the subject.

'Well, money is a coin- and note-based form of currency, commonly used around the world in exchange for goods and services.'

'Thank you for that. You need to come up with some new material. And you know what I mean. I want to contribute – the costs of the petrol, the food, things like this dinner.'

I am so used to counting every penny that a pub meal feels like a huge extravagance, even though I am probably the least poor I have been for years. I have a month's worth of wages in the bank and no rent to pay, and the redundancy settlement should arrive within the next six weeks. I am relatively rich, by my standards, and I don't want to be a parasite.

'You can if you want to,' he replies slowly. 'But it's not necessary. Money isn't really a problem for me.'

'Oh. Are you one of those eccentric millionaires then? I always wanted to be one of those when I grew up. Sadly, I only succeeded with one.'

'Something like that. It's not an issue, do whatever makes you feel comfortable.'

He is an interesting man, Luke Henderson. An enigma

wrapped in a mystery wrapped in a really tricky cryptic crossword puzzle. Not exactly evasive, but definitely private. Kind, thoughtful, and maybe a tiny bit sad as well.

We are all guilty of making assumptions about people, aren't we? Based on the way they look or live or talk. When you meet a man in his middle years living in a mobile home, you assume he hasn't led what you might think of as a traditionally successful life – but Luke is blowing all of that out of the water. The part of my mind that likes to make up stories about people is going bananas.

Our food arrives, and Charlie immediately rouses himself as the aroma of sausage and mash nears his nostrils. By the time we finish up and head back to the motorhome, it is almost dark – that magical time in summer when the light seems to shimmer between day and night. We arrive at the site we have booked half an hour later. Luke shows me how to hook up the van to charge the leisure battery and advises us all to make the most of the facilities. Taking a shower in a full-sized cubicle, using washing machines and enjoying the luxury of a toilet you don't have to empty yourself are all fantastic opportunities to be snapped up, he assures us.

Charlie ignores all of this and lies on the grass next to the van instead. He is gazing up at the sky in some kind of exhausted trance, so I leave him to it while I visit the small camp shop and the facilities block.

The place is still lively, lots of families enjoying

themselves, toddlers riding bikes around the lit pathways, couples sitting outside their motorhomes and caravans, drinking and chatting. I hear different types of music as I wander through, everything from Wham! to something classical with strings. It is lovely, flush with a sense of communal pleasure. There are tents pitched over in a nearby field, and I wonder if there is a hierarchy – massive big motorhomes at the top and two-man pop-ups at the bottom, or maybe vice versa?

I take a nice long shower and get straight into my PJs and flip-flops, because I am a party animal like that. The changing rooms have hairdryers, which I use with a sense of wonder – mine was lost in the landslide, and I fear I have already gone feral. Somehow, wild and messy hair doesn't seem at all inappropriate when you're on the road. I have always dressed as smartly as I needed to for work, but I do feel a sense of relief at being able to abandon early-morning mascara disasters and tights and high heels.

I meet Luke back at our place, and he has set up the camping table and chairs. He has a can of his Wobbling Frog out and a glass of wine for me. I get my laptop from the motorhome, thinking I might do some research about tomorrow, and then sink down into the seat gratefully, taking a sip and sighing in contentment.

'This is really nice, isn't it?' I remark, gesturing around us. 'Everyone seems really laid-back and happy and mellow.'

'Don't let it fool you,' Luke replies, grinning, his teeth white against the evening darkness, 'they can turn.

If you're driving up front in a motorhome, and you see another one on the road, you have to wave at each other. It's a rule. If you don't, they might actually hunt you down and kill you.'

'Oh. Right. Best to be polite, then. Did you luxuriate in the shower?'

'Not as much as I'd have liked. Got chatting to someone – occupational hazard at campsites, people can talk about their motorhomes for hours on end. But it was quite interesting; he has solar panels on his, which I've been thinking about for a while.'

'Wow. You really can get everything with them, can't you?'

'Oh yes. Some have Jacuzzis and saunas, and built-in champagne bars.'

'Really?'

'No. But you sounded hopeful.'

'I'm only flesh and blood, you know.'

We smile at each other, and I realise that he is not the only one who has been lonely. I can't say that I have missed this – adult conversation, banter – because I have never really had it. I was still a child myself when I was with Rob, and since then it has only been me and Charlie. I find that I am enjoying it, a lot. Maybe too much.

Charlie stands up, stretches and groans, and says: 'I'm off to bed. Gonna FaceTime Dad for a bit and then crash. Laters, old people. Don't get too drunk.'

He disappears back into the motorhome, and Betty follows him. They are deeply in love with each other, those two.

'So,' says Luke, once we are alone again. 'What's the story with his dad? Is he still in his life? If you don't mind me asking. Don't feel obliged.'

I bite my lip and wonder if I do mind. I decide that I don't, and reply: 'Well, it's a story as old as time – boy meets girl. Girl gets pregnant at eighteen. Boy dumps girl to backpack around Europe and is never seen again.'

'Right. That must have been tough, doing it all on your own.'

'It had its moments,' I admit, 'and for most of it, I had no clue what I was doing. The first baby I ever held was my own. And yes, Rob is still in Charlie's life – in a way. Another story as old as time, I suppose – the absent parent gets to be the fun one, don't they? That can sting a bit, if I'm honest. But mainly ... it's been great. I mean, Charlie's great.'

'He certainly is. You did a great job raising him, so, whatever you did, you did it right.'

I pause and let that soak in. When you're a single parent, you focus so much on your failures – on what you can't give them, on what you get wrong, on every consequence of every decision you make. It's easy to get wrapped up in that, to feel as though you have never been enough. That you have let them down in some way, haven't given them the perfect family, the perfect life.

But the truth is that the perfect family doesn't exist – and all parents make mistakes, single or not. I know that logically, but don't always feel it. Hearing someone else point it out feels good, like a balm applied to a sore spot

I've had for so long I've just learned how to ignore it.

'Thank you,' I say simply.

'And what about you?' Luke asks. 'Charlie's great, but how did all of that affect you?'

I bite my lip and realise that's a tough question to answer. It's also one that nobody has really asked before. I was so young back then, and I'm never quite sure what my life would have looked like if I hadn't been forced to deal with so much, so soon. 'That's hard to explain,' I reply. 'Sometimes it all seems so long ago I can barely remember it. But I suppose it shaped me – in good ways and bad ways. The bad ways are ... well, the clue's in the name, I think. I worry a lot. I find it hard to relax, like I always have to be on guard duty. But the good ways – well, I try to focus on those. It made me independent and resilient. It made me realise how much I was capable of, maybe ... I don't know. I'm in transition at the moment, Luke, so you can't expect sensible answers!'

'In transition ...' he says quietly. 'That's a good way of putting it.'

We spend a few moments in silence, sipping our drinks and relaxing in the still-warm evening air, until he says: 'I chose "Wuthering Heights" because it was my daughter's favourite song. She was called Katie, and her grandmother was a huge Kate Bush fan. She used to play it to her all the time, telling her she was named after her – she wasn't, but that didn't matter. They watched the video, that old one, and after that, whenever she could, Katie would grab a sheet or a towel and dance around to it, wafting it around like a cape. She always got the words a bit wrong, though, and she used to sing "it's me, I'm a tree". It was ... lovely.'

He is staring away from me as he talks, one hand gripping his beer a little too tightly. He is smiling at the memory, the sides of his eyes crinkling, but there is no mistaking the sadness of his tone. Or his use of past tense.

'What happened?' I ask quietly, washed with an icy sense of dread. I know what is likely to come next and I feel my heart start to splinter.

'She died four years ago. She was only nine. A type of leukaemia called ALL.'

His voice is low, the words clipped, the sentences brutally short. This is, quite obviously, hard for him to talk about.

'I'm so sorry, Luke. What was she like?'

He looks at me in surprise and shakes his head slightly. 'Nobody ever asks that,' he says, 'they're usually just too freaked out. That's one of the reasons I stopped talking to people about it. Stopped talking to people at all really ... but she was perfect: funny, clever, kind. Full of life, even when the treatments were torturing her. She had her mum's blonde hair, and my eyes, and her own sense of mischief. Yeah. She was perfect.'

The look on his face is a heart-rending combination of pain and pride, and I swallow the lump that starts to form in my throat as I reply.

'She sounds it. I'd love to see a picture of her some time.'

'I have some,' he replies, sounding hesitant. 'Maybe I'll show you one day.' He stands up abruptly, knocking his can to the floor and cursing as he retrieves it, the remaining beer fizzing out onto the grass. He hovers above me, looking stern, and says: 'Right. That's me done for the night.'

He is tense, his mouth a grim line, his eyes flickering from side to side as though he is looking for a threat. I reach up, place one of my hands on his. I wind our fingers together, and say: 'Thank you for telling me about Katie.'

He doesn't meet my eyes, but I feel a returning squeeze of pressure before he pulls his hand from mine, nods firmly and heads inside. He pauses on the steps, and says: 'Sorry if it was too much. I don't know why I told you all of that. Maybe because you'd told me about your situation. Maybe just because I feel … like I can trust you.'

He doesn't give me the chance to reply, just disappears quickly inside, as though embarrassed by the whole thing. He feels like he can trust me … I don't underestimate the power of those words. Trust is not a thing to be trifled with. I can't remember the last time I totally trusted another adult human being, and I realise that I am starting to trust Luke. I at least attempted to give him a genuine answer to his questions, instead of retreating to my default setting of making everything into a joke.

I stay where I am. It's been an unexpectedly emotional evening. I am sad and shocked and worried I might cry. It is not my grief to hijack, and although I briefly wonder if I should go inside and check on him, I know that Luke needs some space. It seemed to take a physically tangible toll on him, talking about it at all, and he might need a few minutes alone.

I sip my wine and, as soon as I am sure he is not going to come back out, allow the tears I have been clenching to roll down my face. For Luke, for Katie, for his wife. For everyone who has suffered such an unimaginable loss. My life has not been easy, but Charlie is tucked up in bed, safe and happy, and that makes me the luckiest woman on earth.

Chapter 10

'Zombies?' I say, confused. 'Our next stop is zombies?'

We are all sitting outside the van, eating croissants and drinking coffee. Luke was up early, and bought treats and a spare fold-up chair from the site shop. The baseball hat is on the table amid the plates and mugs, and Charlie is cringing as he stares at the tiny scrap of paper in his hand.

'I know!' he says, despairing. 'It's really stupid, isn't it? But … well, I'd had a drink, and I was just thinking about things I like, and about all the zombie films I'd watched and the video games I play and … look, all I can say is it made sense at the time!'

Luke starts laughing, and it is a fine laugh – deep and genuine and utterly infectious. He seems more like his normal self today, although his early solo start implies that he perhaps didn't have the best of night's rest. I'd been vaguely aware of him tiptoeing around somewhere near 5 a.m. but had fallen straight back asleep. 'Well, zombies it is then,' he says, once we have all calmed down. 'We made a pledge, and now we must honour it. Let's see what we can find out about zombies in the locale …'

He starts googling on his phone, while I clear away and wash our dishes. At first, I am confused as to why no water comes out of the taps but remind myself to switch on the pump. Duh. Luke has already filled the tank, emptied the waste and our leisure battery is fully charged. This, I am sure, is as ready as it gets for a motorhome. I dry the crockery and wrap it, as I have been shown by the master. I also do a quick scan of windows and skylights to make sure we're good to go.

By the time I go back outside, Charlie is looking excited, gazing at Luke's phone screen and nodding.

'Mum, you wouldn't believe how many zombie films have been made in the UK! You know in *World War Z*, when they're driving through Philadelphia trying to escape?'

'I do indeed. Brad Pitt being all macho and pretty at the same time.'

'Well, that wasn't Philadelphia, it was bloody Glasgow! And, at the end, when he goes to Nova Scotia, it wasn't even Nova Scotia – it was some place called Lulworth Cove in Dorset!'

His voice is slightly higher than normal as the words tumble out; he is so thrilled he can barely contain himself.

'Wow,' I say, smiling, 'the magic of Hollywood, eh? But … Glasgow isn't in England, and Lulworth Cove is a long, long way away. Anywhere closer to home?'

'On it,' says Luke, continuing his quest.

Charlie pipes up: 'We looked at *Shaun of the Dead*, but it was all London, and, you know, that doesn't really fit with the vibe, does it?'

'What about *28 Days Later*?' Luke asks, frowning at his screen.

'A classic,' Charlie replies firmly. 'Fast zombies, though. Really scary. You need your zombies to be slow if you want to escape.'

'Well, I don't suppose we need to worry about that, love – because, you know, zombies aren't real?' I say, patting him on the shoulder.

'Ha! You've clearly not spent much time in the amusement arcade on a Sunday night. So, where are we going, Luke?'

He sounds so thrilled, like a little kid sitting in the back of the car playing the ever-popular 'are we nearly there?' game.

'OK,' Luke replies, after some championship-level scrolling, 'this could work. One of my picks was the Lake District – it'll be in the hat somewhere, and now seems insanely mundane.'

'It does,' adds Charlie, 'the way we're going, we'll be pulling out bits of paper that say "the far side of Jupiter".'

'Nah,' I say, shaking my head. 'Never Jupiter. I hate Jupiter. It's so full of gas. Totally up itself.'

'Yeah, I know,' replies Charlie, grinning. 'it's such a show-off – I mean, who cares if it's the biggest? If Jupiter was a person, they'd be an absolute cock, like one of those giant meathead men who goes to the gym and eats seven turkeys a day and has steroids for breakfast and parks their jeep in the disabled spots.'

'Or one of those people who go on talent shows

and say they're the world's best singer in the video clip and when they audition, they're terrible, and you find yourself wondering why they didn't have any friends who told them that before they humiliated themselves on national television,' I add.

'Yeah. Total loser of a planet!'

Charlie holds up his palm, and I slap it with a high-five.

Luke is leaning back in his chair. 'I love your double act,' he says, 'you should start a YouTube channel.'

I examine his tone for any sign of sadness, but all I find is genuine amusement. After last night, after learning that he lost his own child, his little Katie, there is part of me that worries about this kind of thing – the easy knockabout chatter I share with Charlie, the bond that isn't perfect but always strong. I have had eighteen years with him, already far longer than Luke had with Katie, and Charlie and I can talk like this for hours. Now more than ever, I appreciate just how lucky I am.

'Well, maybe not a YouTube channel,' I say, 'but I did do some writing last night. Did a review of our day on one of those touring websites. I thought it only fair that I share that picture of Charlie asleep in the pub in Haworth with drool on his chin.'

'You didn't, did you?' he says, looking aghast.

'No. But I do have the photo on my phone, so watch your step, sunshine. Anyway ... I enjoyed it, writing it all up. Might start doing it for myself, keeping a diary.'

'Will there be any rough caresses or thrusting against the walls of the school gym?' he asks, winking. He has clearly been reading those damned exercise books again, and I blush slightly.

'Moving on . . .' I say, keen to do exactly that. 'Where to then, Luke?'

'A place called Ennerdale Water,' he says, 'in the western side of the Lake District. Apparently the closing scenes of *28 Days Later* were filmed there.'

I don't remember the movie too vividly – I think I watched it once with Charlie when I was half asleep after work – but he clearly does.

'I know the bit you mean,' he says. 'The survivors are holed up in a farmhouse and they spell out HELLO with curtains and stuff on the hillside until the rescue plane spots them. It looked like it was in the middle of nowhere. That'd be really cool. Have we got time for me to go and use the showers?'

We tell him he has, and he traipses away with a towel and his washbag. I watch him disappear and decide that he seems to have grown even taller in the last week. Or maybe he's just standing up straighter, who knows? Something about him seems different anyway. Maybe it's the outdoors lifestyle, I think, then remind myself that we're not exactly living off the grid. Could it only be yesterday that we left our old life behind? We have travelled for hundreds of miles, crossed from one part of the country to another, and spent two nights in a motorhome. It is surreal how quickly everything has changed.

Even thinking about my old home unsettles me slightly, and I suspect that I haven't quite finished processing it all. I have jumped from 'my house has fallen off a cliff, my life is ruined' to 'I am the new Jack Kerouac' with alarming speed, and I would not be surprised if, at some point, I trip myself up.

I'm not even sure how much of this new-found sense of contentment is real and how much of it is simply a coping mechanism. Am I doing all of this just to distract myself, or am I genuinely looking for a change in the way I live my life? Big questions that need to be answered – but not today, I decide, switching off. Not today.

'So, how are you this morning?' I ask Luke, who is finishing his coffee and watching two birds flitter in and out of a nearby tree. They are quite plain apart from brilliant orange patches on their heads.

'Goldcrests,' he says, following my gaze. 'And I'm fine, thank you. I ... well, I'm sorry I went all silent last night. It's just a hard thing to talk about, and I haven't done it for so long and, being truthful, I didn't want to start crying in front of you. Didn't want to blow my tough-guy image.'

He is trying to make light of a dark situation. It is an instinct I recognise, one that Charlie called me out for quite recently.

'Tough-guy images are overrated,' I say quickly, 'and I'd still want you next to me in a zombie apocalypse. I reckon you're the kind of guy who could swing an axe while sobbing and pull it all off.'

'Like Brad Pitt?'

'Exactly like that. Luke ... please don't apologise,

for anything. Just know that if you want to talk about it – about Katie – then I would love to listen. But if you don't, if it's just too hard, then I understand that as well.'

He nods, and stares at the goldcrests, and then looks back at me. Our eyes meet and he says: 'This is going to be quite a journey, isn't it? And I don't just mean to the Lake District.'

I know exactly what he does mean, and I share the sensation. I feel a strange combination of liberation and fear right now – the knowledge that things are changing, and not just my work or home life, but my internal life. It's as though I am a closed-off flower spreading its petals to the rainfall, to the sun, to the sky, desperate for the nourishment I didn't even know I'd been missing.

I am starting to have the niggling feeling that I have been hiding from things that could potentially scare or hurt me for a long time now. Things like trust, and close friendships, and even thinking about deep emotions, never mind confronting them. In my defence, I have been busy, but I have also made choices – to focus on the things I could control, and to ignore the ones that made me feel unsteady. Making another choice – to come on this crazy road trip – is having all kinds of unexpected consequences.

'Well,' I say as calmly as I can, 'I suppose we can still adapt the same general principles – don't go too fast, always clearly indicate when you're going to change lanes and don't crash. Especially the last one.'

'Don't crash,' he says, grinning. 'I like it. Maybe I'll adopt that one as *my* life motto?'

'It's possibly a slight improvement on "everything's better with biscuits", I'd say. So, is there anything else we need to do before we get on the road?'

'I think we're pretty solid. You want to start looking at a route while I put the tables and chairs away?'

I nod and we both go about our business – mine being slightly less labour-intensive than his.

Charlie comes back before long, sending Betty into spasms of joy. He falls onto the couch as though he is trying to prove the theory of gravity, and she jumps onto his lap. He kisses her face and scratches her ears and calls her his little princess, and she licks his face in return.

'Dad said he has that book, the one about the stone circles,' Charlie says, as Betty rotates three times and thuds into a curled-up ball on his knees.

'Oh, right, brilliant – well, it must be good then, if it's got your dad's seal of approval!' I reply, adopting the fake-enthusiastic voice I always hate hearing when I talk to Charlie about his father. He, of course, doesn't know it's fake, so that's all right. I don't hate Rob, or even really resent him – he wasn't much older than me when I fell pregnant, only twenty-one. I can't hold it against him that he freaked out, that he ran – but I do kind of hold it against him that he's been such a piss-poor parent ever since. He's almost forty now and he's never even sent Charlie a Christmas present, never mind contributed to the cost of raising him.

The money side of things isn't even the part that upsets me, truth be told – we have coped, and there are more important things in the world. It's the emotional aspect I've struggled with – the dipping in and out of Charlie's life as and when it suits him, being this fun peripheral figure, always full of stories of adventure and mystery. Truffle-hunting in Croatia, working on a yacht charter in the Bahamas, a season at a bear-spotting resort on Vancouver Island, leading student expeditions in New Zealand – you name it, he's done it.

He's travelled far and wide, lived loud and large, and experienced so much of the world – all while I managed to move from one side of England to the other and raise our son. I have no regrets about that, no bitterness – I still think I got the best end of the deal. But I'd be lying if I said it didn't sometimes hurt listening to Charlie talking about his dad with near hero-worship; relaying his stories second-hand, telling me about his exciting adventures at remote mountain camps as I shopped for budget-brand breakfast cereal. I didn't want Rob's life – but maybe I wanted Charlie to think about me with the same admiration, the same respect.

All of which, of course, is extremely childish and silly – and because I know that, and need to cover it up, I always go over the top in my responses. Please, I tend to say, tell me more – I LOVE hearing about your dad's adventures!

'Apparently he's famous, the bloke who wrote it. He's called Julian Cope and he was in a band in the eighties and then he wrote this, and it's like the bible on British prehistoric sites.'

'Wow. Excellent. I'll look him up, maybe I'll know the band …'

'Don't think so, Mum, apparently they were a cool post-punk group.'

And there, in that one sentence, is exactly what makes me feel childish and silly about the situation – the assumption that while his dad will, of course, know the cool band in question, I for sure will not. What makes it even worse is the fact that he's probably right. I'm more Spice Girls than post-punk.

'OK, right. Anyway. We're going to set off soon – look up Ennerdale Water and see if there's anywhere you'd like to go on the way, all right?'

We are soon on the road again, and now even more enthused by *The Modern Antiquarian*, Charlie picks out a stone circle that is, roughly speaking, on the way to our zombie-connected beauty spot (words I never anticipated being used together before now). Before that, he announces that he wants to call in at a place called Malham Cove in the Yorkshire Dales National Park.

Some of the winding roads we have to travel down on the way are so narrow they make me wish the motorhome could hold its breath, but eventually we make it without getting stuck, or knocking down any of the pretty drystone walls. A few sheep look at us suspiciously, but I can live with that. I reckon I could take them in a fight.

We park near a small information centre and follow the signs to Malham Cove. We walk through a village that is spread along the side of a burbling stream that tumbles over rocks and tree roots, ancient-looking stone bridges crossing from one side to another. We are surrounded by green hills and wide blue sky, and the place feels tiny in comparison – the pubs and shops and the smithy and other signs of human achievement dwarfed by the grandeur of nature.

Charlie has downloaded some information leaflets and walking routes and guides us through the village and up to a gate, where we obey the sign and put Betty on the lead. I swear she looks at us with disapproval.

We walk down a steep hill, covered with rocks and grass, scattered with grazing sheep. It is still early, and we are alone apart from one man and a Labrador going in the opposite direction. As we near the bottom of the hill, we all stop and stare, not quite believing what we are seeing.

The stream gurgles along and expands at the bottom, bouncing over large boulders towards a kind of basin. Surrounding it is a huge cliff of white limestone, curving and enormous, its sheer face veering hundreds of feet into the pale blue sky. It is breathtaking, and alien, and like nothing I have ever seen before.

'Wow,' says Luke, standing and staring, hands on his hips, 'now that is impressive. Do you think it was a waterfall?'

'It was,' says Charlie, after looking at his phone, 'but not now, unless there's been huge rainfall. It was formed at the end of the last Ice Age, whenever that was ... It's amazing, isn't it? It's like the cliffs at Dover but mashed up a bit and plonked down in the middle of the country. Can we walk down?'

We go through a small gate and find ourselves

surrounded by rocks and water. It's been dry for days now, but we still need to pick our way across the floor of uneven pebble and slippery plants, edging closer to the cliff itself. I peer up and see a climber dangling from the side of it, yellow helmet bright in the sun.

It is an incredible place, silent apart from the cries of circling birds and the sound of the water. It feels ancient, somehow holy, and completely magical.

'This is the best thing I've ever seen,' announces Charlie, taking some pictures with his phone. 'I can't believe we're still in England.'

He is a teenager, and prone to exaggeration, but he is right – it's so strange and eerie and beautiful, it is hard to describe.

We eventually tear ourselves away and make the climb up a steep range of steps at the side, which leads us to the top of the cliff. The ground is made up entirely of irregular white blocks, and Charlie tells us it is called a limestone pavement and gets momentarily excited when he finds out that one of the Harry Potter films was shot here. I'm not surprised – it feels otherworldly, and we are all silent as we sit and gaze out at the views of the village, the lush green dales around us.

'Where next, Captain?' says Luke after a while, and Charlie informs us we can do a circular walk to a place called Gordale Scar and on to a waterfall called Janet's Foss before we loop back to the car park.

It takes a while, but it is so worth it. The Scar is strange and stunning, reached after a short hike through a field and another lively stream, which I am told is called a beck. We let Betty cool her feet in the water, and, as we turn a corner, are yet again faced with another unbelievable sight – a huge gorge that has been cut into the limestone, waterfalls tumbling dramatically down over the rocks.

'This place actually looks a bit familiar,' says Charlie, gazing around. He looks at his phone, and after a few minutes a huge smile appears on his face. '*The Witcher!*' he says triumphantly. 'They filmed some of *The Witcher* here!'

'What's *The Witcher*?' asks Luke, shrugging when Charlie stares at him in horror. 'What can I say? I don't watch a lot of TV!'

'It's a fantasy show on Netflix,' I explain, 'and it's pretty good for all kinds of reasons. I can't believe I'm actually walking in the footsteps of Henry Cavill . . .'

'Who's Henry Cavill?' Luke says, frowning.

'Actor,' replies Charlie, grinning. 'She thinks he's hot and has an embarrassing mum crush on him.'

'This is true,' I answer, 'and I refuse to apologise for it. Henry Cavill is a god among men. I might be a mother, but I'm not actually dead.'

'A god among men . . .' says Luke as we make our way back along the path. 'I feel quite emasculated.'

'You shouldn't,' replies Charlie, 'you're pretty hot too, you know, for an old man!'

He bounds ahead with Betty, and Luke laughs.

'I don't know whether that was a compliment or an insult,' he says as we follow on, heading to the footpath to Janet's Foss.

'Possibly both,' I explain, avoiding his face. I have been noticing Luke's hotness a little too much for comfort, and it unsettles me. I find myself thinking about him in ways I don't want to think about him, ways that I haven't thought about a man for a long time. This new arrangement we have is working just fine without me developing another 'embarrassing mum crush'. He is a fast becoming a friend, and that is enough. That is a win.

We reach the Foss after an adventurous downhill walk, clambering over rocks to reach yet another magical spot. It is tucked away in what feels like a fairy glen, secluded and shady despite the warmth of the day. There is a central pool, a pretty waterfall flowing into it, surrounded by rocks so big you can sit or lie on them.

'Can we go in?' asks Charlie, as Betty takes the plunge. 'I think this might be my new thing, wild swimming.'

'Better than heroin addiction, I suppose – but we don't have swimmers or towels with us. I can offer you bottled water, half a croissant and a small first-aid kit, but no trunks.'

He stares at the clear water longingly, and Luke adds: 'It's a hot day. We could take a dip in our undies and dry off in the sun.'

I opt out of that, as, for some reason, a woman in bra and knickers seems a lot weirder than a man in boxers. Maybe just to me, I don't know. I am happy to paddle, wading into the chilly water up to my knees to cool myself off. I deliberately avert my gaze as they strip down, and wait until they are submerged before I look back up.

Sometimes in life, you have those rare moments of perfection – moments that you know you will remember forever, frozen like a photograph in your mind, stored to revisit in more challenging times. This is one of them: sitting in the sun-dappled morning light, my toes wet, watching them enjoy themselves. They splash and dive and swim; they stand beneath the white froth of the waterfall; they laugh and they clamber out and jump back in.

Not so long ago, I thought my life was damaged beyond repair – now I can't keep the smile off my face. I say a small and silent prayer of thanks to whoever might be listening, because in this place, in this unearthly beauty, it feels entirely possible that someone is.

When they finally emerge, shaking themselves free of water, droplets golden in the sun, Charlie says: 'You look blissed out, Mum. What are you thinking about?'

You, I think, and how much I love you. How privileged I am to have such a wonderful human in my life. Luke, and how lucky I was to meet him at the time I most needed help. The beauty of the world, its endless potential, the scary but scintillating prospect of a whole different future opening up in front of me. Of loneliness and loss and how easy it is to find yourself thinking that you need to carry it all on your own shoulders; of the joy at realising that maybe you don't. That if we dare to take a risk, to step outside our own isolation and our own worries, there is a kaleidoscope of wonders just around the corner. Of the mysteries of what is yet to come.

'Oh, you know,' I say, smiling up at him, 'just Henry Cavill.'

Chapter 11

We spend the night parked up on an isolated field in the midst of sweeping mountains and conifers. The lake itself is perfection – quiet, secluded, chilly even after a day of sun. It really is easy to feel completely disconnected from the real world that we know exists around us.

After getting permission from the land-owner, we settle on a spot that is surrounded by hills, sheep our only neighbours. There is no traffic nearby, no other people, nothing but us and this primeval landscape. We hire kayaks, and eat, and lie around on grassy banks, and talk of everything and nothing. It is the warmest it has been so far this summer, and it feels inconceivable that the storm that caused so much destruction happened in the same universe.

Much of the area around the lake is traffic-free, so we make the short hike back to the van as the sun starts to sink, and Luke grills up some fish on the barbecue. He's quite the chef, I have discovered, having mastered the art of cooking on the move. I had years in an actual house with a full-sized kitchen and never made much progress.

After our meal, we settle into a mutual silence. Charlie is sprawled on the grass, looking at his phone. Luke is playing his guitar, picking out tunes that I half recognise. I am writing – another review of our day.

'What ya doing, Mum?' Charlie shouts up, without ever taking his eyes from the screen. Who says the younger generation can't multitask?

'Being all creative and stuff. That piece I wrote yesterday has been quite popular.'

'Wow – are you, like, Insta-famous now?'

'Yeah. I broke the internet by describing the toilet facilities in Malham. But, well, it got a little thumbs-up sign from a lot of people, and some nice comments saying how well I'd brought it to life. The whole thing, not just the toilets.'

I steel myself for the inevitable mockery, but I am actually quietly proud of myself. I enjoyed writing it, and the fact that people enjoyed reading it is a bonus. It feels nice, gives me a tiny warm glow inside. Writing again feels a bit like coming home, rediscovering part of me I assumed I'd lost.

'That's great,' Charlie replies, surprising me by not taking the piss at all. 'You should set up a blog or whatever. Chronicle our amazing journeys ... you could call it "The Lady in the Van" or something.'

I meet Luke's eyes and we both smile. Uncultured youth.

'I think that's already been done, love ... plus, I don't know how to do things like "set up blogs or whatever". You know I can barely manage WhatsApp.'

Charlie sits up, and Betty looks at him disapprovingly. She was sitting on his chest after all. 'I'll do it for you. I'll make you a page, keep it simple, so just do some words and maybe pictures and then I can upload them. It'll be fun. I can look back on it when you're old and I'm changing your nappies and say, "Ah well, she wasn't always like this . . ."'

'You should,' adds Luke, before I can reply to the nappies comment. 'I read it. You're a good writer. You have a way of making things feel vivid. And you're funny, too. It could work.'

Huh. He's read it, and he liked it – for some reason that gives me a little glow of pride.

'Yeah,' says Charlie, now looking even more interested. 'I can set up some social media around it – Insta and Twitter and TikTok.'

'Easy there, tiger – that doesn't sound like me at all!'

'It wouldn't need to be you. It would be me, in disguise. Family effort – me, you and Luke.'

There is a slight pause right there, in our chatter and in Luke's guitar playing. A family effort. We have not been together for long, but I know what Charlie means – and I'm not entirely sure how I feel about it. This is temporary. This is transient. This is fun – but it is not family.

Charlie seems unaware of what he has said and blusters on, planning world domination and sponsorship deals: a book, a TV show, a collection of Luke's recipes. He has a whole franchise planned within minutes, while I'm still reeling from the fact that he now seems to see Luke as part of our family.

I know Charlie has always wanted more – always wanted a bigger family unit. I wonder if that is why he has fallen so easily into this, accepted our changed circumstances with such apparent nonchalance. He's taken to Luke with such speed and such ease, and, to be fair, I can totally understand that – so have I. But for Charlie, I wonder if it is more? If Luke is somehow becoming a father figure to him?

I'm also finding it strange that neither of us seems to be missing our old life. That neither of us has as yet had a swearing fit because of something we lost in the storm, or had a meltdown about being so unmoored, so unsettled? What does it say about our old life that we both seem to have abandoned it so readily? If you'd have asked me what our life looked like before the day of the storm, I'd have said it was good, content. There were worries, there were anxieties, but I didn't feel like they were dominant. I think, with a bit of space and distance, that I now see I was fooling myself – I was riddled with tension and could never even imagine a way out. I told myself I was happy. I told myself it was how I wanted my life to be. I told myself it was the best thing for Charlie. Now I am starting to wonder if that could have possibly been the case – I am not missing a single thing about home and am pondering whether it was all style over substance. Having a pretty garden does not make your life perfect, and losing everything has made me realise that I actually had little to lose. As for Charlie, there has to be more to his new-found bounce than the usual carefree approach to life that teens can have – maybe he was ready for a change, too.

I don't have time to process any of it, because Charlie has already decided that this is game on and disappears back inside the van to start looking at domain names. Wowzers.

After he has gone, I turn to Luke and say: 'I think he's wasted going into science. He should be doing business studies.'

'Can't knock his enthusiasm. He might be right, you know – you should give it a go. If nothing else, you'll enjoy it. Charlie was telling me that you used to want to be a writer. Maybe it'd be good to find your passion for it again.'

I am momentarily disconcerted by the idea of Charlie chatting to Luke, letting him in on all my guilty secrets. But Charlie is an easy-going lad, open, full of warmth – it doesn't surprise me that he is finding this easier than I am. He has had less time on the planet to develop callouses, to understand the need for self-protection.

'Passion? I'm not sure that's the right word. Anyway, what about you? What's your passion?'

'You're trying to change the subject, this isn't about me. But, to answer your question, I don't know yet what my passion is. I'm still looking and, in the meantime, I settle for contentment. But is he right? Is that what you wanted to do?'

'Many years ago. Before real life took hold. Then it just seemed ... silly.'

'Well, maybe this is your chance to revisit it. This is

hardly real life, is it? You're taking a vacation from real life. And doing something you love, something you're obviously good at, is far from silly.'

'Thank you, Yoda. And you? Is this a vacation for you as well?'

I know, of course, that this is a way of life for him – but he is usually alone. Is the fact that we are with him changing things for him as well?

'Again, I don't know, Jenny. Having you two with me ... yes, it makes everything feel different. More fun. More ... happy, I suppose. But I also know it's not permanent, I know you'll find your feet again, and we'll part ways, and I'll ... well, I'll probably go back to doing what I was doing before.'

He doesn't exactly sound sad as he says this – more resigned. As though he knows that's what he deserves. We are both at such strange junctions in our lives.

I look around, at the majestic hills and the lush trees and the dome of silence that seems to surround us, and acknowledge that he has a point. 'It's not, is it? It's still so warm as well. It'd actually be nice to sleep outside.'

'You can. I have groundsheets, sleeping bags. I've done it myself a few times. You wake up coated in dew and with a few new insect friends, but it's a pretty special experience. What do you say? It'd make a good entry on your new blog!'

I snort with laughter, but nod my agreement. When I was younger, I did this a lot, and since then I have spent a few nights in tents with Charlie, but I have never gone full wild-camper since he was born. Perhaps this is the time to try again. I might as well cram in as many new experiences as I can before I have to face up to the reality of boring things like jobs and houses, and finding one of each.

I carry on writing, wondering as I type each word whether Charlie and Luke are right, or if they're just being kind – indulging me in this childish pursuit. I decide that I should just continue doing it while it's bringing me pleasure, which is a luxurious way of viewing anything at all, and one usually associated with the consumption of chocolate éclairs.

Before too long, Luke emerges with arms full of equipment. He spreads it all out, setting up a sheet and a bag either side of the table.

'Charlie says he might join in, so I told him where the stuff was.'

'Another amazing hidden storage unit?'

'Yes. Under my bed. I now call it Larry.'

'We really should have a name for the motorhome, you know …'

'That's true. It'll come to us, I'm sure. I might not stay out the whole night, but I'll join you for a while. Still writing?'

'Just finishing,' I say, closing down the laptop. It is almost 11 p.m. and I am exhausted. 'I was just describing that stone circle we called at on the way, Castlerigg. It was pretty amazing, but …'

'Pretty full as well? Yeah. I reckon those places are best seen very early in the morning or later at night.

Because few things don't say mystic quest as well as coach-loads of pensioners in sun hats.'

He is, of course, right, and I vow to go back there and do it when it is quiet, so I can get a better handle on these ancient folk and their stone shenanigans.

I head inside the van and do my ablutions, check in with Charlie who is now firmly cosied up with Betty, and get into my PJs. There is a slightly awkward moment where Luke and I have to slide past each other on my way out and his way in, and he emerges with a bottle of fine-looking whisky and two glasses.

'Nothing like a nightcap under the stars,' he says, as we both settle into our sleeping bags.

I have my nice notepad and a gel pen by my side in case I get hit by sudden inspiration. I have become a proper prima donna.

'Ha! That sounds like the start of a blog post if ever I heard one!' I reply, scribbling it down.

'See? You're a natural. Now, I know you're probably already thinking that you don't need that sleeping bag, that it's too warm – but take it from a man who's made the same mistake, you do. If you drift off to sleep outside it, you'll wake up cold and in the grasp of a nightmare at 3 a.m. Then all of this silence won't be pleasant, it'll be horrifying.'

He passes me a glass, and I take a sip. It is smooth but fiery, sliding down my throat with reckless ease.

'So, first brandy, and now this. Do you have a secret liquor cabinet called Clive I don't know about?'

'It's not a secret, but it is in my bedroom. Help

yourself whenever you feel the need. I don't have it on display in case I come across like an alcoholic in charge of a large vehicle. That's never a good look.'

I have noticed that he is very careful with the booze, which is probably for the best when you have a magical mystery tour to face the next morning. I wonder briefly about how difficult it would be to upgrade my licence so I could help with the driving, then remind myself that we won't be together for that long. Just a week or two, we said, didn't we?

But as I lie back and look up at the night sky, I simply can't imagine what might come next. How this could ever be allowed to end. The heavens are pure black, dotted with more stars than I have seen in one place for a very long time. Even in our old home, the nearby town had an effect; here, there are no big settlements in the vicinity, no road lights, nothing to pollute the view. It is like being covered with a vast and dazzlingly beautiful blanket, all made of twinkles. It feels like I could float off into it, and I place my hands on the warm grass to ground myself.

'Amazing isn't it?' Luke says, noticing my reaction. 'Easy to forget how big the world is sometimes.'

'I know. It's ... well, I think maybe it's changing me a bit? This whole being in the big world thing,' I say hesitantly.

'How so?'

'I'm not entirely sure. I think maybe I'm only just starting to realise how tied up in knots I was. I was always worried about money, about Charlie, about work, about the bills and the house and the future and the past. I don't think I understood how special it could be to just slow down, look around, look up ... just be, you know?'

'I do. Totally. And all of those things you were worried about were real, and life is hard sometimes, but the value of just standing still is very underrated. We're always in such a rush – what's next, what do I need to do, to achieve, to fix. Nights like this kind of calm you down – there is nothing so big, so important, that those stars up there haven't seen it a million times. That was a big lesson for me as well.'

I turn over onto my side and look at him between the table legs. He is lying on his back, staring at the sky, his arms folded beneath his head. 'How did you end up living like this?' I ask. 'If you don't mind talking about it.'

He turns his head and smiles slightly, the merest crooked lift of his lips. 'I don't mind talking about it, but it's not an easy tale. You might hate me afterwards.'

'Impossible,' I respond firmly.

He gazes at me for a few moments, as though trying to weigh up the truth of that one word. 'I don't think so,' he says sadly. 'I think I might hate myself after I tell you, at least.'

I can hear in the tone of his voice that he means it, that he is genuinely worried that what he has to say will horrify me. Perhaps, like myself, he has been enjoying this vacation more than he expected and is reluctant to unbalance it.

'If you don't want to talk about it, you don't have to. I understand. We all have our pasts, our secrets, things we've done that we're not proud of. But I will say this – what we were in the past isn't necessarily what we are now. Hearing about the old Luke won't make me hate the new Luke.'

'OK,' he says eventually. 'Here goes nothing ... and it's definitely not a time of my life I'm proud of. After we lost Katie, my wife Sally and I tried really hard, but something was broken between us. We'd had years of battling that illness. Our whole lives became dominated by it – caring for Katie; in my case, working, dealing with treatments and hospital stays and doctor's appointments and spending hours on the internet looking for miracle cures. We did everything we possibly could, but in the end, that was all that was left of us. When we didn't have Katie, we didn't have anything. It was like the glue that held us together had just ... melted away.

'We met a lot of other families during it all; some were solid as a rock, others you could see the cracks. When it all first started, after the diagnosis, I was convinced that we'd definitely fall into the rock category. And while Katie was around, we did – for her sake, I think. Then, afterwards ... well. We were both empty, both damaged beyond repair. We talked about separating, but neither of us was quite ready to let go, even though it might have been less painful for us both if we had. I channelled all of that grief into two things: working and being an absolute bastard.'

My eyes widen in surprise. I have not known Luke

for very long, but that doesn't sound like him at all. 'Really?' I ask. 'In what way?'

'I'd stay out for days, some of it because I was putting in insane hours at the office trying to make myself feel better by making yet more money. I worked in finance, and I'd always been good at it, and ... well, I was used to succeeding, you know? Used to getting my own way. I was a total stereotype – flash cars, big house in Surrey, holidays in the Carribean, complete corporate bullshit. The whole thing with Katie made me realise that no matter how much money I had, I couldn't fix everything. But that particular nugget of wisdom took a while to register – at first, I was even more ambitious, even more driven.

'Looking back, it was just an excuse not to go home. Not to be in the house where we'd raised her, not to walk past her bedroom. Not to be sucked inside and sit for hours on her bed, holding her cuddly toys, inhaling the sheets that smelled of her ... not to have to see the pain on Sally's face, or to deal with her grief when I couldn't even shoulder my own. We were both suffering so much, but we just couldn't reach out to each other. And that's when the cheating started.'

He glances over at me, and I see the sadness and shame on his face. The judgement he has already made about himself, the pain that is still there, just beneath the surface. I stay silent – there is nothing I could add at this stage that would make him feel better, and anyway, I suspect he doesn't want me to even try.

'It was meaningless stuff,' he continues. 'One-night

stands. Again, any excuse to stay away – to go to their place, or a hotel, or, on one insane occasion, the boardroom ... ridiculous. I don't even recognise myself when I think about all of that. It's like watching someone who has stolen my body do all those stupid and hurtful things.'

'I don't recognise that version of you either,' I say, reaching out to briefly pat his arm. I feel the need to console him, but I'd be lying if I said I wasn't shocked. I simply can't imagine him behaving like that, when all I've seen of him has been kind and honourable.

'Well, that version of me existed, and he did a lot of damage. Sally wasn't stupid, she knew I was pulling away. She never challenged me on it, even though part of me wanted her to. I don't know why. But, eventually, maybe because of some hidden death wish, I got careless – charged a hotel to our joint credit card. Along with champagne and chocolates. I'll never forget the look on her face when I walked into the kitchen and she was sitting there at the table, holding that innocent-looking sheet of paper. A sheet of paper that destroyed whatever we had left.'

'Was she angry?' I ask, thinking it was a silly question as soon as it leaves my mouth.

'That's the thing – she wasn't. Angry would have been better. It would have been easier if she'd thrown plates at me, called me names, cut my suits up with garden shears ... anything that indicated she still cared, that there was still some passion left – still something to fight for. Anything other than what I saw – which was sadness and hurt and disappointment. Mainly, underneath all of that, resignation. She'd known, really, what was going on – but, either consciously or not, she'd turned a blind eye to it. Then I forced her into a position where she couldn't ignore it any more. I broke her heart, or at least the pieces of it that were left after Katie.

'We have moved past it – she's remarried, has a beautiful little boy, we are still friends. You don't go through what we went through and just abandon each other – we will always share the memory of Katie. But still – I will never, ever forgive myself for it. It was brutal.'

I have never met Sally, but I have been on the other end of heartbreak. Of that loneliness and pain. On top of losing a child, it must have been intolerable – for both of them. Rob left me battered and wounded, but I still had my child, and I still had hope. My heart bleeds for Sally – but the big difference here is that Luke is so clearly devastated by what he did. The fact that she has forgiven him speaks to both her kind spirit and his genuine regret.

'Luke, that's horrible. But you were wounded, insane with grief ...'

'All of that is true, but the way I handled it ... well, as I said, I'll never forgive myself. I don't deserve to forgive myself.'

So much is becoming clear to me now: his lifestyle, the spartan existence, the way he has effectively put himself in solitary confinement. It's not that it makes him happy – it's that he thinks he doesn't deserve to be happy. I am horrified by the things he did, but I can still feel his pain, see the way he is suffering.

'So Sally has forgiven you?'

'I think so,' he replies, smiling. 'I'm the godfather to her son, at least, which is a good sign.'

'So she's the one you were talking about, that day? The person you loved, but you'd hurt? The person who helped you when you needed it?'

'Yes. She's the one.'

'She sounds like an amazing woman.'

'She was ... she is ...'

'Then maybe you should trust her judgement?' I say, quietly. 'If she's forgiven you, maybe it's time to start forgiving yourself?'

I wonder, as I say this, how I would have reacted if Rob had ever asked my forgiveness – if I would be as open to it. I'll never really need to know, because it simply never happened. Rob is not built from the same stuff as Luke.

He turns to meet my eyes, and there is a moment of connection there that is so deep and genuine that it terrifies me. I want to get up and run for my emotional life.

'That,' he replies, 'sounds like a very wise idea. Maybe I'll manage to try it some day. So, in response to your original question – you definitely got more than you expected with that one, didn't you?'

'I did. But that's OK. Please carry on.'

'Well, after that, I moved into a hotel for a while. I continued to be the high priest of self-destruction, until I hit rock bottom. I woke up naked in Regent's Park, without my clothes, wallet, watch or briefcase. To this day, I have no idea what happened – but I do remember getting poked on the arse with a stick by an elderly woman walking her dog. It was one of those moments you don't cast aside.'

'I can imagine.' But I'm lying here and I can't imagine it. I can't imagine this big, capable man so utterly stripped of dignity, in so much pain. It hurts to even picture it, and despite what he's told me, I still feel overwhelmed with sympathy.

'Anyway, as wake-up calls go, that was a pretty spectacular one. I did some serious thinking about what I was doing with my life, and whether this was the kind of behaviour Katie would want to see her dad indulging in. Once I phrased it to myself like that, it was easy – I shed my skin.

'I negotiated a pay-off with the company I worked for, I sold the properties we owned, and Sally and I decided on divorce. I told her she could keep the house and gave her half of everything, even though she didn't want it, and I bought the magnificent beast I now call home. The only thing I kept from my old life was a few bits of Katie's, and the equally magnificent beast I share the motorhome with – Betty was Katie's dog. She'd always begged for a puppy, but we were too busy, then when she got ill, well … we just wanted to give her everything she asked for, you know? Slushies for breakfast, Kate Bush on repeat, a baby dachshund …'

'And how has it been, since you left?' I ask. 'You seem quite … content?'

'Yes. That's a good word for it. Not exactly happy, but content enough. It took a while, and to start with I was very lonely. Especially on campsites, where you are surrounded by happy families, you know?'

'Yes. I do know. That is a feeling I am very familiar with – everyone always seems so perfect, don't they, on the outside looking in? I always felt like that when I went places with Charlie. Being a single parent is weird. Most people are friendly, but some women seem to feel like you want to steal their husbands – usually the overweight ones with beer bellies and England tattoos. Charlie would always try to pal up with other kids, but I always felt bad for him . . .'

'Did he seem to feel bad?'

'Well, no – but that's what parents do, isn't it? We blame ourselves for everything we perceive to be going wrong in our kids' lives. And did you notice that thing earlier, where he called us a family? That freaked me out a bit.'

Now, more than before, I am conscious of the fact that Luke was once a father, and that being thrust into a makeshift family might be a complicated thing for him.

'I did notice,' he replies. 'But don't take it too seriously – it was just a turn of phrase. Fits his brand better!'

'I know, you're probably right. But he has always wanted a bigger family. I've tried to be enough for him, but I know I'm not. I'm just one pretty ordinary woman.'

'You don't seem that ordinary from where I'm standing . . . well, lying.'

'That's the whisky talking. I am ordinary, and I don't mind that. But he can be extraordinary, and it's my job to make sure that happens.'

'Wow. I didn't realise I was in the presence of God!'

'Oh shut up!' I say, throwing my pen at him. It hits him on the forehead and he feigns injury, which makes us both laugh and breaks what has become a slightly surreal mood.

'Well, what about your own family?' he says, once we have calmed ourselves down. 'Isn't he close to them?'

'Close?' I echo, turning onto my back and gazing back up at the sky; hoping that the stars will shine down some wisdom along with the silver and gold threads of light. 'No. I wouldn't say that. In fact, they don't even know he exists.'

Chapter 12

I wake up the next morning to the gentle touch of Charlie's foot in my side. I mutter variations on ouch and roll around a little. I have hair stuck in my mouth and Betty is using my face as a lollipop, but other than that I have survived my time in the wild outdoors. I am practically Bear Grylls, but with backache. Maybe Bear Grylls gets backache too, but he's too macho to show it on camera.

I roll over again and stare up at Charlie, who immediately takes a photo of me.

'Got ya!' he says, hopping away chuckling. 'That'll be perfect for the Sausage Dog Diaries!'

'The what?' I murmur, sitting up and wiping my face clear. I glance over and see that Luke's gear has been folded up and assume he is out hunting, or using the Mona Lisa.

Charlie thuds down next to me and says: 'That's the name of your new blog. I tried loads of different things, but they were too similar to others – the internet is a pretty crowded place! Anyway, when I looked for this one, there was nothing. Apart from loads of ads for actual diaries with pictures of dachshunds on them. So, that's its main title, and the subheading is "Hitting the road and finding your joy!" – I liked that. Thought it sounded a bit new-agey, a bit self-helpy, very current? Loads of middle-aged women like you probably dream of hitting the road and finding their joy!'

'I'm not middle-aged!' I splutter.

Charlie shrugs. 'Depends on when you die, I suppose. Anyway, what do you think? About the blog?'

'I think I need coffee,' I reply, stretching my arms over my head.

Right on cue, Luke emerges from the van bearing steaming mugs. I think I might actually love him.

He passes me my coffee and asks: 'Did you hear the news? The Sausage Dog Diaries? Hitting the road and finding your joy?'

'I will definitely feel more joyful about it once I've had this. Why do you look so sprightly?' I say, staring at him with open resentment. It doesn't seem fair that he is wide awake, fresh from the shower, looking ready to tackle the day.

'Must just be tougher than you, I guess,' he replies, grinning. 'That and the fact that I went back inside and slept in my own bed once you started snoring.'

'I don't snore! And I'm not middle-aged, and you can both ... flip off!'

They both make oooh noises and I wave them away. I take my time over my coffee and feel a lot better when I finally push down half of the sleeping bag. This is something that needs to be done cautiously, in stages. It is mildly warm but not as yet scorching, which leads me to believe that we are making another very early start.

'Have you done the draw without me?' I ask suspiciously.

'Yes!' announces Charlie, looking delighted with himself. 'And it was mine again!'

'Oh lord,' I mutter, 'what is it this time? Mummies? Vampires?'

'No, even better – theme parks!'

I close my eyes and shake my head. Theme parks. My mortal enemy. I have never been one of those people who actually enjoys being tipped upside down and spun in a circle. I even get a bit scared in a waltzer. I remember taking Charlie to the fairground at Great Yarmouth once and that was enough. I also met Charlie's dad at a local fair, which may or may not have contributed to my aversion.

I was one of those teenaged girls on the rides, screaming loud enough that the attendants always pushed us the most, pretending to like it. Rob was one of the attendants doing the pushing. He didn't have close family, he told me, and he worked casually at things like this, and playing with his band. The warning signs were all there, but I was too giddy to see them – in all kinds of ways.

When I got off the ride, I was dizzy and I dropped my candy floss, and he got me a new one for free. He was good-looking and he was dangerous and he made me feel dangerous too. He made me spin even when I wasn't on a ride. From such delightfully romantic beginnings, a relationship was born, and then an actual human was born, and now that actual human wants me to go on rollercoasters with him.

'What about Betty?' I say, as soon as the thought occurs to me. 'She can't go in theme parks. Even if she was allowed, which she won't be, she'd hate it – I mean, all that noise, and the bright lights, and the screaming, and the going upside down?'

'Are you talking about Betty or yourself?' Charlie asks, frowning.

'Maybe both. I think this might be a day that the girls sit out on, OK, son?'

'Well, we'll see,' replies Charlie, sounding genuinely a bit deflated. 'But do you want to hear the plan?'

Yes, I think, as long as the plan involves me staying on solid ground.

'OK,' he continues, 'me and Luke have checked up on stuff, and we reckon we can do three in one day! How cool is that?'

'Wow, super cool,' I respond, glaring at Luke.

He shrugs and gives me a 'how was I to know?' look. I realise that he wasn't to know, of course, and that maybe we need to lay down some rules about this road trip, because I won't be finding my joy if I have to sit in a small metal object and get hurtled through the air.

'We'll start at Blackpool Pleasure Beach, which looks amazing – they have this ride called The Big One, and it's the tallest rollercoaster in the UK – it's, like, sixty-five metres up!'

This really does get better and better.

'That's not too far away,' he carries on, 'maybe a

couple of hours. Luke's booked tickets already, and we can easily be there by the time it opens. We stay there till about twelve, then head to a place called Warrington, where there's a little one called Gulliver's World. There's some big rides, but also a lot for babies, so you might be fine there, Mum! Anyway, if we leave there by about 2.30, we can be at Alton Towers in time to get the last couple of hours there! Alton Towers!! How fantastic does that sound?'

Uggh. It sounds terrible.

'More fantastic than anything I could have possibly imagined,' I say. 'Thank you both so much. But what about Betty, for real? It's too hot to leave her in the motorhome, even though she has her little fan and the cooling mat ...'

I gaze up at Luke imploringly, and he pulls a 'sorry' face before speaking.

'Erm ... well, I'd thought of that and booked her into a doggie day care for the first one. There's a woman right by the Pleasure Beach who specialises in looking after the pets of people who go to the theme park.'

'How very enterprising of her,' I reply, hating her guts. 'Will Betty be OK with that, with being left with a stranger?'

'Have you met Betty? There are no strangers to her, just friends waiting to be licked. She's a social butterfly.'

'Right. What about the others?' I ask, hoping against hope that wherever Alton Towers actually is, it is also completely devoid of dog minders.

'Struck out at the middle one, thought we'd take

turns,' he says sheepishly. Typical – the one that sounded most like I could cope with it.

'And the last?' I don't even want to say its name.

'Yeah, sorry ... found someone to have Betty overnight there. And actually booked us into some proper accommodation at the theme park, because then we can ... um, go back in the next morning?'

My eyes narrow, and I hiss: 'Well, aren't you Mr Resourceful?'

He grimaces in response, and I hit him with my next objection: 'This sounds very expensive?'

This is not only a way for me to try to get out of it, it's also true – it's one of the many reasons I've never done this kind of thing with Charlie before. That and my wussiness.

'It's my treat,' replies Luke, looking at me steadily, as though daring me to argue. 'I've secretly always wanted to go to these places, but felt too embarrassed to do it as a grown man on his own. You know, that looks weird, doesn't it? So thank you for providing me with the perfect excuse to be a big kid again.'

If Katie had still been around, he wouldn't have need an excuse. The thought scatters sadness across my thoughts, and I'm glad for Charlie's excited chatter.

'You're welcome!' he says, grinning. 'Oh come on, Mum! Embrace the new! It'll be fun!'

I suspect the only thing I'll be embracing is a sick bag, but I nod, and say I will try.

Charlie seems appeased and goes back inside, a bounce in his step. I emerge fully from my sleeping bag pupa and shake my limbs loose until everything feels almost normal again.

'I'm sorry,' says Luke immediately, 'he didn't mention that you weren't exactly a fan.'

'No, he wouldn't, would he? I have raised an evil genius.'

'But, look – when we stay at the hotel at Alton Towers, there's also a water park?'

'Right. Well. I do like swimming.'

'And there's a spa?'

'Oh. Even better. What else?'

'An eat-as-much-as-you-can buffet breakfast?'

'OK. You've sold me. Just don't gang up on me and make me do anything I don't want to, all right? And we don't need to take turns on the middle one. I'll stay with Betty. I'll tell Charlie I'm working up some content for the blog, that'll placate him.'

Luke nods, and grins at me. 'It might be fun, you know. We all do need to step outside our comfort zones every now and then.'

I stare at him, and wonder just far out of my comfort zone I need to be – I lost my job, my house fell off a cliff, and I have just noticed that I somehow have midge bites on my cleavage. I remain silent and take a deep breath and sip some more coffee. I look around, at the green and the blue and the many shades of nature, and I remind myself of how happy I felt yesterday. Luke is right; I need to relax, to slow down, to avoid tying myself back up in those knots I was talking about only a few hours ago.

'Yep. All right. I hear you, and I will try to . . . gosh, find my joy!'

I cringe as I say it and walk towards the steps of the van. I pause in the doorway, one hand on the frame, and gaze behind me. At the wide open spaces, at the sunlight falling through the leaves, at this man I now feel like I know so much better. I can hear Charlie laughing inside and know he is watching some silly video on TikTok, excited about his day. Who could be churlish in the face of so much bounty?

'You know,' I say, tapping the door frame of the motorhome with my palm, 'that could be a good name for the magnificent beast you call home.'

'What could?'

'Joy.'

He tilts his head, and looks the van over. His eyes crinkle up with a smile, and he says: 'You know what? I think you could be right. So, what say you, me, Charlie, Betty and Joy hit the road again? The Big One awaits!'

I grimace and go inside.

I take far longer than usual getting dressed and eating a bowl of cereal, because, frankly, I don't want to set off. Because the sooner we get going, the sooner we arrive at places I have no desire to go. Procrastination is my friend.

When we finally get going, we use the motorway for the first time, which is about as interesting as it usually is. The highlight is a stop at a beautiful service station called Tebay that seems to be a tourist destination in its own right, where we stock up on gorgeous fresh produce and all-important bacon butties. Luke also buys some new biscuits for his granny's tin.

I endure the morning at Blackpool, refusing to go on anything faster than the Dora the Explorer boat ride. I do get a kick from watching Luke and Charlie charge around though, speeding from ride to ride to pack in as much as they can. Luke seems to devolve from being a grown man to becoming even more of a teenager than Charlie, and I see a lot of dads acting the same way – I wonder if there is some kind of tested theme park phenomenon that provokes this response?

I mainly sit around a lot, trying to find patches of shade on another warm day, taking pictures of them. Luke buys us all The Big One baseball caps, insisting that we need souvenirs at every stop, but only the two men in my life actually take on the ride – I actually feel a bit sick looking at it from ground level.

When we finally leave, Charlie is still on an adrenaline high – chattering about it, describing it, reliving it, sharing stories of how Luke screamed like he was in a slasher movie when they reached the top. He is still wired by the time we whizz down the M6 to the next theme park, where I gratefully bow out. Betty and I spend a very pleasant hour and a half writing and sniffing bottoms. I'll leave it a mystery as to who did what. We've parked up by a grassy area, and I take her out for a little trot and get together some sandwiches ready for the adventurers' return. When they finally turn up, they are both laughing and soaking wet.

‘Last stop the log flume?’ I say, looking them up and down.

‘Yeah,’ says Charlie, ‘it was perfect in this weather! Lunch. Awesome. We saw dinosaurs.’

It’s a garbled sentence really, so I just nod as he slumps down on the sofa and points the fan at his face. Within seconds, he has inhaled his sandwiches and moved on to a banana. Luke produces a bowl of strawberries from the fridge, and they disappear so quickly, it is like a magic trick. Charlie looks up hopefully, and I pass him the Scottie-dog biscuit tin. It feels impossible to keep him fed at the moment – but then again, he is using a lot of energy.

‘So,’ I say, once the starvation has been averted, ‘dinosaurs? Real ones, like *Jurassic Park*?’

‘Well, no, Mum, because that’s a film and dinosaurs are extinct. Silly.’

‘Well, you know me, I have a PhD in Silly.’

‘Oh, I’m sorry – I didn’t realise you had a qualification. Should I call you Dr Silly from now on then?’

I respond by throwing a tea towel in his face, because that seems reasonable.

Luke shows me his pictures of the actual dinosaurs – a walk-through exhibit that probably enthrals little ones, and possibly Charlie on a good day. He says he’ll send me some copies for my blog, and I wonder how I have somehow turned my life holiday into work.

Except . . . well, it’s not actual work, is it? I’m enjoying it and I’m not getting paid, so it can’t be.

As we hit the motorway yet again, I decide that as

we are having a boring stretch of the day anyway, I will do some chores. I have been putting off checking my emails and feel the vivid colours of my current world fade to grey as I log in. I feel like it's Monday morning all over again.

I do a quick scan, see that there is a lot of junk, confirmation that Nina has been sold – RIP Nina – and a reminder to book my slot in the Next VIP sale, which I think I will give a miss. There is also some paperwork to do with my redundancy, which I deal with quickly.

That done, I give Barb a call – I already feel like I haven't seen her for years, and she was such a kind ally.

'Oh hello!' she says, the sound of glasses and laughter in the background. 'We're just having a barbecue! Anthony installed a hot tub, so we have my sister and her tribe around to celebrate …'

I have been to Barb's house a few times, and the image makes me smile. She is so efficient, so hard-working, so precise – but also so bright and colourful. Like a robot rainbow. I know that the garden will be perfectly mowed with stripes down it, and the food will be served on matching tableware, and the drinks will be summer cocktails that she has made from scratch. Oh to be more Barb.

'Sounds fab. I'm in a motorhome on the M6, heading to Alton Towers.'

'Oooh, get you, the motorway – fancy pants!'

I have no idea why she views the M6 as fancy. I glance out of the window and see the usual dazzling blend of laybys, concrete bridges and green signs. She's clearly never been on it herself.

'How is it going then, the big adventure? How is ... I've forgotten his name?'

'Charlie?' I supply, knowing full well that's not what she means.

'No, you tease! The other one ...'

'Luke. And he's fine, thanks. It's been a lot of fun so far. I've slept outside and we've done some wild swimming.'

There is a pause, and I can imagine the look of horror on her face. The chlorinated hot tub is probably Barb's idea of wild swimming.

'You mean, like, in an outdoor pool? A lido maybe?'

'Oh no – I mean like in an actual river, and an actual lake. With fish and aquatic insects and mud and plants that tickle your toes.'

'Uggh! How horrid. But I'm glad you're having a nice time. Did you get the letter about the redundancies?'

I confirm that I did, and we catch up briefly on our colleagues, sharing our surprise that sixty-seven-year-old Barry has opted to relocate to Kidderminster. We wonder if maybe he is trying to escape his wife, who he has complained about solidly for the last two years.

'So, I have some letters for you here, and some travel brochures,' Barb says, and I hear the background noise change as she goes inside. 'Some junk stuff. One from Charlie's school maybe?'

I ask her to open it and discover that it is a letter inviting him back for a farewell assembly next week. I glance over at him, see that he is asleep, and decide that I will ask him later. I really hope he doesn't want to go – I am worried that finding my joy is a tentative state of affairs, and that if I am forced to go back to the town where we lived so soon, forced to face the memories so quickly, my joy will evaporate and I will be finding my desperation instead. That's not as catchy a hookline really. Still, if he wants to do it, wants to go back and see his friends, then I will find a way to make it happen.

'There's a couple more ...' Barb says, and I hear her riffling through them.

'This is so exciting!' I announce. 'The suspense is killing me – what is it? Is it a telegram from the king? Is it an invitation to a high-stakes baccarat game in Monaco? Is it tickets to a masquerade ball in Venice?'

'Erm ... looks like a gas bill?' she replies, sounding disappointed on my behalf.

'Oh. OK. Could you take a pic and send it to me so I can sort it out please? Anything else?'

'One more ... looks official.'

'Is it in a brown envelope?' I have an irrational fear of brown envelopes, as they are forever linked in my mind with tax, driving licences, and other scary government-based organisations.

'No, white ...'

She opens it up and is quiet, while she presumably reads it.

'Oh dear ... not really a nice one, this, Jenny! It's from your insurers, saying they're considering not paying out on your home contents claim until they have investigated a bit further. Apparently they suspect it was due to erosion, which you're not covered for because that's a specialist policy you don't have. I'm so sorry. They're absolute bastards, aren't they? Excuse my French!'

Barb never swears, and I can imagine the perfect pink blush as she feels ashamed of herself. She is, however, right in her choice of word. I had suspected there might be problems, because, well, why wouldn't I? I wrack my brains to remember what Bob said on the night it all happened, and although there was definite reference to storms and rain and sea currents, sadly I do seem to recall that erosion was mentioned as well.

I know I don't have a 'specialist policy', and wonder right now how big of an idiot that makes me. For all I know, it was mentioned in the small print of my lease or something – but, seriously, nobody expects this to happen, do they?

I tell Barb not to worry about it, and promise to stay in touch before I hang up. I feel a bit deflated, a bit worried, a bit anxious. Even without the insurance, I remind myself, I am financially OK for a while longer – but it acts as a trigger, that letter. It trips me up, catches me unawares, stabs me in the back. I have been ignoring reality and very much enjoying it, and now I feel sucked back in.

I try not to let it take over, try not to let it defeat me, but by the time we drop Betty off at her doggie holiday pad and reach Alton Towers, I am not in the best of moods. But I don't want to bring down Charlie and Luke, so I fake it in the hope that I will eventually make it.

We park the motorhome, and Luke explains some

complex logistics – he can't leave it there overnight, so he plans to go back to the place where Betty is staying and park it there, then cycle back to the hotel and meet us. As we board the monorail that takes us into the park, I am still dizzied by how much all of this is costing. Even though Luke is cool about it, I'm not sure I am.

'Hey, guys,' says Charlie, forming the words around the stick of rock he has in his mouth. He got it earlier and it says Blackpool down the middle. He tugs it out and asks: 'If you were a piece of rock, what would you have written inside you?'

'I'm not sure,' I answer, 'but yours would probably say "evil". Or maybe "hungry". Or maybe both.'

'Ha! That's a good one. Mum, I think yours would be "red wine", or "go away, I'm tired". Luke, I reckon you're more of a "wobbling frog" dude. Maybe, if the rock was big enough, you could be "pretty hot for an old man". So many possibilities . . .'

Luke and I share a smile, and I ponder the question with far more depth than it warrants. Right now, at this precise moment in time, if I were a stick of rock, it would say 'anxious' down the middle. I have the urge to bite my fingernails, which is odd as I have never done that before in my life. Hey, who says you can't teach an old dog new tricks?

Once we have checked in at the very pretty hotel, we head to the entrance of the theme park. Lots of other people seem to be leaving, and the pathways are awash with red-faced toddlers and fractious kids and exhausted-looking parents and couples carrying huge cuddly toys they have presumably won at stalls. The brutal heat of earlier in the day has faded, and the park itself is actually a lot more attractive than I expected. There are lots of green spaces and sparkling water features, an old building that looks like it was maybe a manor house once upon a time, and a main street lined with shops and cafes.

We equip ourselves with cool drinks and more snacks for Charlie, and the boys consult a map to see where they want to go first. Luke has bought some kind of pass that lets us get fast-tracked onto certain rides, which probably cost more than Nina.

I am angry with myself for suddenly seeing everything in financial terms, for sliding back into my old routines and my old thought processes, but I don't seem able to quite stop it. I am making it an issue when it's not, and I am disrespecting Luke's generosity by continuing to scratch away at it. I suspect it's a combination of talking to Barb and being in places I hate. It's not really the money I'm worried about – it's everything. I've successfully managed to shut down most of my usual worry-worms on this trip so far, and I don't want to let them sneak back in.

'Are you OK?' Luke says quietly, as we join the queue for a Mum-acceptable ride – i.e. a very small rollercoaster that seems to be full of toddlers. 'You seem a bit down.'

Charlie is ahead of us and is chatting to two teenaged girls who are taking their little sister onto the ride.

'Ah, no, I'm sorry – I'm OK. Just a bit of disappointing news from home. I don't want to talk about it, really. Not now anyway. Just ignore me, I'll snap out of it.'

'You don't need to snap out of anything,' he says as we shuffle forward a few paces. 'You've been through a lot, and there are going to be downs as well as ups. I don't expect you to be "on" all the time – nobody can be.'

'Charlie seems to be managing it,' I reply, nodding towards him.

'Well, Charlie is eighteen, and talking to two pretty girls at a theme park. That's the definition of paradise in most young lads' minds. You're in a slightly different position. If you want to go back to the hotel and have a bit of time on your own, just say so – I can hang with Charlie. You could go to the spa or watch TV or have a bath, whatever you like.'

I briefly think about it, but I know that I wouldn't be able to relax. I know I'd just start thinking about the insurance and how unfair it is after I've paid them for all these years, even when I could barely afford it. Then I'd think about all the things I can't replace, and how the money wouldn't help with that anyway. Then I'd think about Charlie's leavers' assembly and how that would have been a definite date in the diary not so long ago. And then, and then, and then ... It would be an endless spiral to nowhere good at all. I know myself well enough to be able to predict it, and it annoys me – how is it that we can see what we're doing wrong, and understand why we're doing it, but somehow can't quite break the pattern?

'Thank you,' I say, smiling and trying to put some oomph into it, 'but I actually can't think of anywhere else I'd rather be than right here with you two.'

'OK then. That's settled. Are you ready for the crazy adrenaline spike that is this very tame rollercoaster?'

'I was born ready!' I say, shaking my fist.

I actually do kind of enjoy it – it is fast enough for the breeze to cool me down, but not so fast that I fear I will revisit my sandwiches.

When we get off on the other side, Charlie and Luke are planning to head to something called Nemesis.

'Nemesis?' I say. 'What a charming name!'

'It's not one for you, Mum,' Charlie answers, shaking his head. 'You sit in a carriage that dangles down, and it goes at, like, 50 miles an hour, and it does a corkscrew, and ... well, even I think it looks a bit scary!'

I stare at the toddlers getting off the little ride we've just done. I look at the picture of Nemesis on Charlie's phone. I feel the churning anxiety that is starting to burn inside my stomach, the knots that are retying, the fear I am fighting that has absolutely nothing to do with theme park rides and everything to do with the rest of my life. With the cottage, with the losses, with the conversation I had with Luke last night.

I can't change any of that. I can't fix past mistakes, or wish my house would fly back onto land like a video rewinding, or control many of the things I know I am likely to start worrying about now the process has started. But I can change this – I can change this one thing, right now, at this exact moment.

'I want to go on Nemesis,' I say loudly – loud enough to convince myself. 'Take me to Nemesis!'

'Mum, are you sure?' asks Charlie, looking slightly worried about me. I don't blame him. I'm worried about me too.

Luke grabs hold of my hand and waves it in the air, like I am Rocky and I have just defeated Apollo Creed.

'Yes, she's sure! She's a champ! Come on, let's run – it's always more fun when you run . . .'

I am swept along with the two of them, falling quickly behind because they are both over six foot and I am very much not. They wait for me, and we go to the queue and we show our fast-track passes and before very much time has elapsed at all, I find myself sitting in what feels like a very flimsy piece of metal, trapped under an overhead restraint, being flung around at a squillion miles an hour. I am sitting between Charlie and Luke, and my hands are on my lap, fists clenched. My heart is pounding, and as the carriage starts to clang and bang and chug up a steep metal track, I know I have made a terrible mistake. It is too high. It is too loud. It is too dangerous. My breath starts to speed up, coming in short panting gusts, and my eyes feel wrong – I am blinking rapidly, trying to clear the fuzzy bright light on the periphery of my vision.

Our carriage pauses at the very top of the hill, and I am petrified. I think I might actually pass out and can't believe I allowed myself to get carried away like this. I've gone from I Am Woman, Hear Me Roar to I Am Woman, Hear Me Cry Like A Baby within minutes.

'It's OK!' Luke says, leaning over so he is right next to my ear. 'It's all right – we've got you!'

He unclenches my fist and twines his fingers into mine, and on the other side of me, Charlie does the same. They both grip hold of me tightly, not letting go. I look from one face to the other, see their concern, their encouragement, their reassuring smiles. I stare straight ahead and tell myself it is all going to be fine, that I am not alone, that I can do this. And then we drop.

It only takes a few minutes, but by the end, I am a wobbling wreck of a human. My legs are jelly, and Luke has to help me out of my seat, keeping an arm around my shoulders as we walk away. Charlie is buzzing around us like an inebriated fly, jumping and laughing and saying: 'I don't believe you did it! You rock, Mum!'

That makes me feel a bit better, a bit prouder, a bit stronger – but it doesn't negate the nausea, and I am grateful to move along, to get away from the evil thing of steel and speed. We follow the crowds through to a place where there are photos up on screens, and we find ours – it is hilarious. I have my eyes clamped shut and my mouth is a huge screaming 'O', my hair flying behind me. At my sides, Charlie and Luke are still holding my hands, looking a lot less terrified but still pretty crazy. Luke puts our order in and we wait while they are loaded into a bag for us. I realise that these are the first 'proper' photos – not on-my-phone photos – that I have amassed since I lost a lot of my old ones.

'So,' says Charlie as we make our way back outside, 'what's next, Mum? The Wicker Man? Oblivion?'

'Well, son, they both sound perfectly delightful – but no thanks. I did it, and I'm pleased I did, but that wasn't something I want to repeat in a hurry. I'm going to find some grass and become horizontal for a while. Run free, little man, run free …'

He looks disappointed for a split second, then his phone beeps, and he suddenly doesn't care any more. 'Would it be OK with you guys if I went off on my own for a bit?' he asks, grinning. 'Tasha and Lily have asked if I want to go on some rides with them …'

'Tasha and Lily?' I repeat, momentarily confused. 'Oh! The girls from earlier … Yes, that's fine. I don't mind. Luke might want to come with you, though.'

I know, of course, that Luke will not want to go on a double date with my son and two teenagers – or at least I hope he won't. It just amuses me to make Charlie think it for a moment.

'Nah, off you go, Charlie,' Luke replies. 'I'm feeling like a lie-down myself.'

We make arrangements to meet him back at the hotel for dinner and find a shady spot by the side of a lake. It is nearing closing time, and the park is emptying out. Slow, tired lines of people are straggling towards the exits and the car parks; too much fun had by all.

I stretch out on the grass, thrilled by the simple touch of the ground against my body. The ordinary joy of being flat and still and stable. Luke joins me, and we are both quiet, listening to the random sounds of music from rides and passing chatter and the birds on the water.

'So. Do you feel better after that?' he asks eventually. 'Felt like a bit of a watershed moment.'

'Yeah. I literally faced down my Nemesis. I don't know ... I was starting to feel the stress creep back in. There's a dispute about the insurance payment, predictably enough, and while that isn't actually a disaster, it was just ... dragging me back into the whirlpool, you know?'

'I do. And if you need any help challenging them, let me know. My brother's a lawyer, he'll always write a letter that sounds like he's about to smite them with Thor's hammer.'

'Wow. Nice image. Maybe you should have been the writer ...'

'Nope, I'm numbers, not words. That's your bag. Is that why you were worried about how much this was costing earlier?'

'Probably. Although I might have been anyway – these places aren't cheap. It's one of the reasons we've never been before. That and my terror.'

'Your former terror, now vanquished.'

'Maybe.'

He rolls over onto one side and props himself up on his elbow, looking down at me. The sun is behind him and he looks dark and mysterious. His hair is slightly longer than when we first met, and I realise he keeps it so brutally short because it is the kind of hair that curls if you don't. I'd quite like to reach out and touch it, but that would be, you know, weird.

'You do remember what I told you last night, don't you, about my working life?' he asks.

'Yeah. Of course. I remember everything you told me last night.'

Her bedroom. Her sheets. Her cuddly toys. Forever burned into my mind, that terrible image.

'Well, believe me when I say I'm not worried about money, or about a day at a theme park. I live cheaply most of the time – the odd ale, fuel, camp fees, food, not much else. It's simple, and I don't spend much, and I have plenty. In fact, it's actually really nice to be able to do this – to use some of it on fun, on something frivolous, something that brings someone else pleasure as well as me. So, please, don't be a selfish moo and deprive me of that!'

'A selfish moo?' I repeat, laughing. 'What kind of a phrase is that?'

'One of my gran's. She called everyone a moo when she was annoyed with them. Selfish moo, silly moo, greedy moo, cheeky moo, naughty moo ... I was called pretty much every type of moo by the time I was ten!'

'You talk about her a lot. Were you close?' I ask, more than happy to stop talking about money. There is nothing guaranteed to put me on the misery train faster than talking about money. That insurance letter has been one heck of a downer.

He flops back down and says: 'Yeah. We were. My parents were busy people, and my brother and me spent a lot of time there when we were kids. She was the first person I ever lost, and I still miss her. When Katie was born, one of my first thoughts was that I was so sad she didn't get to meet her. We gave her my gran's middle name – it was Marjorie, so you can see why we didn't make it our first choice ...'

'Yeah. That's never quite made a comeback, has it? So, are your parents still around?'

I realise I sound slightly nervous as I ask that, because Luke is in his fortiess, and I am in my thirties, and this is the age where parents still being around isn't always guaranteed. I feel a sharp tug in my chest as I even think this and take a deep breath to try to shoo it away.

'They're still alive, no need to sound so worried! They're still busy people, and they live in New Zealand now. They were both GPs, and now they're retired and spend their time climbing hills and visiting lakes and generally having a good time.'

'Wow. That sounds awesome. What about your brother?'

'He's younger than me and lives in London and has three kids. Anything else you need to know, Officer?'

'I'm being really nosy, aren't I? I'm sorry. It's just the way I'm made.'

He sits up and grabs a bottle of water from the back-pack next to him. He passes it to me first, because he is a gentleman, it seems.

'I don't mind,' he replies, looking off across the lake. 'It just takes a bit of getting used to. I think I've talked more about myself over the last week than I have in the last four years. It makes me feel both better and also more ... exposed, if that makes sense?'

'It does,' I say, nodding. 'And I get it, I really do. I might not have gone off grid and lived in a motorhome or anything, but I've led a pretty quiet life. Me and Charlie against the world kind of vibe. I've never had really close friends, I've just been too busy . . . and maybe too much of a wuss.'

'Well, as we saw today on Nemesis, you are a wuss no more! But what about your family? You didn't talk much about them last night, but obviously there's some kind of rift. What happened?'

I close my eyes and wonder how to enscapsulate it all into a few sentences. How to distil decades of mistakes, regret and hurt into a few words. It feels impossible, really – and it also feels dangerous. Like something I shouldn't do, because if I start letting it all unravel, before I know it, I'll have a giant ball of wool at my feet and will be totally naked.

I feel a gentle touch against my hand, feel Luke's fingers briefly make contact with mine. I want to grab on, to hold tight, to console myself the way I did on that rollercoaster. But I don't, as that might only make it harder.

'You don't have to talk about it if you don't want to,' he says quietly.

'We say that to each other a lot, have you noticed?'

'We do. Like we're both so aware of how easy it might be to take a wrong step. That doesn't make it a bad thing – maybe it just means we're, I don't know, respectful of each other's boundaries? Oh God, I sounded like a self-help book there, didn't I . . .'

'A bit, to be honest – but, hey, I'm writing a blog about finding my joy, so I'm in no position to judge!'

I sit up, drink some more water and look down at Luke sprawled on the grass. He takes up a lot of space. He is dressed in baggy shorts and an Iron Maiden T-shirt, and I can't imagine him suited and booted and working in corporate finance. I will never know that version of him, and that is OK – we all change. We all grow, and evolve, and who knows how many new skins we will wear before the end?

'Well,' I say slowly, 'if you'd asked me about my family years ago, I'd have had a simple answer. I'd tell you they were controlling, manipulative, domineering. I'd have told you about how stuck-up I thought they were, how they had my whole life mapped out for me with no regard to what I wanted. How they tried to trap me and stop me from living the life I wanted. I'd tell you about their snobbery, and their judgements, and their cloying insistence on what was right for me and what wasn't. I'd have said they were suffocating me, that they only loved their fantasy version of me, not the real one. I'd have told you all of that, and meant every word.'

'And now?' he says gently. 'Now you wouldn't?'

'Now … I'm not so sure. Now I'm an adult myself, and the mother to an eighteen-year-old. Now I have more life experience of my own, and understand the way a parent wants to protect their child a lot more than I did back then. When I have rows with Charlie, when he accuses me of treating him like a child, I can see both sides of it. Basically, now I'm not entirely clear on any of it.'

'What happened?' he asks.

'Nothing. Everything. Maybe somewhere in between. I was seventeen when I met Rob, Charlie's dad. I was on track for all the usual good stuff – A levels, university, career and, at least in their minds, I suspect, marriage to a suitable man. Financial ease, couple of kids, everything all very nice and ordered. Then I went and made it all messy. I fell in love, in that deep and completely committed way you only ever seem to be capable of when you're that young.

'Rob was older than me, and he was . . . well, he was a drifter, a dreamer, even back then. He'd left school at sixteen, never had a proper job, played drums in a band.'

'Oh no. That's a red flag,' he says, smiling. 'The drummers are always the crazy ones.'

'Yeah – tell me about it! But none of that mattered to me. He was the love of my life. He was my world, and there was no way I was ever going to be parted from him, you know? I didn't think I could actually breathe without him.

'My parents were not pleased and didn't try to hide it. At first, it was little stuff – they tried to keep me in at night, booked me up with other things, tried to distract me. Told me I was too young for something so serious, that I needed to concentrate on my schoolwork. Then they stepped it up, gave me a curfew, told me I couldn't see him any more . . .'

'I bet that went down well. Nothing quite as effective as telling a teenager they can't do something to make them want to do it even more.'

'Exactly. My older brother was allowed to do whatever he wanted, so it always seemed like this huge double standard – I went on long rants about the patriarchy and all sorts … and, yeah, it didn't work at all, keeping us apart – in fact, it made it all even more exciting. There was a lot of conflict, a lot of very hurtful things said on both sides. I think they still assumed I was their malleable little girl, and I assumed they were evil, nasty old control freaks trying to brainwash me into being a Stepford Wife, and the truth … well, the truth is there was probably a bit of both going on.'

'It got bad, I take it? Bad enough that you left?' Luke sits up beside me, frowning.

'Oh yes. It got very bad. The curfew didn't work, so they started locking me in my bedroom at night, which made me crazy. Even more determined. So one night I climbed out of my window and snuck off to be with him. When they saw I wasn't there, they called the police and got Rob arrested for abducting me. It was an insane drama. I was seventeen, and once the police realised I was with him of my own free will, they let him go – but it felt like there was nothing to go back to after that. I only went home once more, to get some of my things, and then I walked out and told them they'd never see me again. And later … even when I was alone, with a baby, and Rob had done what they probably suspected he would all along and walked out on me, I still somehow couldn't go back on that. I don't know if it was pride, or me just being stubborn, or if I genuinely did think I was better off without them. It all feels so long ago now. But fast-forward a lifetime or so, and here we are. I have Charlie. I had a home and a job and I didn't feel like I'd done a bad job of it all, really – didn't feel like I'd missed out. Except now ...'

'Except now,' he continues for me, 'some of those things have literally fallen off a cliff, and everything feels uncertain, and you're wondering about it all? About your parents? About the past?'

'Not just the past,' I say firmly. 'About the future. That thing Charlie said about us being a family. The way he's always loved being with his friends who have siblings. The questions I know he has about me, about my background.'

'Has he asked?'

'Yes, kind of. But not seriously until the last few years. By that point, I was so deeply embedded in it all, you know? I tried not to think about them myself, to the extent that I think I'd almost stopped. Whenever he raised the subject, I'd try to answer in a bland way that wasn't exactly lying, but also wasn't exactly answering – and he's a nice lad, he could see that it upset me, and he never pushed too hard. I think maybe I've been a selfish moo, Luke.'

This is the first time I've admitted this properly out loud, and it says a lot about the way I feel about Luke. I feel safe with him, I realise – able to be myself, even when I don't like what I'm being.

'I wonder if I'm being fair to him, keeping all of this a secret?' I continue. 'Keeping him away from his relations? I made the decision to cut them out of my own life before he was even born, and I did it when I was younger than he is now, because it felt like they'd boxed me into a corner. It was the only option I felt I had. But do I have the right to make that decision on his behalf? I don't expect you to be able to answer that, by the way …'

'Good. Because I can't. It's a tough call. All I can say is that from what I've seen, you've done a good job. You've been a good mum. So I'd say maybe trust your instincts? I think you'll come to the right conclusion – but you don't have to come to it right now. You're still reeling from everything that happened, so you're going to feel a bit off balance. Maybe keep doing what you're doing, keep finding your joy, or whatever it is we're doing on this crazy trip – and then perhaps the answers will start to feel a bit clearer.'

I stand up and swipe the grass off my legs. I feel more robust physically now I've recovered from Nemesis, but a wee bit wobbly emotionally after that info dump. I reach out, extend my hand. Luke grabs hold and I pretend to heave him up, making comments about the biscuit barrel, and we make our way to the pathway.

'Back to the hotel for me, I think,' I say. 'Might accidentally fall into the bar for a little glass of wine …'

'Sounds like a terrible accident that could most definitely happen. I'll get Joy moved and see you back there. Won't be long. I might accidentally order a beer or two as well, as I don't have to set off first thing for a change. Hey, do you want to see what I got from the photo place? It was some kind of package deal I just said yes to because I felt a bit sick . . .'

I nod and he pulls some printed photos out of the bag, enclosed in cardboard frames. My traumatised face, immortalised in print. Then he shows me a fridge magnet and a key ring.

'These are for you,' he says, passing them over.

'Well, that's very kind. It's a shame I don't have a fridge, or the keys to anything that still exists.'

'I know that – it's an aspirational gift. Kind of like, here are the first steps towards having those things, if that's what you decide you want.'

'So,' I say, as we reach the gates and follow the wooded path to the hotel, 'I'm not just finding my joy, I'm finding my fridge and finding my door and finding my car?'

It's a tall order, I think. I'm not sure I feel capable of it all, and suspect he has more faith in me than I have in myself right now.

'Exactly! But before any of that, you can find your wine, and find your nice dinner, and find your very own squishy hotel bed . . .'

'That,' I say firmly, 'sounds like a most excellent plan.'

Chapter 13

We end up spending a few more nights in the area, as there is a great camping ground nearby where we can tend to all of Joy's needs, and because Tasha and Lily and their family are staying there and Charlie wants to have more time with them.

He has never had a serious girlfriend, and I have never pushed him on which way his interests lie. It has simply never mattered to me, as long as he is happy. I am guessing from the lingering glances he shares with Lily, the older of the two, that his interests most definitely extend in her direction. I wonder if I should give him a talk about toxic masculinity and avoiding teen pregnancies but decide that I don't need to. He is not even remotely toxic, and I am in no position to lecture anyone on the latter.

We are invited to their motorhome for a barbecue on one of the evenings, where Luke and their dad spend endless happy hours discussing their vehicles and their travels, and I get embroiled in embarrassing conversations with the mum, where I explain that Luke is not Charlie's dad, and no, also not his stepdad, and no, also not my boyfriend. She looks so shocked when I explain the truth of the situation that I resolve there and then to simply say 'yes, he's my boyfriend, cute isn't he?' in the future.

I get a better grip on Joy's functions and tackle exciting tasks like replacing the gas bottle and emptying the waste tank, and we spend our days exploring the nearby countryside and our nights sitting out and chatting and eating as though we are in the Mediterranean, not the Midlands. It is really rather splendid, aided by the fact that I stay off my emails and concentrate instead on the Sausage Dog Diaries.

Charlie does all of the boring stuff for me and also posts ferociously on social media. Lily is a whizz on it all as well and sets me up with all kinds of hashtags and promo ideas. I leave them to it, because it is not my scene, but smile in encouragement when they tell me I already have some followers. Apparently sausage dogs are 'hot right now', and a lot of the people who read my posts on the camping forums have joined in the fun. By the time we decide to move on, I have over 200 people signed up to the blog.

That is a slightly scary amount of people – what if I'm rubbish? What if I make a spelling mistake, or post a picture of my boobs by mistake, or, even worse, put an apostrophe in the wrong place? Writing on the forums felt anonymous and safe; this feels terrifying. I've always seen writing as a form of escape, but this seems to be becoming more than that, and I'm not sure I'm ready. I'm not sure I have the confidence for it.

I adapt my usual policy – Just Don't Think About

It – and simply carry on doing what I like doing. Luke tells me this is the equivalent of dancing like nobody is watching, and I think he is right. It is enjoyable, and distracting, and it feels good to exercise a part of my brain that has long been dormant.

After the third night, we decide it is time to move on, and we make a draw from the hat. For the first time, the tiny ball of paper turns out to be one of my picks.

'Oxford?' says Charlie, sounding disappointed. 'But that's just a place! That feels like cheating!'

'I'm sorry, son,' I say, patting him on the shoulder in consolation. 'But thems the rules – and off to Oxford we go. If it makes you feel any better, we could pretend I put *The Golden Compass* instead? Or *Inspector Morse*?'

'No idea what that one is, must be something from the last century, but yeah ... OK. *The Golden Compass* will do.'

We set off disgustingly early, because Charlie wants to call in at a stone circle, and after our experience at the last one, we aim to be there before anybody else. He tells us, as we arrive just after 7 a.m., that there is an old story about a witch who turned a king and his men to stone, and also that witches used to come here 'skyclad'. This, he explains with a smirk, means naked. I assure him that I am not a witch and therefore will not be following suit, but he should feel free to take a nude gallop around them if he feels the call.

'That'd be weird, Mum,' he says as we get out of Joy into pale morning sunlight.

'It would, but I don't want to restrict your development as a human being. Plus, I grew you in my own body, you know, it wouldn't be anything I've not seen before.'

'I'll do it if Luke will ...' he mutters, earning himself a jokey kick on the backside from the man in question.

We make our way down a pathway through a wooded copse, thick with lush vegetation and alive with birdsong. We are near a main road, but somehow the noise of the passing traffic seems to disappear as we emerge out onto the open space where the stones lie. It is almost eerie how fast that happens, and I pause to relish it.

In front of us is an enormous ring of pale pockmarked stones, almost shining in the early light. Some are upright and tall, some seem to be having a lie-down. I suppose they've earned a rest after being here for a few thousand years. We wander from stone to stone, and I can't resist running my hands across them, wondering what they were for and who built them and how. So many centuries of human lives have passed while they have stood here – through wars, through revolutions, through aeons of change, they have remained, still and silent and strange.

Whoever built them is long gone, together with their motives, but they were still human beings – still people with hopes and dreams, still connected through that long stretch of time to us, now, standing here together as we gaze at them. It is mysterious and majestic and utterly mind-bending.

We spend a good hour there in that magical place,

drinking coffee from the flask, wandering from stone to stone, finding something new and gnarly about each of them. Charlie tries to count them but gives up when he reaches fifty and gets confused.

Eventually, we settle on the grass in the middle and just soak it all up. The birds, the sunshine, the stones; the still, calm sense of serenity. These ancient dudes definitely knew how to pick a top location.

After a while, a small family arrives – mum, dad, toddler, cockapoo – and we take that as our cue to leave. We have had our mystical moment – now it is time to pass it on to someone else to enjoy.

As we stand up and dust ourselves down and prepare to walk away, Charlie says: 'Hey, you know in the Julian Cope book? It tells a story about how women used to come here when they wanted babies, and put their boobs on the stones to make them fertile!'

I involuntarily cross my arms over my chest, and they both laugh at me.

'What?' I say, genuinely concerned. 'You never know! I might trip and fall and accidentally land with one of the girls on a baby-stone ... and nobody wants that!'

Charlie pulls a face and mutters the word 'girls' in mock-horror, and we leave happy and content, and in my case brimful of 'just imagine'. We put some money into the honesty box, clamber back into Joy and continue on to Oxford, which is less than an hour away.

Luke has found a place for us to stay overnight on the outskirts of the city, a few miles out and essentially at the back of someone's very large garden. It's amazing how many places there are out there willing to share their space with a great big motorhome.

We chat to the homeowner and fill two backpacks with what I now see as essentials – water, snacks, phone, swimmers and towels – before getting the bus from a nearby stop.

We emerge onto a long main street edged by picture-perfect stone buildings, already awake at 9.30 a.m. I presume the students are gone for the summer, but there are still lots of interesting-looking people striding around with purpose, already some tourists, and dozens of bicycles whizzing past us. Presumably, everyone is in a real hurry to get back to curing cancer or solving mathematical equations or pondering ancient Sanskrit texts.

We follow the flow of people further into the town, and when we reach a large cobbled square with a round, domed building in the middle of it, it starts to look familiar.

'I remember this ...' I murmur, turning in a full circle, taking in the colleges and the church with its soaring spire and the quaint passageways.

'What? You've been here before?' says Charlie, looking confused.

'Only once,' I reply, 'on a school trip. It was an open day. My English teacher wanted me to apply here, and a minibus full of us came to visit. It's not changed at all ...'

I realise, as I take in the sheer antiquity of the buildings, that they haven't changed in centuries. It is busy and bustling and real, but it is also so very beautifully old. If you took away the people on mobile phones, you could literally be in another era.

'Wow,' says Charlie, staring at me with a strange expression, 'you were clever then, Mum?'

'Clever enough, I suppose. Are you about to say "what happened" and laugh at me?'

'No,' he replies quietly. 'You're still clever, whether you went to Oxford or not. And as for what happened, well, I know that, don't I? I happened.'

He sounds wistful, and I reach up to hold my hand to his cheek. I might have to stretch, but he is still my baby.

'And, Charlie James, I would make that deal a million times over – I'd swap every single one of these hallowed halls for one minute with you, I promise!'

He smiles, and looks a bit embarrassed, whether at his own display of emotion or at mine, I'm not quite sure.

'What is that, anyway?' he says, pointing at the central building, with its magnificent pale columns and massive doors and intricate stonework.

'It's called the Radcliffe Camera,' replies Luke. 'And it's part of the Bodleian Library. When you join, you have to actually declare an oath and promise that, among other things, you will never kindle flame within its walls.'

'How do you know that?' I ask, loving the olde-worlde language.

'Erm ... well. I was a student here, in another lifetime.'

'What!' declares Charlie. 'So you've BOTH been here before? I feel betrayed!'

His expression is so comically outraged that I have to stifle laughter.

'Why?' I ask. 'We never made any rules about only visiting new places. We made no rules at all, in fact – I refer you back to "zombies", young sir.'

'I know, but … well, it's better when it's new, isn't it? When we're all doing it for the first time? Together? So we can all ooh and aah in the right places, like we did this morning at the stones?'

'I do know what you mean,' I assure him, 'but you'll just have to deal with it. Luke can be our expert guide for the day, and I barely remember it anyway.'

I am, in fact, lying about that – I remember it vividly. I grew up in Cornwall, one of the most beautiful places in the world, but my life had been dominated by local villages and the occasional exciting trip to the big city, otherwise known as Penzance, which isn't even a city. Coming here had felt like visiting some exotic metropolis, and I'd spent the whole day in a fug of wonder, overwhelmed at the thought of actually maybe living here one day.

My teenaged brain filled in the gaps: the dusty attic room hidden up flights of higgledy-piggledy steps; the exciting friends I'd make and who I'd have intellectual debates with all through the night; the handsome boy with the floppy hair I'd meet in the college bar; the stories I would write as I retraced the steps of Tolkien and C. S. Lewis and Iris Murdoch … it had all seemed so wild, so thrilling. And then I met Rob, and it felt tame in comparison.

I wonder, in that moment, how I would have reacted in my parents' shoes. It has been easier, over the years, to not engage with their perspective, but I am increasingly finding myself doing just that. Maybe it's Charlie's age, maybe it's this road trip, but, for whatever reason, it's sneaking in and raising all kinds of questions.

Back then, to them, it must have felt like a monumental and disastrous shift – from their good girl with the good grades who was going to go to Oxford to a lovestruck rebel obsessed with a drummer. I have no idea, though, how things would have worked out if they hadn't pushed me, pressured me, tried to keep me away from him. Involved the police. Perhaps the infatuation would have run its course, perhaps I would have tired of him, matured enough to realise that I wanted to do something else with my life.

I'll never know, of course – and I meant every word I said to Charlie. I can't regret any step that led me to here, to now, to being his mum. And maybe having 200 followers on a camping blog isn't exactly Oscar Wilde, but it's good enough for me.

Charlie still looks a little miffed, but then Luke tells him about a place nearby called the Covered Market that has the world's best cookie shop, and all is good in his universe. I give Luke a secret thumbs-up sign behind Charlie's back; he has already found the key to my son's heart.

First we do a circuit of Radcliffe Square and wander

through the courtyards of the Bodleian, and Luke shows us a pretty stone arch called the Bridge of Sighs. He points out various colleges and tells us stories of his time here, and promises to take us to his favourite pubs at some point during the day.

We cross over the High Street and he guides us down to the colleges that are next to the river, walking across Christ Church Meadow. It is a vast and glorious open space to find in a city, a sprawling vista of green fields and trees and flowers, all backed by the grandeur of Christ Church College. Christ Church looks like every TV image of an Oxford college and is so beautiful it feels unapproachable. It is the supermodel of colleges.

Down across the meadow we go, past grazing cows with long horns, which is something you don't see every day in an urban setting. This isn't really like any other city, though, I remember – it's unique and strange and incredibly charming. Betty barks at the cattle, who are approximately 7,000 times bigger than her, as if to say 'come on then, if you think you're hard enough'.

'So, this bit of the Thames is called the Isis,' Luke tells us as we walk along the waterside and over a bridge. 'And these are the college boathouses on the left. Not so busy now, but in term time, it's heaving down here, even early in the morning. The college teams all come down to practise, and the river is crammed with boats, and the coaches cycle along the path yelling into megaphones ... and when there are contests, like in Eights Week in the summer term, which is inexplicably called Trinity, it's packed with students cheering their teams on, and family visiting, and everyone gets very drunk on mammoth jugs of Pimm's ...'

'That sounds like a lot of fun,' replies Charlie, clearly trying to visualise it.

'It was. You know, a hundred years ago, when I was a lad, and life was a simpler thing ...'

'Your life seems pretty simple now, to be honest,' says Charlie as we amble back up the path. 'You're not exactly high maintenance, are you? I mean, you don't even have Netflix.'

'This is true,' Luke responds, smiling. 'I am but a simple creature.'

I smile, but I know that isn't in fact true at all. He may appear simple on the surface, but his life has been anything but. I imagine him here, in his late teens and early twenties, young and carefree. The younger him had no idea of what joys and what pains lay ahead – but I don't suppose any of us do. That's not part of the deal with life, is it? We can plan and work and set a course, but none of us can be sure of where we will end up. Maybe the trick is accepting that, and just trying to enjoy what you have when you have it.

We walk through a small pathway to a place with the amusing name of Magpie Lane and make our way to the famous Covered Market, home of the Cookies of Yore. It is a marvellous place with a medieval feel, traditional butchers shops and greengrocers nestled in rows with boutiques and craft stores and cafes. We fuel up on chocolate chip and macadamia nut and continue our exploring for the rest of the morning.

We have our lunch at a pub called The Bear, which has a collection of thousands of different ties in frames on its sloping walls, and we call into shops and visit a surreal place called the Pitt Rivers Museum, which has a macabre display of shrunken heads that totally freak me out. Not knowing where life will take you is one thing – but I bet none of these chaps expected to end up as part of an exhibit on the other side of the world, being gawked at by twenty-first-century tourists. Charlie, naturally enough, is fascinated. After that, we make a long walk to a place called Port Meadow, where we swim in clear water as cattle at the side gaze down at us with curiosity.

The day is long, and full, and tiring. As we lounge on the riverbank drying off, watching children play and lapwings soar in the sky, I realise that I could quite easily fall asleep. Charlie is snoozing, with Betty tucked into the crook of his arm, and Luke is sitting up, chewing a long stalk of grass and gazing out at the landscape.

'I was really happy here,' he says quietly. 'Had so many good times. Feels like a million years ago now. I stayed involved with my college for a while, came to events, stayed over for reunions – they call them gaudies, because why use a normal word when you can use one that's based on Latin? But after Katie got sick, everything felt too hard. I couldn't face the prospect of seeing all those old faces, catching up with old friends.'

'Having to tell them about Katie?'

'Yeah. That, I suppose. I mean, it's not exactly a great conversational gambit, is it? "Hi, how are you, haven't seen you for years – I've been fine, apart from my daughter dying ..." I hated telling people about it even when I had to, and the idea of putting myself in a situation where I had to do it repeatedly for a whole night ... well, that wasn't my idea of a good time. So I dropped out of the whole circle. Dropped out of everything really.'

'Are you not in touch with anyone from your old life? Friends, family?'

I ask this as though it is strange, but in reality I am exactly the same.

'Not really,' he says, frowning as he thinks about it. 'Sally, obviously. But, thinking back, it was so easy to leave everyone else behind – work colleagues, people I knew socially – that I suspect none of them were especially important relationships anyway. I didn't find it hard to not look back. I just kept driving. Sometimes I wonder if I was just a coward, running away like that.'

I sit up next to him, lay my hand over his. 'You did what you felt you had to do. Don't judge yourself so harshly. This is the way you live for now, and it's helped you survive. One day, things might be different, *you* might be different. This is one moment, not forever.'

He turns to look at me, and there is an intensity in his eyes that momentarily startles me. 'Right now,' he says, twining his fingers into mine, 'maybe I wouldn't mind that. If you had to pick a moment to last forever, this wouldn't be a bad one, would it?'

I feel a flush of heat that has nothing to do with the fading sun, and everything to do with the touch of his skin against mine. Everything to do with those green eyes, that wide mouth, the hair I always want to stroke. Everything to do with Luke.

'No,' I murmur, 'it really wouldn't.'

We are silent, both still, as though afraid to speak or to move in case we break some kind of spell. The sounds around us seem to become faint, the rest of the world retreating into the background. I am immobile, frozen, both desperate to know what will happen next and terrified of it. This is indeed perfect, I think – this moment. Nothing needs to come next. I wish we could hit the pause button, that I could sit here nuzzled against this man, holding his hand, feeling this sense of peace and communion and underlying want.

Of course, I don't have a pause button, and the world stops for no woman. Charlie wakes up, snorting loudly as he stretches his arms, and Betty decides to run off and bark at a duck. The spell is broken, and I pull my hand away from Luke's, shaking my head to clear the fuzz. We make eye contact for one second more, and he smiles.

'OK?' he mouths quietly, and I nod.

Yeah. I'm OK, I think. Nothing another dip in the river wouldn't cure, I'm sure.

'Can we get some food?' Charlie says, and I laugh out loud. I can always reply on Charlie's stomach to save me from the most tempting and dangerous of situations.

Chapter 14

I am vaguely concerned that there will be some lingering awkwardness between me and Luke, and then tell myself off for being an idiot. Or a silly moo, as his gran might have said. Nothing happened – nothing at all. We barely held hands. Certainly nothing to worry about ... and yet worry I do.

I suspect it's not just awkwardness I am concerned about, it's how it made me feel. The fact that it made me feel at all, perhaps. That part of me – the part that shares heated moments with handsome men in wild beauty spots on sunny days – isn't just dormant, it's dead. Or at least I thought it was.

The idea that it might have just been lying there, curled up in a sleeping ball waiting for its chance to jump up and ambush me again, is frightening. I am wary of such things – I am wary of romance, of love, of passion. Of my own inability to manage them. The last time I felt anything resembling this was almost two decades ago, and it did not end well. I know that I was only seventeen then, but still – I am aware of the frailty of my heart, and I do not want to risk it being broken, or even gently bruised. The rest of my life is topsy-turvy, and the least I can do is try to protect myself from any other potential pain. Luke is, in the nicest way possible, messing all of my usual settings up.

If Luke is having any of these concerns at all, if he feels even slightly disconcerted by the Thing That Didn't Happen But Might Have Done, he hides it well. We go back to Joy, and Charlie revels in the fact that we are in a suburb rather than a wilderness by ordering a pizza. The delivery man is surprised to be knocking at the door of a motorhome, but it was a good call, as we are all by that time ferociously hungry.

As we eat, I check in on the Sausage Dog Diaries and read some of the comments that have been left about my earlier posts. I giggle at one that mentions a photo of Luke emerging bare-chested from the a river.

'Hey guys, there's a new comment on the blog,' I say, from my spot on the sofa. 'ChazOnWheels666 says Luke is "pretty hot for an old man". Charlie, is that you?'

'What makes you think that?' he replies, grinning. 'Sorry ... couldn't help myself!'

'Seriously? When are you going to stop with the old man line?' asks Luke. He is sitting on one of the front seats, which is swivelled around to face us, and he has a paperback in his hands.

'I don't know – maybe when they invent a time machine?' says Charlie, winking. Cheeky. 'Actually, Mum, have you seen that other comment? There's one that asks why you're doing the journey, and it has a lot of likes. Your public wants to know more about you.'

'My public?'

'Yeah. You now have over 700 followers – word has been spreading. Lily's been doing loads of socials for you, and the blog's even mentioned a few times on other forums. One describes it as a "light-hearted but vivid account of life on the open road". Get you.'

'Yikes. In all honesty, I'm a bit befuddled by all of this. I mean, I know Betty's cute, but really ... why do they want to know more about me?'

'You have to admit,' says Luke, laying the book down on his lap, 'that it is a pretty good origin story. You literally couldn't make it up.'

'Yeah, he's right, Mum. Do a piece about it, and we'll post it with some photos of the cottage – before and after shots. Seriously, it'll be really interesting, and maybe you can make it sound all inspiring and shit?'

'All inspiring and shit? We lost everything!'

'Ah, but did we really?' he says mysteriously, and winks again. He must have something wrong with his eye.

'I'll think about it,' I say, already doing exactly that. Maybe he's right. Maybe I should put the whole Sausage Dog Diaries thing into context – it would certainly explain why I'm hitting the road and searching for my joy; being essentially homeless can be quite the catalyst when it comes to lifestyle changes.

Before long the exertion of the day catches up with us, and we start our usual night-time routine – checking the windows and screens and black-out curtains are closed, taking turns in the Mona Lisa, getting changed in the still-woefully-unnamed shower room, turning the sofas into my bed and taking Betty out for a piddle. It's funny how all of these once alien actions have now become an effortlessly choreographed dance; it's as though our bodies have adjusted to all the angles and spaces we share, adjusting to our new reality.

By the time everyone is settled and shouts their now-traditional goodnights to each other, I lie awake with my laptop, the fairy lights still shining in the dim cabin. My mind drifts to Luke, alone in the double bed just metres away from me. I remind myself that my son is also in his bed, just metres away from me, and that even if he wasn't, it would make no difference. I am being self-indulgent.

I start drafting up a blog post to distract myself and am surprised at how cathartic it is. It's one of the reasons I always used to love writing – the way you could vent your emotions in a safe space, blow off mental steam, even if it used to be about far less serious things when I was a younger woman. I certainly never had to deal with cliff erosion and freak storms. If I'd been writing a blog back then, there would probably have been a lot fewer actual problems, but a lot more angst about the ones I did have. Maybe, I think, I'd have written one about my day in Oxford. I smile at the thought of the two versions of me in the same city, and how different those two points in my life were.

I cover everything from my bad news at work through to my car breaking down, and getting home to find my refuge destroyed. It all sounds surreal even to me, and

I was there for the whole thing. I explain how I ended up on this adventure, Luke's kind offer, the way the three of us have become friends. I finish with a tribute to Betty, and how she is the ultimate ice-breaker, the crusher of awkward moments, the glue that holds us all together. She is actually sleeping curled up on the end of my bed as I type, and I mention that as well, before I take a picture of her. She adores Charlie, but maybe I'm starting to win her over too.

I re-read it and make a few tweaks before I send it to Charlie. People will either read it and go 'Ooh wow, what a mad thing to have happened,' or they will decide that I am living in some kind of delusion. I can't control which and decide I will not read the comments on this one just in case.

I tuck the laptop away, and roll over onto my back, staring at the roof of the van. I am exhausted, but I still can't turn my mind off. It keeps sneaking away, and running in the direction of Luke. I wonder if he is feeling any of this, and decide that he is probably not. Men don't tend to operate on the same levels of crazy overanalysis as the female of the species.

Eventually, I manage to keep my eyes closed long enough to drift off, and ten minutes later, Betty wakes me up. Actually, I realise, as I sit up groggily, it is not ten minutes later – it is in fact around four hours later, and it is morning. Betty needs a wee-wee, and frankly so do I.

I tiptoe around as quietly as I can, and then go outside with the dog. It is a lovely morning, not too hot as yet, and I sit down on one of the camping chairs and admire the garden around us. It is a cultivated wild space, scattered with patches of long grass, gracefully swaying hollyhocks and lusciously bright lupins. Aaah, I think, I miss my lupins. Maybe I will get some potted plants for Joy. Nothing brightens up a home like flowers. Except, of course, that Joy is not my home, and this is only temporary. This is transient, this is short-term, this is a holiday. I need to remember that.

Betty is prowling around the greenery, giving everything a good sniff, then comes hurtling back towards the van, her ears flapping. I hear the door opening behind me seconds after she has, and Luke emerges. He looks dishevelled, a little tired, his T-shirt bunched up on one side.

He flops down next to me and runs his hands through his hair. Short as it is, it's still somehow messier than usual, pushed into ridged tufts.

'Bad night?' I ask, raising my eyebrows.

'Not the best. Must have been the pizza.'

Yeah, I think, that'll be it.

He wipes the sleep from his eyes and gazes out at the garden, in that way people do when they're not really seeing anything. Seems like we both struggled to get any rest, and now here we are, sitting awkwardly together looking like death warmed up in a microwave. It is, I think, silly. We are both grown-ups, and maybe need to sort this out. You simply can't avoid each other when you are living like we do; there is no place to hide in a motorhome.

'OK, so – I didn't sleep well either,' I say, quietly, on the unlikely off-chance that Charlie has crawled out of his pit. 'I was a bit worried about ... well, about us.'

He rubs his eyes yet again, then turns to face me. He looks sad, and I don't like it. 'Yeah?' he replies. 'About yesterday? We had a bit of a moment, didn't we?'

'That's a good way of putting it. We did, and I'm not sure it would be a good idea to have another one. Those moments have a way of adding up and taking on a life of their own. I ... well, I really like you, and Charlie really likes you, and this is working, isn't it? Against the odds this is working.'

'And you don't want to mess it up? Yeah, I get that. It was weird for me too. I've not exactly been a ladies' man in the last few years, and that's fine. That's what I wanted – a bit of time off from myself. From all the mistakes I made. I'm not sure I deserve any "moments" just yet ...'

I recall the shame he still feels about his behaviour after Katie's death; the way he betrayed both his wife and his own sense of self. I hadn't looked at it from that angle, and I can totally see why this has distressed him. He is going to be his own harshest judge until he feels able to let it go.

'Right,' I announce firmly. 'Well, let's just forgive ourselves yesterday's one little blip, shall we? We're only human. It's natural to reach out every now and then, we're not robots. There was no harm done, no taboos broken. I just wanted to clear the air about it. So are we good?'

He blows out a puff of air, and nods.

'We're good,' he says finally. 'And thank you. I'm not sure I'd have even talked about it. I'd have probably done the bloke thing and pretended nothing happened. This is better.'

He looks relieved, and I have the urge to reach out yet again – to touch his shoulder, to reassure him. That would, of course, be ironic in the extreme, and I resist.

'Excellent. Wow. We're so mature, aren't we?'

'We really are. We should probably get some kind of award. Coffee?'

'Always,' I reply and smile as Betty trots back inside at his heels.

I feel better for having discussed it, better for having set a few guidelines, but also ... disappointed? I mean, what did I expect? For him to declare his undying love and say he wanted me desperately and that he couldn't live without my touch? He is not that person – we are not those people. We are both wounded, both damaged, and it would potentially be a disaster. Besides, I've only known him properly for a few weeks – even if it does feel like a lot longer.

'Charlie's up,' he says, as he comes back out with the drinks. 'And I warn you, he has the baseball cap.'

My son staggers down the steps, cap in one hand, can of Coke in the other, a Danish pastry stuffed in his mouth. Very efficient.

He puts the can down on the table and eats his pastry with alarming speed, then shakes the cap in front of our faces. He is wearing an Alton Towers T-shirt and his swimming trunks, and his hair is a mass of wild dark curls. These men need the attention of a barber as a matter of some urgency.

'OK,' he says, after his last swallow, 'this has been grand, but I assume we're not staying in a garden for any length of time. Next place soon. And, Mum, I posted your piece – it was really good. I especially liked the bit about the photos and why they made you so upset. It was really scary when you started chasing them all over the place, you know, but at least I kind of understand it a bit better.'

'I'm sorry, son,' I say sincerely. 'I can see how frightening that must have been.'

''S'OK. Luckily a big strong travelling man was around to rescue you, eh?'

His eyes flick from me to Luke, and I wonder if he overheard any of our conversation, or if he is simply wondering; simply curious. If he is even testing the waters on a spot of matchmaking. Charlie has never seen me with a man, never known me to be part of a relationship. I have no idea how he will really feel about it but remind myself that it's not a pressing concern, as I remain resolutely single.

'Where are we off to?' Luke asks, changing the subject. Good man.

Charlie pulls out a scrap of paper and unravels it. He pulls a face, then looks at me and says: 'Think this must be another one of yours, Mum. At least it's not just something boring like "Manchester" or whatever. Not that Manchester looks boring, but you know what I mean . . .

Right, shall we get ourselves sorted? Start looking for a route with lots of weird stop-offs on the way?'

'That's a great idea, Charlie,' I reply, trying not to laugh. 'But it's hard to look up the route when we don't actually know where we're going.'

'Oh! Yeah ... forgot that bit. Well, apparently we're going to Jane Austen – so good luck with that one. It is yours, isn't it? Bet you only picked it 'cause of Colin Firth in his soggy pants. All the mums love that, don't they?'

'Oh yes they do,' I respond. Even mine.

I was only young when it came out, that version of *Pride and Prejudice*, but I still vividly remember watching it with my mother, and her being very vocal in her appreciation of Mr Darcy's attributes. She was normally a very proper woman, but the power of the britches overcame her reserve.

'You go and sort yourself out,' I say. 'I'll find something that we can visit that connects to the wonderful Jane.'

'OK,' Charlie replies, 'cool. Don't make it boring, though. Which will be hard, because Jane Austen is boring.'

'You are being really liberal with the "boring" word this morning, love. And Jane Austen, I assure you, is not. She was funny and insightful and clever. Only people who haven't actually read her books say she's boring.'

'If you say so. Laters.'

I turn to Luke and stare at him. 'Are you about to say Jane Austen's boring too? Because I will fight you.'

He holds up his hands in surrender and stands up. 'No way! I can't get enough of empire-line frocks and polite conversation with the vicar at the county dance personally . . . I'll leave you to it.'

Once the philistines have departed, I start looking up locations on my phone. Top Jane Austen spots are scattered around a lot of southern England – Hampshire where she was born and lived most of her life; Reading, where she went to school; the Sussex coast and, of course, Bath. I do a bit more scouting, looking at some of the settings for her books, and eventually find one that will be quick and easy and hopefully fun.

It takes another hour or so to all get dressed, clean up and sort out Joy, and then we assume our positions. Luke manoeuvres the van out of the garden and down the drive, pausing at the exit with the motor running. He turns around and shouts out: 'Where to, Captain?'

'Box Hill in Surrey!' I say. 'It's only an hour and a half away, and it's the place they had the picnic in *Emma*! There are some nice walks and a cafe and a bookshop, and it's near a place called Dorking . . .'

This is normally the part where Luke looks pleased, and excited, and gives me a jaunty salute. This is the part where the fun normally starts.

Except, this time, none of that happens. There is no grin, no salute, no reaction at all other than a frown. He seems deflated, his expression neutral, his tone flat as he responds: 'Yep. I know where it is.'

He turns back around and starts driving.

I glance over at Charlie, who is on his phone and has

not noticed this exchange at all. Something is wrong, I can tell, and I would dearly like to clamber up to the front of the van and sit in one of the passenger seats next to him. That is logistically impossible while we are driving, so I settle for asking: 'Is that OK? I'm not really bothered about going there. We could go somewhere else, or skip Jane Austen entirely …'

'No. It's fine,' he replies shortly. 'I'm fine. I just need to concentrate.'

At that point, he switches on his music – Alice Cooper, insanely loud – and conversation is no longer possible. I stare at the back of his head. Even his shoulders look more tense than usual, and I spend the rest of the journey worried that I have somehow unintentionally upset him. That the conversation we had this morning didn't go as smoothly as I had imagined. I realise that this is supremely arrogant, though, making everything about me, and wonder what else could be wrong.

The journey passes quickly, and we make the drive up a steep hill along a winding road and park. Betty jumps down out of the van and immediately starts sniffing the air, as though she is trying to find a trace of something. She runs over to Luke as soon as he climbs out and starts scooting around his ankles, making a high-pitched yipping sound I haven't heard from her before.

Luke leans down, scratches behind her ears, and says: 'I know, girl, I know …'

He strides ahead of us, putting Betty on a lead because she is so unsettled, and we follow. Even Charlie notices, and we share a questioning look as we trail behind.

We catch up with him at a viewpoint and follow his gaze. It is a view worth lingering on: a glorious patchwork quilt of green fields, thick hedges and glorious woods. The countryside is spread out before us, flowing for miles, dotted with distant signs of habitation, red roofs and white brickwork.

All around us are rolling hills and wide grassy spaces, glorying in the sunshine. There are people here, and a car park, but if you cut all of that out you can definitely imagine it being the same as it was in Jane Austen's day. You can picture Emma Woodhouse, handsome, clever and rich, making the long trek up here with Mr Knightley and the rest of the Highbury socialites for their picnic. Emma, if I remember rightly, is a bit of a bitch that day – and getting told off by Mr K is the beginning of quite a journey for her.

If it wasn't for Luke's demeanour, I'd probably be looking it up on my phone and getting him and Charlie to act out scenes in silly voices with me. Luke would be a great Mr Knightley, and I'd make Charlie play Emma just for kicks and giggles.

I reach out, put my hand on Luke's arm. Breaking our new rules already, I know, but there is definitely something wrong with him. 'Are you OK?' I ask gently.

He tenses beneath my touch, and I pull my fingers away quickly.

'Yeah, Luke, what's up man?' Charlie echoes. 'Even Betty seems a bit freaked.'

Luke turns away from the view and faces us. He runs

his hands over his hair, and replies: 'I'm sorry. Look, come on – let's go for a walk. Shake it off.'

He doesn't explain what he wants to shake off, but we walk alongside him. He points out a place called Swiss Cottage and tells us it's where John Logie Baird used to live. The building itself is hidden by dense greenery, so we can't see it, but a circular blue plaque backs up his claim.

'Who's John Logie Baird?' asks Charlie, taking a photo of it anyway.

'Inventor of the television,' I reply, grinning.

'Oh wow! I feel like I should fall to my knees and worship ... I can't even imagine a world without television ...'

We continue along a shaded path, clambering over gnarled tree roots, until Luke stops in front of a gravestone. Its inscription tells us that it belongs to Major Peter Labelliere, an eccentric resident of Dorking who was buried there head-downwards in 1800. Charlie looks it up on his phone and tells us the Major apparently thought the world was upside-down, and this made sense to him. Each to their own.

Eventually, we emerge out onto a gentle slope, and Luke pauses. He sits down on the grass, and Betty climbs onto his lap, licking his hand.

'OK,' he says, as we join him. 'I can't shake this off. Charlie, has your mum told you about my daughter, Katie?'

Charlie flicks his gaze at me, swallows and shakes his head.

'Well,' Luke continues, 'I had a little girl. She died a few years ago, when she was nine.'

Charlie's face pales, and he blinks very fast, before saying: 'I'm so sorry, Luke. That's a nightmare.'

'Yeah. Thanks. Anyway, we didn't live too far from here, and at the weekends and in the school holidays, this was one of her very favourite places in the world. We'd drive here early in the day, bring a picnic, spend hours rambling through the woods and up and down the pathways. The deeper you go, the more it starts to look like something from Middle Earth, you know? Perfect place for exploring.'

His words unleash a torrent of guilt inside me – even though I had no idea of this place's significance to Luke, I feel dreadful for having unwittingly brought him here.

'When she was smaller,' he continues, 'her favourite part of all was the play trail. Better than a park any day – tucked away in the woods, trees to climb, log bridges to clamber over, forts made out of branches. There are some stepping stones over the river as well, she loved those. We had to carry her across to start with, then she got braver each time, until eventually she could do it by herself.'

He pauses and smiles, and I know that he is remembering. That those images of his baby are forever etched in his mind, both consoling and corrosive at the same time.

Charlie is rapt, his brown eyes shining with tears, and I sneak my hand into his. He squeezes my fingers as Luke continues.

'So, even when she got sick, we used to bring her. It depended on how well she was, whether she could manage much of a walk or not. But, during her good times, when she'd responded well to her treatments, she could seem almost like a healthy little girl. Once we got Betty, she came with us too – it's a pretty perfect place for dogs as well. That's why she's a bit high-strung this morning, I think. If I let her off the lead right now, I suspect she'd fly away into the distance, all the way to those stepping stones.'

I recall the dog's reaction when we got out of Joy this morning; the way she was sniffing the air. It made me think she was searching for something, and I was right. She was searching for Katie. I stroke Betty's soft feathery head. She is a very good dog.

'After we lost her, we scattered her ashes here as well. We all came – my parents, Sally my wife, her mum, our siblings, Betty, of course. It was a strange little pilgrimage, on a day very like this one. It seemed odd that the sun even dared to shine, but Sally pointed out that it was what Katie would have wanted. She would have wanted us to have one last day of fun, even if it was without her. And that ... well, that was the last time I was here.'

He leans forward and nuzzles his face into Betty's fur. I suspect there are tears that he does not want us to see, and he is entitled to that. I'm feeling pretty tearful myself.

'I'm so sorry I brought us here,' I say. 'I'm so sorry you're going through this.'

He looks up and manages a sad smile. 'No, I'm glad we came,' he replies. 'I didn't know how I'd react, how I'd feel. As soon as we parked, I wanted to get back in and drive away again. But ... well, I'm glad I didn't. It's long overdue, coming back here. Seeing this place, remembering those times ... it's not easy. But it's also not all bad – this was Katie's happy place.

'I can picture her here in all those different ages – being carried as a baby, toddling around the tree trunks, running as fast as she could down the hills. Even later, when she was ill, it always made her smile. She never complained about anything – and that's what I need to remember most of all. If she was brave enough to get through all that she had to deal with, then I'm brave enough to deal with this. I can make it my happy place too. So don't apologise for bringing me here – thank you for bringing me here.'

Charlie seems unnerved, as you would expect from an eighteen-year-old being plunged into a whirlpool of adult emotion. He chews his lip, and says: 'Have you got a picture of her?'

Luke smiles and replies: 'Your mum asked me the same, and I never showed her one. But yes, of course.'

He pulls his wallet out of his shorts pocket and passes us a small square photo.

'That's her school picture in Reception,' he explains. 'I have more, back in the motorhome and on my phone, but I love that one.'

I handle the picture like the precious artefact it is, and Charlie leans in to look at the same time. I can't help but smile; she has messy dark hair that has escaped her plaits in wild, errant strands, and huge brown eyes. Her grin is infectious and speaks of a deep vein of mischief. Her school shirt has a paint stain on it, and her cardigan is hanging off one shoulder.

'Her mum was not pleased with that photo at first,' Luke says, taking it back and staring at it. 'She'd done her hair all nice for picture day, and she didn't have that paint stain when she left the house! But that was Katie – she didn't care. She was a little bit wild already, even at four. And that's why I love that photo. I wish I had more – I wish I had school photos that stretched all the way through, and could add graduation photos, and even wedding photos, but ... well. At least I have this. We didn't have her for long enough, but what we had was perfect.'

I think of all of Charlie's school portraits – the progression from Reception to Juniors to High school; the different haircuts and missing teeth and various uniforms, his transformation from cute little nipper to handsome young man – and know how lucky I am. Losing some of those photos in a storm is nothing in comparison to what Luke has lost.

'She's absolutely gorgeous,' I say. 'Like you say, perfect.'

'She looks really cheeky and a lot of fun,' Charlie adds, which makes Luke grin. I notice then that it is the same grin as Katie's – the little girl must have looked physically more like her mum, but there is a resemblance there.

'She was. And thank you. Now, look – this has been a lot, and it's been heavy, and I'm sorry about that. The whole ethos of this trip was supposed to be joy. So, this is my suggestion – how about you two go back up to the cafe and get something to drink, and in your case, of course, Charlie, to eat as well, and I'll meet you there in a while? I think me and Betty are going to go on a trip down memory lane, and I think it's something we should do alone. We're going to go back to that play trail, and over the stepping stones, and we're going to be sad and happy for a while, and then we'll come back. Is that all right with you guys?'

'Of course it is,' I reply as we all stand up again.

'Yeah. I haven't eaten in, like over an hour,' says Charlie. 'Anyway … do you know what it's time for now?'

Luke and I look confused, and Charlie announces: 'Group hug!'

He dives in and wraps his arms around Luke's waist, and laughing, I join in. Luke grabs us both in a big bear hug, and Betty jumps up at our ankles. We stagger around for a few steps, then finally disentangle. Again, I have that strange feeling that Charlie has become great friends with Luke in such a small amount of time – but then again, so have I. It's like we've all been in some kind of emotional fast-forward. It must be one of the side-effects of living in such close quarters and being together twenty-four/seven.

We make our farewells, and walk back up to the visitor centre and cafe at the top of the hill. After safely bagging an outdoor table, drinks and a selection of cakes, Charlie and I settle down together. A black Lab on the next table along keeps trying to sidle towards us, looking at Charlie's plate hopefully in case he drops any crumbs. Good luck, fella, I think.

'That was nice of you,' I say, 'that group hug. I think he needed that.'

'Jeez, Mum, I needed that! What a horrible thing to have happened. How long have you known?'

'A few days,' I reply. 'I hope you're not annoyed with me. It wasn't my story to share, if you know what I mean?'

He nods and drains half his glass of orange juice in one go.

'Yeah. That's OK. I just feel sorry for him. Why does the bad shit always seem to happen to the good people?'

'That, my son, is a question as old as time. Anyway, just want to say – that wasn't easy, and you handled it well, and I'm very proud of you.'

He shrugs, as if to say 'naturally you are', and chews his lip. He does that when he's thinking. It's like his poker tell.

'So,' he says eventually, dragging the word out, 'that was Luke's story to tell, and I totally get that. But what about your story?'

'What do you mean?' I reply, feeling suddenly tense. 'Nothing to tell. I'm very boring. Not so much a story as a chapter. Or possibly a limerick.'

He points a finger at me, notices there's some cream left on there and licks it off. 'Don't do that thing, Mum.

Don't make a joke – or what you think of as a joke – to try to distract me. I've been thinking about this since we were in Oxford. You know last year when I was looking at unis, and you took me to open days?'

'Of course. I bagged a fine collection of free pens and jute tote bags.'

'Well, that was you once, wasn't it? Looking at unis, thinking about your future, making plans. And before you start making a speech, yes, I get it – you don't regret having me. I believe you, because I am very awesome, but that's not what I mean. What I mean is that you had parents. You had a mum and dad and a family home, people who maybe took you to open days, and helped you through your exams like you did with me, and all that boring stuff. And I know next to nothing about them. I'm eighteen, Mum, and I'm about to start the next stage of my life – but I feel like I'm doing it without filling in the blanks, you know?'

I take a sudden interest in spreading the cream and jam on my scone, and in over-stirring my coffee. Eventually, I do it so much I create a brown whirlpool and it sloshes over the side of the mug.

I examine what he has said from every angle and weigh up my possible responses. This is not, of course, the first time that Charlie has asked about my childhood. In the past, I have evaded it – just said something bland like 'it was really normal and boring, nothing to talk about'. He has accepted that, but with increasing reluctance, as he has got older and more independent in his thinking. I don't think it will work any more – and

I also don't think it's fair to expect it. It's time for me to stop being selfish, and at least try to open up to him.

'Are you about to fob me off again?' he says, sounding annoyed with me. 'Because, please don't. I know that for some reason this is hard for you to talk about, but if Luke can sit there and cry into Betty's fur and still find a way to talk about what happened, then surely you can budge a bit too? I'm not just being nosy – it's my family as well. Dad doesn't have any to speak of, and when I asked him about yours, he got super-cagey and said he couldn't remember much from back then and I should ask you instead ...'

I look up in surprise. It hadn't even occurred to me that he would ask Rob, but why wouldn't he? He obviously feels like he has no other choice. I am, however, slightly amused at the thought of Rob's face – my parents hated him, and the feeling was entirely mutual. In fact, the answer he gave was probably the most tactful one he could have come up with.

'OK,' I say simply, dropping the spoon. It hits the saucer with a clang, and the black Lab that is now entirely under our table looks up in surprise. 'I'll try. And yes, it is hard for me, so go easy, all right? What do you want to know?'

Charlie looks so shocked, it is comical.

'Close your mouth,' I say, 'a wasp might fly in.'

He does as he is told, and then speaks.

'Are my grandparents still alive?'

'Ummm ... I think so. I'm not totally sure, but I have been known to drunk google them occasionally, and last time I did it, I saw a picture of them on the parish council website. At the village fete. About two years ago.'

The sentence is simple, but the emotions behind it are not. Seeing their faces, older, more wrinkled; their silvering hair, my dad's slightly shrunken frame – the same but not the same – had made me cry. It was like seeing a photo of a place you used to love, a place you used to feel at home in, but knowing that it's been destroyed by an earthquake and you can never go back.

'And what are they called?'

'Bridget and Owen.'

'And do I have any, um, aunties or uncles or cousins?'

'One uncle,' I reply, 'my older brother Richard. I have no idea about the cousins.'

'And where do they live? Where did you grow up?'

'Cornwall,' I reply quickly.

'Why are all your answers so short?'

'Because, as already established, this is hard for me. I'm doing my best.'

He nods and reaches out to pat my hand. 'I know. I'm sorry. It's just ... I'm kind of scared that I'll only get five minutes or something, and after that you'll clam up again ... and I really want to know more about them. Why did you leave? Why aren't you in touch with them? Did they do something awful to you, Mum? If they did, just tell me, and I'll never mention them again, I promise ...'

I realise that his imagination is conjuring up all kinds of worst-case scenarios, and none of them are fair. What happened between me and my parents was awful – but I am starting to come to the conclusion that we did it to each other. Being away from my normal life, from work, being on the road, and, if I'm honest with myself, probably my conversations with Luke, have forced me to see the other side with more light and shade. We were all convinced that we were right; all firm in that belief. They were parents who were sure they knew best. I was young and was sure that parents who tried to get your boyfriend arrested could have nothing but evil intent. None of this is easy to explain to Charlie – I don't want him to hate his grandparents, and I don't want him to blame his dad for being the catalyst for the whole thing. I also, being truthful, don't want him to resent me. It's quite the conundrum.

'Charlie, love, I can assure you that it's nothing like that. It's complicated, and I'm not just saying that to shut you up. It really is. And your dad has a point – it was a long time ago, and we all have a way of rewriting history to suit our version of events, don't we? Long story short, we fell out – very, very badly. I left. I had you. I started a new life without them in it, because that's what I was sure I needed to do.'

This is a lot for a teenager take in, but I try not to underestimate him. He is far more emotionally astute than most lads his age, I know.

'And you've not been in touch with them ever since? Do they ... do they even know about me?'

'I've sent them a few postcards over the years. Just to let them know I'm alive. There was a phone call that

. . . didn't go well. And, no, they don't know about you. To start with, I was still so angry with them, still so hurt by them – and I maybe didn't think they deserved to know about you. I also didn't know how they'd react, and I couldn't handle it if they rejected me. The one time I did reach out, it felt like she might . . . my mum.'

'Reject you?'

'Yes. I probably overreacted – everything was very heightened. It was just after your dad and I split up, and I was . . . well. I wasn't doing so well. I called, she was angry, and I hung up. It wasn't the most mature of displays by either of us. Then the years just slid by, and the longer I left it, the more impossible it seemed to be to fix, even if I wanted to.'

'Wow,' he says after thinking it over for a few minutes, 'that really is a mess, isn't it?'

'It is, love. Yes.'

'OK – I only have one more question for you.'

I nod, and he hits me with it. As questions go, it's a biggie.

'Can we go and see them?'

Chapter 15

I agree to Charlie's request, despite the lump of anxiety that lodges in my throat, where it makes itself comfy and takes up permanent residence. It is time, I decide. Time for him to meet them, time for me to face my past, time to see what an alternative future might look like.

My mind has readily provided various catastrophes to keep me tense, of course. Turning up and finding out they've moved. Turning up and them refusing to speak to me. Turning up to find that one or both of them ... isn't around any more. I am in turmoil, lurching from one disastrous scenario to another with no break between them.

This is only allayed when Luke has been filled in, and he and Charlie step in and hold an intervention. They both tell me that if we are going to do this, if we are going to head to Cornwall, then the new rule is that between now and then, we have to concentrate solely on having as much fun as humanly possible. In Betty's case, canine-ly possible.

I agree and promise I will try to switch my mind off, to save the worrying for when it is actually relevant and not let it ruin the journey in between. Some of the time, over the next few days I am faking it – but some of the time, the approach genuinely works. At the very least, we visit lots of great places that provide content for the ever-expanding Sausage Dog Diaries.

We take our time getting from Surrey to Cornwall, stretching the journey into four overnight stops and countless trips to some astonishing places. As delaying tactics go, it is a superior example.

We do one more draw out of the hat, and the paper says 'James Bond'. I assume it is mine, as I wrote down James Bond as one of the choices, but Charlie thinks it's his, and Luke the same. Turns out, amusingly, that all three of us wanted to visit something to do with James Bond. Charlie makes a joke about this journey giving us a 'licence to chill', and I steal it to use on the blog.

It turns out that Skyfall Lodge – James's old family home in Scotland – was actually built on a common not far away from Box Hill. Yet again, we are amazed at the sneaky nature of movies, as we wander around the walking trails, and try to imagine all the explosions and helicopters and Judi Dench legging it through the night with a torch in her Dame-like hand.

After that, we meander on our journey, wandering through the South West of England. We visit a stone circle just outside Bristol that is absolutely amazing, and climb to the top of a hill fort called Solsbury, near Bath. When we reach the summit, Charlie plays the Peter Gabriel song 'Solsbury Hill' and we all join in. Then we drive down through Wiltshire, where we crawl into a long barrow at a place called West Kennet, wander around Avebury, and visit Salisbury Cathedral.

In Dorset, we climb down the steps at Durdle Door, and visit Thomas Hardy's cottage and hunt for fossils on Charmouth Beach. We recreate *The French Lieutenant's Woman* in Lyme Regis, and drive on into Devon, where we walk part of the Tarka Trail and ride on steam trains through lush green valleys and go on boat trips. We swim in fast-flowing rivers, and jump from stone bridges into lakes, and hire kayaks, and eat so many cream teas there is probably now a national shortage of scones.

I try my very hardest to keep my fear at bay, to ignore the rising tide of tension that threatens to engulf me with every mile further west we go – but as we drive across the border into Cornwall itself, I know that I am fighting a losing battle.

The landscape starts to unfold around me, the lush green hills, the villages, the winding coastal roads that lead down to fishing villages and harbour towns, and it feels both hauntingly familiar and startlingly new.

Charlie, fully entwined with all of Luke's guidebooks, behaves like he is filled with helium. He is almost floating with the wonder of it all, with the ancient chapels and the roadside fruit stalls and the ever-present tang of salt in the sea air. We take him to Godrevy Beach, where he hires a wetsuit and board and takes a surf lesson. We drive down to the Lizard, and eat ice cream while perched on the rocks overlooking the Atlantic, the waves crashing into the peninsula like a scene from a Daphne du Maurier novel.

We trek across the slipway to visit St Michael's Mount, then get the boat back, sitting at the edge of the shoreline as the sun sets, casting the mount and its castle into silhouette. We call off at tiny village pubs, and Luke plays his guitar as we gaze out at the sea, and we spot dolphins and seals and porpoises from rugged clifftops. We eat the freshly baked pasties that were a mainstay of my youth, and walk through fields of yellow and pink wildflowers, and pick our own strawberries, and sleep under myriad twinkling stars.

If it wasn't for the fact that I feel as though I am driving towards my own execution, it would be glorious. I can tell that Luke has picked up on my tension; notice the way he tries to distract me, engages us all in word games and singsongs, reassures me with the occasional brief pat on the hand or shoulder.

'How far away are we?' asks Charlie, as we make our way to the far west coast where I grew up.

Not far away enough, I want to say. Instead, I simply tell him that we are almost there, trying to hide the tremor in my voice, the tremble in my hands. The landmarks are all there now – the crossroads with its weathered wooden sign; the big rock the locals say is cursed; the footpaths that lead through swaying fields of crops down to the coast. We pass the local pub, and the long thin strip of road that plays host to the nearest shop and cafe. I see the street that leads to my old school, the bus stop where I used to get off and join the flow of uniformed humanity towards our day of learning and goofing off. I see the tight corner where Richard crashed his car not long after his driving test, and eventually I see the sign for Foxgloves. The place of my youth, now a foreign land.

It is easy to miss, a hidden turning on the right, and part of me would like to miss it. To play dumb, to pretend that I am lost, to claim that they must not live here any more. One look at Charlie's enthralled face assassinates that idea. I couldn't do that to him – but I am also not ready to simply drive along that road again just yet, either physically or emotionally.

'Stop!' I shout to Luke. 'Just pull over for a minute!'

He does as he is asked and stops the van. He switches off the engine and turns around, his face concerned.

'Are you all right?' he asks. 'Did I miss it?'

'No ... it's just ahead ... but I need a moment. I'm not sure this is right, just turning up. I mean, they're old – I might give them a heart attack or something ... I think I should call them first.'

I see Charlie and Luke share glances and know that I probably look and sound desperate. I can feel the flush on my cheeks, and my own heart pounding, and my skin seems hot and prickly all over. I am fooling nobody, not even myself – this break is for my benefit, not my parents'.

'Do you have their number even?' asks Charlie, undoing his seat belt and coming to sit next to me.

'Well, I don't know. I remember the landline number. Though they might have changed it, or have mobiles, or ...'

'Just call it, Mum,' he says gently. 'It won't be as bad

as you think. If I'd been gone for eighteen years and then turned up, wouldn't you be pleased to see me?'

I stare at him and ponder the question. The thought of that ever happening seems ludicrous, but I know how easy it can be – to take too many steps away from each other, to say things that feel final, to make promises you don't want to keep but feel you must. To break the thread that ties people together. But ... yes, he is right. If that awful thing ever did happen, I would be pleased to see him. I nod, and take some deep breaths, and pick up my phone.

I dial the number that I haven't dialled for so many years, but which is still engrained in my muscle memory, and I listen to it ring out. I imagine the phone, on its neat little table in the hallway, next to a notepad and pen and my mum's super-efficient address book. I have no idea what I am going to say.

Please don't answer, I think, as it rings out.

I am about to get my wish when someone picks up.

'Hello, 9627,' says my mum, as she always did – reciting the last four digits of our number, as though to inform the caller of any mistakes they might have made, and give them the chance to recant.

I hear her voice, and my own seizes up.

'Hello?' she repeats. 'Is there anybody there? Speak now or I'll be hanging up!'

My mum is – was? – a headteacher, and she uses those years of experience to her advantage. She can be incredibly imposing, even over the phone. I immediately sit up a little taller as soon as she uses her 'don't mess with me' voice.

'Mum?' I whisper. 'It's me.'

'Who is this?' she snaps back. 'Is this a joke?'

'No, Mum. It's Jenny.'

I am greeted with silence, and wonder if she might hang up after all. Charlie and Luke are hovering on either side of me, caught in my spiderweb of tension. Maybe he was wrong, I think – maybe she won't be happy to see me. Maybe she's still angry, still disappointed, even after all these years.

'Jenny?' she repeats finally, her tone devoid of her earlier confidence. 'Is that really you? Are you all right?'

It makes me smile, that question. It makes me realise that whatever else she might be – controlling, infuriating, bossier than Margaret Thatcher on steroids – she is still a mother. And all mothers want to know if their kids are all right. Part of me expected her to go immediately on the offensive, but all I hear is genuine concern.

'Yes, Mum, I'm fine. I … I wanted to come and see you. I have someone I want you to meet. Would that be OK?'

Another pause, a loud bark in the background. For a split second, I think it might be Jem, the springer spaniel I grew up with – then I remind myself that Jem was nine when I left and will be long gone now. I missed the rest of Jem's life, and so much else besides.

'Yes. That would be OK, Jenny. Where are you?'

'Ummm … at the end of the path, just out on the road?'

'At the end of *our* path?'

'Yep.'

'Well, for goodness' sake, come in then – you know how busy that road can get, you'll cause an accident!'

Ah, I think, smiling resignedly. There she is – my real mum.

Chapter 16

Luke navigates us between the two stone pillars, and we drive slowly along the pathway that leads to Foxgloves. The house itself is surrounded by fields, part of a farm that has been in my father's family for generations. The trees that line the route are lush and green and heavy, their branches almost touching overhead, their leaves and blossoms swinging against Joy as we progress.

I gaze out of the windows, waiting for the clearing I know is coming up. I glimpse the fields beyond, see the languid chewing of black and white cows, the darting of birds overhead. I wonder how many times I have walked, run, skipped, cycled, driven up this exact same road. This is where I learned to ride a bike, where I used to bounce on my pogo stick, where my friends and I would play. Where I snuck out to see Rob ... Now I can't even properly visualise the last time I came down it. I was furious, I was in tears, I was leaving for good. All so very long ago.

As we get closer to the house, Charlie pipes up: 'You didn't tell me you had llamas!'

I follow his gaze and find that, yes, he is correct. Off to the right, enclosed in a paddock, is a small herd of llamas. A surreal thing to find in the Cornish countryside.

'That's because we didn't,' I reply. 'That was where the milking shed was . . . they must have relocated it, I suppose.'

We pass the big oak trees at the top of the drive, and I see small wooden boxes tucked into their solid branches, maybe for birds or bats. The heavy metal gate at the top of the lane is open, which is unusual – it was a cardinal sin to leave it like that back in my day.

Luke drives us through, and we park up on a new gravelled area that used to house a set of storage sheds.

'Wow, that's a really pretty house,' says Charlie, gazing through the window.

I suppose it is, now I see it through less familiar eyes. Wherever you grow up is your normal, isn't it – and for me, it was this place. A square stone farmhouse, ivy climbing over its solid walls; a heavy wooden front door surrounded by hearty vines of wisteria, dripping with lavender flowers. It isn't huge, but it is imposing. More handsome than pretty, I'd say.

Off to the side lies another field, this one small and wild, swathed in the deep pink of the foxgloves that give the place its name. Behind the house will, I presume, still be the small flower garden that was always my mother's domain, where she grew roses and hydrangeas and lilies.

It is so strange, seeing it again. I suppose it never really left my memory, I just chose not to revisit it very often.

'So,' says Charlie impatiently, 'shall we, uh, get out?'

I nod and tell myself it'll all be fine. I mean, what's

the worst that can happen? I don't even try to answer that question, instead I run my hands over my hair and smooth down my T-shirt and suddenly feel hideously aware of every crease in my clothing, every tangle in my ponytail, the fact that I'm wearing cut-off denim shorts and flip-flops.

'You look fine,' Luke says, taking hold of my hand and gripping it firmly. 'And she won't care about any of that anyway.'

'Ha!' I snort in reply. 'You've clearly not met my mother. I heard a dog, by the way, so maybe keep Betty on the lead until we know whether it's friendly or if it eats dachshunds?'

He nods and hooks her up, and I open Joy's door. I stand on the stairs for a moment, too nervous to move, and I see that my mother is doing exactly the same. She has opened her own door and is standing at the top of the small flight of stone steps. Her posture is perfect, and her arms are folded across her chest. Our eyes meet, and there is a second where I simply cannot move.

And then she runs down those steps, and I jump down my steps, and we both fly towards each other. Within seconds, we meet in the middle, and then I am in her arms, and she is stroking my hair back from my face, kissing away tears that I didn't even notice shedding. I can't quite describe that feeling – the feeling of being back in my mother's embrace. I am safe and secure and it is as though nothing could ever harm me again. All of the pain, all of the worry, all of the anxiety of the last years are swept away, and I simply sob on her shoulder.

'It's OK, darling,' she murmurs, rubbing my arms and holding me back so she can look at me more clearly. 'It's OK. I'm so happy to see you. I've missed you so much ...'

I swipe my eyes clear and look at her properly in return. Her hair is shorter than it was, cut in a bob that ends at her chin. It's now more silver than brown, and it suits her. She's gained a little weight, feels more comfortable than she used to, and there are lines on her face that were never there before – but none of that matters. It is still her, and I don't think I realised until this exact moment how much I have missed having her in my life.

'Me too,' I say, clinging on to her hand and letting my eyes roam over her, catching up on every new line.

She is returning the appraisal, and I wonder how strange it must be for her – I left here as a seventeen-year-old child, and I stand before her as a grown woman, marked by the passing of time, changed by the life she's led. I hope she's not too disappointed by what she sees.

'Not so bad,' she says, smiling, tucking a stray strand of hair behind my ears. 'I half expected tattoos!'

'No tattoos,' I reply. 'You?'

'Nothing apart from a busty mermaid on my left calf,' she says, still staring at me intensely. 'And the blessed face of Saint Monty Don on the other.'

I don't remember my mum having a sense of humour, but she must have. Maybe I've simply chosen to block out all the good things about her; maybe that's made it easier to stay angry with her, to stay convinced she was purely bad. To stay away.

I hear footsteps shuffling on the gravel behind me and Betty's snuffling sound as she sniffs the ground. For a few moments there, I completely forgot that we weren't alone.

I hold my mum's hand, surprised to see the skin wrinkled and her knuckles more pronounced, to feel the papery flesh. I lead her to the others.

'Mum, this is my friend, Luke,' I say simply, nodding at him.

She says hello, and runs her gaze over him, taking in the brutally short hair, the crumpled rock T-shirt, the motorhome in the background. I have a fleeting worry that she will snub him somehow, judge him and find him wanting, and am surprised at how protective I feel. Luke treats her to the full-wattage smile, and I swear to God she almost sighs. Maybe she is judging him, and not minding what she sees.

'And this,' I say, looking at my son, who is suddenly all gangly arms and nerves, 'is Charlie. Your grandson.'

Her eyes widen, and her hand flies up to her mouth. I see tears squeezed away as she registers what I have said, and I think that this is the first time I have ever seen my mum cry. I always used to take that as a sign of her inhumanity, her harshness, her lack of empathy – but now I remember that moment in Luke's motorhome, just after the house fell, when I had a mini-meltdown. 'You never cry, Mum,' Charlie had said to me. Of course I do, I'd thought at the time, I just hide it from you. Maybe my mum wasn't inhumane and harsh back then – maybe she was just really good at crying on her own.

She walks towards him, reaches up and holds his face in both her palms. He looks a bit like he might cry as well as she envelopes him in a hug. He is a good head and shoulders taller than her, and he doesn't seem to know what to do with his arms.

She pulls away and says: 'Charlie, I'm so pleased to meet you. We have a lot of catching up to do, don't we?'

'That'd be really cool,' he says, grinning. 'This is Betty.'

He picks the dog up, and she immediately licks my mum on the face.

'What a dear! Is she good with other dogs?'

Charlie confirms that she is, and Mum replies: 'Righto. Well, shall we all get in out of the sun? Cup of tea maybe? I didn't know you were coming, but I made some lemon drizzle cake yesterday ...'

'Excellent,' says Charlie, 'my favourite.'

In fact, his favourite cake is Black Forest gateau, but I am impressed at his superior levels of flattery.

He walks in behind Mum, and Luke hangs back with me.

'Are you all right?' he whispers, as we climb the stone steps and enter the hallway.

I look up at him and smile. 'I think so,' I murmur back, 'but ask me again in an hour's time.'

As soon as we are inside, a blur of white and brown runs in and zooms around our ankles. I do a double take and remind myself that, no, it can't really be Jem – but he looks just like him.

'Jem's line,' mum says, seeing my expression. 'I've lost track of how many greats. This is Frank. He's only eighteen months old, and a complete hooligan.'

I kneel down and stroke him, amazed at how much he looks like my childhood pet. After I left, I initially missed Jem more than I missed anyone else, and it is almost too emotional being here, in the coolness of this familiar hallway, looking into the deep brown eyes of his doggie doppelganger.

Frank breaks away from me to investigate Betty's nether regions, which she reciprocates, and then begins to lick her ears. Frank and Betty: A Love Story.

I stand up and look around the farmhouse. It is the same, but not. The hallway has been decorated, the slightly fussy floral paper replaced with deep green paint. The phone table is still where it was, but the phone is new. I glance through the open door to the living room and see that, again, it has been decorated, and that the Chesterfield sofa that almost seemed as old as the house has gone, replaced with a beige velvet suite.

'Make yourselves at home, Charlie, Luke,' my mum says, gesturing through to the lounge. 'And, Jenny, perhaps you could help me with the tea?'

I follow her through, along the hallway, and as she opens the door, I gasp.

'You've got a new kitchen!' I utter, turning around and taking in the shining new cabinets and ultra-modern appliances. It is completely different from the slightly shabby version I remember, with the battered pine table and the old Aga.

'Yes, well – we're not spring chickens any more, are we? Thought it was time to enjoy a few creature comforts in our dotage ... So, Charlie. How old is he?'

She is busying herself with the kettle, with getting a tray together, with retrieving milk from the enormous fridge, so I can't see the expression on her face. Perhaps that is a deliberate thing, I think, as I realise why she is asking the question.

'He's eighteen, Mum. He's Rob's son.'

'Ah,' she replies simply, slicing up the lemon drizzle cake and arranging it on a plate. 'And Rob ... how is he?'

We are suddenly on very dangerous ground. I can tell from the way she is holding herself, from her lack of eye contact, that she knows this as well. So much has happened since I last saw her, and I can only imagine how hard it is for her not to pin me down and interrogate me immediately. But this is awkward terrain for me too – I don't want to lie, but perhaps the last vestiges of my pride don't want to let me confess that she was right all along, that Rob was the ne'er-do-well they always suspected, that I made a terrible mistake and should have listened to them.

'He's fine,' I reply breezily. 'We're not together any more, but that happens, doesn't it? He's doing well. He lives in Paris. He's in regular contact with Charlie.'

I have no idea why I am defending Rob, trying to make the situation sound better than it is, but somehow I am.

Mum turns around to face me at last, and I steel

myself for judgement, for a sniping comment, for a veiled told-you-so.

'And how long has he been gone for?' she asks directly.

Now she has asked that particular question, I know that I cannot lie – apart from anything else, I can't expect Charlie to cover for me. Charlie doesn't even remember his dad living with us, and she will discover that.

'He left when Charlie was two,' I say quietly, biting my lip and looking at my feet. Flip-flops. Jeez. I could have at least painted my toenails.

'So you raised that lovely boy all alone? Luke isn't . . . more than a friend?'

'No, he's not. And yes, I did.'

I find it in myself to meet her piercing stare, and feel a rush of adrenaline. This is how it can be with me and my mum; this is how I remember it. Even if we both try really, really hard, we seem able to skip forward to conflict, real or perceived, within seconds.

'Well, it looks like you did a marvellous job, darling. He seems like a lovely young man, and you must be very proud – of him, and of yourself. Now, shall we go through?'

She sweeps away past me with her tray, and I am left floundering in the alien hi-tech kitchen. That, I think, shaking my head as I follow her, was not what I expected at all. The adrenaline fades, is replaced with something warmer and kinder.

By the time I join them in the living room, everyone is perched on sofas and chairs, and Mum is pouring the tea. Her movements are, as ever, precise and measured, and she doesn't even spill a drop. I remain unconvinced that I am genetically related to this woman.

Charlie bites into his cake and immediately goes into that blissed-out sugar trance I am so familiar with.

'Wow, this is amazing!' he says after the first mouthful. 'Are you sure you two are related?'

It is so close to what I was thinking myself that it makes me laugh, and the low-level awkwardness of the moment is dissipated.

'Jenny was never interested in learning to cook,' my mother says, stirring her tea. 'She assured me that she would be rich and famous and would always have a private chef.'

'Ha! Well, that didn't go to plan . . .' Charlie says, looking around him. It must be so odd for him, after all this time, after all these years of half-truths and evasions, to finally be here.

'So, Mum, where's Dad?' I ask. 'Is he on the farm?'

There is a terrible split second where I wonder what she is about to say – whether he is still around at all.

'Oh. Of course, you don't know. Well, we sold the farm. We still own the fields immediately around the house, and the garden at the back, but the rest isn't ours any more.'

'But . . . Dad loves the farm! It's been in the family for so long . . . and I saw the cows on the way in!'

'I said we'd sold it, Jenny, not expunged it from existence. Nice couple bought it, they've gone organic. Make marvellous yoghurts. I know it must be a surprise, but there was no way around it really. Your father is seventy-five now, dear, and his health has been, well, I suppose you'd call it patchy. He simply couldn't carry on doing so much of it himself, and Richard made it clear that he didn't want to take it over. It got to the stage where we were paying more and more people to do the work for us, and it simply wasn't viable. He was upset at first, but he's settled into it now. It's meant we can have a nice retirement, and a shiny new kitchen, and he was consoled by his alpacas.'

'Yeah – what's with the llamas?' asks Charlie, leaning forward.

'Alpacas, dear, alpacas. There is a difference – alpacas are shorter, and lighter, and have different ears. Well, he saw some at a county show and fell in love with them. We started with four, and now we have fifteen. They're actually splendid animals – very engaging, low maintenance, immensely calming to be around. Your father takes tourists on walks with them at the weekends. Very popular it is too.'

'Really?' I ask incredulously. 'Dad and tourists?'

My father was a lovely man but not always overly enamoured by the many visitors our corner of Cornwall attracts in the summer. In fact, he was known to drive his tractor especially slowly on purpose just to annoy them.

'I know – he's mellowed with age. He enjoys meeting the new people now, and it fills up his time, gives him a sense of purpose. I called him – he even has a mobile, after Richard and I bombarded him with threats! He was in the village, he'll be here shortly. Charlie, do you like cricket? Your grandfather would love to play with you, I'm sure.'

I gulp back laughter at the thought of Charlie playing cricket – or in fact any game that doesn't involve a screen and a handheld controller – but he replies eagerly: 'Well, only a few times at school, and I wasn't exactly at county level – but I'm willing to give it a go!'

Wow, I think. Wonders will never cease. This is a day of small miracles.

'And Richard,' I ask, 'how is he?'

'He's well. He moved to Falmouth – the lure of the big city! – and runs his own marketing company. He's divorced, sadly, but as you said, that happens. Rebecca – you remember Rebecca? – well, she still lives here, which is lovely because we get to see a lot of his children, Ethan, who is seventeen now, and Shannon, who is fifteen.'

My brother is four years older than me, and I remember him mainly as the bane of my life. This is not uncommon with big brothers, I suspect, and from what I've seen of other people, the relationships usually balance out. Ours never did, because he was in his final year at uni when I walked out on the whole family. I didn't even say goodbye to him, which I now deeply regret.

Rebecca, I do remember – she was his girlfriend all the way from year ten, and I'm not surprised they married young and had kids. I'm also, perhaps, not surprised that they're divorced – she never wanted much more than to stay here and raise a brood, and he had bigger plans.

'Will I get to meet them?' asks Charlie, sounding thrilled. 'My cousins?'

'I'm sure that can be arranged,' Mum replies, then frowns. 'Although I have no idea how long you're staying for, or even if you are ... I couldn't help noticing the magnificent motorhome you were driving, Luke. Are you on holiday? Do you need to get back to work?'

Ah, I think – here we go. The very subtle questioning; a slight prod to try to establish Luke's bona fides.

Luke smiles and replies simply: 'Not at all. I actually live in the motorhome on a permanent basis, and I don't have a job.'

He says this completely unapologetically, and I love that about him. My mother doesn't know his story, doesn't know what led him down the path he treads, and he has no need to explain. Good for him.

She just nods and moves back to Charlie, asking him about his A levels and his plans for the future, sounding impressed at his university of choice, showing interest in his degree and generally charming him.

I catch Luke's eye, and he gives me a quick wink. It is nice, feeling that he is on my side, feeling that I have an ally. This reunion has gone much better than I could ever have expected, but perhaps old habits die hard, and I still feel a slight prickle of guardedness around her now that the first flush of emotion has passed.

Charlie is just starting to tell his grandmother about some of our adventures on the way here when I hear the back door slam. My dad may have mellowed with age, but he still can't close a door without a bang, it seems.

He walks into the room, and I stand up to greet him. My heart both swells and dips when I see him in the doorway, looking at me as though I'm a hallucination. It would not be overestimating things to say that he is a shadow of his former self. He was always a big man – not fat, but solid, from a combination of manual labour and a love of food and beer. He played rugby in his youth and always looked like he could step onto a pitch at a moment's notice. Now, he seems a quarter of his usual size and looks as though he has shrunk in height by a couple of inches. His skin is drawn and what hair he has left is grey. He is, however, still dressed in what I think of as his uniform – baggy blue thick-gauge cord trousers, a check shirt and a waterproof gilet. It might be cracking the paving stones out there, but my dad never goes anywhere without his waterproof gilet.

He comes over to me and grins, and some of the sparkle returns to his eyes.

'I heard a rumour,' he says eventually, 'that a certain young lady had called in for tea. Come here, love, and give your old dad a hug!'

I do as I am asked, and it is a wondrous thing. He might feel different as he embraces me, but he still smells the same – a combination of Dad and Old Spice. It is the smell of home, in many ways.

'You all right, then?' he says simply. 'You look fantastic. Always knew you'd be a heart-stopper! And who do we have here then?'

He wanders over to Charlie and Luke, listens to the introductions, shakes their hands, gives Betty a pat.

'So, Charlie, fancy a spot of cricket?' he asks, miming a batting gesture. 'There's plenty of light left in the day yet. Or rugby maybe? Luke, you look like a rugby man, am I right? What position did you play?'

'Flanker,' says Luke, nodding, 'very much retired.'

'Well, I still have a ball around somewhere ... or if you're all tired, we could play tomorrow, if you like – after you meet my alpacas. You are all staying, aren't you?'

We have not discussed this, Luke and Charlie and I. I was so focused on simply getting here, on dealing with seeing them again, that we somehow never tackled the issue of what might happen next. Did I expect to just pop in, say hi, here's your grandson, see you in another eighteen years? Will they want me to stay here, in this house? Should I stick with Joy? Would Luke even want to stay, or is this all too real, all too awkward? Maybe he'll find it easier to just go on his way now we're safely deposited ...

'Go on, Jen, say you'll stay, at least for bit?' my dad repeats. I hear his plaintive tone, and see Charlie's hopeful face, and know that there is only one answer to that question.

'Yes, Dad,' I reply, my eyes flickering to Luke, 'we'll stay. At least for a bit.'

Chapter 17

I wake up the next morning at 6 a.m. There is no need for me to, but I guess my body clock has adjusted and these days expects me to be up, dressed and ready for adventure before breakfast. I am in an actual bed, in an actual room, with an actual ceiling and walls. It feels strange – this is the first time I have had such privacy in a while, and I'm not sure I like it quite as much as I thought I would. It is weird, not having Luke and Charlie within shouting distance; not having Betty clambering up to greet me. Even having so much space is slightly disorientating – it's amazing how quickly I have gone full wild.

I slept in my old room, but thankfully it has not been preserved like some creepy Museum of Me and is clearly used by another teenaged girl these days – I presume my niece, Shannon. So weird to say that, and I find that I am actually looking forward to meeting her. Maybe she'll help me reform the Sugababes.

The walls are painted a pretty shade of lilac, and there is a dressing table and mirror in the corner scattered with abandoned tubes of lip gloss, hair clips and the long strands of earphone wires. She's probably been complaining to her mum for ages now about how she's lost them.

The bed is now a small double rather than my old single, and when I poked around in the wardrobe, I found a small selection of teenaged girls' clothes. It is a bit strange, truth be told – like I am in some kind of time-slip movie where I am inhabiting a different version of my own life.

I know that there is no chance of getting back to sleep, so I get up, pad along to the bathroom, do my ablutions and get dressed. As I make my way downstairs, I look out of the landing window and see Joy in all her glory and feel a tug of what I can only describe as homesickness. I wonder what Luke is doing, whether he is up and on his first coffee, if he's doing a crossword or reading a book, if he's gone for a walk with Betty and his binoculars. It might feel odd for him too, being alone again – or, for all I know, it's a blessed relief. He was the one who chose to stay outside, instead of using one of the spare rooms.

I amble into the kitchen on autopilot, as I have done countless times before in my younger life, yawning and searching for sustenance. Frank is also awake and dashing around my ankles looking for love. He follows me into the room, and I get quite a shock when I see that my mother is already there, sitting in her dressing gown at the table, a mug of tea in front of her. Her hair is a mess, which is very unusual, and she looks exhausted.

She glances up, and her eyes widen in surprise, and I see her process of regaining control. Funny how I never noticed any of this when I was a child; never noticed how hard she works at being her.

'Jenny,' she says quietly. 'Join me, I'll get you a … what? I don't actually know what you'd like any more.'

'Coffee please, Mum. White, no sugar.'

She makes my drink, and we both sit down again. Frank disappears off to another room, obviously deciding that we are no fun at all.

The new table is shiny and clear, and I find that I miss the old one, with its scrapes and scratches. It was battle-scarred and looked like it had stories to share.

'Are you OK, Mum?' I ask, gazing at her over the steam. 'You look tired.'

'Glass houses and stones, dear. Couldn't you sleep?'

'I did, actually. I'm just … well, it takes a bit of adjusting, doesn't it?'

'In all sorts of ways, yes. I am so happy to see you, darling, I really am. And to meet Charlie of course. But … it's been a bit of a shock. I know you sent those postcards, but I never knew, you see, if you were really safe. I've had to get on with life – with work, with Richard and his family and their ups and downs, with looking after your dad. But, underneath all of that, I suppose I've always been worried about you. Now you're here, and I can see you are fine, but I can't quite switch it all off …'

I gulp down some coffee, and it burns my throat, and I feel kind of like I deserve it.

'I can imagine that, Mum. And I'm sorry, for all that worry. I know now what it's like to be a parent, and I know I'd be exactly the same if it was Charlie. But I'm here now, and I am indeed fine, and maybe we can make up for lost time.'

She nods firmly, as though trying to convince herself, and pats my hand.

'I am absolutely made up of questions,' she announces, 'but I don't want to come across like the Spanish Inquisition … Where have you been living?'

'Most recently, Norfolk, for a long time actually. At first, London, then Kent. Then I followed work to the east coast. We had a lovely cottage there, where Charlie has lived for most of his life, but it … well, funny story actually, Mum, but it fell into the sea!'

She looks understandably shocked and replies: 'Goodness! That doesn't sound especially funny, Jenny – it could have been a tragedy!'

'I know. But it wasn't. And anyway, that's how we ended up doing this – travelling with Luke. And if we hadn't done that, then we might not have ended up here, so it's all worked out in a way. Who needs a large-screen telly anyway?'

'Oh, I do, sweetheart – my eyes aren't what they were! But I know what you mean. You do seem … happy.'

That, I realise, hasn't always been the case. If by some freak coincidence I'd bumped into my mum a year ago, I'm not so sure she wouldn't have seen through me – used her Mum X-ray superpowers to look beneath my skin and see that I was actually lonely, anxious, wrapped up in fear and regret. I don't think I even knew that myself – it's taken some pretty strange events to understand what was really going on.

'What's up with Dad?' I ask, keen to distract the Spanish Inquisition before she gets her knives out.

'It's his heart,' she replies gravely. 'He was diagnosed a few years ago, and mainly it's managed, with medication and some lifestyle changes. No more full English for breakfast every morning. It was one of the motivations for selling the farm, of course. Hopefully, next month, he'll be going in for a bypass, which we're told will make a huge difference. But for now, he's easily tired, gets out of breath, sometimes gets a bit low . . . it is what it is.'

She shrugs, but I can hear the pain in her voice, the way she is trying to hide her fear. They didn't have me and Richard until they were in their thirties, but Mum first met Dad in primary school. I never thought of it as a great love story – they were just boring old Mum and Dad, who got on my nerves. They weren't exactly Rhett and Scarlett. But now, older and hopefully a thimble-full wiser, I see that it is a love story – to have remained committed to the same person for the whole of your life takes stamina, hard work, tolerance and a truckload of genuine affection. Now it is clear that she thinks that love story might be reaching its final chapter, and she is struggling.

I am awash with so many different emotions, I can't even process them. Sadness, that my superman of a father has been so reduced. Sympathy for my mum, his Lois Lane. And, most toxic of all, I suppose, guilt – guilt that

I haven't been here to help, and the creeping suspicion that maybe I contributed to it all. What if the stress of what they went through with me added to his burden?

'I'm so sorry, Mum,' is all I can manage. It covers all of it, in its own way. And I mean it – I'm sorry for her, for me, for my dad. For the whole mess.

'Seeing you has perked him up,' she replies, waving away what she perhaps perceives as pity. 'Seeing you, meeting Charlie. It will help and at least put a smile on his face . . . So. Luke. What's going on there, then, with your dishy flanker?'

I actually find myself blushing and stammer out: 'Nothing! He's not "my" dishy flanker. He's . . . his own dishy flanker! Nothing going on at all!'

'Yes. I can see that,' she replies, narrowing her eyes at me. 'Totally innocent reaction on your part there, dear. So, this is how he gets through life, is it? Travelling in his motorhome? How does he pay the bills?'

'That's not really any of your business, Mum, is it? He's a good man.'

'I wasn't suggesting anything other!' she snaps back, and I see that we are yet again on a cliff-edge. 'I was merely asking a question. Forgive me for being interested, you tend to have a few questions when your daughter walks through the door after eighteen years of absence!'

I close my eyes, take a deep breath. This isn't what either of us needs. This is how we used to be, and that did not end well. I am not seventeen any more, and I need to stop overreacting to everything she says.

'I know,' I say slowly. 'I'm sorry. But this is hard for me as well, and I'm doing my best. Let's call a truce, shall we? I haven't seen you for so long, I don't want to argue with you.'

She nods, and I see her also try to calm herself.

'I don't want that either,' she replies, 'and I'm sorry too. I don't know, Jenny, maybe we have eighteen years' worth of bickering stored up as well as everything else? I see how Shannon and Rebecca wind each other up, how easily they fall into sniping, and it looks horribly familiar to me. Mothers and daughters, eh? Perhaps it was ever thus.'

She might, of course, be right – but we are both grown women, and should be capable of acting like it if we try our very hardest.

'We'll be OK,' I say, holding her hand on the kitchen table. 'We'll adjust. Do you have anything I can take out to Luke for breakfast? We didn't get the chance to stop off for supplies on the way here.'

This is a complete lie, but its intentions are good – we both need a break, and giving her something to do, something to organise, will restore her balance, make her feel more capable and in control. It will also give me time to well and truly bury some of the snarky one-liners that my seventeen-year-old self still seems to want to throw at her – number one being to ask her not to call the cops on Luke just for not having a job.

It does the trick, and she bustles about making toast and assembling it on the tray with little ramekins of jam and marmalade. I can tell from the jars that it's all homemade, and smile at the thought. The kitchen might be new, but some things haven't changed – she used to spend days on her preserves, hated waste of any kind.

'I made extra,' she says, indicating the laden tray. 'For you as well ... I thought perhaps you'd like to take your breakfast with Luke this morning.'

It is a peace offering, and I accept it as such, smiling and giving her a quick kiss on the cheek.

Frank appears at my heels again as I go to open the back kitchen door, which leads me out to the side of the house. Here, I see other signs of change – a greenhouse and a rainwater butt have appeared. I pause, and wonder what doesn't feel right, and realise that it is the quiet. Farms are noisy places, even in the morning – but now that the milking shed is no more, it is eerily calm out here.

I curse my feet for making so much noise on the gravel, unsure as to whether Luke is even awake yet, and not wanting to disturb him if he isn't.

Frank has no such qualms, of course, and runs straight to Joy's steps. He scratches at the door and woofs, and I hear Betty bark frantically in return. No way anyone is sleeping through this racket.

I balance the tray on one knee, knock gently, and open the door, carefully climbing up the steps.

As I walk in, Luke is emerging from the shower, a white towel tied around his waist, his skin still glistening with water. I gasp and wonder if we should have named the shower Adonis.

'Sorry!' I mutter, looking away, busying myself putting

the tray down on the table. 'Didn't mean to intrude!'

'It's OK,' he says, amusement in his voice. 'Give me a minute.'

I soon discover that having a young springer spaniel in a motorhome is entirely less manageable than having a well-behaved dachshund in a motorhome, and leave the door open so they can go and play. They disappear in a flurry of fur, and I hope Betty doesn't decide that alpacas are her mortal enemy.

Luke emerges from his room in his traditional baggy shorts and T-shirt, fully respectable. The damage has been done though, and I know that I won't forget that particular image for a while.

'I brought you breakfast,' I say, gesturing to the table.

'I see that. Thank you. Will you join me?'

We both settle into our usual spots, and tuck in.

'Wow,' he says, wiping his mouth, 'this jam is something else.'

'Yes. She's something of a jam guru, my mother.'

'How's it going?' he asks, meeting my eyes. 'Are you all right?'

'I think so,' I reply, sighing. 'Maybe it's going as well as it can. It's all so complicated, though, isn't it? So many years away, so much has changed. It's like dipping back into a TV show after decades of not watching it, and wondering why everyone looks older ... I'm sure it's the same for them. I mean, I turned up with a child in tow!'

'Plus a layabout drifter who lives in a motorhome and doesn't even have a job.'

'Yeah. That too. I'm trying to ignore the little digs, because she's older, and because she's gone through a lot, and because ... well, she's probably entitled to them after the way I behaved.'

'From what you've said, you didn't do it alone, Jenny, so give yourself a break. I think it'll all work out. Life is too short for grudges, for family rifts.'

He is, of course, right – and he perhaps knows that better than anyone.

I nod, feeling instantly calmer. I also feel ... relieved. That's a weird word to choose, but it's the right one – I feel relieved to be back here, in this small space, with this man. Relieved to be able to just be myself again, not to have to watch every word, tiptoe over eggshells, look out for minefields in every conversation.

'How are you?' I ask. 'Was it glorious to have your space back to yourself again?'

He frowns, and finishes his corner of toast, and replies: 'Actually, it really wasn't. I kind of missed you guys. You know, the gentle sound of you snoring like a truck, the delicate aroma of Charlie's farts wafting down first thing in the morning, the queue for the Mona Lisa ...'

I flick a crust at his face in response, because I am a very mature human being.

'Do you want to come on a walk with the dogs?' I ask. 'All that jam might make you fat if you don't stay active.'

'Only if you promise not to snore.'

'Only if you promise not to bore me so much I fall asleep ...'

We both laugh, and I feel all of the niggling tensions inside me unravel.

Luke gets his walking boots on, and I retrieve my trainers from Susan, and we set off into yet another beautiful summer's day. It's almost becoming boring now, the way every morning brings sunshine and clear skies with it.

I lead Luke towards the shortcut to the coast. When I say shortcut, I mean death-defying flight of stone steps that lasts for about half a mile. I guess I'm out of practice with it, and by the time we get to the bottom, I am sweating with nerves.

'I used to run up and down those . . .' I say, as we emerge down onto the sand, the dogs already there and running in and out of the waves.

'Not easy,' Luke replies, as he gazes out at the beach, 'but, wow – worth every step!'

The cove near Foxgloves is tiny, a perfect horseshoe of sand enclosed on both sides by cliffs. The sea can get wild, and it's not a place that many tourists ever discover. We have it entirely to ourselves, and I slip off my shoes as we walk. Nothing quite beats the feeling of sand between your toes.

The water is the same vivid blue I remember, the light catching it in shimmering kisses, the waves frothing onto the golden shore. Seabirds fly to and from the cliffsides, and the only sound is their cries, and the gentle hiss of the water creeping towards us.

'The colours are amazing,' he says, sounding awestruck. 'It's like someone painted it – everything is so bright and pure.'

'I know,' I reply, smiling. 'You should come down to see a sunset. I suppose I took it all for granted, growing up here – the countryside was my play park, the beach was my backyard. Summers were long and luscious, and I went totally feral from July onwards. By the time I hit my teens, it all seemed very mundane – looking at it now, I can't quite believe that.'

'Well,' he says, leaning down to pick up an iridescent shell and examining it, 'that's pretty normal for a teenager, isn't it? You're more interested in your social life than birdwatching.'

'Very true. I wanted to be out in the world, away from a place that felt just too small to hold me. I was so sure that some astonishing future was waiting for me. Little did I know that I'd end up working in an office and living in another very small place.'

'That's what you used to do,' he points out, 'not what you do. That's who you were, not who you are – a lot has changed since then. You've travelled the world, been on a rollercoaster, lived on wheels ... and who knows what you might do next?'

I nod, and know that he is right. I have changed. Even though my living quarters have become much smaller, my horizons have become vast.

'What *will* you do next?' he asks, as we walk towards the large boulders that fringe the beach and perch there, watching the dogs play. 'More short-term, I mean, not in an existential way.'

'I just don't know,' I answer honestly. 'I didn't think that far ahead, which, with hindsight, might have been a mistake. Charlie is loving all of this, and my dad ... well, he's not in the best of health, it turns out. Dodgy ticker. So I think I'll stick around for a while. At least to see how things go.'

As I speak the words, I know that it is the right thing to do – I owe it to my family, to Charlie, and entirely possibly myself, to see this through for a little while longer. I will stay, but I realise that I don't want Luke to go. It might be selfish, but I'm just not ready to say goodbye to him.

'Would you consider staying put here for a while?' I ask, looking up at him.

He is staring at the birds on the cliffs and, I suspect, wishing he had his binoculars.

'I think they're kittiwakes,' he says, nodding in the direction of the cliffs, 'and yes. I'll stay for a while. It's beautiful here, and I've never explored this part of Cornwall. I'll stay – you know I have my two-week rule, though. But for at least that long, if you decide to run away again, you'll have a getaway driver.'

I nod and briefly touch his hand with mine. Two weeks is better than nothing. I am grateful, and relieved, and understand exactly what he means. I am a flight risk, even though I don't want to be. I want to spend more time with my parents and brother; I want to reconnect with them, and I want to give Charlie the extended family he needs, as well as some stability. But I also feel the pressure of it closing in on me – the expectations, the needs of others, the responsibility. I am not seventeen any more, and I have no excuses – if I mess this up,

I will be doing so as a grown-up. That alone is already making me feel like running – but I won't. I have too much to lose by leaving, and entirely possibly a huge amount to gain by staying.

'Is it OK to swim here?' Luke asks, gazing wistfully out at the ocean.

'On a day like this, yes, probably, as long as you don't go too far. There are currents, and if the weather is rough, it gets treacherous against the rocks. It's not the kind of place you mess with, or swim in alone. It looks perfect, but you never quite know what's going on beneath the surface.'

'Ah,' he says, smiling, 'an accidental analogy from the writer of the world-renowned Sausage Dog Diaries.'

'Maybe,' I reply, shrugging. I think about the pretty house up all those steps, and my parents, and all of the love that I know is still there between us. But I can't quite separate it yet from all the pain, all the trauma, from all the hurt we have caused each other. I'm going to dive in, but I'm still wary of those riptides.

Chapter 18

Luke moves Joy around to one of the fields at the side of the house, which has the benefit of sea views and sunsets, and the disadvantage of me being able to see her from my bedroom window. He assures me he can live with the stalking risk, and promises to give me a wave every night.

He does exactly that for the next five nights, always at 11 p.m., when he usually lets Betty out for her last trip, and it sends me off to sleep with a smile on my face. Sometimes, that night-time wave is all I see of him in the day. While he has stuck around, he has also been out and about in Joy, exploring the local beauty spots, going to places my dad has recommended, and taking Betty and Frank on road trips.

I see him most mornings, setting off, and always feel slightly wistful – part of me wishing that I could go with him. I am not a prisoner, and of course I could – but I still feel like I should spend more time at Foxgloves right now. I have been gone for so long, and there is so much to catch up on. My mother and I maintain our truce as well as we can, and I spend a lot of hours with my dad, caring for the alpacas and the hens, walking the country lanes at his much slower pace; being introduced to the new owners of the farm. It is a strange combination of the familiar and the novel – an ever-shifting balance between what was and what is.

Charlie settles into the household as though he has always been part of it, exploring the cove and the cliffs, going to the pub with my dad and generally living the vida loca. He is blossoming, this boy of mine – I saw the beginnings of it on our trips with Luke, the way he opened up, the way he spent less time in front of screens and more time in the real world. Now, he has even more people to spend time with, new places to discover, and many embarrassing photos of me as a baby to mock me with. I wonder if he is still upset about only just coming here, whether we have more talking to do before I can fully convey why it has taken so long – but for now, he seems content to accept the good points of his new situation. He has already been accepted with love and ease, in a simple way that is far apart from my relationship with my family as a teenager.

I am currently showing him one of my favourite old haunts – the tiny two-person caravan that has lived hidden in a corner of the back field for as long as I can remember. I'm delighted that it's still there, a bit weed-riddled, a bit rusty, but still parked up, its towbar propped onto bricks. I am telling Charlie how both Richard and I used to use it as our escape hatch when we were teenagers, and he is very keen to restore it to this particular purpose.

I manage to get the door open, and we clamber

inside. We are used to a large motorhome, and although the theory of the caravan is the same, the space inside is much more compact. One living area, with a little hob and a sink, two battered old seats, and a bedroom. It smells musty inside, and dust motes fly up from every surface. I laugh when I see there is still an ashtray there, along with an empty can of Diet Coke and a sun-bleached copy of *Sugar* magazine.

'Were you a secret smoker, Mum?' Charlie says, feigning horror. He sits down on the sofa, and a small shower of grunge clouds out.

'No, that was my friend Lucy. We used to spend hours in here, and I'm sure you could see her ciggie smoke puffing out of the window for miles …'

'It's pretty comfy,' he says, patting the couch, 'just needs a bit of a clean-up.'

'Yeah, I remember it being comfy … it's also possibly the place you were conceived …'

He jumps up and wipes his jeans clean, as though he has been contaminated. The look of disgust on his face is hilarious.

'Only kidding, sweetie,' I say, patting him on the cheek and giggling. 'That didn't happen until later. Worth it to see your reaction, though. You do know you weren't delivered by a stork, don't you?'

'Of course I know that! I was left under a magical toadstool by a fairy princess …'

Ah yes, I think. That's exactly how I remember it, too.

'Why do you think they don't use it?' he asks, looking around the room. 'Your mum and dad?'

'Not sure, love. They never used it to travel in; I think it was initially my dad's. A bit like a man cave, you know? But then Richard started hanging out here with his friends, and then I did, and I suppose we just colonised it. Maybe after I left they just didn't need it any more ...'

It's also possible, I know, that they simply couldn't face it once I'd gone. Maybe it became a taboo, a reminder they couldn't deal with.

Charlie is opening all of the little windows, having to give some of them a shove, and letting in some much-needed air. 'Do you think they'd mind if I cleaned it up a bit?' he says, using the edge of his T-shirt to wipe dust off the kitchen surface. 'Maybe Ethan and Shannon would like to hang out here as well. We could create a whole new generation of caravan dwellers ...'

He has met his cousins twice, and they are already apparently best friends.

'You'd have to ask them,' I say non-committally. 'Though my mum definitely thinks the sun shines out of your bum, so the answer will probably be yes.'

'She's a woman of impeccable taste,' he replies, grinning. 'I will ask. I might even see if I can sleep out here one night ... I'm really enjoying it here, Mum, being with them all. But every now and then I just miss the motorhome, you know? Well, actually not just the motorhome, but living in it with you and Luke. It was fun, wasn't it?'

'Yeah. Loads. But Luke's still around, you could go and stay there for a night too, I'm sure.'

'I know. I will. But it's not quite the same now, is it? He does his thing, we do ours. Not moaning, Mum, honest – I'm enjoying it here.'

'It's OK,' I reply, nodding. 'I know what you mean. Maybe we should have a word, tell him we've drawn a piece of paper out of a hat, and it says "Luke Henderson must spend more time with his friends" on it?'

'Ha! Yeah. We should. Or at least "Luke Henderson should only go out for a morning or an afternoon in Joy, and then come back to Foxgloves and play rugby with Charlie". Or maybe cricket. Actually, I'm rubbish at both, but it seems to make Granddad happy, doesn't it?'

It really does, I think, as we climb back out of the caravan and make our way to the house. My dad can't do much more than throw the various balls these days, but it does seem to give him vast amounts of pleasure to see his grandkids chasing after them.

Today is a Saturday, and it's the first time since we arrived that Richard is driving over. Shannon and Ethan are coming with him, and Charlie is excited to finally meet his uncle. Me, less so. I still remember him as my big brother, the one who was usually mocking me, jump-scaring me, or making it clear I was cramping his style.

As we emerge onto the gravel driveway, I see that they are, in fact, already here – at least I presume the silver Audi parked up belongs to him. We go into the house, and Richard strolls into the hallway holding a can of lager. He pauses, staring at me, and I see that he has a touch of grey in the sides of his hair; a tiny beer belly poking over his jeans. He looks me up and down and laughs, before saying: 'Bloody hell! When did you turn into a grown-up, sis?'

'I don't know,' I reply, giving him a cautious hug, worried in case he drops a worm down my top or kidney punches me, 'maybe about the same time as you turned into an old man?'

He pulls my hair so hard it hurts and goes over to shake Charlie's hand.

'So this is the famous Charlie,' he says, and I am childishly amused to see that Charlie is taller than him.

'Ethan and Shannon tell me you're the most exciting person they've ever met.'

'What?' says Charlie, looking confused. 'Me?'

'Yeah. You went to three theme parks in one day, didn't you?'

'Oh, right! Well, in that case, yes – I am indeed the man! Nice to meet you ... erm, Uncle Richard?'

'Just call him Dick,' I shout over. 'Everyone else does!'

'Nobody calls me Dick,' my brother asserts, correctly.

'Maybe – but they all think you're one!' I reply, then run away into the kitchen. Ah, it's good to be home sometimes.

I find my mother busy at work peeling vegetables, and she hands me the chopping knife and board as soon as I walk in. I resist the urge to pull a face and say, 'I'll do it later!' which I really want to do – something about seeing Richard again has unleashed my inner teenaged brat.

Instead, I start to slice carrots and am immediately told that I'm doing them too thickly. I grimace and bite my tongue.

'Charlie was wondering if he could use the old caravan,' I say as we work. 'He'd like to clean it up a bit, set up some kind of den for him and the other two. I was surprised you hadn't passed it on to them anyway.'

Her peeling becomes slightly more vigorous, and she eventually responds: 'Yes. Well. If you want the truth, Jennifer ...' She is using my naughty name, and I am not at all sure that I do want the truth. As she's holding a knife, I think I'd actually prefer a pleasant fib. 'We shut it up after you left. Not immediately, but after a while. For the first year ... well, we thought you'd be home soon. We kept expecting you to turn up. Your father was forever trying to get the police to look for you as a missing person, and we even considered hiring a private detective at one point. Your father was convinced that something terrible had happened, that you simply wouldn't leave us like this. He never could quite believe that you'd gone of your own free will, no matter what you said that night.'

I remain silent and concentrate on the carrots. This is obviously hard for my mum to talk about, and hard for me to hear.

'He used to go and sit in there, in the caravan. He'd sit there for hours, on his own, just to be in the same space as you. Did it for months. And then your postcard arrived – the one you sent from London. A couple of sentences, wasn't it? "Mum and Dad – just letting you know I'm still alive and I'm OK." You probably thought you were being sensitive, putting us out of our misery ... but the day that arrived, I found him inside the caravan, crying. You know your dad. He was always a big man, a proud man – but he was just sitting there slumped over the table, sobbing. He said he realised when that card arrived that you were gone because you didn't want to be with us any more, that you were going to stay away forever. That it was our fault. That we'd driven you to it, and he'd never forgive himself.'

It is a simple description, but I can see it vividly – and it almost breaks me. My poor dad. My poor mum. I feel like such a selfish idiot.

'Mum, I—'

'No,' she says firmly, interrupting me. 'I need to say something, and now is as good a time as any, so please don't stop me. You know I always think more clearly when I'm cooking.'

I nod, and stop chopping carrots for the time being. My eyes are blurred with tears and it would be folly to continue. Nobody wants to find a fingertip in their veg.

'I want to say that, in some ways, he was right, Jenny. I've thought about it all incessantly over the years, as you can probably imagine. I've gone over and over it, looked it at from every possible angle – trying to convince myself that we'd done the right thing, that it was all down to you, that we were blameless. I desperately wanted to believe that, but I found that, eventually, I couldn't – I couldn't even fool myself any longer.

'We never gave Rob a chance, which I regret. We

never gave you a chance, which I regret even more – we should have had more faith in you. Should have trusted you. Should have believed that eventually you'd make the right choices. That the right choices might not look exactly like we wanted, but to accept that. Instead, we tried to force you to agree with us. We bullied you, and we coerced you. I can't believe we actually used to lock you in your bedroom, or that we . . . that we called the bloody police! If I'd seen someone else doing that to their child, I'd have called it abuse . . . what on earth were we thinking?'

My mother never swears – she doesn't really need to, she can convey most negative emotions through tone of voice alone. The fact that she has just reflects how messed up she feels right now, how hard this is for her.

I try to speak, to comfort her, but yet again she stops me, holding up her hand and shaking it.

'No, let me finish! We did the wrong things, but for the right reasons – we were worried for you. We saw you letting your whole future slip away – we thought you were going to end up losing everything, and you were only a baby, our baby, our little girl, and we did what we thought we had to do to protect you. And by trying to protect you, we forced you away, into a situation where we couldn't keep you safe at all. We did it all wrong – but we only did it because we loved you, and we didn't think you were old enough to be in such a serious relationship, not with . . .'

She flounders here, and I can see her trying to find an

alternative for what she wants to say, for the words that she is trying to hold back.

'With someone like Rob?' I complete for her.

She looks away from me, as though she can't bring herself to meet my eyes, and nods.

'It's OK,' I say, reaching out to touch her shoulder. 'You were right. It was a disaster. I wasn't ready to leave home, and I certainly wasn't ready to have a child ... He left us, Mum. He left us living on our own in an awful bedsit in an awful building in an awful part of London. We had no money, we had no support, we had nothing – it was brutal. Charlie doesn't even know a lot of this, because what's the point? I wanted to come home so much, so desperately – I was terrified. But I was too proud, too stubborn. Plus, I was sure you wouldn't want me back – you hated Rob so much, and I felt sure you wouldn't accept his baby either.

'I look back now, and I can still remember how angry I felt, Mum, the night I left. How trapped. And, yes, you did handle it badly – I'm not going to lie about that. Everything you did seemed to drive me further away from you and closer to him. Calling the police was the final straw. I know you never thought Rob was good enough for me, and I put that down to you both being snobs.'

'There might have been an element of that,' she admits, sniffling delicately, 'if I'm totally honest ... and it upsets me so much to imagine you thinking we didn't want you, didn't want Charlie. Of course we did.'

'I believe you now, Mum – but at that stage you'd

given me no reason to think that was true. When your parents accuse the father of your child of abduction and involve the law, it doesn't feel reassuring – part of me was even worried that you'd want me home, but not want the baby, and I couldn't accept that. We came as a package deal. Plus, there was that one time I called you ...'

I haven't even told Luke about this. It's such a painful memory that I think I've tried to block it out. But the night I found out that Rob had gone, when I realised that I was truly alone, facing an uncertain future with a baby in tow, I was devastated. We had no money, no security, nothing.

For the first time, I reached out to my parents. I knew I needed help, and I had nowhere else to turn. I remember it so vividly now, even though I've tried to forget all about: standing in a phone box, rain lashing down outside, the door open so I could keep one hand on Charlie's pushchair.

Waiting, trembling with anxiety, while the phone rang out, still unsure about whether I was doing the right thing or not. When she did answer, I couldn't explain, I couldn't tell her – all I managed was to murmur a 'hello, Mum'.

The first words out of her mouth were the ones that effectively sealed the deal for me.

'Jennifer,' she said, after a long pause, 'I'm glad to hear from you. Are you all right? Are you still ... with *him?*'

The vitriol she spoke those last few words with is

hard to describe. It was like she put all her anger, all her regret, into them – and at that moment, I couldn't bear it. I couldn't bear one more person letting me down.

I'd hung up, walked briskly away in the rain, letting the drops wash away my tears. I felt like she'd never accept me again, never mind Charlie.

My mother closes her eyes when I mention this. Of course, she had no idea what was happening in my life, how lost I felt, how much I needed support not rejection. But I now realise that I had no idea what was going on in her life either.

'Yes,' she says finally, her voice sad and low. 'The phone call. Well, all I can do is say I regretted it the minute you hung up. I tried to call back, but it just rang out. I don't know why I reacted like that ... I suppose, with the benefit of hindsight, that I was shocked, then angry at what you'd put us through, and then I blamed it all on Rob. If it was all his fault, it was easier to deal with – it meant it wasn't ours.'

'I understand that now, Mum, I really do. But back then ... well, it was a bad time for me, and I thought I'd made a mistake in contacting you. I thought it was all over – that Charlie was part of Rob, and you'd never get over that.'

'Oh darling – we're not monsters, of course we would have accepted you both! But ... I confess, I do see why you would think that. We had never given you any reason to trust us, had we? We must have seemed like such ogres, such nightmarish authority figures – I can assure you, though, that in private we were absolute jellyfish, just so worried about you and scared for your future. We just felt we needed to keep up a firm front.'

I laugh and reply: 'I get that, Mum – I've done the same myself, countless times. Look, I'm just trying to say that I understand your side of it better now. I was younger than Charlie is back then, and I still have to remind him to brush his teeth! I know you reacted like you did because you loved me. Then, I just couldn't see that – all I could see was that I loved Rob with all my heart, and that being with him was the only thing that made me happy, and that if you wanted to get in the way of that – if you wanted him to go to jail! – then you couldn't possibly care if I was happy or not. It was a mess, and we both helped make it – but it's in the past.'

She wipes her hands on a tea towel and scrapes the peelings into the waste bin. Every movement is measured and precise, and she is showing no signs of her previous distress, apart from a slight flare to her nostrils.

'You're right,' she says, transferring my shoddily cut carrots into a pan. 'It's the past. And I'm sorry to be such an emotional wreck about it. That helps nobody.'

I sigh, and can't help but smile. Her idea of an emotional wreck is most people's idea of calm, cool and collected.

'Why don't you go outside for a bit? I have dinner under control. Too many cooks and all that.'

I nod and leave her to it. It is clear she is feeling exposed and vulnerable and doesn't especially want to be seen like that. I actually feel strangely better, as though we have finally started being honest with each other.

I follow the noise around to the side field and see that not only has Luke returned with Joy, but that he is playing an enthusiastic game of almost-cricket with my dad, Richard and the kids. Dad is bowling – making a very small, shambling run-up before he unleashes an overarm – and Luke is batting.

He wallops the ball, and it flies high into the sky, a deep red orb soaring through the blue. Luke starts running, and the others all scream and yell and give each other instructions on how to catch him out. The others gallop over to hover beneath the now descending ball, and in the end they collide and knock each other out of the way. The ball thuds to the grass, and everyone stops play to take a laughter break. Betty and Frank come to join in the fun, dive-bombing the group, everyone tangling up in a rolling ruck of arms and legs and tails.

It is a perfect little tableau, and it makes me giggle. Sunshine, silliness and smiles. I am surrounded by family – and I realise that I include Luke in that – and I am home. Home for the first time in so long. It is not straightforward, there are still murky waters to be navigated, but at least I am sailing in the right direction for once.

Nobody seems to be bothered with playing any more once they are horizontal, and my dad waves and says he's going inside for a nap.

Luke walks over to me, wiping sweat from his brow. He is grinning broadly, and his T-shirt is sticking to his back, and he seems very happy. I guess I must look the same, as he tilts his head to one side and says: 'You look like you're in an exceptionally good mood. What happened?'

'Oh, nothing really,' I reply, picking a stray strand of grass off his shoulder. 'Just enjoying the view, I suppose. Maybe I'm having a near-life experience ... Where did you get to today? And will you join us for dinner?'

'I drove over to Cape Cornwall and tried to count how many different shades of blue I could see in the ocean. I failed, but I did see some basking sharks off the coast and swim in a big rock pool, and walk through some fantastic hay meadows. Ended up in St Just, foraging for pasties. And yes ... to dinner, I mean. As long as it's OK with your parents.'

I confirm that it is and disappear off for a shower and very possibly a small nap myself. I haven't been sleeping especially well since we arrived, which I suspect is due to a combination of factors all crash-landing at once. Too many things to think about, too many things to feel, too many decisions crowding for space in my mind. That and the fact that my room seems too big now. Maybe I'll have to move into the caravan if I end up staying here permanently ...

Even as the word 'permanently' scampers across my mind, I feel my muscles clench and my stomach knot. I know that it is the right thing to do, I know it is – I just don't feel it as yet. Eventually, I am sure, the rightness of it will travel from my head all the way down to my heart.

Charlie will be heading to uni at the end of September, but between now and then he can have this stability, this base, this big family that he has always craved. He will always have a home, always have people around him, always have somewhere safe and happy to come back to during his vacations. He will have a place to call his own. It will be good for him, in both the short and long term.

My parents need me too, I know. They are ageing, and my dad has his heart op coming up, and I have already missed too much. I want to be here to spend time with him, and also to help my mum. She would never admit it, but I know she's struggling. We will have to work hard at staying patient with each other, but I am sure it can be done. We both seem filled with regret at things said and done in the past, and I believe we can work through it – we can be in each other's lives again.

That tableau I enjoyed so much outside doesn't need to be a one-off. I can stay here, and find work nearby, and rebuild, I tell myself. I won't feel trapped, I will feel content – I will feel useful. The road trip, the blog, even my friendship with Luke, maybe that was all just a precursor – maybe that was just what it took to get me back here. To get me home. To the place where, I really hope, I will actually find my joy.

I repeat these things to myself as I get ready for dinner, drying my hair and putting on a freshly washed sundress and even stealing a little of Shannon's discarded lip gloss. I still only have the choice between flip-flops and trainers, but I can live with that.

By the time I make my way downstairs again, everyone is mooching around in the big dining room, chatting and drinking. It is a grand room, with high ceilings and ornate plasterwork, a huge sweeping picture window framing the coastal views. When I was growing up, we called it the Museum – because we rarely used it, and when we did, it was for formal occasions, and we had to be very careful not to knock over a vase or kick a chair leg or scuff the old oak parquet.

It still looks like the Museum as I walk in, with its framed oil paintings on plain painted walls and its velvet curtains, but the rules have clearly been loosened. The three teenagers are sitting on the floor, playing cards, and Betty and Frank are curled up together on the deep burgundy chaise longue. Richard doesn't even have any shoes on, which makes me feel better about the flip-flops.

My mum has, of course, changed for dinner – because while she might be less demanding about other people's standards these days, hers remain rigidly high. Her hair is a shining silver bob, and her make-up is subtle, and I can smell her Chanel No. 5 from across the room. Dad is pouring drinks from the cabinet, and Luke is chatting to him, waiting to pass around glasses. He sees me come into the room and flashes me a smile. He has swapped out his usual rock-related tops for a navy blue polo shirt, which, by his standards, is pretty much a tuxedo.

I walk over to them, say hi to my dad.

'What's your poison, love?' he asks, gesturing at the cabinet. I swear to God some of the drinks in there are exactly the same bottles I used to pinch measures from as a teenager, sneakily refilling them with water. 'You used to be partial to an illicit vodka, I seem to recall …'

I find myself blushing, embarrassed even as a totally grown-up woman that my dad had sussed me out all those years ago. Maybe I wasn't as sneaky as I thought.

'We knew what you were up to,' he adds, grinning, 'Richard had done the same, of course. When we realised, we started watering it down ourselves, in advance of you pinching it.'

'So, all those times I thought I was being wild and rebellious and drunk on vodka, I was actually just drunk on tap water?'

'Yep – we're not so dumb as we look! What about now? I think you're old enough for the hard stuff …'

'Anything at all, Dad,' I say, realising at the look of glee that crosses his face that I may have made a mistake.

'Go on,' he says, waving his hands at us, 'off you scoot, you two. I'll bring it over when it's done.'

'You look nice,' Luke says, as we make our way towards the table.

My mother glances at us, and I wonder if we are breaching some of her etiquette – in fact, I am amazed she hasn't put out name cards.

'So do you,' I reply, raising my eyebrows at him in what I hope is an amusingly saucy fashion. 'You scrub up well.'

'Yeah,' he says, shrugging. 'I've been told I'm pretty hot for an old man.'

I see my dad lurching towards us holding a glass of bright green liquid decorated with a swizzle stick and a jazzy little umbrella on a cocktail stick.

'My own invention,' he declares, placing it down in front of me. 'Gin, crème de menthe, a few secret ingredients ... enjoy!'

I thank him and wait until he's gone to tell Luke he made a solid choice by sticking with a glass of red.

Before long, Mum ushers everyone towards the table and gets the youngsters to help her bring the food through. It is quite the feast – roast chicken, thickly sliced gammon, big bowls of crisp roasted potatoes, salad, heaps of steaming veg, boats of rich gravy. I toy with the idea of claiming to be a vegan these days, but it seems too cruel. I do like a cheap laugh, but now might not be the right time.

'This is a lot grander than I'm used to,' murmurs Luke, as Mum starts to dish up and pass around plates.

'It's not that grand. At least she didn't use the dinner gong.'

'There's an actual dinner gong?'

'Oh yes. To be fair, they picked it up at a jumble sale and used to use it for a laugh, but it makes a hell of a noise!'

Before long, all eight of us are busy eating and talking and drinking, the conversation flowing quite well, everyone seeming to be in a good mood. By the time we reach pudding – homemade raspberry cheesecake and cream from the organic dairy next door – there are more lulls, more pockets of silence as we all sit and quietly contemplate the fact that we have eaten so much that we may require wheelbarrows to ever leave the room.

'So, Luke,' pipes up Richard from his end of the table, 'quite a monster, that motorhome of yours. I saw the antenna – on-board Wi-Fi?'

'Yep, works well,' replies Luke. 'Better than I expected.'

'Have you ever thought about solar panels?' Richard continues.

I am uncertain as to why my brother is so interested, or knows so much about motorhomes, but I do not give that thought a voice. The obvious answer is that I have been away for a very long time, and I really have no idea where his interests lie.

They chat about it for a while, my dad pitching in to ask a few questions, my mum taking a polite interest as she delicately sips her small glass of wine, until Richard asks: 'So, big rig like that, Luke, must have set you back a bit – got to be what, £200K, £300K?'

There is a pause, and my mother uses her very best headteacher voice as she says: 'That is not appropriate conversation for the dinner table, Richard!'

He pulls a face, and it makes me smile – he is forty years old, but that tone of voice can still stop him dead in his tracks.

'It is a really great motorhome,' says Charlie, undeterred. 'And Mum's been writing all about our travels in it. She has a blog called the Sausage Dog Diaries.'

I cringe a little inside but keep my face neutral, steeling myself for the digs that I fear will inevitably come next.

'A blog?' repeats Richard, smirking as he puts down

his beer. 'Bit of a come-down from that award-winning novel you always told us you were going to write, isn't it, sis?'

I sense Luke tense slightly next to me, and he responds: 'Actually, it's great. Very popular. She has ... how many followers now, Charlie?'

Charlie whips out his phone, briefly consults, then looks up in surprise. 'Just over 5,000,' he announces.

Richard frowns and looks over at the screen. 'What are her socials like?' he asks, getting out his own phone. Shannon and Ethan join in, and before long, all four of them are comparing platforms and totting up figures.

'Those are pretty good numbers ...' says Richard, looking up at me with interest. 'You could probably monetise this, you know? One of my clients is a motorhome dealership, and they're always looking for new sponsorship opportunities.'

I grimace – I can't think of anything worse. I have kept my distance from the technical side of all of this and would actually be happier not knowing any of the figures involved. The only way it works is if I pretend I am just writing for myself.

'You'd have to talk to my manager about that,' I reply, nodding towards Charlie. 'I'm just the creative genius ...'

'We need to post some new content, Mum,' Charlie says, after studying his phone some more. 'Have you got a few stocked up and ready to go? We went to so many places last week, there must be more.'

I nod. There is. But it is raising questions that I have

so far avoided – like how do I continue with the Sausage Dog Diaries if I stay here? How do I hit the road and find my joy if I'm not hitting the road at all? These are issues I am not ready to address yet, and I am relieved when my mum firmly tells everybody off and informs them that there is no place for phones at her dinner table.

The evening rambles on for a couple more hours and finishes off with a cut-throat game of Monopoly that Luke wins by a mile. It's the first time I've seen him display a ruthless streak, and it does amuse me to see Richard annihilated by a last throw of the dice that sees him land on Luke's hotel-laden Mayfair.

The teenagers have taken over the attic room for the night, and they are the first to make their excuses and leave, after they've helped my mum clear the table and load the dishwasher. She was always very insistent on us doing our fair share of the chores, and I'm glad to see that she's not gone soft in her old age.

My parents leave next, my dad tired but happy, and then Luke takes Betty off for her night-time business before turning in himself.

Richard and I are left alone in the dining room, and the atmosphere is suddenly less convivial. We were never close, truth be told, and from everything I've seen since I've returned, I think it's unlikely we will suddenly become confidants.

'So,' he says, making the most of Mum's absence to put his feet up on one of the upholstered dining chairs, 'what's it like to be back? To be the prodigal daughter?'

'Hmmm,' I say, checking that she's definitely gone before I also put my feet up, 'from what I remember of that story, the prodigal son's brother wasn't exactly pleased to see him ...'

'Well, can you blame him?' he asks. 'He was the one who stayed, slaving away in the fields, while the youngblood went off partying and having fun. Then the slacker comes home and gets given a coat of many colours!'

'I think you're mixing up your Bible stories ... and I can promise you, Richard, that I have not been off partying and having fun. And anyway – don't you live in Falmouth?'

It is petty and irrelevant, I know that – but I feel attacked, and I have had a few too many of Dad's bright-green cocktails.

'Falmouth is just over an hour away, Jenny. With you, we had no idea where you were. You don't know what it was like, after you left. None of it was easy.'

I close my eyes, and nod. He is right, I know, but I am not overly keen on getting into it.

'Fair enough, Richard. But I was only seventeen, and you also don't know what it was like *before* I left, because you were off at uni in Glasgow. I didn't feel like I had any choice. It might sound stupid now, but I really didn't.'

He pats his jeans pocket, and I can tell that he is pondering sneaking outside for a cigarette. He swills down the last of his beer and looks across the table at me: 'I can imagine, a bit. I know what they were like, even with me – why do you think I went all the way to Glasgow when I could have studied anywhere?'

'But it wasn't the same for you!' I splutter, suddenly struck by the unfairness of it all. 'They never told you where you could go, when you had to be in, who you could see . . . and I'm pretty sure they never tried to get Rebecca arrested just because she didn't suit their idea of the perfect girlfriend!'

'Easy tiger – I'm not comparing it directly. And, yeah, they were definitely more on it with you – but it was there for me as well. All those times it seemed like I was doing whatever I wanted, it was because I'd told them I was seeing Rebecca, and they liked her so that was fine. Truth be told – or not, because I'd never want her or my kids to hear this – but I'm not sure I was ever even in love with her; it was more what they wanted than me, and I just went along with it. Plus, I used her as an alibi – half the time I was out with my mates, or going to barn parties, or otherwise misbehaving. I basically decided that it was easier to lie to them than to confront them.'

I ponder this and try to really remember that time in our lives. Richard had always been portrayed as the perfect son, with the perfect partner. It is disconcerting to picture him secretly disobeying them for all of that time.

'I suppose,' I say after a few moments, 'that you always had the farm thing as well, much more than me.'

The 'farm thing', as I call it, was an ongoing source of mild disagreement for a few years in the run-up to Richard going to uni. Dad wanted him to go to agricultural college, to take over the ropes – Richard never did. He stood his ground on that one, but I wonder now what toll it took.

'Yep,' he says, nodding. 'They let me go, obviously. They knew my heart wasn't in it and eventually they accepted that – but I still felt it, you know, that underlying sense of disappointment? The feeling that I'd let them down, somehow been selfish? They never said it, but, well ... as you know, our mother is the absolute mistress of expressing her disapproval in a million tiny ways. She is the emotional papercut assassin.'

This is an interesting twist for me – it is something I had never really understood about Richard. He always seemed straightforward, simple, secure in his role as Number One Son. But then again, I was only fourteen when he left for uni, and probably never noticed him unless he was doing something to annoy me. Like I said, we were never close – but maybe I was wrong about us not being close in the future. Maybe we have more in common than I thought.

'So,' he says, grinning. 'What's up with Luke? Are you shagging or what?'

Ah. Maybe we won't be that close, after all.

I stand up, and chuck a napkin at him as I walk past. 'None of your beeswax, numb-nuts,' I say, giving him a poke in the back of the head for emphasis. As I reach the doorway, I pause, look back at him. 'They weren't bad parents, though, were they?' I ask. 'Even though we're moaning like this. They always loved us, and we were really lucky in so many ways.'

'I know, sis,' he replies, looking at me over his shoulder. 'They always did love us. They still do. And nothing makes you more tolerant of your own parents' mistakes than having your own kids, does it?'

'For sure. I'm positive we'll provide them with plenty to moan about themselves when they're older. Anyway ... goodnight, bro. See you tomorrow.'

As I make my way up the wide stairs, hand skimming along the polished mahogany banister, listening to the familiar tick-tock of the old grandfather clock on the landing, I realise that we all have our own realities. We all remember what we want to remember, understand what we want to understand. Families are complicated devils.

I walk along to my room, and take my time getting into my pyjamas, brushing my hair, fluffing up my pillows. I sit on the edge of the bed and know that I am going to struggle with sleep again tonight. I'm very slightly drunk, and my brain is just too busy. If I get under these covers, I will simply lie here for hours, tossing and turning and switching the pillow over to the cool side and back again. I will get up for water, get up to use the loo, get up to check my phone. It will be pointless.

I open up my laptop, try to do some writing. Shannon has a desk set up in here, some random school texts scattered across it. I resist touching any of the exercise books, just in case she's like me and has written terrible, slushy teenaged erotica in them.

I flick through half-written blog posts, not satisfied

with any of them. I was telling the truth when I said to Charlie that I had plenty left to write about – I just don't seem able to write any of it. I haven't finished a single piece since we arrived here. I have been telling myself that it's because I've been busy, that there is too much else going on, that it is understandable that I need a break – but, whatever the reason, writing has stopped being a refuge, stopped being something that comes naturally to me. I hope it comes back, I think sadly, as I shut down the laptop.

I am still restless, still too awake – that awful netherworld where your body is tired but your mind wants to go and run a marathon. In fancy dress.

I walk towards the window, look at a beautiful night sky. It is a dark shade of blue, tinged with violet, scattered with stars. It reminds me of the night I slept outside, the night Luke told me more about his life, about the events that led him to his travels. The events that, ultimately, I suppose, led him to me, and led me to here, to this place that is so laden with both love and lament.

I glance down, see that there is still a light on in Joy. His bedroom, at the back. I wonder what he is doing, if he is struggling to sleep as well. If he is sad or happy or somewhere in between. I find that I don't like this – I don't like not knowing, I don't like this sense of distance that has opened up between us. I don't like the fact that he is still here, but we are not connected in the same way. Sometimes it feels like he's already left.

I put my flip-flops back on and go back down the

stairs. I peek into the dining room, see that Richard is snoring open-mouthed on the chaise longue with Frank draped across his chest, and creep towards the back kitchen door. I sidle out as quietly as I can, and cut through the flower garden to Joy's field. What is it with me and this house and sneaking out to see men?

I knock gently on the door, smile as I hear Betty snuffling around on the other side. She already knows I am here, of course. Clever girl.

I wait for a few moments, telling myself that I will leave if there is no answer, rather than simply let myself in. He might have fallen asleep while he was reading a book. He might be on the phone to someone. He might be . . .

'Jenny,' Luke says, opening the door and staring at me in surprise. 'Are you OK?'

'I'm not entirely sure,' I reply, gazing up at him. 'Would you mind if I came in?'

Chapter 19

I am trying to sneak back into the house the next morning, feeling like a guilty teenager all over again, when my mother collars me.

She has been sitting in the living room with the dog, and a full view of everything going on outside, and I freeze as she says: 'Jenny! Come here, darling!'

I'd just about managed to get one foot on the lower stair, and consider ignoring her and running all the way back up to my room. Old habits, dying hard.

I sigh and trudge in to see her, a sense of defeat hanging over me.

'Please, sit ...' she says, gesturing at the chair. I wonder when she will start shining a bright light in my face.

'It's not what you think, Mum!' I say pre-emptively. 'I just stayed over for the night. Nothing ... inappropriate happened!'

Frank hears my tone and ambles over to shove his head under my hands.

My mum raises her eyebrows into a delicate arch, and sips her tea.

'You're a grown woman, Jenny,' she replies, looking marginally amused. 'Although I'm not sure a grown woman would spend quite as much time in pink flip-flops as you do.'

I glance down at my feet, and silently curse them.

'I have limited supplies,' I say, defending myself, even though I wish I didn't feel the need to. 'Most of our belongings went over the cliff, and these were cheap.'

'Well, you'll need to borrow something of mine then, or go shopping, because the BBC informs me that the weather is due to break later today. Rain, rain and yet more rain.'

She takes her glasses off the top of her head and points to a small tablet on the table next to her. Imagining my mum using an iPad is quite the stretch.

'I've been reading your blog,' she announces. 'The Sausage Dog Diaries! I have to say I very much enjoyed them. It was strange, I won't lie, but, in a way, I feel as though I know you a bit better now. This version of you, not the one I last saw. You seem to have had a very happy time recently. How is it going, finding your joy?'

She can't quite keep the tinge of sarcasm out of her voice as she says the last sentence, but that is fair. I have mocked the phrase myself plenty of times, even though I genuinely believe in the truth of it.

'It's been a lot of fun,' I reply, gazing through the window, knowing that the physical Joy is just around the corner. 'But that's all it was – it was never meant to last. When Luke first offered to take us on his travels with him, we thought it would be for a week, maybe two. I was testing it out – seeing if it was something that would work for me. It's lasted longer than I expected, and it's been good for me, good for Charlie ... but I think it's time to draw a line under it now.'

'Oh, I see,' she says, staring at me intently. 'And why is that?'

We are on delicate ground here, and I know that my mother is proud, independent, would never want to be seen as someone who needed anybody's help.

'Well, if it's OK with you, I wondered if we could stay here? Charlie is loving it, and I think he needs a proper home.'

'And what about you, dear? What do you need?'

'I need a home too,' I say firmly. 'As you say, I'm a grown woman. I can't be traipsing around the country forever. I need to settle down, get a job, get back to real life.'

She nods, and gazes beyond my shoulder. I hear my father heading to the kitchen, swearing about 'yet another bowl of bloody oatmeal' as he goes.

'I've often wondered if real life isn't a touch overrated, Jenny, but I know what you mean. And, of course, you are more than welcome. This will always be your home, yours and Charlie's, for as long as you want it. Maybe you could start the Springer Spaniel Diaries instead, once Luke has moved on?'

I smile and nod, and give Frank a stroke.

When Luke moves on ... such simple words, but such a complicated concept.

I tell my mum I need to have a shower, say good morning to my dad, and make my way upstairs.

I go about my business on autopilot, then sit down with my laptop. I manage to finish a few blog posts and send them over to Charlie. I am not feeling especially joyous right now, but I hope they will do the trick. A night in Joy has definitely helped unlock my muse.

I lie down on the bed, spreading out like a giant starfish, and stare at the ceiling. I needed to get away last night. I needed to be out of this house, to have some distance between the people inside it, people I love but who bring such complex emotions with them as part of the package. I was feeling claustrophobic, despite the size of the building.

Luke understood that. He let me in, made me tea, quietly strummed his guitar while we chatted. We talked of nothing and everything – about the birds he'd seen, about what it was like growing up on a farm, about his own childhood, about our favourite types of ice cream, about music, about dogs. It was gentle, and easy, and kind.

When I started to make murmurs about leaving, he'd said simply: 'Why don't you stay? You seem like you need a rest.'

Part of me wanted to just crawl into his bed with him, to spend the night in his arms. I wasn't even yearning for anything more than that – I just wanted to be close to him, for us to give each other comfort. We have both been alone for a long time, and I think perhaps he needed that too.

Luckily, he was far more sensible than me, seeing around corners and predicting – correctly – that as we have foresworn any more 'moments', such intimacy would be a mistake. He made up my old bed for me, and shouted goodnight from his, and I had the best night's sleep I've had since we arrived here, despite my dad's cocktails.

He was still asleep when I left, so I took Betty out for her morning doings and put her back in with him when I crept away. Now I am here, lying on this big bed in what used to be my room, already missing him. I haven't discussed it with him, the future – the fact that I will be staying here. The fact that he will be moving on alone yet again. It makes me too sad to imagine, to visualise him on the road with only Betty for company, seeing the sunsets and sunrises and all the beautiful things without anybody to share them with.

I remind myself that he lived like this for years before he met us. That we were always only an unexpected add-on; that he might have enjoyed having us around for a while, but that he certainly doesn't need us. I am overestimating my own importance in his life, I suspect – and he will be fine without us. Perhaps we will stay in touch, send emails or old-fashioned postcards, become fond but distant friends. Or perhaps he will simply drive away, with Joy, with Betty, and we will never hear from him again. This has only been a very brief interlude in my life – less than a month. It has been vivid, and memorable, and important – but it was only ever ephemeral.

Besides, I think, kicking off my flip-flops, I need to buy new shoes. I need to help my parents. I need to be a grown-up again, for them and for Charlie.

As soon as I think about my son, he magically appears. He makes a cursory knock and then shambles in, still wearing last night's clothes. I have raised a sloven.

'I was just thinking about you!' I say, as he collapses down on the bed next to me. 'And you materialised – I think I may have developed supernatural powers . . .'

'Probably picked them up at all those stone circles,' he says, stretching. He is so long, his limbs are drooping over the edge of the bed, and he yawns so widely, I fear his face might crack.

'I wanted to talk to you anyway,' I say, reaching out to push his curls away from his face. He slaps my hand away, as is only fair.

'Oh yeah? About what? I got the blog posts by the way. I'll sort that today. I think Richard might be onto something, you know, with the sponsorship and stuff? Maybe you could make your millions and never have to do another boring job or have a row with insurance people ever again . . .'

I bite my lip as he says this, upset that he was even aware of my feelings on those issues. I don't know why – he is eighteen. He is entitled to know that his mother is not in fact superhuman – but I don't like the fact that my anxieties have bled into his own life.

'Maybe. That's something else to discuss, I suppose. But I was talking to my mum this morning, and I've been thinking about it a lot, and I've decided we should stay here. I know you're loving it, being with your grandparents and your cousins. I know you've always wanted a bigger family, and now you have it. It'll be good for us both, a fresh start. Mum's really happy too, and there's plenty of room for us here.'

He is uncharacteristically silent, and his normally figdgety boy-man body is entirely still.

'Are you pleased?' I ask, sensing his tension. 'I thought you'd be pleased ...'

'Did you?' he mutters back. 'Didn't it occur to you to possibly ask how I felt about it before you made any decisions on my behalf? Did it occur to you to ask if I wanted to live here, not just assume I'd agree with anything you suggested?'

'Charlie, I'm sorry, son, but making decisions on your behalf is kind of part of my job description! You need a home, love. You need somewhere to feel safe, somewhere to come back to when you're away at uni. I know it's not the world's most exciting place, but I genuinely think it'll be good for you!'

He stands up and looms over me. I sit upright, perched on the edge of the bed, and frown at what I see. His fists are clenched, and his face is rigid with anger.

'Mum, I have my own mind, you know, and I'm perfectly capable of using it. I've really loved being here – meeting my family, getting to know everyone. But I never imagined it being permanent ...'

'Well, what did you imagine?'

'Oh, right, now you ask?' he spits. 'Well, I've been thinking too. I've been looking to my own future, and I'm not sure it's exactly the one you have mapped out for me.'

'What do you mean?' I say, standing up to face him.

Teenagers are nothing if not unpredictable, and of course I have argued with my son before – but this has totally wrong-footed me.

'I mean that this road trip has changed me as well. It's made me think a bit more about what happens next. I'm not sure I want to go to uni this year – in fact, I've already spoken to the Admissions people about deferring.'

'What?' I splutter, taken aback. 'Why? You haven't even got your results yet! Why do you want to defer? You can't imagine we'll just stay on the road for all that time, can you?'

'What if I did? Would that be so bad? And anyway – no. That's not what I thought. That's what I thought you might do, but not me. I've been talking to Dad a lot, you know, through this trip?'

I nod, feeling fingers of dread slip around my heart. He has, yes – they have Facetimed more recently than the rest of his life put together. Something about our road trip has opened up some common ground that wasn't there before, given them a shared link to explore, to communicate through. I have been telling myself that that is a good thing, no matter how ambiguous my own feelings are about Rob – he remains Charlie's father, and it is positive for him to be close to him.

'Well, he's invited me to go and live with him for a bit.'

'In Paris?' I say, sounding as shocked as I feel.

'As that's where he lives, then yes! He said we could do a bit of a road trip of our own as well, go around the country, and he's got friends in Spain and Italy we could visit ...'

Oh, I think, feeling my stomach curdle, I bet he has. Rob has never laid down more than half a root in his life. He is by nature restless, always searching for his next adventure, his next thrill, his next experience. The next thing that might actually make him happy. He's done this for as long as I've known him, no matter what the collateral damage – which was, in fact, me. Me and his own child.

Life was hard when he left, but we survived it – I survived it, and gave Charlie what he needed. Gave him love and stability and did all the boring things, like make him eat his vegetables and wash his pants and go to parents' nights at school. I made him do his homework, and drove him to his mates' houses, and dealt with the hormonal moodiness, and took him to univeristy open days. I kept him safe, kept him secure – I protected him. And now Rob thinks he can just waltz into his life, without having done any of that, and take him away? Derail his life, his plans? Suck him into his own ageing-hippy world?

Rob always had a tentative relationship with reality and, back in his twenties at least, a far more committed relationship with booze, with recreational drugs, and with partying. Nothing I have seen of his world since then convinces me that that has changed.

No, I think, I cannot let this happen. This is not fair. This is dangerous, and it is my job not to allow my son to blunder into anything dangerous, no matter how much he wants to.

'Charlie, no!' I shout, interrupting him mid-flow. I hold my hands up and say, firmly: 'No – that is not what is going to happen here! I won't let you do that. You are going to stay here, with me, until September. Then you are going off to London to start your degree. Your dad might seem like a lot of fun, and maybe you can visit him sometimes, but there is no way you're spending a year with him. This is not up for discussion, OK?'

He screws up his face and glares at me. We have not argued for so long that I had almost forgotten how violent these spats can be.

'Not up for discussion?' he repeats slowly. 'I can't actually believe what I'm hearing, Mum! I don't know if you've forgotten this tiny fact, but I'm eighteen, not eight! I don't even need to be discussing it with you at all!'

'Yes you do!' I reply snappily. 'You might be eighteen, but I have your passport, and you don't have any money, and you're just not going to Paris, OK? This is the end of it!'

He looks at me with what I can only describe as disgust, and I wonder how we got here so quickly – from lying on the bed together chatting to being sunk into this pit of aggression.

'You know what, Mum,' he says, striding off towards the landing, 'you are a complete cow sometimes. I don't think our house fell off a cliff at all – I think it was so sick of you and your bullshit that it jumped!'

And with that he exits, leaving me only with the echo of a slamming door.

Chapter 20

I decide that we both need time to cool off. I have learned from experience that there is no point chasing him down the hallways, trying to talk to him. He is not in the mood to listen, and, to be entirely honest, neither am I. I know he spoke in the heat of the moment, I know he doesn't really hate me, but they still sting, the things he said.

He needs space and so do I. I stay in my room for a while, licking my wounds, until Richard pops his head around the corner.

'You OK, sis?' he asks, frowning at the sight of me curled up in a soggy ball on the bed. 'Charlie asked if he could go over to Rebecca's, spend the day with the kids. I asked him if it was OK with you, and he said, direct quote, "She's not the boss of me." I didn't want to argue with that one, but thought I'd just check if it was all right with you before I dropped them off . . .'

I sit up, rub my swollen eyes, and reply: 'That's fine, Richard. Probably a good idea. We . . . um, we had a row.'

'Yeah,' he says, sidling further into the room. He gazes around, at what he probably now thinks of as his daughter's space, and then focuses on me. 'I gathered.

These things happen. It's really weird seeing you in here again. Mum says you're thinking of sticking around?'

'I am, yes,' I say firmly, 'me and Charlie. You've dealt with all of this on your own for too long.'

'All of this?' he echoes.

'Yes. Dad's health, I mean. He's going in to hospital, isn't he? Mum will need some help when he comes out. It's my turn.'

Richard sits down on the small chair by the dressing table, idly picks up a lip gloss and stares at it as though he's never seen such a thing in his life before.

'OK. If that's what you want. But ... look, I don't want to sound like a prick ...'

'Stop talking, then,' I snipe, childishly. 'Sorry.'

'That's all right. It was a good line. But what I wanted to say was that we'll be fine, you know. We've done OK without you. It was tough for all kinds of reasons, but the sky never fell in. Dad's op is a big deal, but it's also routine, and he's pretty fit otherwise. Mum was planning to hire a nurse for the first few weeks, and set up a bedroom downstairs for him, and he should be up and about before long anyway, better than new. She's got it all under control.'

Of course she has, I think – she always has. Maybe I've been deluding myself imagining that she needs me, that I'll be any help at all. Right now, I feel like neither use nor ornament.

'Right. OK, thanks. I still think we'll stay, though. But ... again, thanks. And it's fine for Charlie to go with you.'

Richard nods and makes his farewells, and I decide that I need to be busy.

I do some of the things I have been putting off, such as checking in with the insurance people, who tell me they have agreed a part-payment due to the complexity of the situation. I accept their offer, because I don't have any energy left to fight about it, and some is better than none. I spend a long time looking at employment websites that cover the local area, and find that I'd have a lot more success if I was searching for a seasonal job in a cafe or a gift shop than I would anything substantial and permanent. The hidden side of the countryside idyll. There are a few possibles though, including a data-processing role in Penzance, and one at a car-hire company near the airport that needs an admin manager. Neither of these exactly sets my heart on fire, but now I come to think of it, having your heart set on fire actually sounds really uncomfortable and potentially dangerous. I bookmark them, planning to apply for them when I feel less discombobulated by life.

By lunchtime, I see that my mum's predictions look as though they will be correct, and the sky is darkening with clouds. It is strange, seeing anything but azure blue up there, and it reminds me that life here isn't all picnics and sea swimming and cricket on the grass.

I check my bank balance, borrow Mum's ancient but well cared for Toyota, and drive to a small retail park that lies off the A roads between us and the nearest town. There I purchase such exciting items as wellington boots, a kagoul and a pink umbrella patterned with frogs. I invest in a new rain jacket for Charlie, as well as some walking boots – if I imagine he is staying, if I plan for it, then it will happen. I simply can't allow myself to think otherwise. I am sure that he will calm down, that he will start to understand, that we can have a measured and reasoned conversation about it, rather than a screaming match. He is young, and he has been through a lot – but he is still Charlie.

I stay out for the rest of the day, because I am unused to retail therapy, and am starting to see its appeal. It is the ultimate distraction from the stuff that really matters. I even call in at a garden centre and buy some lupins – maybe Mum will donate a corner of her flower garden to me and I can have my own little flower patch. Maybe I will feel more settled, more solid, once I start to see things bloom around me.

When I get back to Foxgloves, I see that Joy is gone and remember that Luke was planning to visit the area around St Ives today. I go back inside, put away all my new treasures, and leave the potted flowers outside. The rain has started to trickle down, and they will enjoy a nice drink until I can get them somewhere more permanent.

I forage for food for us all, and join Mum and Dad watching a documentary about the birds of the Caribbean, each of us sitting with a tray on our lap eating plates of beans on toast. I feel like we are all in a nursing home.

I try not to think about Charlie, and what stage he is at in his come-down. I also resist the urge to call Rob and give him a verbal boot up the arse – it would be satisfying, but also, I know, extremely counterproductive.

It will help nobody if Charlie starts to see me purely as the enemy. I am starting to realise that shades of our conversation this morning – if it really qualifies as a conversation – had distinct echoes of some of the rows I had with my own parents, and that didn't exactly end well. It seems unlikely that Charlie will run off with a drummer and get pregnant, but I still know I need to be careful not to push him away. To back him into a corner. Of course, I see all of this approximately ten hours after the fact, which is less helpful than having seen it that morning, when I was threatening to keep his passport and essentially hold him hostage. I am determined not to repeat the mistakes of the past, no matter how hard it feels. I don't want him to go, but I understand that keeping someone against their will can end much worse.

By 8 p.m., there is still no sign of him, and the first real slivers of worry start to creep in. I try not to let my parents see it, and instead attempt to contact him on the phone. No answer. I send a quick message, but with the same result. Eventually, I resort to going through Mum's address book by the phone in the hallway, and find Rebecca's number.

I go back upstairs as I dial and, when she answers, realise how strange this is.

'Hi, Rebecca,' I say quietly. 'It's Jenny. I know I haven't spoken to you for almost two decades, but . . . well, I was wondering if Charlie is still with you?'

She laughs, and replies: 'Jenny! Indeed, long time, no speak! I'm sorry I haven't popped over yet – maybe we could go out for a drink sometime?'

'Yes, that would be lovely, thanks ... but, Charlie?'

'Well, he was here, hanging out with the beasts – but he left maybe a couple of hours ago? The rain had started, and he borrowed Ethan's bike. I offered him a lift, but he said no. Is everything all right?'

'Fine,' I reply breezily. 'He's probably just gone off to explore. I'm sure he'll turn up any minute now.'

'I'm sure you're right,' she says, but I hear a reflection of my own fear in her voice. Being the parent of a teen-ager is not for the faint-hearted. 'Let me know when he lands, all right?'

I assure her I will, and hang up. Two hours. On a bike, in the rain, in a place he still doesn't really know very well. My brain immediately starts to conjure up a smorgasbord of disaster, and I make myself sit still, take some deep breaths. Going full psycho will not help me, or Charlie.

I stand up, go to the window and pull the curtains to one side. The sky is bruised grey, the rain coming down heavy and thick, and the frantic sway of the oak trees tells me the wind is up as well. I see that Luke is back, put on my new boots and kagoul and rush down the stairs. I can hear my parents in the living room, bickering about who last used the remote controls and where they are now, and make it past them without being spotted.

I let myself out, apologising to Frank as I shut him

in the house, and run over to Joy. I bang on the door, hard, and Luke opens up. He is obviously just in from the rain himself, his hair soaked and the shoulders of his T-shirt drenched. He has a towel around his neck, and smiles when he sees me.

'Come in!' he says brightly. 'I was just putting the kettle on …'

Betty appears at his ankles, but I am too upset to engage as I step inside.

'Charlie's been gone for the whole day,' I say, too tense to sit down. 'He left Rebecca's house on a bike about two hours ago, and at most it's twenty minutes away. And we had a row. And I was angry, and he was angry, and I've spent all day doing stupid things and assuming I'd see him later and sort it out … and now I don't know where he is! Can you help me? I don't want to upset Mum, or especially Dad …'

He takes hold of my shoulders, and gently pushes me down onto the sofa before taking his spot opposite me. 'Yes, of course I can help. But you need to calm down a bit first. You might have had a row, but that doesn't mean anything bad's happened. What was it about?'

'Umm … a lot of things, I think. But on the surface him wanting to go and live with his dad for a year instead of going to uni.'

'He wants to defer, and go next year? Or is it a complete change of heart?'

'Next year, he said. But—'

'But you're freaking out worrying that everything that can possibly go wrong will go wrong, and that his whole life will be ruined? And that maybe, even just a teeny bit, he might end up preferring his dad to you?'

I stare at him with a mix of annoyance and frustration. I want to say rude words to him, but essentially he's right. The 'preferring his dad to you' bit hadn't even really registered before now, and it is only a tiny bit of it, but it is there.

'All of that, probably. And I didn't react well – I reacted like my parents, all those years ago. I know how well that ended …'

'Let's not get ahead of ourselves, eh? He's probably just sulking somewhere, trying to punish you. Is there anywhere you think he'd go?'

I chew my lip, and give it some thought, and eventually have a small light-bulb moment.

'The caravan!' I say, immediately standing up again. 'He's been cleaning it out, and that'd be the perfect place to sulk … I did it myself many times …'

I jump down all of the steps, and run as fast as I can towards the caravan's hidden spot in the back field. The trees and bushes are thick back here, dripping with accumulated rain, and I stand on tiptoe to try to see through one of the windows. I clamber up the steps, and crank the door open. Inside, I see some signs of teenaged habitation – a discarded packet of crisps, a half-empty bottle of water, yet more abandoned earphones.

I shout Charlie's name, even though I can tell the place is empty. A quick check in the tiny bedroom confirms it. By this time, Luke has caught up with me, and I look at him in despair as he comes in from the rain.

'He's not here!' I semi-wail. 'And he's not answering his phone, and ... oh God, what if he's hurt, Luke? What if something's happened to him?'

'We're not there yet,' he replies firmly. 'And you mentioned his phone. Can you track it?'

Of course, I think, fumbling my own phone out of the zip-up pocket on the front of my coat. Why didn't I think of that? Probably because I'm a complete bloody idiot, I decide, as I scoot through the log-ins and security checks and finally reach a screen that shows me a map. Charlie only agreed to sign up to it when he once left his phone in the amusement arcade and I had to buy him a new one. I was furious at the time, told him off for being irresponsible, but now I'm so pleased he was.

I stare at the screen, and the little flashing beacon that tells me where the phone is – or, I notice, where its last known location was. What does that mean?

I look it up, and see that it sometimes means the battery is dead. Even better. My son is missing, out in the wilds, with no way of getting help.

'Where does it say he is?' asks Luke, peering in to see. 'It looks like it's somewhere near here ...'

He enlarges the map, and I see that he is right. I visualise the real-life version of what I'm looking at, and that's when I realise that what I'd been feeling up until now was nothing. Now I am experiencing true panic.

'This says it's by the gate down to the coastal path,' I murmur. 'The shortcut that leads down to the cove ...'

I meet Luke's eyes, and I can tell from his expression that I don't need to say anything more. He clearly perfectly recalls what I said about it when we walked there: that it could be dangerous, that there are currents, that in harsh weather the rocks are treacherous. That you shouldn't ever swim there alone …

'Don't jump to conclusions,' he says, before I can speak. 'Now, we're going to go back to Joy, and get those head torches of ours, and we're going to go and check, OK? Charlie isn't an idiot, you have to remind yourself of that.'

I nod, but I'm not sure I believe him. I mean, look at his genetics. He's related to me after all.

I follow Luke back to the motorhome while he grabs his coat, the head torches and a large handheld one. Betty escapes from the van as he tries to close the door, running ahead of us, her small brown form soon disappearing into the murky evening sky.

'She'll be fine,' he says as we set off, me worriedly calling Betty's name. 'I've walked down to the cove with her every morning, she knows the way, and she might even help us.'

I nod, and we set off towards the path.

I want to run, but Luke lays a calming hand on my arm, shakes his head, and adds: 'It won't do Charlie any good if you get hurt, will it?'

He is right, of course, but it is so hard to slow my pace – especially when we reach the gate, and I see an unfamiliar bike propped up against it. Ethan's bike, I have to presume.

'Charlie!' I yell, as loud as I can. 'Charlie, where are you!'

My words are swept away on the wind, but I continue to shout his name as we start to descend. The steps are slippery with rain, and the only real light is the bobbing glow from our torches. There is no beautiful sunset tonight; it is as though the sun has never even graced the sky. The mood of the whole place has been transformed; what once felt dazzling now feels dangerous.

We make slow progress, Luke in front of me, occasionally holding out a steadying hand to help me down. I am frantic with worry, cold with dread – I can hear the waves crashing in against the rocks, see the white spray of the breakers illuminating the darkness. I imagine my boy down there, in trouble, needing me, and I scream his name once more.

We are about halfway down when we hear Betty barking. We don't see her until we are much closer, and she runs up to woof at us. She circles and heads back down, and Luke speeds up his pace, leaving me behind as he clambers down the steps two at a time. I follow as fast as I can, cursing my own limitations.

'He's here!' Luke shouts, and I slip and slide the last few steps to find them.

Charlie is sprawled on the ground, one leg splayed out in front of him. His hair is soaking, plastered to his pale skin, and his clothes are drenched. Betty is licking his face, and I breathe a sigh of relief when I see that he is stroking her.

He is stroking the dog. He is moving. He is alive.

We crouch down next to him, and Luke shines the

torch over his body. I grasp Charlie's face in my hands, kissing his cheeks, pushing his wet curls back, telling him repeatedly that he is OK, that we are here, that everything is going to be all right.

'It's OK, Mum,' he murmurs, his eyes huge and wet, 'I'm OK. Busted my ankle on the way down. I tried to crawl back up, but I didn't get very far – too wet, and I kept slipping. My phone's dead. I'm sorry ...'

I kiss him some more, see him grimace as Luke examines his injured ankle, and reply: 'No need to be sorry, love. I'm just glad you're OK. I thought—'

'Thought I'd gone swimming, on my own, at night, in the place you told me to never do that?'

'Um ... yes ...'

'No. I came home, saw you all watching telly. Just couldn't hack it, so I went to the caravan for a bit, and then I just ... I just wanted to come and sit down here, and watch the waves for a bit, you know? It was daft. I'm sorry. I feel so stupid now.'

'No, no ... it's OK. It's fine. Accidents happen – it doesn't make you stupid. Nobody expects them, it's why they're called accidents ... don't worry. We'll get you home, you'll be all right ...'

I stand up, and Luke joins me.

'He's right – my medical definition would be busted ankle as well. I don't think it's broken, but I'm not sure. Pretty swollen already, and he's cold and wet and probably in shock. We should get him to hospital. Should I call an ambulance?'

'No,' I say, feeling something approaching calm settle

back over me. 'They'll take too long around here, and they'd never get down the steps anyway. Charlie, do you think you can make it back up, if we help you?'

'Yeah, I think so . . .' he says, and I can tell he's trying to be brave.

Between us, we manage to get Charlie upright. Luke whips off his own coat and fits it around Charlie's much slighter form before we tell him to wrap his arms around our shoulders. He can barely put weight on the bad ankle, and it is awkward and difficult, but we manage to pick our way slowly back up the steps. There is some swearing, from all three of us, and a few breath-taking moments where we almost lose our footing, but eventually we make it. We leave the sound of the waves behind us, and emerge onto the clearing by the gate.

We are all exhausted by this point, but there is more to come – one look at his leg tells me he definitely needs X-rays. I help Charlie hop towards my mum's car, and Luke goes to put Betty back in the motorhome. She's earned an extra-special treat tomorrow, I think.

The keys are where I left them, tucked inside the glovebox – a car thief would have to walk miles in this neighbourhood – and I start up the engine. Charlie is in the back seat, covered up in the travel blanket that my mum always keeps in the boot. Bless her organisational skills.

Luke climbs into the passenger seat, and part of me wants to tell him he doesn't need to come with us, that he should go back to Joy and warm up – but I am glad to have him by my side, and simply smile my thanks.

I pause before we set off and send my mum a text: *Everything is fine, but Charlie has twisted his ankle. Taking him to A&E to get a quick X-ray, be back soon.*

I drive off in a flurry of gravel before she can see it, come outside and get involved. They don't need to see Charlie like this; they don't need to know how close this came to being even worse – they don't need the stress, especially in my dad's condition.

In the end, the 'be back soon' part of that message turned out to be on the optimistic side. The nearest A&E is miles away anyway, and the sudden bad weather has caused a deluge of accidents. It is hours before Charlie is seen, once the triage nurse has established that he isn't about to die. Such strange places, hospitals – that weird combination of adrenaline and boredom.

When Charlie is finally wheeled through for this X-ray, I glance over at Luke, see his perfectly bland face, and the way his clenched fists give the lie to his surface calm. I realise that I have been so caught up in the moment, caught up in my own worries, in Charlie's needs, in the drama, that I have not even considered how this must feel for him. He is a man who has spent more than his fair share of time in a hospital with a child, and this must be brutal for him.

I reach across the chairs, take hold of one of those hands, unclench one of those fists, and look directly at him. His eyes skitter away, like he doesn't want to face me.

'Luke,' I say insistently, 'it's OK now. Thank you, for everything – but we're all right for now. Why don't you go and take a walk, or get a coffee, or even get a taxi back to Foxgloves? I know this must be hard.'

He nods, an abrupt jerking of his chin, and stands up. 'OK. I could do with a breather. I'm not leaving, though – I'll be around, at the end of the phone. Just call me when you need me. Promise?'

'I promise,' I reply and watch him walk away towards the exit. There are flashing lights outside, and as the automatic doors hiss open, I see an ambulance pull up. Luke is lit up in their flashing strobe, and I see him duck his head and walk quickly past. He doesn't even have a coat, I realise – Charlie still has it.

Just then my name is called, and I dash over to the nurse who is scanning the busy room looking for me.

'He's fine,' she says, taking one look at my face and obviously realising I need the reassurance. 'It's just a sprain. He's just getting it bandaged and taking some painkillers. It should heal up quickly enough – rest for a while, ice if needed, and keep it raised if possible. As soon as he can put pressure on it more easily, though, get him up and active. OK?'

I nod and follow her through to a cubicle. Charlie is lying on the bed, his now-dressed foot propped up on a pillow. He still looks exhausted, but his colour is back, and he manages a smile when he sees me.

'Sorry, Mum!' he says as I perch on the edge of the bed next to him. 'I didn't mean to cause all this trouble! I was just . . . I was angry, and I needed some time on my own.'

'Believe me, love, I understand. I did as well – I

just went shopping and spent a load of money instead of spraining my ankle, though. Maybe they're both self-destructive in their own way. And I'm sorry about our argument. I hate it when we argue, Charlie.'

'Me too,' he says, sounding relieved – I have said the first sorry about the row, which in teenaged world means that he is now allowed to give a little as well. 'It always feels like the world isn't quite spinning right when we fall out, doesn't it? I'm sorry I was such a prick about it all, but you did ambush me.'

'I know,' I say, nodding decisively, 'and I've also had a whole day to think about it. I did ambush you, and I did make decisions on your behalf, and I should have talked to you first. I know exactly how it feels to be on the receiving end of that. But I also made that decision because I think it's the best one for you. I've been making decisions without talking to you for a long time, and I hope I've not made any huge mistakes so far. I just want to—'

'Protect me?' he asks, raising his eyebrows.

'Yeah. That. And kill you sometimes, obviously.'

'Fair enough. But look, Mum – I don't want to fight again, but I do want you to listen to me. I'm really not a kid any more. And yes, before you say anything – I know the events of the last few hours don't exactly win me any maturity prizes, but, as you said yourself, accidents happen. I haven't decided to defer uni on a whim. I've thought about it a lot.'

I bite my tongue and resist all my urges to interrupt

him. He is asking to be treated like an adult, and accusing him of behaving like a child will not help.

'Have you?' I reply quietly. 'I had no idea.'

'I was going to talk to you about it earlier, but life kind of got complicated, didn't it? I was considering it already, and the road trip just kind of made my mind up ... I don't want to go to uni just yet. I want to see more of the world, and more of my dad, and more of ... you know, stuff!'

I am taken aback that I had no idea he had been considering deferring – but I know I shouldn't be. Teenagers are made up of ninety per cent secrets. We are close, but I have never told him everything about me – so why should I expect the same in return?

'OK. I'm just worried about it, that's all. Worried that maybe you'll get distracted. That you'll forget all your plans. That—'

'That I'll turn into my dad?' He laughs when he sees the shocked expression on my face, and adds: 'What? How thick do you think I am? Did you assume I thought Dad was this perfect role model? I'm not blind, Mum. I know who raised me. I know who was always there for me, who did all the hard stuff. You've never said it, but I'm capable of figuring things out on my own – I know he left us in the lurch, and I know he's far from perfect. But I also know that I want to do this – I want to travel, I want to see more of the world, and yes, I want to get to know my dad better. I'm not going to suddenly drop out and join a commune and spend the rest of my life smoking dope in the foothills of the Himalayas or anything. I've worked hard for my A levels, and I want to go to uni, want to have a career, all of that – just not right now. You have to trust me, and trust yourself – you didn't raise an idiot!'

I feel humbled, and touched, and surprised, and in awe of this amazing human being. But I also still feel troubled – unconvinced. Scared, I suppose, to let him go.

'OK, thank you for that,' I reply, holding his hand. 'And I understand, I really do. And we can definitely talk about it more—'

'Mum,' he says, squeezing my fingers. 'I know a bit about what happened, between you and your parents – Ethan and Shannon are proper gossips. But do you remember what it felt like, back then, when you were this age and they were trying to control you, when they thought they knew what was best for you?'

'Yes, and I hated it, Charlie … but in some ways they were right! They just wanted to protect me from making a terrible mistake!'

'That terrible mistake being, eventually, me?'

'No – you know that, love! You were the best thing that ever happened to me, and I can't even imagine a life without you in it. But it wasn't easy, Charlie – and I so want your life to be easy!'

'But, Mum,' he says, grinning, 'where's the fun in that? Anyway … I'm pretty sure they could use this bed for someone else. Let's go home.'

'Home?' I repeat, as I help him up. 'Which one? An empty space in Norfolk, Foxgloves, Joy, the caravan …

I'm not quite sure where home even is any more.'

'Don't be dense, Mum,' he says, as he leans on my shoulder and hops, 'surely you've figured it out by now? Home is wherever you're happy.'

Chapter 21

Charlie's ankle heals annoyingly well, and annoyingly quickly, and the day when he is leaving comes around annoyingly soon.

I had to accept his reasoning, take a giant leap of faith and do what he asked of me – trust him. I also had to have a long conversation with Rob on the phone, where I expected to have to lay down ground rules, herd his lunacy and generally be the boss. I was pleasantly surprised to find that he was not only reasonable, but equally as committed to Charlie coming back for uni next year, even promising to ensure that he does so tattoo- and piercing-free.

I suppose, I admitted grudgingly to myself, that I am not the only one who can change – and the Rob of now is not the Rob I used to know. He will never be Mr 9–5, or someone you'd call in a crisis, but after we talk, I have to accept that he is also not going to drag my son – our son – into a whirlpool of psychedelia and instability. He even paid for Charlie's flight, which shocked me. I should have been more open to the fact that this could be a good idea, that Rob could be a positive part of Charlie's life and not just a messy part. I am still not one hundred per cent sold on it all, but I am more settled with it than I was.

And now, we are all here, taking up most of the space in the lobby of the tiny local airport, where Charlie will catch a flight to Paris via London. Rob will meet him at the other end, and the next set of his adventures will begin – getting to know both another country and his own father.

Richard is here, bringing his children and Mum and Dad with him in his car, and Luke and I travelled in my mum's. Now, his bags are checked in, and we are all standing in a huddle, saying our goodbyes. Charlie works his way around the group, variously exchanging handshakes, cuddles and fist-bumps, saving a huge man-hug for Luke – one of those where they are hugging but also slapping each other's backs, so it looks marginally like a fight.

It is finally my turn, and I hold on to him so tightly, I hear him gasp. I wrap my arms around him, and squeeze, and I really don't ever want to let go. He might be grown up, but he will always be my baby.

'Mum,' he says, peeling my arms away from his waist. 'Unless you're coming too, you need to let me go . . .'

'I don't want to let you go!'

'I know – but it's time. Love you loads, and I promise I'll stay in touch, OK?'

I reluctantly back away, but reach up to place my hands on his cheeks. I am crying, and he looks like he might cry, and the whole thing is pretty horrible. I haven't been away from Charlie for more than four nights since he was born, and that was when he was on a school trip. This is hard, for so many reasons – but having seen his excitement, shared in his plans, I know it is the right thing to do. For him, at least – the jury's still out on me.

'Promise me one more thing, though,' I say, staring at him intently, as though I am storing up memories of his face to last me while he is gone. 'Don't do anything too sensible, OK?'

He laughs and promises he won't – then, with a jaunty wave and a final round of goodbyes, he is gone. I stand and watch him disappear off towards the security checks and feel like all the life has been sucked out of me. I am an empty-nester who doesn't even feel like she has a nest. Or an empty-nester who has returned to her own childhood nest, at least.

'You'll be all right, dear,' my mum says from behind, laying a hand on my shoulder. 'I know it doesn't feel like it now, but you will.'

I turn around, find a smile for her. At least Charlie is leaving with my blessing, I think. At least I know where Charlie is going, and that he will be safe. At least I will be able to speak to him, hear his voice, see his face – which is a lot more than she had.

'You did the right thing,' she adds, a sad smile on her lips. 'Letting him go.'

We both know what she is referring to, and I know that she is correct. I know it was the right thing, but it doesn't feel great yet. I thank her, and we all disperse to the car park.

Luke and I leave just after them, and I am silent as I drive. The weather has been ping-ponging between glorious sun and howling storms, with little transition between them. We are experiencing the classic British 'four seasons in a day' phenomenon.

I navigate the winding roads, and concentrate on what I am doing, and allow myself to feel sad. It is OK to feel sad, I tell myself – and it will pass. My poor, sore heart is like Charlie's ankle, it just needs time to heal. And maybe the application of an ice pack, or a few of Dad's green cocktails.

As we hit the stretch of road that curves alongside Carbis Bay, one of those unexpected patches of sunshine descends. I glance down at the suddenly blue ocean and make a decision.

I drive us in the direction of a picnic spot I know and park up. Luke joins me, and we silently gaze out at the wonders spread below us. A wide crescent of golden sand, lush green banks tumbling towards the shore, and the white-tipped waves racing into land.

'Beautiful,' Luke says. 'Like no place else I've ever been. And I've been to quite a few places.'

'I know,' I say, smiling up at him. 'I took it all for granted when I lived here. I suppose now, I get a second chance to enjoy it all again. I have a job interview next week.'

'Ah. And who is lucky enough to be potentially gaining your skills?'

'A data-processing company. Exciting, isn't it?'

'Well, it might be, who knows? If the last phase of

your life has taught you anything, it's probably to keep an open mind.'

I nod, and tell myself that he is right. It could turn out to be the most thrilling data-processing company to ever grace the earth, and anyway, it's only part-time – I want to keep plenty of hours free to help my parents.

We sit together at the picnic tables, and I idly trace a love heart and initials that someone has carved into the wood. SJ Loves MN apparently. I wonder how old it is, and whether their relationship has stood the test of time.

'He'll be fine, Charlie will,' Luke says, firmly. 'And so will you.'

'Oh, I know we will – it's just still a little raw. It will all be OK, nothing a bit of time can't fix. Thank you. For today. For everything.'

I place my hand over his on the top of the wooden table, and he twines his fingers into mine. I have a sense of what is coming, of what he is about to say, and I know that it is yet another one of those things that is right, but still hurts.

'I think I need to move on, Jenny,' he says gently, his green eyes deep and vivid as we look at each other in the sunshine.

'Right. Where do you think you might go?' I reply simply.

'Not entirely sure longer term, but I think I might start with a visit to see Sally and her family, and my brother. I've neglected those relationships, and this has all been a pretty vivid reminder of how important it is to ... nurture them instead. After that, who knows?'

I nod, glad to have been of some use – even if it's just by setting a perfect example of how not to get on with your family.

'I understand,' I reply. 'I know you've already broken your two-week rule, and I appreciate it. You and Betty need to be off to find your new adventures, wherever they may lie.'

I turn my gaze away, look at the bay, the sea, the nearby dustbin crammed with McDonald's boxes. Anywhere apart from at him. At this man who has meant so much, taught me so much, changed me so much. This man who has become such a big part of my life, and who now needs to leave me.

I will be OK, I repeat silently to myself. I will be OK. This is my new life motto.

'You could always come with us?' he says quietly, and I turn my gaze back to him. I look at that face, the wide mouth, the laughter lines around his eyes. I imagine waking up and seeing it every day, and hate the way it makes me feel. How much I want something that I can't have.

I squeeze his fingers tightly, and try to find a smile. 'I'm sorry,' I say simply. 'But I can't.'

Chapter 22

That evening, when I glance out of my bedroom window and into the drizzling gray rain, I see one of the saddest sights ever – Joy, her rails all tucked in, her windows and skylights all shut, her adaptor cable and wire stretching to the side of the house as she charges up. I catch a glimpse of Luke through the lit-up window, and see him wrapping mugs and hooking cupboards shut. I imagine Betty curled up on the sofa, and his music playing, and all of the activities that go on before Joy embarks on a journey.

They are familiar routines to me now, usually both comforting and exciting – routines that signify the next leg of our travels. Routines that are the boring prelude to drawing a scrunched-up piece of paper out of a baseball cap, planning a route, finding a random stone circle to visit or a fairy glen to swim in. Routines that mean, yay, we're hitting the road again, and who knows where that will take us? Now, the road will only be taking us in different directions. Now, it means saying goodbye.

Tonight, as I watch him go about his business, those routines signal none of the fun stuff – at least not for me. It is the end of an era – though, admittedly, a very short era. I am grateful for having had it, that brief spell of freedom, and also grateful for where it led me – back to my real home, back to my family. To people I love, people I have missed. It has given me the chance to forgive and be forgiven.

Solemnly, I close my curtains against the dying evening light and make my way downstairs for dinner. I offered to cook for my parents, but they said they couldn't face beans on toast yet again and would take their turn tonight.

It has been a day of bittersweet goodbyes, I think, as I walk slowly down the stairs. I have lost both of the men in my life, and that will take some time to settle – but I also have to remember what I have gained. I am back in Foxgloves, which I never thought was possible. I am in my mum and dad's lives, which is a complicated but joyous thing. I can make up for lost time, be the daughter they need, and even rebuild my own life. I can start afresh, older, wiser, more useful. I am only young, still, no matter what Charlie says – and I have a lot of life left to live. I will do at least some of it here, in this beautiful place I can now call home again.

I have been giving myself pep talks like this all afternoon, and as I make my way towards the shiny new kitchen, I am halfway to believing it. Maybe a third of the way, at least.

I amble through the hallway, Frank coming to greet me. He snuffles at my hand, but seems subdued, and I wonder if he understands, on some basic doggie level, that Betty is leaving us, or if I'm just projecting my own feelings onto a big, slobbery fur-baby. Both are possible.

I find my parents sitting at the dining table, mugs of tea in front of them. There is no food apparent, which momentarily disappoints me, until I realise that I actually have very little appetite at all.

'Jennifer,' my mother says seriously, 'please join us.'

I immediately wonder what I have done wrong, and glance at my dad to try to find a clue – my mother is always inscrutable. She is absolutely impossible to scrute, whatever that may be.

'Don't worry, love,' he supplies, gesturing to the chair across from them, 'it's nothing bad!'

He might say that, but as I take a seat, with both of them facing me, I can't help feeling that it is. I suppose it might at least be good practice for a job interview. I do hope they're not going to ask me where I see myself in ten years' time, because, frankly, I have no idea.

'So, we've been having a chat,' he continues, his arms folded on the table in front of him, 'your mum and me. And we've decided that we're kicking you out.'

'What??' I splutter, not quite believing what I'm hearing. 'What do you mean? Why? What have I done?!'

I am a fraction of a second away from adding 'but it's not fair!' when my mother holds up a placating hand. She has a slight smile on her lips, which, for her, is almost a belly laugh, and she says: 'Now, now, none of that! First of all, we don't actually mean exactly that – if you really want to stay here with us, then we would be delighted to have you. Your father is simply indulging in his flair for the dramatic.'

'Guilty as charged,' he admits, looking sheepish.

'Well, what do you mean then?' I ask, frowning. 'I know I've been gone a long time. I don't blame you if you're still upset, but I thought we were working through it, I thought you were glad I'd come back ...'

'It's nothing like that, silly child,' she replies dismissively. 'Of course we're glad you came back! This has been complicated for all of us, but I never want you to doubt that you walking back into our lives was the best thing that has happened to us for a very long time. We've loved having you here – but we simply don't think you should stay.'

'But I want to stay!' I reply, still beyond confused at what she is trying to explain. 'I want to be here with you two. I want to be part of your lives. I want to help when Dad has his surgery.'

My mum nods briskly and picks up her phone from the table. She finds what she is looking for and holds the screen up to me. I look, and see a photo of a middle-aged woman with curly brown hair and a big smile.

'Umm ... she looks nice? How is that relevant?'

'This is Elaine,' she says, putting the phone down again. 'She's a fully qualified nurse, experienced in the cardio wards in several hospitals, now working privately. She is the person we have already interviewed, already decided we like, and already asked to come and help us after your father's bypass. Don't take this the wrong way, Jenny, but I suspect she'll be more useful.'

It is a lot to take in, and it has been a tough day, and I am tender – it is difficult not to take it the wrong way.

'You're saying that you don't need me here? Don't want me here?'

'You're half right, sweetie,' my dad chips in. 'Of course we want you here – but we don't *need* you here. Those are two very different things, aren't they? I appreciate that you want to stick around and help out your old pops, but it's really not necessary.'

I pause and look at their faces. Their new lines, their new wrinkles, their new strands of grey and silver. But when I look beyond that, I see them as they used to be – just as my parents.

'Look,' I say, laying my hands on the table, 'I hear what you're saying, and I appreciate it, but I think I should stay. I've been away for long enough, and I want to make up for it.'

'Jenny, darling,' my mum replies earnestly, 'that was all so long ago, and it was as much our fault as it was yours – a marvellous team effort by the whole family, in fact! I hope you know that whatever we did, we did for the best of reasons – we were trying to protect you. But we went about it in such a terrible fashion, we really did – we got everything wrong, and we have never regretted anything more. We see now how well you've done, how fabulously you've raised Charlie, and we feel nothing but pride. But you are, and always will be, our baby, and we still only want one thing – for you to be happy. And neither of us thinks that staying here with us is what will make you happy.'

'It will, Mum – I have a job interview and everything! I can be happy here, I know I can, I promise I'll try!'

The two of them look at each other and share a smile.

'We don't want you to have to try,' Dad says, 'we want you to just be happy. And we think you will be, if you go with Luke.'

'If I go with Luke?' I echo, not at all sure of what they are trying to say.

'Yes,' he replies simply. 'Go with Luke. We've seen the way you two are together. I've even read your infamous Sausage Dog Diaries! You should carry on with that life – you should find your joy. You might find some peace here, Jen, but you won't find joy. And we're old now, and wise, and we know that joy doesn't come along often – when it does, you need to grab it with both hands!' He makes a clapping gesture in the air, as though he is catching something, and Frank looks up in interest.

Mum is looking on, tapping her fingers on the table-top, and I can see that she has more to add. I raise my eyebrows at her, and she speaks: 'You know I can be a frightful snob, dear. And I must confess that when I first met Luke, that part of me came to the fore. I didn't like it, but I found myself judging him. But since then ... well, as your father says, we've seen you together. Darling, you light up when he walks into a room. You come alive when he is near. He lifts you up when you are down, and whether you realise it or not, you're so very good together. I may be old and past it, but I can still see when two people are in love.'

I stare at her, dumbfounded. I open my mouth to argue, to tell her that is the stupidest thing I have ever heard. To explain that we are nothing more than friends. Two people whose lives accidentally crossed, two people who have become closer than either of them perhaps expected – but still just friends. Part of me is even resentful at them daring to try to tell me what to do with my life again – we have spent eighteen painful years apart, and maybe I don't feel they have as yet earned the right to tell me they know me well enough to give me advice.

That aside, they have the wrong idea. I want to tell them that they are wrong. Maybe even to convince myself that they are wrong. I want to tell them that, yet again, they have firmly grasped the incorrect end of the stick. I want to deny all of it, and yet … and yet I cannot. I remember all the moments Luke and I have shared; the casual touches of skin against skin that left me yearning for more; the heat that could build from a simple glance; the way he makes me feel safe and calm and excited to be alive all at once. The way he comforts me, confides in me, draws out the very best in me. The way I felt just minutes ago, as I looked out of my window and saw him getting ready to leave.

Could they be right? Could I have been in denial about this? I am not experienced in the ways of love, the ways of partnership – my only real encounter with it left me battered, bruised and cynical. I have spent so long alone, so long convincing myself that I need nobody else, that perhaps I have refused to let myself see the signs that my parents seem so convinced are there.

My mum reaches across the table, takes my hand

in both of hers. Papery skin, delicate bones – but still strong. 'Are you scared?' she asks, leaning across towards me.

I nod dumbly – I am scared. I'm terrified.

'Good,' she says briskly. 'All the best things in life are scary to start off with. Now, as I see it, you've shown incredible courage all through your life. You had the backbone to defy us when you were a girl, to leave behind everything you'd ever known because you thought it was right for you. You've raised a child, all alone, which takes astonishing amounts of spine and bravery. You've built a life for yourself on the foundations of your own abilities. Now, dear, I think you need to find a touch more of that courage – and take a chance on Luke. On the two of you. You will always have a home here. Charlie will always have a home here. And believe me, dear, we plan on sticking around for a good long time yet! You will always be our daughter, and we will always love you – but it's time to live for yourself. Not for us, not for Charlie – but for you.'

She leans back in her chair, and crosses her arms over her chest. She narrows her eyes at me, and shakes her head.

'Jennifer,' she says, nodding towards the door. 'What on earth are you waiting for?'

Chapter 23

Luke has the door open as he works, and I pause just outside it, gazing in, feeling the fine drizzle coat my hair. I see him standing near the kitchen, holding a map and frowning. Planning his next move, I presume. He is wearing the same faded Motorhead T-shirt that he was wearing on the day of the storm; the day I met him. Ages ago, in a different world.

I take a deep breath, note the way my pulse quickens as I look on. The way I feel lighter already now that I am near him; the way I want to reach out to him, the way I am magnetically tugged in his direction. I note all of this, and I know that my parents were right.

This is Luke Henderson. I have not known him for long, but I know enough to understand that I love him. I love him, and I want to be with him, and I want to be brave enough to tell him all of this – no matter what happens next. He might be horrified, he might be repulsed, he might be overjoyed – but I need to at least tell him.

I climb the stairs, and he looks up in surprise. He puts the map down and takes a step towards me. This is the part where we would normally make small talk.

Where we would normally avoid touching each other, avoid having a 'moment'. Where we would normally pretend that this thing between hasn't grown out of all recognition, taken on a life of its own. Where we would normally skim the surface of our friendship, both afraid of what might lie beneath.

I close the distance between us, deciding that this will not be normal. Deciding that this will be a moment – the most important moment we have shared so far.

Before he can speak, I press my body against his and wrap my arms around his shoulders. I let my hands finally touch his close-cropped hair, stroke the side of his face, run my fingertips over his lips. I turn my head up towards his and meet those green eyes. I ignore the question in them and pull him down for a kiss.

It is deep, and it is long, and it is glorious. I have thought of this act so many times, imagined it and blushed at it and reprimanded myself for it – but now it is here, and it is even more than I thought it would be.

His hands tangle into my hair, his hips crush against me as he backs me up against the wall, and we simply lose ourselves in each other. I revel in the feel of his muscled back beneath my hands, in the scent of him, in the way the world around me disappears, and only this kiss exists.

This kiss, and, of course, Betty. She dances around our feet, confused by what we are doing, jumping up and scrabbling against our legs with her little paws. Eventually, we cannot ignore her, and Luke pulls away, laughing. His tanned skin is flush, and his eyes are intense with need, and his voice is deep as he mutters: 'Was that really our first kiss?'

'The first one for real, yes. I'd be lying if I said I hadn't thought about it a lot, though.'

He runs his gaze over my face, reaches out to smooth back my hair, his hands trailing down my shoulders and arms until his hands entwine with mine.

'What made you finally do it?' he asks. 'Not that I'm complaining.'

'Would it be weird if I said my mum and dad told me to?'

'A bit, yes ... but I guess I should thank them ...'

He pauses, and shakes his head, and I see him struggle to regain his composure. I feel exactly the same, and want nothing more than to touch him, to kiss him, to hold him. It is as though all of the need and all of the desire that I've been denying for so long has come calling all at once.

'Why now?' he asks, taking a step back. 'Was this, like ... I don't know, one for the road? A goodbye kiss? Something to remember you by?'

I take his hand in mine again, and stroke the skin of his palms. It is a blessed hand, and I do not want to let it go, ever again.

'No,' I reply firmly. 'At least I hope not. We've danced around this for so long, Luke, for reasons of our own. Perfectly valid reasons. We both have our histories, our bruises, and I think we've both been alone for so long, we've forgotten how else to be. My mum told me I had to be brave, so this is me being brave – I love you, Luke. I don't just like you. I don't just see you as a friend. I don't just enjoy your company. I love you, in every way a woman can love a man. If you hate that idea, if it terrifies you or makes you want to run screaming in the opposite direction, then I understand that – but I also know you deserve to hear it, and I deserve to say it. To at least give us a chance at, well . . .'

'Finding our joy?' he asks, quirking his lips into a half-smile and giving me a look that literally makes my knees weak.

'Yes,' I murmur, 'if that's a proposition that you would be at all interested in . . .'

There is way too long a pause after I say that. I feel exposed, raw, all too aware of what I am risking here. I have done this on impulse – literally run headlong into this confession. What if he doesn't feel the same? What if he does, but his wounds are still too deep? What if he still doesn't think he deserves to be happy, or, even worse, what if he doesn't think that he'll be happy with me? What if he does actually want this to be just 'one for the road'?

Yes, he kissed me back – but that could mean nothing. That could have just been a primal reaction in the heat of the moment. What I feel for Luke has snowballed, changed, evolved – for me, this isn't just about the physical. I am in love with the man, and if he doesn't feel the same, it might break me.

As the seconds tick by, my tension builds, and a sense of dread starts to envelop me. I've been a bloody idiot, I am starting to think.

Then Luke pulls me close, kisses my forehead, wraps me tightly in his arms. I couldn't move even if I had any interest in doing so.

'I love you too, Jenny,' he says, murmuring the words into my ear. 'I've known it for a while, and it scared me. I didn't want to even admit it to myself, and I didn't want to put any pressure on you, especially when you seemed so set on staying here. It's been torture, lying alone out here, knowing you were just up in that room – so close but out of reach. Knowing that we would be so much better together than we are apart . . .'

I lay my head against his chest, and simply let myself breathe. Let myself feel safe, and hopeful, and yes – joyous.

Better together, he said, and that is exactly it. I didn't even know what I was missing until we made each other whole.

Chapter 24

Two months later

It is early October, and the landscape is showing subtle signs of change. In the flower garden, the Michaelmas daisies are holding on to their purples and lilacs, and the gladioli are swaying in graceful stalks of pink and yellow. The foxgloves are fading, but the hedgerows are still bursting with life.

We are enjoying an Indian summer, our days dappled with sunlight. Gentle breezes bear the smell of the ocean, rising up over cliffs that are still scattered with sea campion and scarlet pimpernel.

Luke and I are walking Frank and Betty on the beach, smiling as we watch them chase each other around the sand, a chaotic trail of pawprints in their wake. We hold hands as we stroll, barefoot, and it is still thrilling, still miraculous, to be holding his hand. To be able to live like this. To live so fully.

We are talking to Charlie on the phone, his face filling the screen that I hold up in front of me as we walk. Luke is pointing out seabirds perched on the crags, and I am telling him how his granddad is doing, and Charlie is filling us in on all of his own adventures. He has visited a stone circle called Carnac, continuing our theme, and has already mastered the basics of ordering beer and food in French. He looks relaxed, happy, somehow older – in a good way.

'So,' he says, as we balance on the boulders and slip our feet back into our trainers, 'this is the big day, is it? Are you all prepared?'

'Yup,' I reply, grinning. 'Except we don't even have a baseball cap set up, Charlie!'

'Ha – see what happens when I'm not around? Everything falls to pieces! So what's the plan?'

'There isn't one,' Luke says, before he shouts the dogs over to follow us back up the steps. 'We're just going to wing it!'

I have become much more adept at managing the steps now, almost back to my native abilities as we clamber back up to the house.

I see that my parents are there, waiting for us by the front door. My dad is looking well – his operation was a success, and although he was a terrible patient, his recovery has been surprisingly swift. He is, in fact, as he predicted he would be, better than new. We have been forcing him to take it easy, but it is a joy to see him walking with so much ease, moving back into the upstairs bedroom, throwing cricket balls with glee. It won't be long, he tells us, until he's back batting. He says he also plans to take up power-lifting and train for an Iron Man contest. We hope he is joking, but neither my mother nor I are quite sure.

I hand the phone over to my dad, and the two of them chat to Charlie while Luke and I do a final check on Joy. We are fully charged, fully stocked, and fully ready to go. My mum has supplied us with vast quantities of homemade jam and bread and scones, and my dad has checked over her engine and tyre pressure – not that it was necessary, but it clearly made him feel useful.

Frank looks on mournfully as Luke shoos Betty inside the motorhome, slinking down to his belly, his ears flat.

'Poor thing,' I say, scratching his head. 'You're going to miss Betty, aren't you?'

'We're all going to miss Betty,' my mum says, reaching out to tidy my hair away from my face. 'And we're going to miss you, too. But Christmas isn't far away, and it will be marvellous, darling, to have everyone in one place, won't it?'

Charlie is flying back for Christmas week, and Richard says he'll bring the kids over for dinner, along with Rebecca, and I have to agree – it actually will be marvellous. I am now fully confident in the fact that my parents don't need me to stay – I have kept them under careful surveillance, and spoken to Dad's nurse, and consulted with my brother. They may be in their seventies, but they do have a lot of living left to do, and they are perfectly capable of doing it without me hovering in the background.

'It will, Mum, yes,' I reply. 'And Luke and Charlie will finally get to hear Dad do the dinner gong!'

'Well, he seems to think he's Superman at the

moment, darling, so he may well destroy it with one mighty blow!'

Dad brings the phone over so we can all say a final goodbye to Charlie. We gather around the screen, all taking our turns at waving at him.

'Good luck!' he says, grinning. 'And I'll be keeping an eye out for new Sausage Dog Diary posts, Mum – don't be slacking just because I'm not there in person to nag you, OK?'

I promise that I won't, and I mean it. Richard followed up on his suggestion about the motorhome dealership, and it looks as though I might actually get a sponsorhip. Luke and I have stayed here quite happily until we knew my dad was out of the woods, but we have also been out for many day trips together, and I have most definitely rediscovered the joy of writing. That and a few other things, I think, smiling as I feel his arm slide around my waist.

When it is finally time to leave, my dad engulfs me in a hug, and firmly shakes Luke's hand, imparting some last words of wisdom about how to avoid traffic on the A30.

My mother and I stand for a moment, and simply look at each other. I am now seeing her more for who she actually is, not just a parent. I am seeing her as a woman, a mother, a wife, a friend. A flawed but deeply caring human. A source of strength to us all, an inspiration, a maker of supreme cakes, the loser of remote controls, a grower of flowers, a keeper of memories. She is all these things and more.

I wonder what she sees when she looks at me and hope she sees the same as I do – a woman who is finally ready to live.

'Mum,' I say quietly, reaching out to hold her hand. 'Thank you. For everything.'

She squeezes my fingers and replies: 'I'm your mother, darling – there's no need to thank me. Now, you two had better scoot, before I lose my dignity and start crying!'

I give her a quick hug before she can object, and Luke and I climb up the steps into Joy. This time, I join him in the front seats. He starts the engine, and I feel that familiar thrill of excitement – at not quite knowing where we are going next, at wondering what the day will bring, at being open to absolutely all of it.

Our parents wave us off, and we drive down the lane. The greenery is less heavy than the day we arrived, and I spot the cows in the next field and wave at them as well.

Luke puts on the brakes when we reach the end of the path, before we join the main road. He looks across at me and gives me the full-wattage smile. I melt a little inside, as I always do, and lean across to kiss him.

We are setting off on a new journey, a new adventure – but I already feel like we have been on the trip of a lifetime. We have seen new places, tried new things. We have both chosen love, despite the fact that neither of us was looking for it. We are entirely new versions of ourselves compared to that very first day, back in the place I used to call home.

I don't know where we will head next. I don't know

what our future will hold – but I know that we will face it together, and that's what matters.

'So,' he says, once we are ready to finally leave. 'Where to, Captain?'

Acknowledgements

All books take on a life of their own as you write them, and this one quite unintentionally became something of a love letter to England. I'm lucky enough to have enjoyed numerous family road trips, filled with the usual delights – 'are we nearly there yet?'; 'where's the carrier bag, I'm going to be sick!'; 'why is there no Wi-Fi?' scattered among the oohs and the aahs. We've counted cows from the car window, and sung songs, and shared picnics, and enjoyed it all – the wild swimming that's left us freezing but full of life; the 5 a.m. starts; the ever-changing reaction of children to being presented with yet another stone circle and being told to 'just imagine'. My poor kids will either be scarred for life, or do exactly the same to their own offspring at some point.

Along the way, we have had regular companions in some of the books mentioned in this story – you can look them up yourselves if you want to know more. In particular, Julian Cope's *Modern Antiquarian* has been a constant – we rarely go anywhere without the much-used 'Copendium', as it's known. Planning to drop a child at Uni? Check if there's a stone circle on the way!

Driving to see family in another part of the country? There might be a cool long-barrow along the route! It's added numerous quirky and evocative memories to our family life, and although it might be old, and might be battered (much like myself), it's been a huge amount of fun joining the entertaining Mr Cope on his travels.

Most of the places that Jenny, Luke, Charlie and Betty visit are places I've also been to, places like Malham Cove and Haworth and parts of Cornwall that have left me speechless, they're so jaw-droppingly gorgeous. I love to travel and discover new parts of the world, but sometimes it's nice to remember what we have on our own doorstep.

I have played fast and loose with a bit of geography, not to mention the walking abilities of a dachshund. But it's fiction so I hope you'll forgive me, and just go along for the ride.

Now, the all-important thank-yous . . . firstly, as ever, my amazing and completely barmy family: Dom, Keir, Dan, Louisa, Norm, Tara and Dave. A special mention to my Auntie Chris as well, for being such a lovely person. Also my friends, who keep me sane, make me laugh, and are pretty much the most awesome humans ever – especially Sandra Shennan, Pamela Hoey, Paula Woosey, Helen Shaw, Vikki Everett and Ade Blackburn. Big thanks also to Milly Johnson, for being even more of a constant than Julian Cope, and to my fellow writers Catherine Isaac, Carmel Harrington, and Rachael Tinniswood/Jessie Wells.

Special thanks to Jane and Rob Murdoch for sharing

their motorhome expertise, and for letting me kip over in their own. Any mistakes are mine, and probably because I was a bit drunk when they were explaining how everything worked!

On the professional front, I'd like to thank my agent Hayley Steed, Elinor Davies, and the whole team at the Madeleine Milburn Agency for working so hard on behalf of me and my books. Also, the wonderful people at Orion – my editor Charlotte Mursell, as well as Lucy Cameron, Becca Bryant and Sanah Ahmed. Writing a book is only one part of a very long and complicated process, and I appreciate all of your help in getting it from my brain into my readers' hands.

My final thank you is to those readers – without you, what would be the point? I hope you've enjoyed Jenny's journey, and look forward to seeing you again next time around!

Credits

Debbie Johnson and Orion Fiction would like to thank everyone at Orion who worked on the publication of *Falling for You* in the UK.

Editorial
Charlotte Mursell
Sanah Ahmed

Copyeditor
Jade Craddock

Proofreader
Francine Brody

Audio
Paul Stark
Jake Alderson

Finance
Jasdip Nandra
Sue Baker

Contracts
Anne Goddard
Humayra Ahmed
Ellie Bowker

Design
Charlotte Abrams-Simpson
Joanna Ridley
Nick May

Editorial Management
Charlie Panayiotou
Jane Hughes
Bartley Shaw
Tamara Morriss
Sue Baker

Marketing
Lucy Cameron

Production
Ruth Sharvell

Publicity
Becca Bryant

Sales
Jen Wilson
Esther Waters
Victoria Laws
Rachael Hum
Anna Egelstaff
Frances Doyle
Georgina Cutler

Operations
Jo Jacobs
Sharon Willis

Discover your next gorgeously uplifting and emotional read from Debbie Johnson . . .

A love to last a lifetime . . .

Gemma knows perfectly well how one moment can change your life forever. That's why, for two decades, she's lived life by the rulebook.

But this year, everything is different. The beloved daughter she gave up for adoption all those years ago is about to turn eighteen – and that means, there's a chance of being found.

For the first time in her life, Gemma can no longer run from her secrets. And she begins to realise that when everything is falling apart, love can be found in the unlikeliest of places.

Because sometimes your true family is the one you pick for yourself . . .

It only takes a *second* . . .
For life to change *forever*.

Elena Godwin could never have known that her dream holiday to Mexico would change her life forever. She thought that she was in charge of her own destiny. But on a gorgeous summer evening, her whole world is ripped from her feet in a single moment.

Ten years later, she still can't forget the face of the stranger who held her while everything she knew was destroyed. Thrown back together again, Elena starts to uncover the truth around that fateful night – and questions whether she made the right decision all those years ago.

She only met him for a moment, but maybe it's not too late . . .

What if you had the chance to find a lost love?

Jess still thinks about the man who disappeared from her life seventeen years ago, and the tragedy that tore them apart. So when she discovers a hidden box of letters in her mother's attic, Jess realises that the truth about why he walked away has been kept from her all this time.

Jess sets out to follow the faded postmarks across the country, determined that her journey will bring her closer to him. As each clue falls into place, Jess discovers new things about herself – and the man who once broke her heart. Maybe she can find him. Maybe their love story isn't over.

Maybe one day, they will be together again . . .